BLOOD MOON OVER
BOURBON STREET

BLOOD MOON OVER BOURBON STREET

CAITLIN KELLEY: MONSTER HUNTER VOLUME ONE

THERESA GLOVER

Charlotte, NC

FALSTAFF
BOOKS
WWW.FALSTAFFBOOKS.COM

To Emily, Cate, John and Melissa
and to everyone else who feels unseen.

I see you.
Broken doesn't mean beaten.

I

CAITLIN KELLEY: MONSTER HUNTER

1

The carousel buzzed, but I didn't move. A level thirty-six boss took focus.

Marty, on the other hand, crossed the gray industrial carpet in three long strides to watch the luggage belt grind into action.

I thumbed the touchscreen, tilted my phone, and mumbled less-than-charitable encouragement to the flickering digital characters throwing explosives at each other.

A rumble of thunder.

The crowd groaned in impressive synchronicity as another announcement interrupted the already ubiquitous jazz. I lost the game in the split-second I looked up. At my muttered invective, the woman beside me huffed in disgust and tugged her daughter's hand as she walked away.

Marty stomped back and slid down the reddish wood-grained column to sit beside me. "Didn't I tell you this would happen? I told you not to check a bag. This is why."

"And I thought you'd be a good travel buddy, so let's say my judgement isn't great and leave it at that for the week, okay?"

He sighed, shaking off his pout with a toss of his unruly brown curls. "I'm sorry. I guess I'm..." He shrugged.

"I believe 'being a dick' will suffice," I said and put away my phone. There's a reason they tell you to pack chargers in carry-on luggage, and I, of course, ignored it.

"To be fair, that is kind of my thing." Marty smirked as he bumped my shoulder.

I bit the inside of my cheek to restrain my grin. "Indeed."

Thunder vibrated the glass doors to our right, and the night outside flared purple. In front of me, a swaying woman jumped, waking the little boy in pajamas on her shoulder. His thin frame didn't give away his age, but his bare feet dangled around her waist. He rubbed his eyes and whined as she crossed the baggage claim area to the luggage belt.

"I'm hungry. We should have gotten something in the terminal."

"Nothing was open." I ignored the way my stomach grumbled just thinking about food.

"Oh. Right." Marty pulled his padded duffel bag into his lap and grunted under the weight of the tech inside. "Maybe I still have snacks."

A wail of terror shattered my nerves, and I couldn't help but look. The little boy clung to his mother, shaking, his face buried against her shoulder as she murmured to him. Without looking up, he pointed over her shoulder into the baggage claim waiting area.

I leaned my head back against the column, breathing slowly, my eyes closed. Not my kid, not my problem.

My guts clenched with each howl.

"I think I ate everything on the plane."

I glanced at my friend, my voice raised over the little boy's cries. "Seriously? You ate everything you packed?"

He shrugged. "I was hungry. You had some, too."

"I had *a* granola bar. One." I struggled to focus through the kid's cries. Marty'd had enough to feed an army of children for days yet inhaled it all in less than a couple of hours.

"Like I said." He zipped the bag, thrust it under his skinny legs, and folded his hands across his flat stomach. "You had some."

"Mommy, it's the MONSTER!"

My back stiffened.

Monster.

He said "monster."

The boy's terrified screams silenced the baggage claim area except for sympathetic murmurs and snorts of frustration. Even as his mother turned, helpless to soothe him, he pointed, tracking a spot out of my line of sight. When she turned, he recoiled and clung to her.

I leaned forward and looped my arms around my bent knees, following the little boy's trembling arm.

Casual. Be casual. There couldn't be an actual monster walking through the Louis Armstrong Airport. New Orleans had monsters, and plenty of them, but few were humanoid enough for conventional travel. And few would dare make so cavalier an intrusion into human space. Not here.

My hand drifted to my TSA-approved empty pockets as I turned. People swiveled their limited interest where he pointed, but not for long.

A group of men dressed in similar suits hunched over cell phones between two carousels. They muttered back and forth, nudged and showed devices to each other, but remained oblivious to everything beyond their huddle. One muttered a few words, another nodded, but they all focused on their technology. Behind them, two women over-dressed for the airport sneered, glanced at their watches, and rolled their eyes. One snapped her gum and pulled out a mirror to preen. A single young man in shorts, a bright blue polo, and a backpack fidgeted and shuffled his feet as he avoided the crying child.

"You're on vacation, Cee."

"Yup," I said. "That's why I'm sitting."

Nothing about the nervous man seemed remarkable, yet he stood out more than I did in my torn heavy metal band t-shirt, tight black jeans, Doc Martens, and the cobalt blue streaks in my hair. The TSA agent in Atlanta had waved me through without a second look, but this squirrelly dude'd warrant a pat-down, at least. Figuratively, I'd seen him a thousand times, this average, early thirty-something, upper-middle class American guy. From the cut of his shorts to his shabby-chic loafers, he might have been coming from or headed to some lake vacation.

"Stop staring at him, then."

"I'm not," I said. He looked like a former frat boy, tanned, blond, his muscled arms contradicting the hint of a beer belly under his cotton polo. "He doesn't even see me."

He couldn't. Too busy watching the inconsolable child.

The boy peered over his mother's shoulder, "monster" the only recognizable word among his shrill, incomprehensible syllables.

The man winced and ran a hand through his short hair, his mouth twitching as his gaze hesitated on the doors.

Marty snorted, shifting his bag and looping the strap across his chest. "You're about to cause a scene and get us kicked out, aren't you?"

"Nope."

"I can't be on the no-fly list, Cee. I've got places to go, and so do you," Marty continued.

Frat boy-man sucked in his stomach and wove through the crowd, hands up to avoid contact as he side-stepped unobservant people in his path with the extreme caution of a germaphobe. Every few steps, he glanced over his shoulder.

Until his eyes met mine.

The carousel buzzed again, announcing the arrival of chaos.

Frat boy-man stumbled into a thick, forty-something man in a suit, both hands splayed across his back and jostling him against his neighbor. The older man dropped his phone. Frat boy-man didn't acknowledge or apologize, only jerked his hands back and hurried away.

The man in the suit blinked. His younger neighbor emerged from his technology haze and met the older man's blank stare as he crumpled to the floor. The younger man's mouth opened in comical surprise, his phone teetering in his fingers. Another from their group repeated a foreign-sounding word and knelt beside the fallen man, shaking his limp shoulder. As other members of the group noticed, their commingled voices buzzed, punctuated by occasional panicked cries.

The little boy's voice carried above the ruckus. "Don't let the monster get me, Mommy!"

I stood. Slow. Intentional.

Frat boy-man hesitated and turned, far enough away to avoid implication, but his nonchalant curiosity couldn't conceal him. Especially from me.

A woman yelled for 9-1-1 in heavily accented English and dropped to the fallen man's side.

Marty sprang to his feet.

I stepped around the column, losing sight of frat boy-man for a moment as he navigated the crowd. He emerged from the clot of people milling around baggage claim and stared me down before dashing out the glass doors toward ground transportation. "Come on." I snatched Marty's hand and dragged him as I ran.

The doors opened with a hiss and a hydraulic sigh of humid Louisiana air. My skin instantly slicked with sweat, wisps of hair sticking to my face.

Few people waited on the damp concrete sidewalks and fewer vehicles passed. LED signs flashed warnings, alerts, and I ignored them all.

Yellow-orange overhead lights buzzed louder than the bugs swarming around them. No evidence of frat boy-man or his hurried passage.

"He couldn't have disappeared."

"But he did," I said with a sigh. "Weren't you just reminding me I'm on vacation?"

"Yeah, but I'd rather kill a little time hunting than have you brood over every Hurricane and cup of étouffée." He shifted the weight of his bag. "Do you see him?"

"No." I scanned one direction, then the other.

"Why'd the kid call him a monster? He looked normal to me."

"Don't know." The tinted glass made baggage claim shadowy and cavernous. Two brawny men in dark uniforms, EMT printed across their shoulders, parted the crowd. "Know of any humanoid monster that causes incapacitation with their touch?"

"Dude, you are asking the wrong person. You'll have to call *her.*"

I restrained the groan to an inward cringe. Arranging temporary coverage for my absence had been an ordeal, but even suggesting I wasn't doing all the relaxing I'd said I desperately needed would probably cause an issue. She, Sister Betty, would be…perturbed. At best. "I'm supposed to be on vacation," I said. Ignored luggage chugged along the carousel as the EMTs worked on the fallen man.

"Yup. But you won't be until you report this."

And probably not even then. First the report, then debriefing with in-town contacts, following up on the guy being lifted onto the waiting gurney. I'd come to let go of responsibility, but the burden was already heavier than before I left. "Let's get my bag and get out of here. It's going to be an early morning."

2

"Have you called?"

I didn't look up from my writing. "You know I haven't."

In the bed farthest from the desk, Marty stretched, grunted, and flopped back into his pile of pillows, a tumble of muddy-brown hair falling across his eyes. "Never thought I'd be able to sleep in a haunted hotel."

"Your snoring scared everything away." *Except my nightmares.*

"You're still here."

"Uh huh." I drew a line through my last sentence and sat back in the creaky chair. No matter what I wrote, Sister Betty would still give me shit. Sleep shortened by a kaleidoscope of nightmares made it harder to strategize around her inevitable resistance. "I don't count. I'm a glutton for punishment."

"It's a good thing I love you." The old bed creaked as Marty climbed out and stretched, his inky silhouette arching with feline drama in front of the sunlit window. He crossed the room, adjusted his pajamas, and looped his arms around my shoulders. He rested his chin on my head with a yawn. "Writing yourself a script?"

His chin slid against the top of my head as I nodded. Though I'd been at it for over an hour, I had nothing to show but a page of crossed-out half sentences, two crumpled sheets of paper in the trash, and stone-cold coffee.

"Think it will work?"

"Doubt it." I sipped the bitter brew. "I'm just trying to limit how much crap I'll have to take."

"I think she gets off torturing you." He shuffled to the coffee maker and inspected the foil-topped white plastic pods.

I scowled. "Don't talk like that. She's a nun."

"Yeah, well, she wasn't always a nun." He popped a plastic container into the coffee maker.

He was right, of course. Sister Bridgit MacKenna, known in our little circle as Sister Betty, had once been like me. The Catholic Church bankrolled hundreds of operatives around the world to hunt and kill monsters, and though some names inspired awe, few were as notorious as Sister Betty. She was the one they called in for hush-hush jobs, especially when the monsters were big, bad, and out of control.

She'd grown up somewhere in Massachusetts or Maine or something, but monsters orphaned her sometime in her early teens. To hear her tell it, she'd lived like an ascetic, her vengeful life nearly ending in a feverish faint on the steps of Saint Patrick's in New York City. After a few drinks, she'd regale anyone who'd listen with impressions of the rattled Cardinal of the New York Diocese and the stormy night the old man interviewed her at her hospital bedside, his blessed flask in hand. That he didn't throw the feral woman-cub into Bellevue after tales of monsters she'd slain since her parents' death suggested he wasn't quite as shaken as she claimed. Whatever won him over, when Betty healed, the Catholic church whisked her off to Ireland, inducted her into the Holy Order of the Sisters of Mercy of Saint Brendan, and trained her in stealth and the art of monster hunting on behalf of the Father, the Son, and the Holy Ghost.

Retired from active duty, she took vows to train the next generation of monster hunter, with special attention to her previous expertise. How Father Callahan convinced her that I would be a good candidate still baffled me. Yet, she'd agreed to work with the thick, angry, scared pre-teenager he brought to her. Week after week, we worked together with varying degrees of success. Her patience fluctuated, but not her commitment. Even now, I still had more to learn, but everything I knew about monsters and fighting came from her. No one I'd met matched her ferocity or skill.

And she was the sexiest woman I'd ever seen in a habit.

"You're having sex thoughts about Sister Betty again, aren't you?"

"Huh?" Heat climbed my neck. "What are you talking about?"

9

"Please," he sneered, stirring his coffee. "You've had a thing for the hottie in the habit since forever." He took a sip, and I forced myself not to look away. Little bastard loved staring me down. "You get all quiet when you think about her, and it's the same dreamy, far-off look as when you're 'shipping Black Widow and the Scarlet Witch."

"You're insane." I returned my attention to the paper in front of me. "I don't 'ship Scarlet Witch." *With anyone but me.*

"Right. Okay. Whatever you say." He laughed and headed to the bathroom. "I may not the one who needs to be hosed down, but I'm getting in the shower anyway. Good luck."

When the door closed, I sighed and leaned back in the chair. How the hell did he know? It's not like we talked about anything like that. When it came to "yucky love stuff," most of what I tried to explain didn't make sense to him. He understood affection and love, of course, but sex, or even the desire for it, confounded him. It didn't matter. I assured him he was better off without it. He agreed. "Besides, you sex up the world enough for both of us anyway."

Scribbles and crossed-out text taunted me from my abandoned script attempt. No matter what, she was Sister Betty, and preparation didn't change that.

On the other side of the thin wall, the shower hissed and metal shower rings scraped against the rod. I should take advantage of the privacy he offered. And the sooner I finished the work stuff, the sooner I could pull out my book, grab a drink, and crash at the pool.

After one last deep breath, I dialed my phone.

"Thank you for calling the Holy Order of the Sister—"

"Hi, Sister Betty."

"Hmm. Time off hasn't improved your manners, I see." The reproach stung despite her teasing lilt. Though I recognized her teasing, years of taking critical feedback during survival training didn't break easily. "And, m'dear, aren't you supposed to be taking time to—how did you put it? Recharge and restore?"

"Can I say I missed your unflinching kindness?"

"Not if you want me to believe you."

Despite myself, I laughed and slid farther into the chair, trying to relax and sound casual. "Then I'll save my flattery for someone who'll fall for it."

"Wise. I'm sure you'll find plenty of delectable delta tarts more than willing to take the tumble." I imagined her curled up on the couch in post-workout sweats cradling a bowl of cereal, the phone pressed between her shoulder and ear, her rust-colored hair bound up in a messy bun. "Now tell me why you're up so early. And why you're working."

"I wanted to talk to Father C."

"He's not here," she said, her words colored with the hint of battling intercontinental accents. "The Archdiocese of Santa Fe called him in. Something about a kerfuffle in Albuquerque between the local hunter and law enforcement."

"Damn." I leaned on the desk, grinding the heel of my free hand against my eye.

She laughed. "I'd scold you for language if I thought you'd stop."

"Or if it bothered you."

"I have taken vows, dear." Vows or not, Sister Betty's faith wasn't rigid and humorless, though I never doubted her piety after seeing her with a rosary in hand. At her most stern, her affection shone through. With a soft cough, she changed the subject. "Why do you need Father's help, Caitlin?"

My bones quivered. She only used my name to get my attention in training, and even so far away, it compelled an automatic response. And an answer. "We had an encounter at the New Orleans airport."

Rustling on the line and I imagined her sitting up, serious and attentive. "In such a public place? What happened?"

I told her about the child in the baggage claim and the shifty frat boy-man. "Are there any humanoid monsters that cause incapacitation by touch?"

"What do you mean?"

I gave her as much detail as I could remember.

"Hmm." More rustling. Maybe crossing the room to the library. "It doesn't sound familiar. You're sure it was humanoid?"

"He looked like he stepped out of the casual wear section of Rye & Ballast. Only his behavior stood out."

On the other side of the wall, the water stopped. The clatter of metal rings on the shower rod jangled over Marty's voice as he sang. Badly.

"I'll have to do some research and call you back."

The weight of work resettled on my shoulders. So much for a break. "I'm not packed to fight. All I've got's a few amulets and a knife from my checked luggage."

"I don't expect you to fight. You'll have to debrief to the regional hunter, of course, but at most, you'll support if things go bad. You're on vacation, after all."

"Have I told you I love you lately?"

"Not since the last time I saved your life."

I winced, remembering that incident in Philly. One of my first assignments. She'd warned me about the monster and needing back up, but I'd ignored her advice. Thankfully, she'd ignored my insistence on going alone and bailed me out. Lesson learned. "Well, I do."

"Great. I'll do some research, chat with the locals, and let you know the plan."

"Awesome, thank you." We said goodbye and ended the call as Marty emerged from the bathroom, wrapped in a towel.

"You don't look like she gave you too much trouble." He walked back to his bed by the window.

"For a change, she didn't." I told him about the call.

"Get changed and let's go. We'll get beignets and this frozen Irish coffee I heard about."

I stood and stretched. "Sounds divine. I'll get in the shower and—" My phone buzzed, an image of the Scarlet Witch illuminating the screen. Sister Betty. "That was fast," I said as I answered.

"We've got a problem. The local monster hunter's dead."

3

The third round of knocks caught me trying to slap white powder out of my black tank top. "Just a minute," I said, unable to keep the irritation out of my voice. Locked bathroom doors usually suggest occupation, but whoever waited on the other side refused to take the hint. With a last glance in the mirror, I wiped powder from my upper lip only to have more fall on my shirt.

I swore, then winced as I imagined Sister Betty's admonishment. Then I swore again because it would piss her off.

Another knock.

"Seriously?" I yanked open the door.

A bent old woman scowled up at me as she leaned on her cane. Her clothes were more ancient and wrinkled than her leathery skin. "Baby, you need to find another place to do..." she gestured at me with crooked fingers, "that. This lavatory is strictly for the call of nature. Miss Almeda'd ask you t'leave if she knew what you were up to. Now, if you'll excuse me..." She tapped my leg with her cane and gestured for me to leave.

"But I wasn't—"

She shook her head. "I'm not the police, baby, just here t' use the facilities." She tapped my calf again. "*Tout suit*, if you don't mind."

I could argue or refuse to leave, but she reminded me of my grandmother. My grandmother believed "no" only opened the door for negotiation. Something told me this Yoda of a woman might have actually challenged my grandmother's stubbornness. I didn't have to know her to see she'd fight dirty if that's what it took.

Instead of getting my knees clubbed, we traded places.

A hot puff of humid air greeted me as I stepped outside and crossed the brick-paved courtyard. Though it barely stirred the greenery or the leaves of the palm trees planted against the brick walls, the "breeze" carried the heavy yeast and sugar perfume of fresh beignets from the café behind me. At the bar on my right, humming fans tossed the bartender's blue and green ponytail over her shoulder. She flashed a quick smile as she leaned on the tile-covered counter but never stopped flicking a menu in front of her to move the heavy air.

Laughter from the covered stage on the other side of the courtyard drew my attention. Two men chatted as they set up a drum kit while a third, older and heavier man tuned a guitar. Drooping ceiling fans rotated slowly over their heads, though I couldn't imagine they had much effect on the oppressive air.

A bird skipped across the bricks in front of me, flying up to the back of a metal chair to check me out before continuing its search for abandoned treats.

Marty waited at one of the little iron cafe tables under another lazy ceiling fan. Watching the men on the stage, he leaned over an open brown paper bag, a beignet pinched in his fingers and a napkin pressed against his chest. A soft cloud of white powder burst around his mouth as he bit into it. He eyed me as I pulled out a chair beside him and sat.

"Don't say it."

A curious bird perched on the back of one of the empty chairs at our table. It watched Marty drop his beignet back into the bag.

"What?" He wiped powdered sugar from his mouth with a second napkin, the first fluttering against his chest. "That you look like someone who sneezed while snorting their first line?"

I glared at him and snatched a napkin from the tabletop dispenser to beat at my shirt. "I said don't."

"But it was funny." He grinned. When I didn't answer or smile, he continued. "It's not a big deal. I'm sure locals are used to seeing tourists covered in this crap." He rubbed his fingers together, sugar falling from them like fine snow.

"Right." Still, the bag of beignets taunted me, my stomach rumbling at the faintest scent of them on the air. They made a hell of a mess, but they were worth it. "I'm not a tourist."

"Relax, will you? Sister Betty said this was a simple retrieval."

"Nothing is ever simple when it comes to supernatural creatures. Besides, if it's so simple, why wouldn't Sister Betty give us the details? Not to mention, since when do we 'retrieve' monsters who can drop an adult human with their touch?"

"Dunno." He wiped the frost from his plastic cup before taking a long drink of the creamy, frozen concoction. "I don't know why you didn't get one of these. They're heaven."

"I'm working, that's why." I glanced at my watch.

"Oh yeah," he picked up his phone, "while you were..." he gestured at the faint white shadow of sugar across my chest, "doing whatever you were doing in there—"

"It's the beignets, dammit." I yanked another napkin from the dispenser and brushed my shirt again while he giggled.

"Like I said, while you were in there, I found an interesting tidbit." He tapped the screen with both thumbs, then handed me the device. "I'm not sure how true it is, but there are spiritualists who claim New Orleans is such a paranormal hotbed and so attractive to supernats because there's a power nexus in the middle of the French Quarter."

I scrolled through the site. "Any way to verify it?"

"Not really. Or at least, not with scientific credibility. It's still in the realm of 'hooey' and 'mumbo jumbo,' scientifically speaking."

"But if it's true, there's plenty of human energy here to keep it juiced up."

"Yup. Transient human energy." His expression indicated this was significant, so he'd probably explained it before. I weighed my options and decided to pretend I understood.

"This could make life interesting." I glanced at my watch again. "We need to go. I'm not sure where this place is."

Marty picked up his phone and waggled it at me. "Got you covered. It's about two blocks away. Want another beignet?"

I plucked at my shirt again, the ghost of the sugar less noticeable. "Nah, they've done enough damage."

"We'll have to come back," Marty said, pulling the rest of his fried and powdered sugar-dusted pastry from the bag. "This is a sweet park."

"Yeah." Everything from the archway over the entrance proclaiming the name of the brick courtyard, to the fountain, to the bronze statues of jazz legends, to the men preparing instruments on the covered stage conjured my earliest daydreams of what New Orleans would be. But, despite the decadent treats, abundant alcohol, and the sun warming my tense shoulders, a job waited. And depending on the New Orleans diocese, maybe more before heading home.

Some vacation.

"Stop brooding." Marty stood beside the table, crumpled bag in hand. "Let's do this."

"You don't have to come." The metal chair scraped across the brick as I pushed back and stood. "You could enjoy the city or lounge by the pool." I shrugged. "Or, I don't know, drink yourself into a stupor at the carousel bar in our hotel. Or bar hop your way down Bourbon Street. Whatever."

With the smile that always annoyed with its hint of secrecy, he winked. "And let my partner have all the fun? No way."

In garish daylight, Bourbon Street looked tired and hung over. Aproned workers scrubbed the sidewalk with stiff-bristled broom, though it did little to dissipate the miasma of stale beer, garbage juice, and urine. Kitschy souvenir displays drew more tourist attention than the long rainbow-colored rows of drink machines churning frozen, alcoholic concoctions.

Cool air surged over me as a pair of tourists in shorts and t-shirts opened an air-conditioned haven of craven consumerism.

Maybe it was the AC and not the souvenirs.

Marty pointed out restaurants where he planned to try jambalaya or red beans and rice as we walked. "Before we go, I have got to have a po' boy. I need to check some reviews to figure out where, though."

His childlike excitement and flushed cheeks made me laugh. "We're going to eat our way through the city, is that it?"

"Hell yes," he said, lifting his frosty plastic cup in a toast. "Let *les bon temps roulez* right in to my bel-ly!"

I laughed. "You are such a dork."

The sun emerged from behind a cloud. A woman down the street echoed my laugh, alcohol lacing the sound with manic joy. Nothing like a town with no qualms about a morning buzz. I looked, but there were too many people to identify her. Wherever she was, I hoped she'd have fun for me, too.

We turned down a tight side street away from Bourbon. Small, European-sized delivery trucks parked half on the sidewalk. Marty and I stepped into the wet street to pass them. Clean stucco walls suggested more upkeep than I expected. Windows and flower-filled window boxes cowered behind wrought-iron bars from lost and industrious revelers. The sun's reflection flared off a beer bottle wedged into the protected lush greenery as we passed. Aside from the occasional sticker on a parking sign, the NOLA party industry had failed to leave its mark on the neighborhood.

I glanced at the number painted on the tile embedded in the rough textured, cream-colored wall. "This is it, isn't it?"

Marty tucked his drink into his elbow and fumbled with his phone. After a few taps, he said, "Yes. This is it."

We looked up, our eyes drawn to the ornate wrought-iron balcony and the lush vines trailing from it. Low hanging leaves swayed in the breeze. The building wasn't tall, but it was old and well-kept, and in this city, that meant big money. I stepped up and rang the bell, listening to the faint chimes through the open French doors overhead.

"Did Sister Betty tell you anything about this woman?"

At the approaching footsteps behind the door, I only shook my head. She'd mentioned her "influence," which probably meant an endowment for the Church. Or a known bequest. Either way, I assumed it meant money and plenty of it.

The door swung open, and a silver-haired liveried butler greeted us.

If I could have kicked Marty to close his gaping jaw without being seen, I would have. Instead, I introduced myself to the older man and hoped he'd pick up on the tone shift. "Good morning, my name is Caitlin Kelley, and I've—"

"The mistress is waiting for you." He stepped aside with a wide sweep of his muscular arm in welcome. "Please, come in."

4

Any chair in the world would have been more comfortable than the spindly-legged antique the butler offered me. Even with extensive training to concentrate under pressure, most of my focus went to immobility to avoid stressing the fragile wood. Little remained to focus on the slender woman seated in front me, never mind what she said. Everything else went to the wolf of a dog staring at me from his spot at her feet.

Though I'd wanted to kick Marty for his slack-jaw first impression, his easy manners and friendly conversation with the elegant woman let me get my bearings. The two chatted, her strange accent and clipped words a contrast to Marty's adopted southern-isms and undeniably northern rapid-fire delivery. I lost the thread of their conversation as I looked around. Despite the open French doors behind us, the room smelled stale, unused. It reminded me of libraries. Or museum storage rooms. It could have been part museum. Most of the furniture, artwork, books and pottery lining the shelves and fireplace mantle were old. Not shabby old, but the kind of old that sold for thousands of dollars.

In my casual work "uniform" of black jeans, a tank top, and Doc Martens, I felt entirely out of place.

The dimness in the room did little to help me focus. I felt sleepy, my senses dulled as I struggled to concentrate on the woman in front of me. Weak, curtain-filtered light softened her features, making them as ageless

18

as her voice. I tried to pick up on anything remotely unusual magical or otherwise, but the intermittent burr of the giant wolf-dog's growl made it impossible. Flat on its belly, snout between its massive paws, its shoulders tensed and twitched, ears swiveling to follow the conversation. Amber eyes watched me through half-closed lids, nostrils flaring with each intake of air. The translucent silk ribbon looped around its muzzle failed to make me feel secure.

Silence between the woman who'd introduced herself simply as "Helen" and Marty caught my attention. They stared at me, expectant.

Of course. I'd missed something.

"I'm sorry," I said, making an excuse.

Like an indulgent matriarch, Helen smiled. "There's no need to concern yourself with him." Her bare right hand dangled over the arm of the chair, and the gray-brown wolf-dog sat up. She stroked the space between the dog's ears, and though he didn't relax, his eyelids drooped.

"He is...unusually large for a pet." I shifted, wincing as the chair groaned beneath me. "What kind of dog is he?"

The wolf-dog gave a thin whine.

"He's not a pet; he's family. Poor thing doesn't get out often." She scratched his ear and under his jaw. The dog closed his eyes and pressed his face into her palm.

"Family or not, shouldn't he be restrained?"

"Oh, he is." She lifted the ribbon in her left hand. Her gloved hand. "But even if he wasn't, Fen wouldn't harm you."

I nodded, though I didn't believe her. "Will that hold him?"

The gossamer ribbon shimmered as it caught stray rays of weak light. "Of course. It's the only restraint I use." She ran it through her fingers, bare hand over gloved hand as she contemplated it. "When will you be able to start?"

"I'm sorry, Ms.—"

"Please, call me Helen." She inclined her head, a sweep of golden hair hiding half of her sweet smile. One blue eye stared at me, her lashes too pale to see but long enough to cast a hint of shadow on her cheek. Returning her hands to her lap, she lay her bare right hand over her gloved left, the ribbon between them. She sat perfectly upright, her legs crossed but covered under her long skirt. Statuesque. Not even her foot swayed. The intensity of her stillness unnerved me.

"Helen, there's been a misunderstanding. What you're asking isn't something I do."

"You deal in the supernatural, yes?"

"Well, yes, but—"

"Then I see no conflict."

Silence fell so complete, even the noise outside drained away.

"It's not that simple."

She smiled and lowered her head, the curtain of her hair hiding her face. The wolf-dog sat up, and she absently stroked the dark gray fur between its ears. "It is, Miss Kelley."

"I don't think you understand. I'm a monster hunter, not a dog catcher. I'm the one they call when things get dangerous. When people die. I'm the one that kills the things that go bump in the night and want to kill us. I've been sent to capture the monster I saw in the airport, so as far as your dog's concerned, I can't help you. If your pup got loose, he's your problem, especially in a city I don't know." I stood. "Really, you're better off calling animal control—"

Helen sat back, her bare hand laying on her gloved one. "No, you don't understand, *cherie*. This is not about whatever you encountered. There's more to this world than even you've learned." She gestured to the chair I'd vacated. "Please. Sit."

In my peripheral vision, Marty shrugged as if unable to come up with a polite alternative.

I didn't move.

Helen's eyes flashed, her face hardening under the shadow of her hair. "I insist, Miss Kelley. Your services have been retained."

My rebuttal died before it fully formed.

Retained?

Creeping dread gnawed at me. *Retained* was new. A first, even.

I shut my mouth and sat, waiting for her to continue.

Her hard edges softened as she relaxed. "I apologize for being so blunt, but sometimes even a lady must."

I'd have blisters on my tongue from biting it so hard but nodded and gestured for her to continue. Frozen Irish coffee would make for good therapy, and Marty should be game for another, especially after this weirdness.

"This job isn't just finding a dog, or a black dog, but the Black Dog." I heard the capital letters as she spoke. "Are you familiar with the legend?"

Both Marty and I shook our heads.

"Most people who've heard about the Black Dog only know the legends. Most of them are incorrect, of course, but all legends contain some truth. This one started in Northern Ireland centuries ago. The home of your ancestors, Miss Kelley. The last stones of a once great castle still stand on the cliffs. Before the castle stood a village, whose name is long lost to time, and this is where the Black Dog began."

M y head didn't stop spinning when Helen's story ended. "So, you're telling me this Black Dog legend is real and now it's hunting in New Orleans?"

"With a plethora of famous, profitable dead, I'm sure you see the problem."

Problem. As if there was only one. As if supernatural, undead dogs killed by the Church to protect the sacred burial grounds prowled the streets of a major city every day. As if the presence of this dog didn't threaten the very lucrative afterlife business in New Orleans. As if this job meant as little as some menial task and not a potentially life-threatening feat.

"Maybe that's why I didn't see anything at the hotel last night," Marty said, as if talking to himself.

Helen continued. "This requires the utmost sensitivity. The Black Dog is to be captured, not killed, and returned to my collection."

My brain struggled to respond. "This legendary portent of death and calamity is something I'm supposed to scoop up without killing, without dying, and before it culls any of the important ghosts in New Orleans? Hey, yeah, no problem. How about I find the Holy Grail while I'm at it?" The wolf-dog scrambled to his feet and growled as I stood.

"Hush, Fen." Helen tugged the ribbon.

My hand slid to the short blade stashed in a waistband sheath as the animal lowered his head between his paws, ears up and vigilant.

I took a deep breath and pinched the bridge of my nose. "I apologize. That was unprofessional." Clasping my hands behind my back, I tried to regain my composure and smile. "This is a bit much to take. I need to do some research, consult with my team, and I'll come back tomorrow."

"I'm afraid that's not an option, Miss Kelley."

Marty paused half-way out of his chair.

"Excuse me?"

Helen pulled an envelope from between her leg and the chair and held it out to me. "There isn't a decision to be made."

"There's always a decision. Like I could walk out right now and you'd be on your own to find your undead demon doggy."

She leaned farther forward, the letter in her fingers.

"What's this?"

"Read it."

I took the thick envelope, immediately recognizing the wax seal of the Holy Order of the Sisters of Mercy of Saint Brendan on the flap. Knots in my shoulders tightened, and a weight settled in my stomach. Not good.

The wax seal cracked as I opened the envelope. When I finished reading, I handed it to Marty and walked to the open French doors. A weak breeze shifted the curtains around me. Only a sliver of the empty street showed through the open doors. The faint riff of a jazz melody crested, broken by the sound of a car horn.

"Cee?"

Never before had I gotten a letter like that from Sister Betty's order.

Marty touched my shoulder.

Never before had I been ordered to a job like this.

"You okay?"

Never before had the Pope personally assigned me.

"Yeah," I said, steeling myself as I turned to face Helen. "I don't know who you are, but you've got my attention. You've obviously got connections, so I'll find this damned dog of yours, but after that, I'm leaving New Orleans. No one jerks me around like this."

"Cee!"

Her slow smile spread like honey. "I am not 'jerking you around,' Miss Kelley. As you know, the local hunter is dead."

"Did you have something to do with that?"

The wolf-dog stepped between us.

"Don't say something you'll regret." Her smile stiffened. "I will excuse your shock, but I will not tolerate your disrespect."

"If there's nothing else," I said, "I have a job to do."

Her bare hand gripped the pink ribbon, her gloved hand stroking the slack end, but she did nothing to pull back the wolf-dog or to discourage his bared teeth and raised fur. "That is all. For now."

Marty re-read the letter in his hand.

"Guillaume will show you out."

As if summoned by his name, the door opened, and the butler appeared. He gave a half bow and swept an arm toward the open door, unfazed by the growling animal.

Helen nodded at me, as if in dismissal. "I expect to see you soon. The information you'll require is waiting at your hotel."

I didn't answer.

She stood, my anger suddenly distracted. Her clothes hung strange on the left half of her body. It seemed smaller. Lopsided. With a subtle, controlled tug on the pink ribbon, the wolf-dog stopped growling and stepped back. She gave a little nod. "Good day."

Guillaume cleared his throat, gesturing toward the open door.

Annoyed, I shrugged off Marty's attempt to guide me to the door. "This isn't over."

"No," Helen said, "it's not, but you're not the one running the game."

"I don't play games."

She laughed, an indulgent sound. "You've been a player since the night your sister died, Miss Kelley. Did you think your role in Rome was accidental?"

Ice formed in my guts. My knees wobbled.

How the fuck did she know about Rome? Or Shannon?

"Perhaps I struck a nerve," she said, her eyes fixed on me.

My back went rigid. "Your research is impressive."

"Not as impressive as my reach." She walked towards the open French doors, the wolf-dog reluctant to follow until the ribbon stretched taut between them. She didn't turn. "And now, as you said, you have work to do. Good day."

"Whoever heard of a ghost tour with no ghosts?" The two college-aged women wove between tables, one settling the strap of her expensive designer purse between her breasts as she snorted. "Of course, I demanded a refund."

"Hey. Will you focus, please?" Marty tapped the table and gestured to his tablet as the two walked away. "I'm brilliant on my own, but this requires expertise I don't have."

I shook myself, rubbed my eyes and muttered an apology. First the airport, now being retained by Helen and chasing a supernat dog instead of taking my vacation. Not only that, the assignment came directly from the Pope by way of Sister Betty's order. On so little sleep, it made my head ache. With so much out of the ordinary, I didn't know where to start untangling it.

"Are you daydreaming about Sister Hot Pants? Do we need to feed your carnal appetites? What's the sex equivalent of a Snickers?"

Though a thousand rejoinders crossed my mind, none of them came out of my mouth. "No, nothing like that."

"Then what?"

How had Helen procured that letter? And why had Sister Betty not warned me? Surely, she'd known. Nothing happened in that order without her knowledge. Or so I'd thought. And if the directive came from the Pope, who hated me as much as any man could, what the hell did it mean for my future?

Nothing good.

Maybe last night's nightmare of being attacked by a homeless man had been a premonition of the shitstorm to come. If premonitions were a thing. Or maybe it had been my brain's revenge for the delicious gastronomic travesty of the chili cheese fries I devoured before bed. Thank you, room service. Or maybe the nightmare was just stress.

I could have said any of this, but the pity in Marty's eyes made my jaw clench. An encore of misplaced sympathy for the girl with invisible wounds. Exactly the last thing I needed.

I shook my head, avoiding his gaze. "I love you, Mar, but you wouldn't understand."

His smile deflated. "No, I wouldn't. But I'm trying." With a shrug, he added, "In my own unique and charming way, of course."

Shaking my head with a snort, I stared into my cup of melting beige slush dusted with coffee grounds. Charming or not, he was right. My thoughts needed to be here and strategizing, not thousands of miles away or obsessing over questions I couldn't answer.

"Is it the Rome thing?"

The gentleness in his voice brought the sting of tears. I swallowed hard, chastising myself. It shouldn't still bother me. The past is past, and I needed to get over it. I'd been working on getting stronger, getting faster. It wouldn't happen again. After a long sip of the creamy frozen drink, I cleared my throat. "Yes and no."

"Regret pissing off the Pope?"

No matter how shitty things got, the image of the spluttering old man trying not to curse as he stomped around the Vatican guest house still amused me. He might hate me. He might fuck up my life forevermore, but he'd never take that memory. I smiled in spite of myself. "Never."

Marty propped his chin up with both hands and grinned. "I still wish I could've recorded it. You should get an award for making his head explode."

"Nah, it's not hard to do."

"I don't know. That dude seems more chill than most of his predecessors. Well, seemed. Until you."

"He didn't excommunicate me, so that's something." I picked at the corner of my notebook. "Though he probably should have."

"Stop."

"You know I'm right."

"I know you're beating yourself stupid with this Catholic guilt shit."

The waiter cleared his throat. Neither of us had noticed him. "Anything else I can get you?"

"No, thanks," I said. "Just the check."

He produced a small, black vinyl folder from the pocket of his bistro apron and stood it, open, on the table. "Have a great afternoon."

Marty watched him walk away. "Is it me, or did that sound like 'fuck you'?"

"Yeah, I thought the same thing." I tucked the church credit card in the pocket at the top.

"Visa. Accepted everywhere Jesus needs to be," Marty said.

"Can I get an amen?" I winked at him. "So we'll start—"

"We weren't done with our conversation."

"Maybe you weren't, but I am." I gestured to the waiter.

"You can't blame yourself, Cee," Marty said after the waiter collected the folder and left. "You're never going to save everyone, especially people who don't want to be saved."

The muscle in my jaw twitched, and I rested it on my hand to hide the spasm. "She didn't know what she was doing."

"Maybe not in the moment, but she did what she did of her own free will."

Echoes of her screams and the interminable wet crunching still haunted me. Awake and asleep. "No one deserves what she got. I should have—"

"No." Confidence and calm made him sound like a different person. "There's no way to win that game. You did everything you could. Even Sister Betty said so, and she'd be the first to correct you."

Instead, Sister Betty had flown to Rome to hold me through the tears. It wasn't the first time someone had died during a battle, but it was the first I could have—*should have*—prevented. I took another long drag off the straw. "Let's drop it, okay?"

"When you do." He sat back in the chair, his arms crossed.

"You're not a shrink, so—"

"Maybe you need one."

Whatever I intended to say fled. I stared at him, open-mouthed.

Like a nasty accusation rising from the past to haunt me, he'd said it.

Knowing my history, he'd said it.

The dagger of his words hung in the air.

His shoulders softened, and his arms dropped. "I only mean—"

I almost collided with the waiter as I stood. "Don't." I snatched the folder from his hand. The pen tore the slip as I scribbled a signature and grabbed my card. "It's pretty clear what you meant," I said, dropping the folder on the table.

"Cee—"

Weaving around tables, wait staff, and diners, I cut across the dining room and through the lobby. Steamy New Orleans humidity oozed over me as I hurried down the shadowed sidewalk.

"Caitlin!"

I dodged tourists, jaw clenched. This was supposed to be a vacation. Marty was supposed to be the no-pressure guy, the friend I could relax with without expectation or judgment. Now, again, I faced the same accusations my parents brandished like sacred relics of denial. Of rage. Of grief. The parade of psychiatrists, the landslide of pills. Every month, some new doctor, some new "treatment." They believed in my mental illness more than they believed a monster killed Shannon.

Father Callahan assured me their denial protected them from harm.

But I paid the price. In every cautious look, in every glance they shared. In the nervous way they talked to me. I felt it all. I lived in a world they refused to believe and protected them with my silence.

I fought to keep them safe. As payment, they insisted I needed a shrink.

And now, Marty.

"Caitlin!"

The streetlight changed, and I crossed without regard to the oncoming traffic. They could hit me or not, it made no difference. I wasn't running so when the hand grabbed my shoulder, I expected it to be Marty. Acid words rose to my tongue as I spun to break his grip and confront him. Instead, I stumbled and blinked.

A man in dirty clothes grinned at me. Bits of brown leaves stuck in the tendrils of his scraggly beard. His white tongue poked through his yellowed teeth to roll over parched lips. "Yer a pretty girl," he rasped, his right hand rising to my shoulder again, "a pretty little thing for the collection."

Without a thought, my left hand swung up to block his grip and knock it away. I stepped back as he howled, gripping his arm. He rolled across his back on the wet sidewalk, clutching his arm, his knees drawn to his chest as he rocked. "Why you hit a' old man? What I do to you?" The soles of his shoes flopped away from his feet with each movement, the thin gray material only attached at the heel.

Marty skidded to a stop on the wet pavement, almost falling over the man. "What the hell happened?"

"He grabbed me, I turned, and when he went to grab me again, I blocked him. Then," I gestured towards his theatrics, "this."

Few of the passing people stopped, but they stared as long as they could. A few pedestrians stopped to watch, some holding phones. The man didn't seem to notice, his antics unchanged. I shook my hands to ward off adrenaline shakes. And to prepare. Though thankful for the knife at my back, the general lack of weapons pissed me off. I scanned the area for anything useful and adjusted my stance. Nothing about this man should make me so nervous, and yet...

Marty leaned over him, sidestepping a collision when he rolled. "Mister? Mister, are you okay?"

The old man raised his voice and rolled, cradling his arm against his chest. "No reason for none of this. Assaulting a' old man!"

I met Marty's gaze and shook my head, answering his unspoken question. "Standard block. Nothing special." I repeated the movement with the same speed and power I'd used.

Squatting back on his heels at a safe distance, Marty pulled out his phone. "I'll call it in."

"Be careful."

As he rolled and howled his pain, the old man watched Marty.

Something about him wouldn't let me relax. Something on the edge of memory. Something...familiar.

I inched closer to see his face, careful to stay out of range.

In the wrinkled wreckage of sun-damaged skin, grizzled eyebrows, and layers of caked-on dirt, his eyes sparkled. The clarity of his rich mahogany eyes contradicted everything about him, even the broken way he spoke. A separate consciousness stared back at me while he carried on. When the sunlight glinted in his eyes, they flared gold.

And then, I knew.

Everything happened in a second.

The longest second of my life.

I lunged, knocking Marty to the ground and out of striking range of the knife that flashed out of the man's sleeve. A woman screamed. We tumbled across the uneven sidewalk, followed by the scuttle of the man scrambling after us. Searing heat tore through my calf. I kicked the hunched, feral old man, knocking a bloody knife from his hand and gaining a little space from his elongated teeth as he retreated.

Swearing under my breath, I grabbed a broom leaning against the wall and swung it. The old man dodged with freakish agility, just as the man from my nightmare. His blade glinted, and I swung, narrowly missing his stomach. Behind me, Marty yelled, his words unintelligible and—

Pain exploded in a black burst as something crashed into my back and knocked the wind out of me. My broom clattered to the sidewalk seconds before I fell to all fours, hands and knees scraping against uneven pavement. Unable to draw air, I still turned, trying to find the bastard.

"Caitlin!" Marty collided with me, grabbing my shoulders and pulling me up to face him. "Breathe."

I struggled to pull in a thin breath.

"Breathe, babe, come on."

I coughed and doubled over, Marty grabbing me, preventing me from crumpling to the ground. A shallow gasp and I tried to break free, to find the old man.

"He's gone. He ran." Marty shook me, and I coughed again. "Relax for a second and breathe."

Never had I wanted to breathe so bad, if only to tell him to shut up.

Another cough and I finally drew a full breath. Black and white sparks danced on the edge of my vision. I knelt, bracing my bloody, scraped palms on my destroyed jeans.

"Are you okay?"

I nodded and looked around. "Where'd he go?"

Bystanders murmured to each other, putting cell phones back in pockets or purses.

Great.

Covert ops usually meant I was in and out before people knew any danger existed. Bystanders never intervened, but someone always had a phone or camera ready to capture the disaster for posterity. And Facebook. Or, God help us, Facebook Live. Sister Betty'd probably insist on calling in DEMON, the Department of Extra-Dimensional, Magical, and Occult Nuisances, the governmental "No Such Agency" that handled all varieties of supernats and other scary stuff. When the magic didn't interfere with recording technology, DEMON's expertise in cleaning up evidence of the things most people didn't believe in kept public panic out of the equation.

Marty gestured to a gap between two buildings farther down the street. "In there."

I tried to stand, and he caught me.

"Nope. You're not going anywhere. The police—"

"Will be out of their league without a local hunter," I said, my breath wheezy as I twisted away from him. "Dude's supernat. I'm guessing a were-something." With a wiggle of fingers in front of my face, I added, "Gold eyes, big teeth."

"Can't we—?"

I only managed two steps before the crescendo of sirens filled the street, and cut him off. The blue flare of lights reflected off a restaurant's plate glass window across the street. I stopped, leaning against the wall. "He's *our* problem."

A short, thick woman with a strong Midwest accent marched up to us. "I caught that crazy man on video, and I'll be glad to show it to the police. I saw him attack." The pride in her voice made me want to laugh.

Marty thanked her. I checked my bleeding flesh through the newly ripped knees of my favorite jeans. He'd teased me this morning about my anti-tourist "uniform" when I got ready, but I'd worn them anyway. Another premonition?

The intensity of the sirens grew until they finally parked the cruiser in the middle of the road behind us. Two officers slid out and eyed us only to be intercepted by a tall, muscular man too rigid to look comfortable in his shorts, polo, and boat shoes. He postured like a cop, I realized. As I caught the gist of what he said, I suppressed a grin.

"Off duty?"

"Yup. Tourist, but feeling awful important as a witness."

The older uniform gestured to the younger, obviously giving him direction to take the off-duty's statement before wandering our way. Twenty years ago, he'd probably been a peak specimen like his partner. He hitched his belt, his swagger calling back to the strut of a division-leading former athlete. "Morning, folks." He smiled with that uniquely Southern mélange of welcome, irritation, and condescension reserved for trouble-making outsiders. "Mind telling me what happened here?"

I sighed, covering it with a posture that, I hoped, looked like I was still recovering. "Yes, sir. My name is Caitlin Kelley. Are you familiar with—"

He bristled, and I instantly regretted the question. "Ma'am, I was born in this parish, and I've worked this city for thirty-eight years. There isn't much around here I'm not familiar with."

"Yes, of course, I'm sorry, Officer…" I looked for his name tag, "La Fontaine. I apologize if I sounded disrespectful."

Though I wouldn't have imagined it possible, his chest puffed out more, and his Cajun accent intensified, the bayou echoing in his voice. "S'all right, ma'am." He gestured to my bleeding knees. "Looks like you've had quite the morning."

"You could say that." I tried to smile though I already disliked him. "I've got ID in my back pocket, and I'd like to take it out."

Officer La Fontaine straightened, his mouth a sour little knot. "I assume by the way you're telling me that you've got more than just ID."

"Yes, sir." I explained the knife. "It might have fallen out in the fight, but I haven't checked."

Marty shifted. La Fontaine's head snapped in his direction, his right hand hovering over the butt of his weapon. "Stay put, son."

Awesome. All the cops in New Orleans and we get Officer Twitchy. I berated myself for bungling the approach and getting him so riled. I knew better. Sister Betty had taught me better. "Pat down or partnership," she'd said, "your choice."

The criminal-style pat-down would be unavoidable now.

When I debriefed with Sister Betty, I'd get another lecture about relationships with local law enforcement. Not that I didn't deserve it.

Of course, the pat down was as annoying as expected. La Fontaine made sure of that.

When he finally finished, I handed him both driver's license and federal ID declaring me an authorized agent of DEMON. He spent far too long scrutinizing them. Had to be part of the power trip. Everything was current, since I'd renewed both a few months ago. Or maybe that triggered his suspicion. Either way, he eyed me, then called his partner. "Boudreaux."

The younger man hastily thanked the off-duty tourist to join his partner. "Yessir?"

La Fontaine flicked his first and middle fingers toward his partner, my IDs pinched between them. "Y'ever hear of this?"

How La Fontaine hadn't was more surprising, but I didn't mention it. Sister Betty would be proud.

Boudreaux took them and squinted at the federal ID, then shaded the plastic. His pale brow furrowed and his gaze darted between me and the card. "Yessir."

"That's what I—what?"

"Yessir." Boudreaux's voice dropped to a whisper. He stepped closer. "The captain mentioned a few weeks ago. They're the monster hunters affiliated with the Church."

La Fontaine pulled off his sunglasses, his lip curled in a sneer. "Are you out of your ever-lovin' mind?"

"No, sir." The younger man didn't move, even when the bigger man stepped closer. "We're supposed to cooperate, provide resources and—"

"Enough." The older cop snatched the cards back and settled his sunglasses over his scowl. He seemed to consider how to handle the situation. "What am I going to get if I call to verify who you are?"

I shrugged. "What are you looking for?"

The knot of his lips tightened. I wondered how the hell he'd untangle them.

"It's the Feds. They'll confirm my operative status, clearance, credentials." Hiding my amusement made me rather proud. "If, of course, federal agencies are credible enough for you."

A drop of sweat rolled down the rolls frustration carved into his lumpy forehead. "And what exactly does the federal government have to do with this?"

Ignoring him, I continued. "DEMON is the Department of Extra—"

He stiffened and returned my ID. "How'd they give you the authority to tear up my town, Miss Kelley?"

"Woah, wait a minute." My amusement dissipated. "I'm the one who got jumped. And by something you'll be thanking me to hunt and destroy."

"So you say."

I thrust the cards back at him. "Call them. And while they're on the phone, tell them to expedite the process for getting a new local hunter. You've got a supernat that attacked me in broad daylight and a monster that landed at Louis Armstrong airport last night. I'm already on assignment. You'll want them dealt with before the bodies pile up."

The man bristled, his lips twitching. Boudreaux's lips pressed tight, though to contain laughter or out of trepidation was impossible to tell.

"Officer La Fontaine," Marty said, his hands in full view, "there's been a misunderstanding."

"You're right, son," he said, his thick head swiveling toward Marty, sweat sparkling in the sun. "First that any federal agency can step in to my city without the courtesy of hello."

"Your city?" I couldn't have stopped if I'd tried. "Your city? Who the hell are you—"

"Caitlin!"

Something in my brain snapped at the sharpness of Marty's tone. I looked at him, then back at La Fontaine. The officer's red face and short huffs of breath told me all I needed to know. I rubbed my forehead, partly to wipe away sweat and partly to push against the headache growing behind my eyes.

Time for damage control.

I took a deep breath.

"Miss Kelley, the next thing out of your mouth might land you in jail," the man growled, his accent sharpening each brittle word.

"Officer La Fontaine," I said, all cool control, "I apologize for being a complete idiot."

His mouth opened, thumb unsnapping his holster.

He blinked.

His mouth closed.

"Miss Kelley, Beau," Boudreaux inserted himself between us. "I'll interview Miss Kelley and Mr. ...."

"Lavoie. Martin Lavoie." Marty's shoulders bunched too high, ready to intervene. Ever my back up, ever my partner.

Even when I was a dumbass.

"Mr. Lavoie can continue the discussion with you, Beau."

The heavy-set cop's shoulders dropped, his hands relaxing at his sides. "You got Creole blood, son?"

Marty smiled, drawing on his endless reserves of charm. "Not that I know of, sir."

"Bah, that don't mean nothin'." He smiled for the first time since I'd screwed up and dropped the F-word. I should have considered local sensitivity to the feds after the whole Hurricane Katrina debacle. "How 'bout we step in the shade and you tell me what happened."

Marty nodded, and as the cop turned away, he winked. Not for the first time, I wondered if my friend didn't have a little Elvin blood to help him out.

"Miss Kelley," Boudreaux gestured towards the cruiser.

I nodded and thanked him. "I apologize, I shouldn't have—"

"He shouldn't have, either." Boudreaux smiled. "*Ma memere* raised me right, but he's older and my superior officer, so whether I agree or not, I defer and disarm."

"You're wiser and more self-controlled than I." Not even Sister Betty's best efforts had beat those traits into me. The last time she'd had me in the gym under the church, she'd promised to kick the sarcasm out of me one roundhouse at a time. We'd both ended up on the floor, bruised, sore, and sweating on the ancient blue mats.

Spoiler alert: it didn't work.

But, what an afternoon.

Boudreaux's smile glowed like sunset, warmed like bourbon, and made my heart flutter. I tried not to squirm. He'd be dangerous to spend time with. "You learn a thing or two at the academy. Shut up or get out is lesson number one. How'd you survive federal agent training?"

I sighed. The explanation rarely satisfied the curious. "It's not like that."

"But you've got agent status?"

"In a capacity."

"What's that mean?"

"How much time you got?"

6

Hell hath no fury like a pissed off nun.

You'd think I enjoyed it for all the ways I've managed to invoke her wrath.

"I know, I should have handled it differently, so you can skip that speech." Even several states away and over the phone, the cold steel of her glare made my guts quiver. Not in the good way. "What should I do now?"

"Why is it my responsibility to get you out of trouble when, if you'd listened to me in the beginning, you wouldn't be in it?" Her sneakers squeaked. I pictured her pacing the wood floor of the gym in the church basement, the punctuating squeal the sound of pivoting on a toe to change direction for another pass. No trace of her concern over the attack survived her seething irritation. Too bad I couldn't have told her about that part last.

"It's not. I'm asking for advice."

"No, Caitlin, advice is what you ask for when something unexpected happens. This is bailing you out because your mouth got you in trouble. Again. We've been over this."

"And you're treating me like a child."

"Because you're acting like one!"

I didn't have a response. She wasn't wrong. I felt like a child. Had I screwed it all up to make them take the job away from me so I could get my break? I didn't think so. Not consciously, at least. But my fuzzy, jumbled brain was part of the reason I'd asked for the time. Time to sort things out. Time to make decisions about what the hell I was doing with my life. And instead of doing all that, I'd had a job thrust at me.

Didn't even make it out of the damned frying pan.

The ceiling fan wobbled as it stirred the cool air in the hotel room. I lay in bed in my underwear letting my skin pebble with goosebumps and waited for Marty to return with food.

"Caitlin?"

"Yes?"

"You have nothing to say?"

"Nope." I shifted against the pillows. "It's been a hell of a morning."

She sighed. "You make me crazy."

Ditto. In so many ways.

"And you know I'm going to help you, even if it's helping you defeat yourself."

"You always said I was my own worst enemy."

"You are, my dear," she said, her voice soft. "That's what scares me."

"I didn't think you got scared."

"Not by much, but I'm not immune." Rustling on her side. Rummaging amongst her papers, for a pen, perhaps. "Now, tell me again everything that happened, including the names of the officers."

Thirty minutes later, I had a plan, and she'd lost her prickly edge.

"Thanks again," I said and rolled on to my back, the pen and paper and all my notes abandoned on the side table.

"Will you at least try to play nice with the locals?"

"If I say yes, do I still get to take my vacation?"

She sighed. "I know, I'm sorry. If it weren't for Sister Evangeline's death leaving a big swath of the South unprotected, I wouldn't ask this of you."

Neither of us knew Sister Evangeline, but Sister Betty seemed to be taking it pretty hard. From what she told me, Sister Evangeline's territory stretched from Tallahassee through Louisiana, covered San Antonio, and she traveled it on a Harley with a rifle strapped to her back. Envy wiggled through me imagining what kind of badass could handle anything from the bayou nasties to the vampires that inspired those popular novels (and Tom Cruise ruined), and still have the gusto to deal with chupacabra infestations every few years in the San Antonio mesquite scrub.

"Still there?"

"Yeah, just thinking."

"Great! Can you start practicing that before you speak so we don't have to work so hard to bail you out in the future?"

"Har. Har."

She laughed. "You have to admit, that was funny."

"Yeah, okay, fine." I debated bringing up the letter. It could wait. "I'll talk to you tomorrow."

"Stay safe."

I said goodnight again and ended the call. The cut on my calf itched, and my right shoulder ached. *Must have pulled it in the fight,* I thought, yawning so hard, my jaw popped. The cool air felt so good, and I closed my eyes to enjoy it. For just a minute.

"Cee, you're dreaming."

Three tongues slid out of the mouth of the thing hovering over me, each moving on its own. One slid across the leathery upper lip of the hideous mouth; the other two wiggled toward me. I fought the bindings securing my wrists, trying to see past the scaly, furred thing, the hot stink of its breath making my eyes water.

"Wake up."

I thrashed, straining to see around the hulk of the beast, not wanting to draw attention to Marty's presence. The thing couldn't notice him. It hadn't heard him over the screech of its claws on the stones behind me. Instead, it loomed closer, rancid breath burning my eyes as all three tongues reached for my face.

Marty had to escape.

"RUN!"

The word sounded alien and wrong. The world rolled. Everything shook, and even the monster tilted, its tongues lolling. Long, sticky strings of saliva drooped from the nasty curl of its lower lip and arced with the shift in gravity.

"Cee, wake up. You're dreaming."

The mouth opened wider.

"Caitlin!"

And then, I was sitting up, squinting against the harsh light. The sheet pooled around my waist, exposed skin breaking out in goosebumps.

Marty sat on the bed, a white plastic bag dangling from his left hand, his right on my leg. "You okay?"

37

The room looked exactly as it had when I hung up with Sister Betty. Marty's rumpled blankets. Same wobbling ceiling fan. My notebook on the bedside table open to pages of scribbled notes. Orange sunlight burned through the window. The recesses of my brain registered the impending sunset.

"I think so," I said, covering my chest with the sheet.

"Don't cover them on my account. They're pretty and all, but," he shrugged, "meh."

"I know."

"Sounded like a pretty intense dream. Want to talk about it?"

I shook my head. "It wasn't anything special. Probably stress."

Stress with three tongues. My imagination had issues.

"Okay," he said and lifted the bag, the plastic crackling, "food, then!"

"Shirt first. It's cold in here." I slid out of bed and pulled on a t-shirt long enough to cover my panties and grabbed a towel before I climbed back into the soft bed.

"Better than out there," he said as he stood. "I'm sweating like a pig. And still no ghosts. For a so-called haunted hotel, it's spook-free."

"Right." We'd yet to encounter ghosts on any of the jobs we'd worked together. My experience with them wasn't horrific or anything, but I'd rather deal with the corporeal. Easier to fight.

"I hope to see one before we leave," Marty said, handing me a Styro-foam food container and climbing into bed beside me. "It's on my bucket list."

"When you know there's so much weird shit in the world, why do you still want to see ghosts?" I stuffed a piece of fried shrimp in my mouth and groaned as it burst in a shrimpy-greasy little Cajun-spiced explosion. Maybe I should stop teasing Marty about his restaurant review apps. Maybe.

"Why not?" Marty lifted his po' boy and took a monster bite, echoing my groan of pleasure. Whatever he said got lost in the mouthful of food, but I think I got it anyway.

I took a bite, talking through the mouthful. "Isn't what we do enough to scare you?"

"I want to know," he said after he swallowed.

I wiped my mouth with the back of my hand and then licked a drop of sauce from it.

"You are such a cavewoman."

"Whatever." I wiped my hand on the towel. "You'd have done the same. I don't know what this stuff is, but it's heaven."

"God, yes." He took another huge bite and flopped against the pillows to chew.

I took a smaller bite. Food didn't diminish the dream. I thought as I chewed, trying to figure out what about it seemed...familiar.

"Hey-o." Marty poked me in the side. "Food time. Sleep later."

Pointing at my mouth, I chewed and swallowed. "I'm eating."

"Any word from our new friend, La Fontaine?"

"Nah." I dipped a piece of shrimp in the sauce. "Don't expect anything, either."

"What's the plan?"

"Tonight, we hunt the dog and tomorrow we follow Sister Betty's damage control plan."

The hiss of metal scraping metal on our hotel room door made both of us turn.

"What —"

I held up my hand and strained to listen over the whump of the ceiling fan's uneven spin. Something like...breathing.

Shadow blotted out the light under the door.

"Holy shit." Marty's hand covered his nose and mouth against the burnt, sulfurous reek filling the room.

"Shut up," I whispered.

The shadow moved, retreated, a little light seeping in at the corners of the door. More scraping, like a wire brush against the metal, then the shadow under the door disappeared to the left, toward the open hall. Footsteps echoed like low thunder as it retreated.

I threw the blankets back, food tumbling with them, and scrambled out of bed. In my t-shirt, underwear, and bare feet, I ran out the door.

Eerie stillness filled the hall. The strange hour between dinner and bed time that almost always emptied a hotel meant silence. No footsteps. No breathing. No metal scraping. I couldn't even hear TVs behind the closed doors I passed. At the end, where the hall split in opposite directions, I stopped, looking each way. No hint of the recent passage of any person, animal, or specter. I muttered a curse under my breath and spun from one direction to the other.

"Sister Betty would chastise you for language. If she wasn't distracted by your practically bare ass." Marty stepped up beside me. "Cute panties, by the way."

I ignored his comments. "Whatever it was, it's gone."

"You think it was Helen's dog?"

"Doubt it. It wouldn't come for us."

"Maybe it wasn't looking for us."

"What do you mean?"

"She said its role was to guard the dead."

If it was looking for the dead, it would seek out the haunted places where it could herd them like an otherworldly border collie. "So maybe it's herding them."

"Which is probably why I haven't seen any. The little bastard's collecting them. The question is, how do we find it?"

"We go where the dead are. Or should be. Time to gear up." I looked at my bare feet and the hem of the shirt brushing against my upper thighs. "Well, clothes first. Fighting naked sucks."

7

The sun sunk behind the buildings as we dodged meandering pedestrians on Royal Street's uneven sidewalks. I caught conversation in bits, not all of it English, but most of it excitement or anticipation of a night on Bourbon Street. A saxophone wailed a mournful blues riff in the distance under the strange half-twilight broken by street lights. Energy shivered through the air—some of it from the people, some from nearby magic. Maybe a practitioner worked nearby, or perhaps a street magician earned his living with something more advanced than sleight of hand. The buzzy hum of energy made the city all the more dreamlike and unreal. It felt like every postcard I'd ever seen.

I hoped it would feel the same when I could finally enjoy it.

"I'm glad we ate because otherwise, we might have to stop." He turned, following the spicy, intoxicating smell of something deep fried wafting out of an open door. The hand-lettered sign advertised something called boudin balls.

"Focus, foodie."

"Uh huh."

"I called the office. Father Robicheau will be waiting for us. He's the church's monster hunter liaison and was Sister Evangeline's local resource. He's the keeper of the arsenal and will support us while we're in town."

"You mean while we're on this job. Once this is over, we get to go back to that whole vacation thing, right? Hurricanes, étouffée, binge drinking, and lounging by the pool?"

"Yeah, of course. That's what I meant." For a moment, I'd forgotten I hadn't come to work. It seemed so natural. My steps slowed some. Maybe that was part of my problem.

"There's a place I want to check out near the cathedral." Marty outpaced me as I thought. "Not now, of course, but as soon as this is done."

Side-stepping a bent man, I turned to watch him walk away. Did he look familiar? Was he the same man from earlier? He shuffled down the uneven walkway without hesitation or haste, his back bent and head down.

"Cee?" Marty stood at the corner across the street waiting for me.

"Just a sec."

The hairy man in dirty clothes disappeared into the crowd.

Maybe he just looked like the man who jumped us.

The cut on my leg throbbed as if in recognition.

Or maybe...

Last night's nightmare flashed across my eyes. After the first attack, after I escaped and thought myself safe, he'd cut my throat.

The touch on my shoulder made me jump, and I swung, my arm slamming into Marty's chest. "Oh my god, I'm sorry," I said, grabbing him as his knees buckled.

His eyes bulged as his breath wheezed. I dragged him across the sidewalk and propped him against the wall, supporting him as he gasped. After a few minutes, he didn't look as purple or red. His voice rasped when he finally managed to speak. "What...the...hell?"

Despite myself, I giggled when I answered. "You scared me."

He rubbed his chest, coughed, and took a deep breath, only to cough again. "You seriously need to relax."

"I thought you were..." The prospect of explaining that the man who attacked us earlier might be some nightmare come alive seemed comical. Impossible. Crazy. "Never mind."

His breath whistled. "I've seen you fight monsters but never realized how damned strong you are. How much do you work out again?"

"I'm sorry, really. I didn't mean to hit you."

"I'd hate to be on the end of a calculated swing."

Pride I wouldn't have admitted to stirred within me. "Are you okay?"

"You clotheslined me with a steel beam." He rubbed his chest. "Next, you're going to say you expect me to keep walking and help you."

"At least I didn't break your sense of humor."

"Nah, just a couple of ribs." He rubbed his chest again and stood up. "Either we're becoming best friends or I'm in a horribly abusive relationship."

I kissed him on the cheek. "I'll make it up to you, I promise."

With a sigh, we fell in step. "Abusive relationship it is. At least you're not making me withdraw my life savings." He jerked a thumb over his shoulder at the bank behind us. "I was going to ask if we had time to pick up pralines, but I'm not really hungry anymore." Intoxicating cinnamon-scented air distracted him as we passed a shop window.

I thought it best not to answer.

We continued down Royal Street and ducked low-hanging branches in front of the courthouse. A lone musician with a saxophone played "Baker Street" to a mostly disinterested stream of tourists. With a rain-slicked street and full darkness, it would have been practically romantic. Clichéd, but romantic.

"This is it." Marty pointed at the next intersection. The air jangled with music spilling out of restaurants and stores, the chatter of tourists rolling by. "Take a right here."

We turned down the alley, Pirate's Alley according to the street sign, and passed the wrought iron-encircled garden behind the church. In the dusk, it looked strange and overgrown. The rhythmic clang of a tambourine echoed down the street. I squinted, trying to see what lay at the far end of the church, but only caught glimpses between passing tourists. Waves of magic rolled through the alley, keeping time with the music.

"Are you creeped out?" Marty whispered. "Because I'm creeped out."

"Lil' bit," I admitted, looking up at the church rising above the black fence and dark green flora.

A woman passed us, her arms loaded with colorful paper shopping bags, laughing with another, similarly burdened woman. The magic had to be coming from the street in front of the church, unless someone had spelled the stores to make them more enticing. The air crackled and the pulse of New Orleans throbbed through both of us.

"Miss Kelley?"

Marty and I both jumped, almost colliding with strolling tourists. A dark shape lurked behind the fence between the end of the garden and the church's white stone wall. Raising a hand in greeting, the figure leaned into the light from the store across the alley. The clean-shaven man smiled and bowed his head, his face disappearing into shadow again. "My apologies. I didn't mean to startle you."

"Quite alright," I said.

"Sure. I get broken ribs, but a stranger, 'quite alright,'" Marty grumbled.

The gate squeaked as the man in black opened it and gestured for us to enter. "My name is Father Robicheau. Please, come in. We'll use the private entrance. It's less...chaotic than Jackson Square at this hour."

Marty and I looked at each other and followed him through the gate.

I nside, the church echoed with the music from the nave. Ethereal murmurs of lowered voices faded as we passed behind the altar and into a simply furnished private office. "The Archbishop sends his regrets that he wasn't able to meet you personally." His words betrayed no accent, but the polished crispness suggested he'd worked to erase one.

I shook my head. "Save the pleasantries, Father. The Archbishop has no intention of meeting me. I pissed off the Pope so no upwardly-mobile cleric is going to meet with me. It doesn't offend me, but there's no need for the little white lies of social propriety."

The priest stammered, his hands fluttering on top of the desk like wounded white birds. "I assure you, Miss Kelley, it's nothing like that, only—"

"Like I said, I'm not offended, just saving us both a little time."

He didn't respond. If I couldn't hear his breathing, I'd have thought him a vampire. Or a statue.

I cleared my throat. "Forgive me for being blunt, but I'm seeking support for my current assignment. The Vatican tasked me with hunting a black dog for the lady Helen."

His pallor deepened, his hands becoming deceptively calm and still. "What did you say?"

Marty pulled out the paper and pushed it across the desk, a crumb of the wax seal falling to the calendar blotter. "This," he said softly, as if breaking bad news, "is the signed order."

The cleric picked it up and read it. When he finished, he dropped it on the desk and stared at it wordlessly. He looked something like a saint at prayer with the overhead light reflecting like a halo in his ashy-blond hair.

"I don't mean to rush you, Father, but we're short on time." I glanced at the window over his head, the deep blue sky already pricked with starlight. "We've still got to locate and capture the dog. And when that's done, I'm either going to help your replacement monster hunter find the monsters I've already discovered in the past twenty-four hours, or I'm going to fall into the first mixed drink I encounter. Whatever shows up first."

"I thought this was over the day we laid Sister Evangeline to rest." The anguish in his voice made it hard to listen. "She mentored me from my first day in this church." He looked up, as if expecting to see her hovering overhead. "She introduced me to the locals, their culture, and even told me monsters existed and hunted our flock."

Marty and I looked at each other as the priest stared at his desk calendar blotter. A shrug was the only thing Marty offered.

"I thought her eccentric, a bit mad to be honest, even after she shared evidence of these fantastical things. I thought maybe her entire order was…off." His rueful smile directed at the letter in front of him. "And then there was Bubba. Have you met him?"

I shook my head, not wanting to extend the conversation.

"He's exactly what his name conjures. And then there's Agent Hall from some federal agency that isn't supposed to exist." His eyes clouded, a little dreamy. "None of this is supposed to exist."

"Father—"

He raised his hand. "I know. You're on a schedule. I'll be quick. As I said, I thought this would go away." He opened his desk drawer and pulled out a brass key on a red satin tassel. "I never thought I'd unlock this door again. That God would intervene. And then Sister Bridgit called. Then you called." The chimes tolled the hour as if punctuating his observations, accompanied by a lone soprano crescendo from within the church. "I hoped you wouldn't show."

I rubbed my arms to tamp down gooseflesh. The last time I'd felt like this, I'd been hunting a coven of dark magic users kidnapping children. Research led me to an average New England house, but I walked in on some grandmotherly woman brewing something magical right on her Kenmore stovetop. I'm not sure which of us was more surprised. After she transformed into a long-limbed, skeletal demon beast, it hadn't ended well. For her.

The priest raised his arms, his eyes closed. "If this be the will of God, so be it." He paused like that, unmoving for longer than was comfortable to watch, but it gave me a chance to look around the office.

Nothing in the room stood out as supernatural in a non-religious way. A crucifix hung over a bookcase filled with an array of religious and spiritual texts from what I could read at a distance. Marty liked to tease that I needed glasses, but I'd never admit it by asking him what he saw on the shelves.

A small door stood beside the bookshelf, something that might have been used in the 1800s during the reconstruction of the church. Before I could ponder possible uses, Father Robicheau knelt, unlocked the door, and pulled it open. A light clicked on automatically, and as he stepped away, my breath caught.

"Holy…" Marty's voice trailed off either because he caught himself or because he forgot to complete the thought.

A cavern of wonders lay before us, and I got up out of the chair without waiting for an invitation. What lay beyond wasn't exactly a room, nor a closet, but something in between. Arsenal was the only word that came to mind when I saw the weapons hanging on the red velour-lined walls. Even at my utterly average height, I'd need to duck to stand inside, though the contortion would be worth it. Scanning the orderly rows of gleaming metal, I recognized some of the same beauties from my personal collection—a snub-nosed Ruger like the one usually nestled in my boot holster, a matched pair of Sig Sauer's—but there was so much more.

One made me grin.

A katana all but glittered with a seductive come-hither under the recessed lights, the white leather-wrapped handle pristine. I recognized it immediately. No doubt Sister Evangeline and I would have bonded over a fictional, bad-ass, female zombie hunter.

The blade only distracted me for a moment. My heart fluttered as my eyes fell on a beautiful Mossberg 500 twelve-gauge shotgun hanging underneath it.

"Easy, killer," Marty whispered over my shoulder. "Sister Hotpants will get jealous if you drool over another woman like this."

I thumped his chest with a half-hearted backhand.

The far wall with the katana and twelve-gauge felt like a shrine. I slid into the low space and knelt, a matched pair of nickel plated 1911 .45 pistols catching my eye. "Hot damn," I breathed, stroking a barrel with the lightest touch.

"This was Sister Evangeline's collection," Father Robicheau said, "and though many were originally hers or left to her through family, she bequeathed them to the Church. You're welcome to whatever you need."

I shivered and picked up one of the 1911s, hefting the solid weight before sighting the barrel. Perfection. The smell of gun oil. Sister Evangeline, whoever she was, cared for her stash.

Each weapon had a place. Each gleamed, well-maintained and clean. No blank spaces.

My stomach wrenched. She must have died unarmed, I realized. I fought the discomfort of not having more than the blade in the waistband sheath.

"If you need transportation, her Harley's still in a local garage."

I blinked, turning. "Harley?"

"Yes." One corner of his mouth twitched with amusement. "Sister Evangeline preferred traveling on her motorcycle. It's a Harley Davidson." He paused, scowling at the well-worn wooden floor. "I can never remember what kind, though she told me many times."

"Can you ride?" Marty asked.

"He—uh, no." I climbed out of the arsenal. "Thank you for the offer, Father. As much as I'd like to, I think New Orleans is safer if I stay on four wheels."

"I don't ride either, but it didn't stop me from taking it out once or twice." He winked before glancing at the white-washed ceiling. "And thanks to God, both the bike and I are still unscathed."

Marty and I laughed with him, then fell silent with him as he cast his gaze to the ground, hands clasped in front of him. I wondered if he was praying. He radiated peace. For a moment, I let go of my suspicion. Maybe I was imagining it. Maybe I saw something that wasn't there. I bowed my head and tried to find the peace to pray. Words didn't come, except angry ones about Rome. About Shannon. About all the others who had died under my protection.

I squeezed my eyes closed and tried not to see their faces.

Father Robicheau coughed softly.

Relieved, I looked up, the strain draining away as we returned to business. "She had a beautiful collection. Before we start picking, what's the ammunition situation?" Whatever the night brought, I wanted to be prepared.

He reached in to the gun grotto and opened a cabinet on the left side. Ammunition boxes filled the shelves in neat rows, each marked with small white labels. When he backed away, I stepped inside the little space, reading the labels. Blessed. Hollow point/holy water. Silver. Cold iron. White phosphorus. "She was ready for anything, wasn't she?"

"Until the day she returned to our Lord," Robicheau said.

I rocked back on my heels, and before I could speak, Marty asked, "If I may ask, how did Sister Evangeline die?"

He sighed. "An unfortunate, tragic accident, and nothing I like to discuss."

"That's understandable." I pulled out a box of ammo. Marty took it without comment and looked around for someplace to put it.

"I was there," Robicheau said, handing him a khaki-colored military grade backpack with MOLLE straps. "When we got to the ground, I prayed with her until she passed."

"Creepy," Marty murmured as he leaned in to take the 1911s from me.

"Got to the ground?" I asked, looking over Marty's shoulder as he packed the guns carefully into the bag.

"Yes. She fell from a helicopter."

Both Marty and I stopped, our questions overlapping. "How did that happen?"

"A tragic accident, as I've said." He bowed his head. "She died in the service of the Lord. If I have any choice, that will be how I go as well."

Right. Didn't like to talk about it. As he'd radiated peace earlier, now, excitement and anticipation rippled off him.

Guess I hadn't imagined much of anything. Good to know.

"I think that's the most any of us can ask," I said. "I'm sorry to press you further, but how did she fall from a helicopter?"

He walked back to his desk, straightening a book on the corner. "The investigator said her seatbelt failed. When we made a turn, she slid, and I, secured as I was, couldn't reach her. Somehow, she survived long enough for us to land, but there was nothing to be done."

"What were you doing up there?" Marty elbowed me, and I smacked my head on the opening of the arsenal trying to dodge. I scowled at him and rubbed my head.

"Surveying the remaining Katrina damage. A coalition of religious leaders asked to assess what the parish still needs. She'd heard of a...nest of some monster or another hiding in the ruins of the ninth ward and came not only as representation for the New Orleans diocese, but for research. We all have our ways of serving Him, of course. I'm not one to judge another for their choices."

When our eyes met, I shrugged at Marty. "Let him talk," I murmured and shoved a closed black case at him. Instinct told me there was more to Robicheau's story, and for someone who didn't want to talk, he'd already volunteered quite a bit without much prodding.

He still might be innocent, but clichés started somewhere.

"What you're hunting tonight, this dog, is it related to the nest Sister Evangeline heard about?"

"No, and we're not hunting exactly. At least not as we normally do." I picked up the Mossberg, hefting its weight, admiring the light shining along the barrel. Beauty. "It's a special circumstance. Retrieval work. I won't bore you with the details."

I shrugged off Marty's confusion and mouthed the words "roll with it" as I hung up the Mossberg again. As much fun as she'd bring to the work I couldn't avoid, this wasn't the job for that kind of firepower.

"Oh no," he said, peering around Marty who moved to let him see into the arsenal, "you misunderstand. I'm very interested in what threatens my flock. I'm charged with the well-being of my parishioners and anything that may harm them. Sister Evangeline and I—"

"Father, I apologize." I duck-walked out of the arsenal. "At any other time, I'd love this discussion. Right now, I have to find this dog so I can take my vacation."

"Of course. I'm glad to provide whatever support I can."

"Hopefully, we'll finish tonight, and this'll be the last time we raid your arsenal."

"Sister Evangeline's arsenal."

"God's arsenal?" I offered with a smile.

His right eyebrow jumped. "Guns in the service of God? Given the history, I'm not sure we'd get far in that argument with Him."

Despite myself, I laughed and shouldered the backpack. "Good point, Father. I hope to return all this to you tomorrow and get out of your hair for the rest of my stay in N'awlins."

Father Robicheau's stiff smile didn't budge. "Let's hope tomorrow will be the last we see each other."

8

The red tail lights of the car shrunk into the distance as we stood outside of Saint Louis Cemetery Number One. "You'd think they'd be surprised when someone wants to go cemetery at night," Marty said, putting the bag on the ground, angling it into the streetlight glow from across the street. Yellow-orange light gleamed off the guns inside.

"Are you kidding? This is probably the easiest place to blend in. Outside of Bourbon Street, of course. And with the cargo we've got, I'd rather avoid as many tourists as possible."

"We should have Uber'd. After Tallahassee, I'm sure my rating is horrible."

"I told you we could have walked."

"And I was too drunk to listen. That's why I puked." He looked around. "So, you ready to strap up?"

The streetlights at the end of the block changed, and a single car approached on the other side of the street. None of the buildings or fixtures had obvious cameras, but it wasn't worth taking a chance. I stared at the wall. "I wish I'd known it was white."

"I told you we should have Googled it."

"And when do I ever listen?"

"Fair point." He slung the bag across his shoulder, hefting the lock at the barred gate. "So how're we dealing with this?"

"We're not," I said, my hand out for the bag.

"What?"

I slid the straps over both shoulders, squatted, and laced my fingers together in an upward facing cup. "Alley-oop."

He stared at my hands, took a step back, and shook his head. "Nuh uh. Last time I ended up with a broken finger."

"Unless you've put in some time at the gym I don't know about, you are going to struggle scaling this wall."

"I could just wait out here."

"With a bag full of guns? In New Orleans?"

He shrugged. "I'll be all right."

"Then let me object. It's a shitty idea, especially if that dog is in there. I'll need back up, no matter how sketchy your aim is."

"My aim isn't sketchy."

"Right." I nodded toward my hands. "Step up."

With a heavy sigh, Marty put one foot in my hands, and I boosted him. As he rolled over the wall, the crash wasn't as loud or as curse-laden as I expected, but then again, it wasn't very tall. He muttered on the other side.

I jumped and caught the top of the wall, the rough stucco abrading my fingertips. "All the better to scrape off fingerprints," I said as I hoisted myself over.

Marty rubbed his elbows and handed me the holsters for the 1911s. "You need to show me how to do that."

"You need to build muscle." I flexed and grinned before adjusting the holster, the leather slung low on my hip, a reassuring weight. "Then, someday, you can carry the big boy guns like me."

"You look like a character from a video game."

I looked down at myself, guns strapped to each thigh. "Nah. My boobs aren't pointy enough."

Even the dark couldn't hide his eye roll.

Low, stone buildings loomed in the half-light that crested the stucco wall at my back. "Don't forget," I said, threading my arms through another holster, "this is a capture mission. Shoot only as last resort."

"Right." Marty adjusted his holster. "And exactly how are we going to capture this hell-hound with lethal force? Club it with the gun?"

"You're the only one armed for non-lethal force." I popped open the black plastic case and freed the tranquilizer gun from the foam inside. "I liberated this from Sister Evangeline's arsenal." Dart loaded, I slid it into the holster under my arm. "Should be just what we need."

"Will that work on supernatural creatures?"

I shrugged and eyeballed the darts. "That's why you're my back up."

"How are we getting it back to Helen?"

"Let's bag it first. We'll figure that out later."

"I love how you plan for all the important details."

I opened my mouth to speak, interrupted by the crunch of gravel.

Marty paused, the second snub-nosed Ruger half-way into his holster.

We waited in the shadows, silent and barely breathing. Another crunch. I pointed at Marty, then down the aisle in front of us. Jabbing a thumb at myself, I gestured to the next row. He nodded in agreement, gun pointed at the ground in a two-handed grip. I chambered a dart in the tranquilizer gun. By the size, it had to be enough. If not, I had five more in my pocket. As long as I didn't stab myself with one.

We crept around the mausoleums. I kept my foot low to the ground, seeking obstacles and grade changes where the streetlights didn't reach. Staring hard into the night and straining to hear, silence buzzed through the graveyard.

Another crunch, this one an unmistakable footstep.

I froze. Marty shook his head and pointed to the far corner of the cemetery.

In sync, we stepped between the rows of crypts, guns drawn. Drunken tourists laughed and sang on the other side of the stucco wall. Under the covering rush of a passing car, the crunch and rustle continued, braver and more determined. I wriggled between two of the crypts into the next row, seeing nothing.

A stone rattled across the sidewalk. The crunching steps stopped, replaced by a growl louder and deeper than Helen's wolf-dog, Fen. My skin crawled. If this thing was bigger than Fen, it would be massive. I hoped the darts would be strong enough to take it down and keep it down long enough to get it to Helen. And that I could reload fast enough to make it matter.

"Oh shit!"

I spun and hurried backward down the path. The menacing growl rose, echoing through the cemetery. When Marty screamed, I sprinted.

One gunshot.

My stomach sank as I looked down the aisles between the close stone mausoleums, my voice a stage whisper. "Marty, where are you?"

He sprawled on the ground at the foot of a crypt, street lights high-lighting his back.

I skidded to his side, holstering my weapon and running my hands over him as I called his name. No obvious blood. No noticeable wounds.

He groaned and shifted, his gun scraping on the ground.

"Don't move." I fished in my pocket for my flashlight. Covering the bulb with my fingers, I clicked on the light and shined it on my friend. He didn't look hurt, until I aimed the light in his eyes.

"Ow." He raised his hand and pushed the light away. "I'm fine."

Fingers still covering the flashlight, I let a sliver of light fall across Marty's forehead. "You've got a good bruise starting." With the other hand, I touched it, and he winced. "And a hell of a lump."

"Not to mention the one you gave me earlier," he said, rubbing his chest.

I rolled my eyes. "What about the gunshot? What happened? Did you see it? Did it jump you?" I scanned the area, expecting to find the body of the dog. Or at least a blood trail.

"Wasn't me." He sat up slowly, rubbing his head. "I saw it, though."

"What do you mean?"

"I saw the dog, and that thing is huge. No way we're lifting it over the wall, even if you manage to stick enough darts to take it down." Marty winced as he pushed himself up to lean against the weathered stone. "Red glowing eyes, by the way. Fucking creepy."

"And the gunshot?"

"I'm getting there. The dog, or some shadow manifestation of it, was in front of me, growling, glowing eyes. All I could think was 'oh, shit.'"

"You said it, too."

"No. Not me." He rubbed his head. "Someone in black stood behind it with a gun. I saw the gun, turned to run, heard the scream, and I guess I ran into the crypt trying to avoid the shot."

Whoever fired was probably still here. Possibly watching.

An itch tickled the spot between my shoulders. I resisted the urge to roll them. If someone was watching, it might already be too late, but if not, I might get the upper hand. We had to sound focused on anything but our surroundings. I hoped Marty would catch on.

"What about the dog?" he asked, eyes clear as he winked.

I clicked the flashlight off. "I'll look around, though it's probably gone."

"How? We're in a walled-in graveyard."

"It's a supernatural creature that's drawn power from cemeteries for millennia. Walls aren't much of an obstacle." I hoped he'd see me hold my finger to my lips. Drawing the 1911, I aimed it at the ground away from Marty.

"I guess not." He tried to get up and staggered against the crypt.

"Stay put. I'm going to see how we can get you out of here without climbing." I pointed to myself, then a route around the crypts. If whoever fired at Marty was still here, I wanted them off guard. Each slow step made as little noise as possible.

The main gate of the cemetery hung open.

That made one thing easier. And everything else harder.

9

Marty's bruise glared at me like an accusation, the deep purple a stark contrast to his naturally tanned skin. "You sure you're feeling okay?" I tried to face yet another failure to protect those around me without looking away.

"I told you, I'm fine and, again, it wasn't your fault." He pressed the ice-filled towel against his head, hiding the ugly purple mark. A drop of water rolled down his sunglasses.

"I'd feel better if you'd get checked out."

"And get medical advice that says I can't have another of these?" He lifted the slushy, fluorescent drink with his other hand. "Hell naw."

The sun warmed my shoulders in the most enticing way. Everything I wanted was here. A little shade under the potted palms and the shadows of nearby buildings, a little breeze, a roof-top pool and alcohol on demand delivered by hotel staff. I shifted on the plastic lounge chair and shaded my eyes. The sooner I figured out how to catch this damned dog, the sooner I could spend my afternoons here.

"You could relax, you know. There isn't much you can do until nightfall."

I shook my head. "I've got legwork to do while you research. Maybe Robicheau knows who's got keys to the gate at Saint Louis Number One. Or why someone would've been there last night."

"Do you trust him?"

"Nope. Something's off with him. I can't tell what, though." It'd kept me up far too long last night, but come to nothing.

"You're always saying things like that—"

"And how many times have I been wrong?"

"If you'd've let me finish, I would've said I agree with you." After a moment, he said, "But I'm gonna start writing it down just so I have an answer when you ask."

"Until then, will you check him out, please? And if you find anything interesting, send a copy to Sister Betty?"

He saluted me with his free hand. The wrong one, not that it mattered. "You got it, boss. But isn't it cliché for the religious guy to be bad?"

"Totally. And yet?" Was I seeing things where they didn't exist simply because cliché taught me to expect it? I'd thought it over for so long the night before that I didn't know what I thought anymore. Nothing had changed except I hadn't slept. There had to be more. Such a persistent gut feeling had to have something behind it.

He nodded. "Something's hinky."

"Agreed. As much as I don't like it, he's our only local resource. Sister Betty said the high-ranking clergy's out of town to handle Albuquerque. If I can't get anything out of him, I'll ask her to intervene."

Sun glinted off his sunglasses as he nodded. "So you go lone wolf. That'll end well."

I flipped him off. "If you didn't have a head injury, I'd smack you."

With a laugh, he put the towel of ice on the table beside him. "It'd still be worth it."

"Call or text me if you need anything, or if you find anything to help us pin down the Black Dog. Or a pattern of 'sudden deaths' like the airport guy. Or anything you can dig up about Father Robicheau or Helen." Quite the vacation. I envied my nerd friend, even with the goose-egg on his forehead. At least he could work by the pool and drink.

"You got it. Be careful, lone wolf."

"Aren't I always?"

———

Though I'd hoped to surprise Father Robicheau by showing up unannounced at Saint Louis Cathedral, my ambition only led to punishment. To my thighs, specifically. By wooden pews. After spending half my childhood in church following Shannon's death, wooden pews never failed to evoke loathing whether during Mass, waiting for my turn at confession, or waiting for my parents to finish a counseling session. The unforgiving seats doled out more punishment than any priest in the confessional or parochial school nun.

And here I was, again, my hamstrings doing penance while I waited. The nervous young deacon who offered to call when Father Robicheau returned from visiting congregation members only ventured out to check on me once, though I saw him peek out at me from a door behind the altar twice. I tried to relax, to appreciate the stained glass and architecture of the nave. History had a heartbeat here, though not the same as other places I'd visited. More unsettling.

When my legs cramped the first time, I'd walked around. An old woman passed me as we approached the candle rails. She lowered herself carefully to the kneeler, bowed her head, and clasped her hands. I stepped away to let her remember and pray in peace.

The deacon approached, wringing his hands as I resumed my uncomfortable seat. "I'm sorry, Miss Kelley, Father Robicheau called to say he won't return until much later. I'll be glad to call you when he returns."

"No, that's not necessary. I'll wait." I tried to feign a relaxed posture.

The deacon, who's name I'd already forgotten, glanced over his shoulder at the sacristy door. "It would be b-best if you, uh…"

"He's in the sacristy and told you to get rid of me."

Nothing could have been more confirmation than the way the deacon's head whipped around, or the way his blue eyes bugged out of his head. "Wha… I don't—no, that's not, he's visiting—"

"Infirm and unwell congregants," I said. "Right. Got it. How about you take me to his office. He has something for me. I'll take care of two errands at once."

His forehead wrinkles deepened as he looked over his shoulder again. The lack of hair above the laurel wreath of spare strands crowning his ears made sense. Poor guy probably worried off every strand. "It's against the rules to admit you to the sacristy or private offices."

I stood to his almost comical relief. "Rules are meant to be broken," I said. "That's what parochial school taught me." With a wink, I walked around him and his astonishment to the sacristy door behind the altar.

The commotion of hurried footsteps on creaky wooden floors greeted me before I opened the door. I grinned. If he was running, discovering what the good Father had to hide might actually be fun.

Sister Betty would be the first to warn me not to do it.

The door opened on silent hinges. I hesitated, my foot hovering over the threshold.

She'd warn me that nothing good came from lone wolf hunts. That "a Scooby-Doo crew of at least two means back up and safety for you." She'd even made me recite the stupid rhyme from memory. But Marty knew where I was, and this wasn't a monster hunt.

"Miss Kelley, I assure you, I will call you when Father Robicheau returns." The deacon tugged at my shoulder, but the taller man had no chance of moving me without my consent or participation. Superior muscle mass for the win.

"That's fine." I shook off his grip and continuing down the hall. "I'll just get what I need from his office while I wait."

He argued.

I ignored.

The office door was closed, but unlocked. When I opened it, a red-faced Father Robicheau sat behind his desk, his hands primly folded on the calendar. "Miss Kelley," he said, a little breathless.

"Tsk tsk," I said to the stammering deacon behind me. "'Thou shalt not lie' is a commandment, isn't it? Seems like the Father has been here all along."

The deacon cringed.

"No, Miss Kelley, Deacon Paul wasn't aware I'd returned from my visits." Father Robicheau stood, gesturing to the seat in front of his desk. "Please, have a seat."

"Father, I'm s—"

"Thank you, Paul. Please leave us now." The strange harshness in his voice silenced the other man. Every nerve in my body tingled, though I couldn't figure out why this felt so wrong. "Bad cleric" was such a cliché that it couldn't possibly be what was going on, yet the "hinky" was undeniable. Once the door closed, Robicheau turned his rigid smile back to me and sat. "How can I help you today?"

"How were your visits?" I sat back and watched him.

The brittle smile wavered with the unexpected question. "Fine, fine. Our devoted members who cannot make it to Mass still require spiritual support. Like Mrs. McGillicutty. Devout woman in her nineties. She's fortunate enough to still get around, but getting here is challenging most of the time." He picked something from his sleeve, his shoulders relaxing. "That and her toy poodle requires more attention as it ages."

I nodded. "Sounds like tending to your flock's a full-time job."

He bristled. "Of course."

"Then we've got something in common."

"Perhaps." Sitting back in the chair, he clasped his hands, elbows resting on the arms of the chairs. "Though I nurture the spiritual well-being of the faithful, not to enable their sinful behaviors. As a matter of fact, I still have things to take care of, so while I hate to rush you, I must ask again, how can I help you?"

Oh, this would be fun after all. I "enabled sinful behavior"? This might run deep and require some assistance from Marty, but what fun it would be to unravel. I might even consider this part of my vacation. Watching him struggle with calm, I tried to hide my amusement. "Of course. I'd like another chance to go through Sister Evangeline's cache. We encountered the Black Dog last night and need to adjust our plan. As well as address another challenge we encountered."

"Oh?" He shifted, his face a kaleidoscope of emotion.

Bait taken. "You may be able to help. Do you know who has access to the keys for the Saint Louis Cemetery Number One? Anyone who might have been there last night?"

He shook his head, lips pursed. "Not that I can think of. The Archdiocese controls access, both for tourists and family of the departed. No one should be there without authorization. How do you know someone was there?"

"Would you be able to get a list of those with access?"

"Why should I do that, Miss Kelley?" A red flush crept up his neck and colored the tips of his ears. "That's not relevant to your assignment."

"As of last night, it is." I shrugged, trying to keep a casual posture as he bristled. "Part of that challenge I mentioned."

He opened his right-hand desk drawer and took out the key without getting up. "Of course, I'll provide support, but I don't see the need for you to have an access list."

"If I can't get it from you, I'll reach out to the Archdiocese."

Something flashed in his eyes too fast to catch. "Do as you feel you must. I'll protect my flock as I see fit." He dropped the key in the drawer. "And all of God's creations, as well."

Interesting.

I stood, my hand out. "How about I look through the stash and get out of your hair?"

"No, I think you've taken all you need for now." With a smile, he slammed the drawer and folded his hands on the desk. "I'll discuss appointing a more appropriate local liaison with the Archbishop."

Curiouser and curiouser. "What do you mean, Father?"

"My job is to protect God's creations. You destroy them. I see us at odds."

I laughed. "Monsters. I hunt monsters responsible for harming your congregation."

"That's how you see them. I don't."

"And how do you see them?"

"As the perfect, righteous justice of God, of course. If He created them, they have a purpose. Perhaps that purpose is culling the sinful. Perhaps they're more holy than all of us." He stilled, his composure returning. "We're not meant to know all, only to obey and submit to His will."

Before I could ask a question, there was a knock at the door.

"Come in." Father Robicheau didn't hesitate.

"Father, Sister Bridgit from the Holy Order of the Sisters of Mercy of Saint Brendan to see you."

My heart jack-rabbited. Both Father Robicheau and I straightened.

In the doorway, she loomed behind Deacon Paul slightly taller than the thin man. The stark white of her coif and the rich black of her veil intensified the sharpness of her dark eyes. Even without makeup, those eyes pierced me to my very soul.

I swallowed the lump in my throat with as much grace as I could.

Father Robicheau's poise flittered away. "Sister Bridgit," he said as she stepped around the deacon and crossed the room, her hand extended. "I wasn't expecting you."

"Where there's a crisis, I follow." With a perfunctory smile, she shook the limp fingers Robicheau offered. "A pleasure."

"This is Miss—"

Sister Betty pulled me against her for a quick hug and muttered, "Play along," before returning her attention to the man in the black frock. "Caitlin and I are well acquainted. She's my protégé and will eventually assume my role in the Order."

We'd been working toward it for years, but hearing her say it to another person made it real. Anxiety over Rome welled in my stomach, but I managed a smile. Time to doubt my ability to take over for her later.

I had time to get better. Stronger. Never again would someone die if I could stop it. No matter what it took.

Robicheau blinked, his mouth agape. "I...didn't expect..."

"God works in mysterious ways." Sister Betty flashed an innocent grin. I almost choked as heat poured through me. That woman. "Now," she said, "let's talk business."

ister Betty crossed her legs under her tunic.

The reprimand I'd have expected from anyone else didn't happen. Robicheau barely had the guts to hold himself together against her, never mind assert himself against impropriety.

"I assume you and Caitlin have worked out access to the armory?" She smiled her dangerous smile. Her words rolled out in a disarming purr disguising the threat of impending menace.

Father Robicheau sat squarely in her sights, and he had no idea.

"Yes, in fact," he opened the drawer and produced the key, "she'd just requested access it again. Which I was about to permit, of course."

"Great." Her foot bounced, making her tunic sway.

I accepted the key, now so readily given, and sat back, waiting for the drama. "Thank you, Father."

"Thank you for your support," she said, her voice low and sultry.

He avoided looking at her, maybe pretending not to see the unseemly wiggle of her tunic. Kudos to him, but maybe it distracted me more since I knew what was underneath. I bit the inside of my cheek to subdue a giggle while trying not to squirm.

"Of course." His sour scowl fought to be a professional, emotionless expression, but lost. He blinked several times, tugging his cleric blacks. "Was that all?"

"Not. Even. Close." The threat in her slow, staccato words stopped him, mid-rise. "There's something foul in your house, Father, and I'm here to clean it out."

"No, no, you're mistaken," he said, his words tumbling over each other, his eyes wide. "I'm just serving God by tending the New Orleans flock."

Sister Betty's predatory grin reminded me why she was one of the most terrifying hunters the Church had ever known. She sat still as a vampire, her eyes locked on the cleric behind his desk. "Are you sure?"

"This is highly irregular, Sister Bridgit!" Father Robicheau pushed back in his chair, sweat rolling down his forehead.

Sister Betty stood, aiming a quick gesture at me to do the same, and we rounded the desk in opposite directions. "Please. Call me Betty. Everyone does."

Robicheau's head swiveled between us, a trapped animal looking for escape. "What is this? Why are you doing this?" Finding nowhere to retreat, he dropped into his seat, cowering.

"You know why. And you'd better start talking before things get..." She leaned over him. Her white teeth, flushed cheeks, and pink lips belonged in a magazine rather than a religious order.

Then there was her stance over the cowering man.

Lethal and sexy.

I swallowed hard, unsure if fear or arousal would win the war within me.

"...serious." She stretched the word, the long sibilant hiss of a snake ready to strike.

Father Robicheau shuddered. "I don't know what you're talking about."

"How about we talk about Sister Evangeline's death?"

Had there been color in his face, it would have drained away. Instead, his skin yellowed, as if aging thirty years before our eyes. I expected him to have some kind of heart attack. "I don't like to talk about it," he finally managed.

"Hard to discuss it without incriminating yourself?" I asked.

"No, no, that's not it, I don't like talking about it because she died—"

"Serving God?" I offered.

His face hardened, wrinkles like rigid cracks as his mouth twisted in distaste. "You have no idea what it is to serve God."

"Funny." I glanced at Sister Betty without letting him out of my sight. "Last I checked, I work for the Church."

The priest huffed. "You have no idea what God's work really is."

Sister Betty laughed. "Enlighten me."

The Father fidgeted. "It's shepherding your fellow man and leading sinners to repentance. But not all sinners are repentant, and some will never seek God's light."

As if on some kind of divine cue, a shadow crossed the window over his head. I slid my hand into my pocket and pulled out my cellphone.

"Put it on the desk, Miss Kelley."

I hadn't seen Robicheau draw the gun he pointed at me. All I could do was blink and stare. Where the hell had it come from?

"Don't make me repeat myself." The hardness in his eyes didn't replace the sad droop around the corners. Even though the bastard had me, I still pitied him a little. A very little, but it was there.

"Father," I placed my phone face down on the table, "we're on the same side." As long as he was focused on me, Sister Betty might pull off some kind of miracle. What exactly, I had no idea.

That was up to her. I had to give her time and opportunity. And take it if it came my way.

"This isn't part of protecting your congregation," Sister Betty added, her hands hidden in the sleeves of her tunic. She had to have some gadget, or weapon, hiding up there.

"Who are you to judge me?" Robicheau's color returned in a rush. "You," he pointed with the gun, "cloistered away in...wherever you hide from the world. You have no idea what it's like, what it takes—"

"You're harming them by hindering us," I said.

The gun swung in my direction along with his scowl. "I leave judgement to God."

"Do you know what we do?"

"We?" He scoffed. The sleeves of Sister Betty's tunic wriggled. "You say you serve God, yet when His creations punish the sinful and unrepentant, you kill the means of His justice. You. Kill. Them." He punctuated his words with thrusts of his gun. "Thou shalt not kill."

I flinched to keep his attention on me. Letting him believe he had the upper hand was so simple, it might actually work. "And yet," I said, "you're ready to kill us."

"Like you killed Sister Evangeline," Sister Betty said.

"Her death was a tragic accident. She—"

I held up both hands, the gun thrusting in my face again as soon as I moved. "Right, seatbelt, banking helicopter, got it. But you knew. You had something to do with it, didn't you?"

A sinister smile oozed across his face. The hair rose on my arms. He didn't have to say anything else.

"You did. Whatever you did, you made sure she died." I heard my own astonishment. How had I not seen it? How had I not suspected something as odd as falling from a routine helicopter ride, especially someone as tactically experienced as Sister Evangeline?

"Shut up."

I caught the glow of Sister Betty's cellphone screen through her tunic.

"You killed your local monster hunter." Marty owed me for being right. Again...

"Shut up!" His arm shook, and he leaned over the desk, the muzzle of the snub-nose .38 dancing inches from my face.

"You murdered your mentor because she protected innocent people from monsters who threatened them!" I leaned in close enough to smell the gun oil, daring him to fire, demanding his full attention. "You murdered her and tell me not to kill?"

"She interfered with God's design. She questioned His decisions and intervened!" He pressed the gun against my forehead, face flushed and breathing in ragged gasps.

"And you're doing the same with us." My words were almost a whisper.

He recoiled. "I am not."

"Aren't you?" I leaned forward again to keep his attention on me. "You've got a gun in my face because I protect people, repentant or sinful, worthy or unworthy, from the monsters who hunt them. So, who's interfering with God's plan, here? Who's really their brother's keeper?"

He squared his shoulders in defiance, the gun no longer wobbling.

We locked eyes.

Time to take the bastard down.

I felt the quick shift in the energy before I saw anything, but as Sister Betty moved, I dropped.

The report of the gun drowned out Robicheau's surprised yelp. My ears rang as I rolled to regain my footing. Hearing only a screaming echo of the gun's report, I shook my head and scrambled around the desk, struggling to keep my balance. In the narrow space between the desk and abandoned chair, Sister Betty and Robicheau became a tangle of flailing, struggling limbs and too much black cloth. Of course, I jumped in, struggling to pry the gun from his hand. His wiry fingers were far stronger than they looked, so I went with the only feasible option.

Breaking them.

The suggestion of sound broke through the howl of deafness, probably Robicheau's scream since he released his weapon. I slid it across the floor and pinned his arms. Maybe I tweaked his broken finger a little more than necessary, but the bastard had threatened me with a gun. And fired it. A little manhandling balanced our debt. Sister Betty's knee seemed to be taking her due with his holy jewels.

A hand on my shoulder.

I twitched, wrenching another finger to keep Robicheau subdued. Another spike in the roar of non-sound.

Standing over me was my new bestie, Officer La Fontaine, red faced and sweating, his gun pointed at me.

Awesome.

Half a dozen cops in body armor filled the room, some clustered around the desk, weapons pointed at the wriggling clerics, a few more in the hall, weapons aimed at me.

Even better.

Nothing says vacation like being held at gunpoint.

His mouth moved, and I shrugged. "Can't hear you, but he's the one you want." I gestured at the wriggling man on the floor as a uniform pulled Sister Betty back on her heels. She held her hands over her head, her face too pale and sweaty.

I reached out to give her a thumbs up to see if she was okay, when both of my hands were wrenched behind my back. "No," I said, or maybe I yelled. I couldn't really tell. "He's the one you want. He fired the gun. He killed Sister Evangeline."

They ignored me.

As someone pulled me out, another cop lifted Sister Betty. The wet shine on her tunic glistened, but pain transformed her face. "She's been shot!" But no matter how I struggled, I couldn't break free.

I tried to relax my jaw and not grit my teeth as I answered. "I told you, already, Robicheau fired the gun. The only time I touched it was to take it away."

"And broke his fingers." He glanced up at me, his pen poised over a steno notebook.

"Either that or get shot."

He wrote without acknowledging my response.

"Once I had it, I slid it across the room and tried to secure him against further violence. Now, will you please tell me the status of my partner?"

"He's being questioned." The detective sounded bored. "But since he wasn't there, he'll probably be released soon."

"He? No, my other partner. Sister Bridgit. The one in the room with me. She was shot. I need to know how she is."

He shrugged. "I wasn't aware anyone had been injured." With a nod at the notebook on the table in front of him, he continued. "You're saying the priest shot the gun?"

I stopped pacing around the spartan, industrial green conference room and stared at him. "Seriously? How many times do I need to answer this question?"

A knock at the door interrupted whatever he intended to say. When it opened, an officer gestured to the detective, and the two whispered at the door, too low for me to hear over the buzzing in my ears. The detective glanced at me but returned to his conversation.

I folded my arms and waited. Never had I been held or questioned this long by local law enforcement. Of course, I'd never had such a contentious encounter with them before getting caught up in such a weird situation. Okay, not never, but not often. Not more than half dozen times or so.

And probably because Sister Betty or DEMON, the Department of Extra-Dimensional, Magical, and Occult Nuisances, usually intervened. Without her, it would take time before DEMON got the message.

Without her—

Nausea roiled in my stomach, and I pushed the thought away.

The two men nodded at each other, and the detective returned to his seat at the table, refusing to meet my eyes.

"And?"

He looked up. "And what?"

"What did he tell you about my partner?"

"Nothing."

"She was shot." I approached the mirror, staring past the detective's reflection, trying to see whomever might be observing on the other side. "I need to know she's okay."

"Miss Kelley, yesterday, you were attacked on the street. Today, you claim a priest held a gun to your head. That this same priest tried to shoot you. In a church."

"Yes, that's right."

"You have to see why this is so difficult to believe."

"What?" I turned around.

He stared at me, implacable, expressionless, pen in hand, waiting for something remarkable enough to write down.

"You think I'm lying?"

"I didn't say that."

"That's what you're implying."

His chin lifted a fraction as he inhaled slowly. "Explain to me the circumstances of the attack yesterday."

"I already have!" The echo of my own voice made the ringing in my ears louder. "And I've already explained what happened in the church. Tell me how my partner is."

"Miss Kelley—"

"No. No more. Charge me if you have to." If they hadn't already filed a report with my name on it, as soon as my name was entered, I'd have backup. Someone from the Church, or someone from DEMON would be here. Either way, it didn't matter. Either way, I'd be released. Either way, I could check on her. Sister Betty could be dying. I could be losing her.

She might already be gone.

Nausea swelled within me.

Without moving, the detective stared at me.

I sat in the chair across from him.

Neither of us spoke.

He sighed. "Your partner is fine. She's being treated for an abrasion and a cracked rib."

Relief flooded through me with such intensity I thought I might slump onto the table. My voice cracked as I thanked him.

Another knock at the door, and it swung in without hesitation. A short man in government-blue suit that fit better twenty pounds ago nodded at me, shifting his battered brown briefcase to his left hand. "Miss Kelley, you're free to go."

The detective stood up. "Who are you?"

Before he'd finished the question, the little man produced a business card with the flick of his fingers. "Agent Cooper Hardin. I'm with the federal Department of Extra-Dimensional, Magical, and Occult Nuisances."

"Department of…" He scowled, standing. "DEMON?"

"That's right, and he's legit, McKenzie." A uniformed cop appeared behind Agent Hardin, his insignia identifying him as the commander. "And don't bother Googling that department. It's one a' them that doesn't exist."

Agent Hardin gave what might have passed for a smile in his world. "They do call it one of the No Such Agencies for a reason."

I grinned. I'd not met Agent Hardin before, but I could tell I'd like him. The little man had gusto.

"Since there's no grounds to hold Miss Kelley, she will be leaving. With any, and all, weapons she had on her person."

"Of course." The commander's jaw twitched.

"But sir," the detective who's name I'd not bothered remembering tried to protest.

The commander shook his head. As he approached, I glimpsed his nametag. R. Albert. He stuck his hand out, thin skinned and flecked with dark spots. Far older than the man it was attached to. "Miss Kelley, my apologies. My team does their best to protect New Orleans, and we appreciate your…unique expertise, no matter how poorly we show it." His drawl made the city's name into something more exotic and vaguely foreign. Combined with the sincerity in his eyes, I lost the conviction of my irritation.

"Of course. If I'd been here in any professional capacity, I'd have come to introduce myself." Probably not true, but it sounded good. I needed to get better with that professional courtesy thing.

"Of course." His smile hinted that he knew better. "Our city hasn't been easy on your kind lately. I'm hoping you can help us change that."

"I'll do what I can," I said.

"Glad to hear it."

The death knell of my vacation rang in the familiar laughter behind me.

"Caitlin, we'd best be on our way to see Bridgit before visiting hours are over. There'll be plenty of time to chat later." Father Callahan leaned against the doorway, one leg crossed in front of the other, arms crossed. His grin showcased his unnaturally white teeth. When I first met him, I assumed him a monster in disguise because of those teeth. All the better to eat me with.

I agreed. Commander Albert led us out, talking all the way, though I didn't listen. Father Callahan talked enough for both of us. No one ever noticed who contributed to the conversation when he was around. Except Sister Betty.

No one could hide from her.

11

"I told you," Sister Betty grumbled, "I'm fine. I'll be out as soon as they let me."

Father Callahan laughed. "Such a patient patient."

With a scowl, she thumped the bed in frustration. "I came to help, and I can't do that from here."

"You did help," I said. "I'd probably be dead without you." Even though I'd suspected Father Robicheau, I'd gone to the St. Louis Cathedral unarmed. Alone. Stupid. And because I was stupid, she'd gotten shot.

At least she hadn't lectured me.

"You'd have figured out some way out of it. You always do." She shifted and winced. "Besides, based on the message Marty left, you were already on the right track. I called the police on the way to Saint Louis Cathedral from the airport when he told me you were headed there on your own."

"They took their time showing up."

"That they showed up at all is a little surprising," Father Callahan said. "At least before the gunshot."

"No, they didn't." I looked at Sister Betty, waiting for her agreement. He fired before the cops showed up.

"They were on the premises. The gunshot was…" Father Callahan shrugged and waved a hand, "incentive to hurry."

I rolled my eyes. Father C never missed a detail, or failed to point out the minutiae. Sister Betty interjected before words made it out of my open mouth. "Regardless, Robicheau's in custody, and with the evidence we presented, I don't think we'll have to worry much about him."

Father Callahan shrugged. "Legal will take over."

"Why didn't you let me know?"

"Timing." Sister Betty shrugged and put her hand over her wound. "We thought we'd figured it out and immediately got on a plane. By the time we landed, Marty'd left his message and you were en route to the cathedral."

"And we need to talk about the letter."

Sister Betty avoided looking at me. "We will, but not now. That dog is still out there, and there's the creature you saw in the airport." She waved her hand as if dismissing the thought. "But the dog first. You shouldn't be wasting time here."

"I'm no closer to figuring out how to catch it."

"Yet another reason I'm here, pigeon." Goosebumps rippled across my skin as our eyes met. "Even before the Robicheau thing, Marty and I were exchanging research about it. Of course, everything I brought's still at the church."

"I'll go get it. Marty's resting at to the hotel. The knock on the head last night laid him low."

"Call me as soon as you have it. We have several things we need to discuss."

"I don't like you going alone." Father Callahan crossed his legs and slipped a hand into his jacket, pulling out a pack of gum.

"Do you have a better option?" It sounded far more sarcastic than I intended.

With slow, deliberate movements, he removed a piece, unwrapped it, and popped the unnaturally blue confection in his mouth. "No, I don't."

"They're probably still processing the scene, so the place'll be crawling with cops." I forced a grin. "It'll be the safest place in the city as long as I keep my mouth shut."

Sister Betty laughed, the sound cut short with a grunt. "So we're banking on miracles now?"

Father Callahan laughed, too. "Now I really don't want you going by yourself."

The tension drained out of the room. "I'll be fine," I said, repeating her words. "I can handle New Orleans at night, and I'll behave myself. I promise. Besides, as long as I'm not dying, the dog shouldn't be a threat."

"That's not exactly true," Sister Betty interrupted.

"The letter said…"

"I know," she said, her cheeks flaming red as she picked at the blanket.

Words failed me. First, she'd kept the assignment secret, though she'd known it was coming. Then, the letter from the Pope about the dog, and now, the part that assured I'd be safe, the most critical part, wasn't true? "What about it isn't true?" Accusation rang in each syllable.

Father Callahan sat forward, propping his arms on his crossed legs. "Now, Caitlin, the letter came from the Vatican—"

"From a man who hates me and would excommunicate me if he could find an excuse. If there's some risk related to facing this creature, I have a right to know."

"You do," Callahan said with frustrating calm.

"I'm not hearing it."

"Because you're not letting anyone explain!" Sister Betty's raised voice shocked us both. "It might attack the living. There's historical precedent, though I can't remember all the details, but if it goes that far, it's almost impossible to contain. Combined with the sheer volume of non-corporeal dead that are part of the city's economy—"

"Right. Dog goes nuts, we're all in deep." Crossing my arms, I asked, "What do I do to stop it?"

"You," Sister Betty said, "can't."

"That doesn't make any sense."

"It's not as simple as you think. We need—"

"If I can't stop it, then it can't be stopped, right?"

"Not exactly."

"Then what? You're not making sense."

"You're not listening, Caitlin, because you don't want to hear." Father Callahan tried to be the voice of reason, but I kept my eyes on the woman in the bed. The woman I depended on for information, for advice and insight. The woman I trusted with my life.

"Who can stop it?"

She lifted her chin and stared back at me, unflinching now. "A volunteer."

"What?"

"The Black Dog—"

"I'm not asking you, Father. I'm asking her."

"It's attracted to death, Caitlin," she said softly, "so to lure it in, someone has to die."

"Bullshit."

"Language."

I ignored him.

"This city is full of dead and dying people. Don't tell me—"

"It has to be a volunteer," she snapped, as if critiquing me through grueling routines. The trainer voice. "Death will attract the Black Dog, and the volunteer will lead it to Helen. But the volunteer will need help to avoid...crossing over. You'll be that beacon."

"No." Not another death. Not another risk like that. I pushed the roil of anxiety down hard. "There has to be another way."

Sister Betty shook her head. "There isn't."

"But it hasn't attacked the living." I could find some other way of capturing the dog. Surely Marty had come up with something in his research. He'd done it before; he'd do it again.

"We can't wait for that, Caitlin," she said softly.

I heard it in her words. A note of sadness. Resignation. Maybe loss. Her eyes glistened with the unshed swell of tears. My heart fell to my feet. "No."

"It's not your choice." Unbearable compassion glowed in her smile.

Losing Sister Betty would be nothing like watching a stranger in Rome devoured by the huge, fanged and tentacled monsters she'd called forth from the Tiber River. I couldn't save Shannon, but I could save Sister Betty. I refused watch someone else die. Someone I loved. Without her, who would I be? How would I face the fight every day?

My chest ached.

Sister Betty couldn't volunteer. She couldn't die.

I wouldn't survive it.

"We've done the research, Caitlin."

"Not enough," I said, standing up, wheeling on Father Callahan. "If anything happens to her before I get back, I'm holding you responsible."

"You're overreacting. This is—"

The closing door cut off his words as I stormed out of the room and down the hospital hallway. I would find another way.

"Your bedside manner needs work."

"I asked how you were feeling."

"With such tenderness and compassion." Marty shifted his laptop to the other side of the bed. "I'm guessing you talked to Sister Betty?"

I sighed and rubbed my forehead. "Yeah."

"I told her you wouldn't go for it, but she wouldn't let me volunteer."

"What the hell?" I looked up and stared at my friend. "Is everyone suicidal?"

Marty slid across the bed toward me, smiling. "It's not like that."

"None of you are dying, even if I have to have you all hospitalized for your safety." I paced the room.

"Pouting isn't cute on you. Besides, you're getting all worked up over nothing."

"Nothing? Nothing? Are you serious?" I ignored the guilt that tore at me when he winced, but I didn't lower my voice. "Since when is volunteering to die nothing?"

"You're overreacting."

"You can't expect me to be okay with this."

"Cee—"

"You know how crazy all this sounds, right?"

"Yes, but I've read the original texts, or as much of them as I can."

"You can't expect me to be okay with this."

"Will you shut up and listen, please?" The bastard actually smiled like this was nothing. Like Sister Betty wasn't planning to die to lure the damned Black Dog to the woman who'd lost the damned thing in the first place.

I turned my back to him.

"Since nightmares have been keeping me awake anyway, I've been researching. I found a couple of texts that took on similar situations where the Black Dog went rogue. First, there's diary of a nobleman in Ireland in the 1100's, O' Donnchadha or something, that outlined a ritual of sacrifice that stopped the problem. How it started then isn't clear, but word seems to have traveled. The same ritual is referenced in a French book, La Fleur de Chien Noir, or 'The Black Dog Flower' written the last time this happened in a province in northern France around the time of the plague. Widespread death set the Black Dog into something like a frenzy, and it attacked the living."

"It hasn't done that yet. Not even any sightings."

"Look at you being a little goth Pollyanna," he said with a grin. "Nice bright side, babe."

"Shut up."

"But, you're right. We're not facing that problem. Yet."

"Then why are we going for the nuclear option?" I crossed my arms.

Marty pretended not to be exasperated. "Okay, we'll play this game." Reaching for a tablet, he kept talking. "With a population constantly in flux, a variety of supernatural communities, and almost as many powerful dead amplified by the power nexus here, it's a matter of time before it happens." He showed me maps of New Orleans with bright color-coded overlays and cemeteries outlined in bold black orders. "And it may have happened since the plague, but historical records are imperfect, at best, especially if it happened under the cover of some major catastrophe, like war."

"You're sure using a dead dog-walker to lure this thing back to Helen is our only option?"

"It's the only solution with evidence of working and the least potential for collateral damage among the living, dead, and supernats in the city."

I rubbed my face and leaned on my elbows. Collateral damage. The euphemism for dead. Dead people. Innocent dead people. And there had been too much of that under my watch. People I should have saved. I trained to save them. It was my purpose, but even Sister Betty had been shot when I should have been able to intervene.

"You're brooding."

"Because someone else is going to die. And not some bystander, not in some accident I might prevent. This is intentional. This is…" I shook my head. The word wouldn't come.

"You might feel better when you see this." He picked up another tablet and tapped it to life. "This document focuses on the sacrifice to reign in the Black Dog."

I squinted at the elaborate, archaic script, my eyes skipping from word to word without really understanding.

"The legend says the protector lays down their life in faith, and their spirit rises to walk. Essentially, this protector becomes the dog's human equivalent, a guardian."

"Okay." I scrolled through the digitized document.

"Nowhere does it say the protector dies." He reached over, flicked the screen, and pointed out a line near the end. "It only says they 'lay their life in faith upon the altar' in sacrifice."

"So, it's not necessarily death?"

"Hard to say, but that's what I took from it."

"Then why were Father Callahan and Sister Betty so focused on her dying?"

His eyes sparkled as he fought a grin. "Were they, or is that what you heard?"

I didn't have an answer.

Marty watched me a few seconds longer, then scrolled through the document again. "There's a chance it means death, of course, that the sacrifice is literal, so maybe they're preparing for worst-case scenario."

"But it might be symbolic. Some spiritual journey. Maybe an out-of-body experience."

Reluctantly, he nodded. "As old as this text is, that's a possibility. Or that it's a holdover from other forms of spiritualism the Church subsumed."

"But it could be death."

When he didn't answer, I looked up.

He nodded slowly. "It's an act of faith. A test."

"I suck at tests, dude."

"Which is why you keep getting them. A chance to try again."

Another chance to survive losing another innocent.

I shuddered.

"Remember, they have to volunteer."

Without asking, he wanted me to accept Sister Betty's decision. He expected me to suck it up and say yes, adding her name to the list in my head. "I get that this has been done before. Or at least the legend is out there, but I need you to explain exactly what part of this is a good idea and how I'm supposed to let Sister Betty die to get this job done."

"Fuck, you're cranky. I thought that was my privilege as the one with the head injury." He patted the pillow beside him. "Come here, drama queen, and let me school you."

Every reason why I shouldn't ran through my head.

"Don't make me kick your ass." He crossed his arms and cocked his head.

"The hell you say." I scooted across the rumpled sheets and sat beside him to see his laptop monitor.

"Here's where the story gets interesting. Helen, as you've probably guessed, isn't quite what she seems."

1 2

"You're telling me a Norse goddess lives a block off Bourbon Street?"

Marty shrugged. "You said you felt energy in her house that wasn't magic. I burned through Google then hit up the Dark Web but didn't find anything until I saw your book." He picked up my library book from his nightstand.

"I told you I read."

"Yeah, but I'm obligated to keep you humble by giving you as much shit as possible."

"At that, you excel. How did you make the connection between Helen and Hel?"

"Pure, dumb luck, really." The pages fanned under his thumb. When he stopped, he handed me the open book. "I had the weirdest nightmare with her as a queen attended by zombies. Scared me awake. After that, I couldn't sleep. I tried working, but my monitor was giving me a headache, so I thought I'd read a chapter. I opened to your bookmark and saw the chapter on Loki's children, so, like the Marvel movie whore I am, I read it to see what might show up."

"Okay, but I don't get it. How'd you make the connection?" I skimmed the chapter.

"Remember how she wore the glove on her left hand and hid half her face under her hair? That's in the book." He gestured at the book. "And had you had even a day of vacation, you probably would have put it together."

But I hadn't. And wouldn't for a while yet. Once I figured this mess out, I still had to deal with the frat boy "monster" in the airport. Maybe I could relax in a couple of weeks.

Marty didn't notice my distraction and kept talking. "She could hide in New Orleans without altering the paranormal balance of the city. There might be a small influx of the dead attracted to her presence, but it wouldn't seem like more than a lunar cycle surge."

"And if she had the Black Dog—"

"Nope. It wasn't hers."

"She said—"

"She lied." Marty smirked and tapped the tablet again. "And this is information only available to the highest-ranking clergy, and I mean Vatican-level high-ranking, so don't go blabbing to Sister Hotpants or I'll lose my back door."

I rolled my eyes. "What did you find out?"

"As far as I can verify from historical accounts, such as they are, what Hel, or Helen, told us about the Black Dog's origins was true."

"I hear a 'but' coming."

He chuckled. "Yup. From what I can tell, though, what we're dealing with isn't just 'a' Black Dog, since many were created over history, but 'the' Black Dog. The first of its kind." He handed me the tablet. Scanning the document, I scrolled, eyes skipping from word to word, too distracted by my own thoughts to actually read.

The first supernat of its kind.

Great.

"Where it's been or when it went astray isn't clear, but a few months ago, the Vatican tracked it to New Orleans. It was probably attracted here since, with so many dead, this has to be like a massive graveyard. Helen wasn't here when the Vatican asked her to intervene, but since she had dealings in New Orleans, convincing her didn't take much effort. Less effort than it took for the Vatican to convince Ganesh to intervene on behalf of the missionaries in Northern India after 2016 cyclones. Despite the history and bad blood, they finally came to an agreement, and from what I hear, it's still in place."

I nodded, remembering Sister Betty's tales of the awkward meetings between the high-ranking clergy and the Indian elephant god. The "remover of obstacles" finally agreed to help out with the heavy lifting.

Though it wasn't the first time the Catholic Church had partnered with deities of other religions, it was certainly the most memorable in living memory.

"The idea was that she'd use her influence to attract the dead that could be culled without negatively affecting the economy, and the Black Dog would instinctively follow."

"But it didn't work." It wasn't a question.

"Nope. Maybe with so many dead it's unfocused or the bait isn't strong enough." He shrugged. "I haven't figured out that part yet."

Something felt...wrong. Or incomplete. "Maybe. But if she's the goddess of the underworld, it should herd the dead to her." I handed him the tablet and pressed the heel of my palms against my closed eyes. "It's not just protecting the dead like it would have in the early Christian churches. Or the tourists, if it sees them as travelers. No, we're missing something."

His fingers thumped the glass of the device in his hands. "What about the nexus theory? If it's real, this place must be like a spiritual battery."

"If the dog's drawing power from the nexus, maybe it's feeding Helen as well. Plus, if the dead prefer her company, like the book says," I tapped a line in the black book with Mjolnir on its cover, "maybe they're drawing off it, too..."

"Maybe she's interfering with the capture to focus power here in New Orleans?"

"Possibly." My head ached. "So much for a simple capture job." I slid off the bed to grab my notebook. "Now I'm up against an O.G. supernat that has somehow survived centuries, crossed an ocean, and hunkered down in a city built on a power nexus and filled with so many dead, it won't leave of its own volition." I jotted in my notebook before continuing. "And all I have to do is catch it, without harm, even though a Norse goddess of the underworld hasn't managed to get the job done."

Marty's laughter wavered with nervous energy. "When you put it that way..."

"Right?" I paused and flashed a wry smile at him. He looked away first. I wrote a few more lines and closed the book. "Thanks for the info."

"But I haven't told you about the rite."

"Doesn't matter. I don't intend to use it."

"You're avoiding it."

"No, I'm going to find another way. One that doesn't involve gambling the life of someone I..." I swallowed the word 'love' before it slipped out. "Care about. A lot."

When I pushed off the bed and started packing the guns into the backpack, Marty asked, "What are you doing?"

"Going to see our local Norse goddess."

"You shouldn't go alone." He swayed as he stood, trying to cover it by touching the bed to regain his balance. Right or wrong, allowing him to come would endanger him, and that couldn't happen.

"You're certainly not going with me. Stay here, back me up. Call Agent Hardin and NOLA PD to let them know I'm headed out there." The backpack's nylon straps made a scratching whistle as I cinched them. "Just in case, of course."

He nodded with resignation, his familiar words heavier and more somber than usual. "Don't get dead."

"Last on my to-do list, especially with vacation pending. Stay out of trouble."

"That's my line! You—"

The heavy door closed and cut off his words.

Halfway down the hall, I smelled it. Sulfur. Brimstone. A hint of animal musk. First, the merest whiff reached me, but as I followed the drunken paisley-patterned carpet, the acrid stench intensified as it had the night before. Burns the size of my palm scorched the florid carpet. I knelt, tracing the edge of one with my fingers. Not just marks. Footprints. No. Animal tracks.

I stood while the argument raged in my head. Marty should know about this. I should wait for Agent Hardin or even Father Callahan. Any back up. I might be hunting a supernatural dog, but Helen, or Hel, might be another matter.

But this time, I had weapons. At the end of the hall, I'd gear up.

I kept walking.

The footprints led around the corner to the right. No different than the one I'd exited, metal-framed doors lined both sides of the hall. Wall sconces lit the expanses between small, glittering chandeliers. At the far end stood a small table, a heavy floral arrangement occupying its entire surface and almost obscuring the mirror hanging behind it.

The pull of the mirror felt like a dream. My rational mind screamed with each step I took toward it. Dark blemishes scarred the silvered background, mottling my incomplete reflection as it ghosted and blurred with each step. In the ancient glass, instead of my standard "uniform" of black jeans and black tank top, a sparkling evening gown clung to me and swung with each step.

I rubbed my palms against my thighs, relieved to feel denim. I glanced down at my beaten black Doc Martens just to make sure nothing had actually changed.

My feet moved toward the mirror without thought, though my veins burned with the urge to run. I needed to run. But not away. I wanted to run toward it. To dive into it. To lose myself in whatever lay on the other side.

This could be bad.

Though I wanted to call or text Marty, my hands wouldn't cooperate. Nothing did. I needed to stop and gear up, but my feet kept walking, each step inches from another scorch mark in the hideous carpet.

The mirror never got closer.

I walked. My feet ached as if I'd walked miles, yet I couldn't stop. An amorphous shadow appeared behind me in the mirror, impossible to discern. In the silvered glass, the hulking mass filled the hallway behind me, blotting out the light. Squinting did nothing to clarify its shape.

I looked. Nothing behind me but the obnoxious carpet and an unnaturally long corridor lined with metal doorways, sconces, and chandeliers.

The black shadow blob stalked me in the mirror.

Could I be asleep? Could this be another nightmare?

I must be awake. I hadn't laid down after talking with Marty. Hadn't closed my eyes.

Or had I?

I jogged forward a few steps, surprised my body obeyed. Immediately, the hallway shrunk, vertigo set in as the mirror zoomed in with the disorienting speed only known in dreams.

Two bright red spots flared behind me in the mirror's reflection.

I froze as a low vibration rumbled behind me, the acrid stench of brimstone sharpening.

No. Not a vibration.

A growl.

Shadow swallowed the light in the hallway, but the reflection sharpened.

I had to be dreaming.

The massive shape might have been a wolf or bear or even a large dog, but at the same time, it was none of them. Nothing I'd ever encountered seemed so wrong. Nothing I'd ever known to roam the night and devour people ever manifested like this. My breath strained against its foul reek. Its oppressive presence made me want to run, made me wish I'd holstered a gun or two instead of foolishly stashing them in my backpack. Damned social conventions and…laws and shit.

Its fur bristled and sparked in the dim light as it growled again.

For a brief second, I yearned for the threat of the wolf-dog, Fen, that curled at Helen's feet. In comparison, Fen was a pup. And playful.

Hellhound.

The only term fit to apply to the beast behind me. Any other name was a euphemism. This was the guardian of graveyards, protector of travelers, and it saw me as an enemy.

A cautious step forward, another nightmarish growl. Power rumbled through my chest, the sound hinting at the power in its massive body. Every hair on my body took notice.

Twin red lights flared in the mirror.

Its glowing red eyes.

Great.

Alone. Essentially unarmed.

In other words, totally fucked.

It snuffled the air in short, sharp bursts, its exhale the sulfured animal smell that brought me here. Wisps of smoke drifted with its breath, tinged with burning carpet. The snuffling dissolved into another threatening rumble. This time, the floor shook when the beast stepped toward me.

Don't run. Predators chase.

Sour fear sweat joined the miasma in the hallway, my stomach churning with burning acid. There had to be a way out. I'd faced worse. Not much, but maybe once or twice. I just had to keep my head and hope some kind of divine intervention would keep my ass alive.

Pushing away the fear and pretending sweat wasn't rolling down my back, between my boobs, or soaking the underarms of my tank top, I glanced around, moving as little as possible. Nothing but locked doors between me and the table and flowers. I strained to see through the shadow of the beast in the mirror. Just the same long line of closed doors reflected behind me.

Now what?

Nothing left but to turn and face it.

Slowly.

As slowly as I could, I turned.

To face an empty hallway.

"What the—?"

The growl again. I whirled to the mirror.

Me. In a sparkling evening gown again, a huge black dog behind me. "I have to be dreaming."

Heat suffused the air around me in a slow vortex. Hot wire brushed my skin, and even my feet felt hot through my Docs. Burning hair joined the stink around me. In the mirror, the shadow circled me. The vague shape snuffled my feet. As it circled behind me, I took a half step forward. Heat dissipated, then the hot wire scrape brushed my arm again, and I swear a cool, wet nose nuzzled my palm.

Okay. Sure. We'll call this an improvement. Preparing to run for my life one minute and wondering if I'd somehow adopted a supernatural puppy the size of a small buffalo the next. An invisible puppy. The size of a small but invisible buffalo.

If I survived long enough to write my life story, no one would ever believe it.

"I really hope you're not going to eat me or try to drag my soul to Hell or anything," I said to the creature I couldn't see.

The sound it made in response couldn't be described as anything but a whine. A deep, terrifying whine from an invisible supernatural creature, but a whine nonetheless.

"Let's go for a walk," I said, talking to the prickling, bristly heat pressed against my legs, "and see if we can get you home. Or somewhere like home, at least."

Each step down the hall took forever. Longer, if possible, than walking to the stupid mirror. Which I'd have to investigate later. Silver mirrors didn't usually reflect supernats, but this one seemed to. And why the hell had it shown me in an evening gown?

New Orleans had too many questions and not enough vacation opportunity for a monster hunter. Marty'd have to include that in a Yelp review.

I shook my head to keep my thoughts focused on the animal heat at my side. It might be as simple as leading it back to Helen, though I didn't know if it would follow me all the way to her. So many distractions, so many opportunities to lose an invisible creature in the crowds, but maybe I'd get lucky. I brushed my hand against the tips of invisible fur, the heat intense and comforting as the dog stepped closer to rub against my leg. Maybe this might be as simple as walking it home. And if it was that simple, perhaps this would all be over. And then, vacation.

But nothing is ever as simple as all that, is it?

Especially not when monsters are involved.

I'll never know how, but I made it as far as the inside of the elevator with the impossible dog. In the elevator, the mirrors reflected it more clearly than the hallway mirror. But when I pulled out my phone to update Marty, it happened.

13

The doors opened. On the other side stood frat boy-man from the airport. His jaw dropped, and I might have said something as eloquent as "hey" before he turned and ran.

Predators chase.

In the elevator mirrors, the hulking dog reflection leapt from the elevator, jaws open to reveal long, shining teeth, toward the man running across the busy, white marble lobby. People dodged the man, some falling as the unseen beast plowed through the crowd. A woman tumbled down the few stairs by the front door, her partner reaching out to catch her. The doorman conveniently opened the door, and frat boy-man and his invisible pursuer spilled out onto Royal Street.

"What's happening?" Marty asked through my Bluetooth earpiece before I could say anything.

Darting through the crowd, I gave the short explanation. "I found the dog, and it's chasing the guy from the airport."

"From the airport? Are you sure?"

"Same clothes, same face."

"In our hotel?"

"The one and only." I raced between two tourists into the center of the road, looking in both directions, seeing nothing. With a string of inventive curses, I stepped onto the sidewalk. "I've lost them."

"Why was it chasing him?"

"He ran. Predator drive. I had the dog in the elevator, the doors opened, and as soon as the guy took off, it chased." A couple of tourists stared at me as they passed. "It's more wild than domesticated."

"Then how did you get it to follow you?"

"Dumb luck," I said, scanning the ground for scorch-mark footprints, one finger pressing my Bluetooth headset into my ear as a truck rumbled by. "Can you access traffic cams or something and see if you can find him?"

"Working on it, but these don't have the same capacity as my computers at home." Usually his first complaint contained mutters about the dubious legality of the request. Maybe the surprise had him off guard. Or maybe, the vacation effect.

A thin stream of smoke rose from a dark spot on the road. I leaned over it into the smell of burnt oil and hot tar, and ran down the street.

"What happened?"

"Found evidence. Still trying to track them."

"I'm not finding anything on the cams. Either they're avoiding them—"

"It won't be a 'them.'" I explained the mirrors as quickly as possible.

"But supernats shouldn't appear in silver-backed mirrors."

"Shouldn't, but this one does." I skidded to a halt, trying to listen beyond the traffic and music and the pulse of humanity already throbbing on Bourbon Street. Though the party never really stopped, dusk called revelers to Bourbon, the bars, and music. The air thrummed with the sound. I closed my eyes and tried to listen to everything under it.

"Got something. Corner of Bourbon and St. Louis. There's a gated alley across from the burger bar. There's some kind of altercation."

I ran, panting as I asked, "You think it's them?"

"Can't tell for sure, but people are running. It's something."

Tourists in various states of inebriation crowded the streets, but I ran around them, ignoring laughter, insults, and complaints about spilled drinks. I turned the corner, hearing the screaming man before I saw the ring of swaying drunks watching the man curled at the foot of the gate.

Someone yelled to call 9-1-1 as I approached the crying, yelling ball of frat boy-man in smoking clothes. Black spots the size of my palm smoldered around him.

"What the fuck do I do, Marty?"

The man screamed as a blood-stained rip appeared in his polo shirt.

"Working on it."

"Work faster." I stepped closer, the wire-scrape of bristling fur brushing my pant leg.

"Can you get its attention?"

I stepped back, the animal's snort turning my Docs into a leather oven. "Yeah, I think I got that." Backpedaling a couple of steps, the heat followed with the reek of sulfur. Hot air puffed in what might have been curious sniffs and investigative snorts. "Send someone out to handle this mess and give me directions to Helen's." Her place wasn't far, but if I had to focus on keeping the Black Dog's attention and navigating the crowd, I'd never see street signs.

"On it," Marty said.

"Miss Kelley." I recognized the voice behind me, but not as one I could easily place.

"Little busy here," I said, backing up, eyes on the soft black spots that appeared in the tarmac patches on the road in front of me.

"Agent Hardin."

"Not a good time." Ignoring more angry complaints as I walked into pedestrians, I hurried back a couple of quick steps, hoping the crowd would part around me. "Marty, why the hell can't I see this thing?"

"It's the protections, Miss Kelley," Agent Hardin said, a few feet away, bookending the empty space between us. His closed hands pointed at the ground, and I caught the glint of metal. "It's enchanted to avoid causing a panic."

"And you know this how?"

"Because we enchanted it."

I looked up at him, taking another step back. "We who?"

"DEMON."

Great. Not only did I have to figure out how guide the dog to Helen, now I'd probably have to convince a government agency that didn't exist to release it to her. No one ever told me that double-dipping into the Church and federal government could be such a pain in the ass. Or maybe someone had and I hadn't listened. Either way, I regretted agreeing to serve both. That whole separation of Church and state thing made a lot of sense.

"I've got a job to do, Agent Hardin, and I can't let you interfere."

"I'm not trying to," he said, flashing a small mirror at the space between us. The stretch of road between us didn't exist in the reflection. Instead, a whole lot of wire-bristled dog took its place. Only dark fur reflected in the mirrored compact. This had to be the biggest damned dog

I'd ever seen. Or not seen. "I've been trying to figure out why it's stalking you."

"Stalking me? Don't you mean why it was mauling that guy?"

"Seriously, can you guys talk about this later?" Marty interrupted. "Get this thing off Bourbon, deliver it to Helen, and then you can chit chat about anything you want."

I ignored him. Keeping the interest of a predator meant becoming prey. Predators chase.

I knew what I had to do.

"The monster," Agent Hardin said, unaware of Marty's protests.

Looking where the Black Dog's eyes must have been, I imagined looking straight in them, offering challenge.

It answered with a growl.

Good. We spoke the same language.

"I hate being right," I muttered as Marty yammered in my ear about public safety. "Now isn't the time, Agent Hardin. I'm thinking I'm going to run this thing back."

"No!" Never had I heard real panic in a federal agent's voice. Especially not one with DEMON. "Don't run. You run, and it will attack."

Marty rattled off directions without reacting to my plan. He understood. Maybe, he even agreed. It required a volunteer. An act of faith. My guts unclenched.

I glanced up to check the street names as we reached the corner, ready to offer up my faith that I'd make it to Helen unscathed. Ready to offer myself as the sacrifice if it meant saving the revelers between Bourbon and her front door.

Predators chase, so I volunteered to run.

"That's what I'm hoping for, Agent Hardin." I registered his surprise before I turned and ran.

Growling followed. Heat burned the back of my neck, and I suspected the burning hair I smelled was mine. My Docs clomped the street as I ran hard, dodging more people than cars, the dog snapping at my heels. I tried not to imagine what would happen if I ran into a car.

With a jolt and clatter of metal, the straps of my backpack yanked my shoulders back, and I leaned forward, keeping my feet as the dog tried to shake me from side to side. The fabric groaned and stitches popped, but I ran faster, the weight of the bag still bouncing at my back. "Marty, call Helen. Tell her I'm running, and this dog's coming for me. She needs to be ready."

"What do you mean coming for you?"

"I mean…" I panted and swung around a corner, narrowly avoiding collision with a crowd of females wearing tiaras, bright pink sashes, and raising plastic penis-shaped yard glasses in the midst of some shrill cheer. They screamed and stumbled back against the wall. "It snapped at me. We're a little beyond playing."

A man yelled at me in some language I didn't understand as he stood over the wreckage of a spilled paper bag. He fell over as a thick shadow passed over him, the dog flickering as it shoved past him and chased me.

"I lost you. Where'd you go?"

"Nowhere, just where you told me."

"Can't see you."

"Hurry up because if it's not chasing me, it'll turn on someone else." Looking for motion to distract the dog, I turned and ran again, seeing the bricked up dead end too late to pivot. Of course.

"Working on your location."

"Nice doggy," I said, taking one slow step backward, trying to turn. The dog flickered into view for a second, a solid shadow with glowing eyes.

"You're in the shit again, aren't you?"

"Something like that. How long until you've got eyes on me?" The sound of people talking drew closer.

The red eyes flared, the dog appearing solid again, bared teeth stark white against its black, smoking fur.

Definitely a hellhound.

"I'm going to need a route out of here with as few bystanders in the way as possible. Invisibility is no longer our friend."

"What do you mean?"

"Not the time for questions, bud. Just get me out of here."

"Working on it."

The Black Dog growled again, advancing, its fur rising in wiry spikes on its back. "Time is of the essence," I said, trying to control my own fear. One false move, and my ass would be high-quality dog chow.

"It takes time, you know. This isn't *CSI* or some crap TV show, you know."

"Literally up against a wall here, bud." My shoulders hit the wall, and I slid along it.

"Holy shit, what is that?" He actually squeaked. Were I not in mortal danger, I'd have laughed.

"Glad to know you're tapped in."

"What the hell *is* it, Cee?"

"Looks like a dog, growls like a dog. For now, I'm saying a dog. We'll deal with the details later. How about you help me get this to Helen's? And with as few distractions as possible."

"Right." His keyboard clacked like gunfire. "I don't know how the hell you get yourself into this shit."

"It's all part of saving the world, yo. Or at least New Orleans."

He gave directions, and I slid along the wall until I turned the dog enough to run again. I sprinted. My breath burned hot in my lungs as I pushed harder, the snap of jaws behind me. This was a bad idea. "Tell her to get that damned door open."

Some bystander screamed, but I didn't stop to look. *Just taking my dog for a run*, I thought, a giggle breaking loose despite my inability to breathe as I forced myself to outpace the beast.

"Marty," I panted, a hot stitch burning in my side, "next time I have a shitty idea, remind me of this, okay?"

"Noted. And I'll remind you that you told me to do it."

"Fair enough."

I turned the last corner as Marty directed. Guillaume stood in the middle of the street, elegant and almost regal in his suit. With one final push, I ran, and he stepped aside as Fenrir appeared in the street. I swore with what little breath I had and made an ungraceful turn toward the door where Guillaume stood. The massive beast of a dog rushed past me to collide in a snarling tangle with Fenrir, still muzzled with the pink, shimmery ribbon. The two wrestled, biting, snarling, and tumbling in a pile of black and dark mottled fur, Fenrir's ribbon tangled around both of them. Though smoke rose from it, it didn't burn or blacken.

I collapsed against the wall and looked up at the butler who regarded me without expression. "Now what?"

He shrugged and smiled. "We wait for Master Fenrir to get things under control."

"What the hell were you thinking running like that? Especially after I told you not to?" Agent Hardin slowed to a stop in front of me, neither sweaty nor out of breath in his full suit. I didn't know whether to be ashamed of my state or to accuse him of some kind of magical intervention.

I laughed, bent over, my hands on my knees. "Agent Hardin, I do a lot of things I'm not supposed to, especially when I'm told not to."

"That's the damned truth," Marty said in my ear.

I ignored him.

Agent Hardin drew his Glock and stepped toward the snarling mass of animal flesh writhing in the street as they wound themselves in the shimmering ribbon. "We've got to get this under control."

The butler placed his hand on Hardin's weapon, pointing the barrel to the ground. "Master Fenrir will handle it."

There are times I regret not having my phone out like some tourist. This was one. Agent Hardin's astonishment made me giggle, though I tried to hide it behind attempts to catch my breath.

"Agent Hardin, with all due respect," Guillaume said, his hand still on the agent's gun, "this really isn't the place for you. It's under control."

"Actually, this is exactly where I need to be." He jerked his weapon away, keeping it pointed at the ground as he circled the noisy animal battle that seemed to be winding down.

I rolled my eyes.

Fenrir hovered over his captive, jaws locked around the black void below the other dog's bared white teeth. The Black Dog's red eyes rolled in panic, only the outermost edges showing white as it looked for escape. The ground shook with the growling of both animals. One problem down. One more to go. "Marty, what about the guy at St. Louis and Bourbon?"

"Ambulance picked him up, but NOLA PD's en route to take over." Marty's fingers rattled the laptop's keyboard. I imagined his tablets fanned out around him, all displaying something different.

"He's not a person," Agent Hardin said. "He's a monster. One we'd been tracking, and lost, before your handler reported him."

Fenrir's body dropped as he flattened himself over the Black Dog. Both animals stopped growling, but the tension persisted as Fenrir's muscles twitched. He waited for submission. It would come. His muscles tensed and released in short pulses, not letting his guard down, but showing willingness to relent.

"Yeah, I got that." My shoulders relaxed as I watched. The alpha had control, which meant I was off the job. There was some kind of frou-frou-la-la drink in my future tonight. "You're welcome for that, by the way."

"For what?"

"That he's in custody. Might have been driven by accident, but I'm still counting it as an assist." I grinned at him, but he just stared back in confusion. "Let me know what he is sometime next week. Late next week. As of now, I'm on vacation." I gestured to the pile of beasts between us. "Since we're done here, I'm going back to my hotel to shower, change," I plucked at my torn tank top, "and drink something with a lot of alcohol in it."

"Done? No, Miss Kelley, you don't understand. We need your help with the monster we captured tonight."

Some people just didn't get the hint.

Guillaume, the butler, approached, then pressed a finger against his ear and turned away from us.

"No, Agent Hardin, *you* don't understand. I'm on vacation." I gestured to the calm, quiet pile of wolf-dog and hellhound at my feet. As I watched, the Black Dog disappeared, leaving nothing but a void under Fenrir. Intense heat radiated off the "empty" space, and I looked up at the agent. "Your doing?"

He ignored me. "Miss Kelley."

Never before had I considered changing my name. The more I wanted to disappear into a pool and a frozen hurricane for a week or so, the more everyone used it.

Instead of acknowledging the agent, I turned to Helen as she glided out her front door, ethereal in the low evening light. I gestured to Fenrir and his invisible subordinate. "I've returned the Black Dog to you."

With a smirk, she asked, "Have you? He's not exactly as I anticipated."

"Huh? Oh, the invisible thing?" I jerked my thumb at Agent Hardin. "I had nothing to do with that."

"It was for the protection of the populous before word got out and caused a city-wide panic, Miss Lokison. Of course, it made him harder to find." He pulled out a small mirror and angled it where Fenrir's head hovered over empty space. In the reflection, two glowing eyes burned.

"Lokison?" Marty asked in my ear. "She's not even hiding it."

"You know each other?" I asked Agent Hardin, raising an eyebrow.

Her blond swoop of hair half-hid Helen's regal smile. Everything about her seemed to glow as the prickle of energy ran over my arms. "All available resources were employed, Miss Kelley." She gestured with her right hand, the left hidden in her over-long sleeve. "Nothing was more important than having him returned."

"And, of course, the federal government has a vested interest in keeping New Orleans safe," he glanced at Helen, "and economically stable."

"Right," I said, dusting off my jeans. "Now that everyone and their interests are safe, I'm headed back to my hotel."

"What about the nightmares?" Agent Hardin asked.

I turned, Marty repeating the last word in my ear. "What did you say?"

"You've had nightmares. As has your partner, Martin. And many others in the hotel. Psychic nightmares."

Blinking to clear away the flashes of the homeless man's return, his fatal attack, I steeled myself against turning to look behind me. Nightmares were nightmares. Not reality. "What does that have to do with anything?"

"They're real, you know. They'll come to pass."

The sinking in my stomach scared me more than the lack of sense that he was lying to get my attention and cooperation. "Dreams are dreams."

He shook his head. "Not these dreams. And I think you know that."

I fought the urge to look around, to seek the scruffy homeless man I'd seen emerge and—

"They come true, you know. Unless you stop the cause." Like the well-trained federal agent he was, he didn't grin, but I heard triumph in his voice. "New Orleans needs your help, Miss Kelley."

II

A TOUCH TOO MUCH

14

Miracles happen every day. Like hearing Agent Hardin over the bounty of mouth-watering Cajun specialties spread before me. Boudin balls. Steaming gumbo. Étouffée and red beans and rice. Jambalaya. Gator bites.

Okay, so "gator bites" challenged my sense of culinary adventure, but the rest smelled like heaven and tasted like sin.

Or that's what Sister Betty said.

She sat across from me at the scarred table in the tiny, dark restaurant. In her gray t-shirt and jeans, her red hair restrained in a ponytail, she looked nothing like a nun. With eyeliner and some quality time with a hair straightener, she'd pass for Scarlet Witch, or at least the dressed-down movie version. Lack of reality-warping powers did nothing to lessen her influence, though. More than once, my beloved, badass mentor took advantage of her long legs to kick me in the shins when my mouth emptied enough to get me in trouble.

Marty, my partner and friend, delighted in every yelp, despite the retribution my glares promised.

"Agent Hardin," I began, but lost the thought as my fork hovered in indecision over the plates cluttering the table's center.

"Please," the federal agent, who looked more like an aging accountant, covered his mouth and swallowed, "call me Cooper."

I nodded with a half shrug, wondering how many of his colleagues in the Department of Extra-Dimensional, Magical, and Occult Nuisances had the same privilege. He didn't seem like the type of person comfortable with others using his first name. Including his parents. Hell, he might have been born in a three-piece suit. Biting back the urge to laugh, I continued. "Cooper, while I appreciate the offer, I don't hunt monsters for money. Or status, so you can stop pushing. Like I told you this morning when you woke me up," I added a little extra emphasis to hint how much he'd endangered his well-being by calling without an imminent threat, "I'm here for vacation. To rest. To take a break."

And so much more than that. To think. To get my messed-up head on straight. So much had happened recently, it left me wrangling my figurative demons as I hunted and slayed literal ones. Superficially, it was simple. Find monsters. Kill monsters. Sometimes, for a select few, catch and re-home them. Above all, protect people. The last couple of jobs, however, had me questioning, well, everything. Sure, I hunted monsters. Caught some, fought more. Some memorable kills even made fine storytelling over a beer and a good meal.

What bothered me was how hard I'd failed lately. I needed time to figure out what the hell happened and then figure out how to get back to not sucking. I'd started working for the Holy Roman Catholic Church out of defiance, to make a stand and protect those who needed it most. It still got me out of bed after a rough night, but somewhere along the line, fighting the things that made midnight snacks of humans got...fuzzy. Complicated. And complicated became confusing.

I glanced at Sister Betty, her arm draped across her body, hand hovering over the fresh stitches in her side where she was wounded as we tried to take down Father Robicheau, the former priest of St. Louis Cathedral and murderous human monster masquerading as a colleague. She laughed at something Marty said, but his bruised head distracted me, a souvenir from hunting another monster. Creature. Whatever.

Not even my closest friends stayed safe on my watch.

If those I cared about most weren't safe, was anyone? And if they weren't, what was I doing? What was the point? If I couldn't protect people, why pretend to be something I wasn't? Why set myself apart as some kind of protector of humanity if I couldn't be what they needed?

All eyes fell on me, and I laughed along with whatever joke I missed.

The incident in Rome hadn't started this weird downward spiral, but nothing had felt right since I watched that woman die because I failed to save her. I remembered her face and the snap of her bones in the monster's teeth. Her voice still echoed through my dreams.

It wasn't the first time someone had died in front of me, nor was it the most gruesome death I'd witnessed. In fact, it reminded me of the night that set me on this path, familiar in a fucked up way I didn't want to examine too closely, but after her death, everything seemed to go wrong. I'd intended to use this trip to sort through it all, starting with Rome, and decide if I still wanted this crazy monster-hunting gig. Decide if I could handle it long-term.

Then, life happened, culminating, at least recently, with the mysterious man in the New Orleans airport and his victim. Even a child recognized the monster for what he was, but I didn't act in time to prevent him from touching the stranger in the suit, killing him instantly. I could have acted, but I failed. The job retrieving the Black Dog for Helen, also known as the Norse goddess of the underworld, Hel, started and ended...hinky. I felt like it should mean something, but I hadn't had the time, brain power, or enough sleep to process it.

"Miss Kelley—"

"If I'm calling you Cooper," I jabbed my fork into a shrimp curled around a slice of andouille sausage from the jambalaya, "you should call me Caitlin." I stuck both in my mouth with a groan of satisfaction. Traveling with my foodie friend and partner destroyed my assumptions about the culinary reputation of New Orleans. If I'd known the transcendental food wasn't hyperbolic rumor, I'd have visited years ago and maybe enjoyed the city instead of being pressed into immediate monster hunting service.

"I know you work for the Catholic Church. We're not trying to interfere with that at all." Cooper flashed a grin at Father Callahan, the priest who'd orchestrated my current career after my younger sister's death. "And, Father, don't hold the department's nickname against us."

Father Callahan nodded charitably and chewed, reaching for a piece of cornbread. Sister Betty passed him the honey butter and received muffled thanks in exchange.

During my training, neither Father Callahan nor Sister Betty specifically discussed the Department of Extra-Dimensional, Magical, and Occult Nuisances. Oblique references to potential government help in particularly nasty situations came up, though both encouraged me to focus on my own creativity, problem solving, and our immediate resources. I'd never even met a member of the no-such-agency comically nicknamed DEMON before. I don't know when or if I would have if Agent Cooper Hardin hadn't shown up in the New Orleans Police Department after our scuffle at the Saint Louis Cathedral. Without Cooper flashing his credentials, I might still be in jail.

Cooper looked at me, expectant.

I only opened my mouth to shove in more food.

Hardin's fork clinked against his plate. His smile vanished as he folded his arms on the table and leaned forward. The overhead light gleamed on his forehead. On most of his bald head. "You've never declined a mission before, so how about you cut the bullshit and tell me what you're holding out for?"

The low buzz of chatter in the crowded restaurant roared up around our silent table. Sister Betty and Marty stared him down. Father Callahan stopped, mid-bite, a drop from his spoon splashing on his plate.

Despite the pressure of their wordless condemnation, Agent Cooper Hardin didn't squirm. His disturbingly blue eyes focused on me, and I stared back, neither of us willing to look away first. "Well?" he asked. "What's your price, Caitlin?"

I set my fork on my plate and sat back, twisting to rest my elbow on the back of the chair. "That's a pretty crass question, don't you think?"

"It's business. I assume this is your tactic for negotiating your role with," he glanced over his shoulder, "our department."

"I don't have a role with your department," I said. "The Church hired me. The Church pays me. If I decide to negotiate a role with your department," I enunciated the word, "I won't take the coward's way out."

Marty and Sister Betty's simultaneous warning of "Cee" and "Caitlin" sounded something like "Ceelin."

I ignored them.

Agent Hardin sat back, folding his arms across his chest, the hint of a smirk tugging his lips. "Just remember I didn't call you a coward."

"I didn't call myself a coward, only the so-called tactic you're accusing me of using."

"What's your deal, Miss Kelley?" He emphasized the formal use of my last name.

The vague tingle of compulsion prickled my skin. Everyone could probably hear my teeth grinding as my jaw clenched, yet I counted to ten and forced myself to relax. "I don't have a 'deal,' Cooper. I told you, this is supposed to be my vacation."

"Which you're choosing over the lives of innocents."

"Even on the airplane, they instruct you to put on your own mask before helping others."

Hardin's lips twisted into a sour little frown.

Checkmate, dude.

That argument had been key in convincing Sister Betty to cover my responsibilities so I could take this damned trip in the first place, but I was even more proud of it as the electricity drained from the air at the table.

I picked up my fork, took another greedy scoop of jambalaya, and chewed while I waited for him to answer. His shitty, accusatory question would not ruin my night. Or the food. Nothing short of bands of roving zombies or a feral vampire attack could put me off this manna.

"Agent Hardin," Sister Betty said, her voice stiff with diplomacy, "suggesting Caitlin has ulterior motives is tantamount to...to..."

"Accusing her of extortion," Father Callahan said.

The little man unconvincingly dressed for New Orleans in his short-sleeved plaid button-up shirt shifted in his seat. "That's not what I'm implying."

"Then you're preying on her sense of justice and—"

"Woah, woah." Hardin held up his hands. "That's not what I said."

"Then what are you saying?" demanded Sister Betty, cheeks flushed, eyes narrowed.

"Only that the needs of the community far outweigh the benefits of a vacation, however brief. Lives are at stake. More with every day she refuses to take action."

"Your department's trying to insert itself—"

"My department's an ally you need," Hardin interrupted Sister Betty. "Especially here in New Orleans. As much as you may know about this city, Sister, you don't *know* the city. You need experts. I have those experts."

"And they've done a fabulous job supporting the city's monster hunter. Oh," she tapped her chin with a fingertip, "no, wait, that's not right, is it?"

Cooper's face burned bright red at the allusion to Sister Evangeline, the city's previous hunter. Her death left a void I'd had to fill as soon as I touched down, including taking down her killer, Father Robicheau, the priest assigned to help her. Now, a federal agent was trying to push me into her role officially and complete a job they hadn't been able to. "If you prefer, I'll leave." He pushed away from the table.

I didn't say anything. Watching him squirm amused me enough to stay out of trouble.

"Cooper, sit." Father Callahan waved at the array of half-empty dishes on the table. "There's still plenty to eat."

Hardin looked at each of us in turn.

"But cut the accusatory crap." Marty picked up one of last two boudin balls. "If Caitlin says she needs a break, there's a reason."

My chest ached. We'd never discussed my reasons, but little got by him. Especially when it got as bad as the breakdown that brought Sister Betty across the Atlantic to help me through it. I needed space. I needed time.

I just couldn't figure out how to explain it without sounding weak.

When my thoughts cleared, Sister Betty, Marty, Father Callahan, and Agent Hardin all stared at me.

Apparently, I'd missed something. Again.

"Sorry, what was that?"

"We're done discussing work tonight, Cooper." Father Callahan waved to the waiter and indicated his empty water glass.

"But the threat—"

"Will be there tomorrow. It's too late to start anything tonight anyway."

Hardin bristled. "Which is why I tried to start the process this morning."

And he had.

The first time Cooper called, I answered the phone and...expressed my annoyance with being awoken for a chat about my employment status. The second, third, and fourth times Cooper called before I'd hauled myself out of bed, Marty answered the phone. The next call I'd gotten was from Sister Betty telling me she'd agreed for all of us to meet Cooper for dinner.

I poked at the food on my plate.

He wouldn't relent until he got the answer he pursued. Though he certainly didn't look the part, he was a hunter in his own right. And why not? Monster hunters had to be as slippery as their prey. Maybe more. Maybe protecting the world required this kind of heavy-handed "convincing." Despite Sister Betty's assurance that DEMON agents were partners, I couldn't imagine working like this all the time.

"Agent Hardin," Sister Betty said, each syllable over-enunciated, "that's enough. You're welcome to enjoy dinner with us, but no more business. If you cannot respect that," she smiled without humor, "then it's time we part ways."

"It's not my intention to focus on business," he said, "only to ensure the vulnerable are acknowledged and protected."

"Listen," I leaned on the edge of the table, "I considered the human cost and arranged for coverage for my responsibilities. If you have concerns about my dedication, I'll remind you that less than an hour after landing in New Orleans, I'd started chasing monsters. The very monster, in fact, you're asking me to track down. DE—" I cleared my throat as his eyes widened. *"Your department* worked this case without success and, while I appreciate your confidence, there's no guarantee I'll find it any faster."

He stared at me, then nodded. "I'll take you at your word as long as you—"

"Dude," Marty said, "she gets it. Let it go."

Hardin stared at Marty.

Marty stared back.

In the eternity that passed, I crossed my legs to bring the Derringer hidden in the ankle holster closer. My eyes never leaving Hardin, I released the strap securing it, more for reassurance than preparation for the inevitable explosion.

Hardin blew a breath through his nose, his shoulders sinking as if deflating. "Fine."

The tension drained from the room, and though I expected his capitulation had more to do with being outnumbered than with surrender, if it meant even a temporary reprieve, I'd take it.

"Hurricanes all around." I turned and waved at the waiter, taking advantage of the truce, no matter how short-lived it might be.

Laissez les bon temps rouler, as New Orleans decreed.

15

Residual warmth loosened my muscles as I rolled my shoulders against the brick wall and laughed with sheer pleasure for the first time since I'd landed. I felt lighter, freer, though that might have been the alcohol. Cooper had abandoned work talk when the first round of hurricanes made it to the table, inspiring all of us to keep the adult libations flowing. Three rounds in and Cooper excused himself for the night, leaving us to explore the controlled chaos of Bourbon Street and all it had to offer.

Sister Betty giggled as her shoulder crashed against the wall beside me, leaning close and raising her voice over the music and tourists. "You're drunk." Ribbons of reddish hair escaped her ponytail, framing her face with long, untamed curls. Neon signs reflected multi-colored flashes of mischievous light in her steel-blue eyes.

All the better to see you...

"No, I'm not." The bright, slushy drink in my plastic cup sloshed over my hand. "But even if I was—I'm not, but if I was—what would you do about it?"

She slid her arm between me and the wall, her hand curling around my waist and making me shiver. "I'd make sure you got back to your room and tucked in. Safe and sound."

Night throbbed around us. Competing bass pulsed from the clubs lining the street. Less actual jazz and more *thumpa-thumpa* dance music. Tourists passed in dazzling waves of sound and motion, light painting their laughing faces the same garish neon colors as the frozen drinks in their hands.

I looked up at her to regain my balance.

She grinned at me.

I grinned back and leaned so close my lips brushed her ear. "Take me home."

The city's rhythm transformed in the dark and made it easy and fun to get lost. Not to mention thirsty work.

True to her wild roots, Sister Betty steered us in to one last bar "for directions" and shots before we managed to find Royal Street and the doorman under the square, white hotel awning. We stumbled down the street, shoulder to shoulder, propping each other up and singing.

I pulled my sunglasses down as we crossed the blinding white lobby. "Bright light, bright light," I squeaked.

Sister Betty snorted a laugh. "You are such a nerd."

"Yeah, but you think I'm adorable." I laughed, and we both swayed, almost falling in the elevator as the gold doors opened.

"You are." She grinned.

A bell ticked off each passing floor.

The elevator could take all damned night for all I cared.

Her faded jeans and gray t-shirt made it damned hard to remember her real vocation. Even drunk, she leaned against the wall with the unconscious grace and fluidity she used when fighting. Only her occasional hesitation or indrawn breath hinted at the bandaged bullet wound on her side. She cleared her throat and straightened. "So tomorrow—"

I groaned. "Tomorrow can wait until tomorrow."

"Well, technically, it's tomorrow, so..." She waggled her phone between her fingers.

"Not until I sleep, it's not."

"That doesn't even make any sense," she said, unable to suppress a laugh.

The elevator lurched to a stop, and we spilled into the hall, giggling and shushing each other. Nothing about the twisting paisley carpet pattern made the hallway easy to navigate drunk, but with our arms around each other, we mostly avoided bouncing against the walls. I held her tight to me, my hand on her hip to avoid the bandage barely a hand's width above. For once, the long hallway seemed more like a gift than a punishment.

"Here we are." She flourished her free arm at my door.

Reeling from the sudden stop, I flopped against the wall to dig the plastic key out of my pocket. "You could stay."

Sister Betty laughed. "I don't think that's a good idea."

"Why not? There's two beds." I shrugged, awkward, doubtful that reminding her about Marty's presence would improve the odds of her staying. Awareness of the invitation's implications grew and threatened to rush in at any moment. "Besides, I brought my thoroughly non-threatening Batman pajamas."

"I'm sure they're adorable on you." Sister Betty tapped my nose and seemed to sober up. "But it's still not a good idea."

I struggled against my disappointment. "Alright. So, breakfast in the morning?"

She raised an eyebrow. "Will you be up before the hour strikes double digits?"

"If not, brunch."

Swaying a little, she laughed. "Then I'll see you in the morning." She kissed my cheek, and I smelled her shampoo, her soap and the faint, sweet scent of whatever she'd been drinking. "Sweet dreams."

I didn't open my door until she disappeared down the hall and around the corner.

The lock mechanism made a funky sound, then clicked open. I shut the door behind me as quietly as possible. In the dark, I thought Marty's breathing meant he was asleep.

Until he spoke.

"Couldn't close the deal with Sister Hotpants?"

I barked my shin against the bed frame and bit back a curse. "I thought you were sleeping." Rubbing the sore spot didn't help. It would bruise before morning.

"Nah." He turned on the bedside light and blinked in the glare. "With all the bad dreams I've had the past couple of nights, I'm not exactly eager to sleep. Especially if Cooper's right. They can't come true if you're not asleep to have them."

I sat on the bed, my back to my friend, ignoring the way the room tilted and spun as I untied my Doc Martens. "Maybe. But, I'm not convinced he's right."

"You're never convinced until someone proves you wrong. That's your default setting."

Touché. "And one of our shared traits." My Docs landed with a thud beside the nightstand. The thick-soled boots looked so out of place beside the antique-styled furniture. "But it's not time to think about this. Not until I get some sleep."

"I could switch rooms with her so you guys—"

"She said no."

"But she won't see your fabulous Batman 'jams."

I laughed despite my frustration and flopped back on the bed. "You're the only lucky one on that score."

"Her loss, friend."

And mine.

Marty tapped his phone before shoving it in his pocket. "We're going to be late."

"It's morning. I'm doing the best I can." The coffee he'd made me hadn't stripped the gravel from my voice, but I felt marginally more human. Once my brain came online, I might actually reach personhood. "This nightmare business is going to be tricky."

Last night, before he finally dropped all the "shop talk," Agent Cooper laid out a strange and disturbing case involving the creature Marty and I first encountered at the airport. The supernat that attacked us on the street might be another of its kind. It unsettled me. I'd chased ghosts and ghouls, fought zombies and vampires, but how the hell do you track down a nightmare? And what do you do once you find it?

"Does this mean you're throwing Cooper a bone and helping out?"

I snorted and wriggled into my jeans. "I never planned to leave him hanging. I just needed like five minutes to myself. A pretend vacation, if I can't get a real one."

"Makes sense." Marty walked over to the desk to survey the weapons we hadn't yet returned to the rectory arsenal in the Saint Louis Cathedral. "What're we taking?"

"To brunch?" I slid a shirt on and twisted to see how it fell in the mirror. "Unless you're worried about the crab cakes being more than fresh, I think we're good."

"Har. Har." He put his hands on his hips. "I was thinking more about what we'd need after brunch, or have you not learned your lesson about wandering around unarmed?"

My meager two days in New Orleans had proved…eventful. After the airport encounter where a monster dropped a victim with a touch, I'd been shot at by a priest hell-bent on stopping monster hunters from interfering with "God's plan," attacked by some supernatural creature on the street, and led a mythical harbinger of death and catastrophe on a wild run through the French Quarter, all while un-, or under-armed.

Is it any wonder I needed a break?

"I've learned it," I picked up my Docs and sat on the edge of the bed facing him, "but Denver omelets and biscuits and gravy don't usually demand small-caliber arms."

"When others eat them, they probably don't." He waved at the array. "But, this is you."

I did kind of hate it when he was right. "You take the Glock. I'll take one of the 1911s." The 1911s were big guns, but my favorite to handle. The weight would be a familiar comfort for me, but Marty wouldn't stand a chance with them on a good day. "How's your head?"

He tilted his chin. "My eye's pretty."

Though the swelling had gone down, he still had a lump where he'd clocked himself on a mausoleum while we hunted the Black Dog in Saint Louis Cemetery Number One. The overhead light made the bruise shift colors as he turned. "Pretty, indeed. But that didn't answer my question. I'm more concerned about the inside."

"I'm fine. Just hungry."

"You don't sound excited."

"About my head?"

"About food. It's kind of freaking me out."

"I'm excited. It's supposed to be top notch. Four and a half stars on Yelp, thousands of reviews." He picked lint from the blanket on the bed. "Might be better than last night."

"Then what is it?"

"We need to get going."

I dropped the laces, hands on my hips. "You never let me get away with a non-answer. What is it?"

"Nothing." He turned and walked to the window.

"If you're not feeling well, we should get you checked out."

"I told you, I'm fine." With a shrug, he pulled the curtain aside and shaded his eyes. "Minor headache, but no concussive symptoms."

"WebMD isn't a—"

"I called my mom."

I shut up.

"She diagnosed me via remote appointment. Video chat and everything." His voice dropped along with his shoulders. "Satisfied?"

"Yes." I focused on tying my shoe, unsure of what else to say. Marty seldom called his parents, since their conversations rarely ended well or at a reasonable volume. "How'd it go?"

He turned back to the table of weapons and lifted a shoulder holster. "It's too hot to wear anything over this."

Evasion. Not good. "True, but legal or not, we're not provoking idiots with open carry."

"Right." He checked himself out in the mirror and me in the reflection. "So we stop to raid the arsenal?"

"Nah." I slid off the bed and rummaged through my suitcase. "I'll throw on something to hide the shoulder holster, and I can pack the Derringer in an ankle holster. Text Father Callahan and ask him to bring something for you."

We worked quietly, him on his phone, me searching for something I wouldn't sweat through in thirty seconds.

"It was okay, by the way," he said, his voice soft. "Talking to Mom."

"Good." I tried to stay casual as I folded a pair of jeans before dropping them back in the suitcase. "Did she give you a hard time?"

"Less than usual when I told her about my head." He laughed without humor. "I have a feeling the lecture will come next time."

His mother, a neurosurgeon of relative renown in the Boston area, never approved of her son's involvement in monster hunting and never missed an opportunity to remind him where he'd be in his medical career if he'd stuck with it. She compared our work to ghost hunting TV shows. Despite Marty's easy-going nature, her jabs spurred intense, heated arguments I'd fled more than once.

"She said I didn't need to worry unless I started vomiting, lose consciousness or," he waved a hand in a vague gesture, "a list of other stuff I wrote down."

"Maybe she was worried." I felt the heat of his glare before I turned. "What?"

"Right." He tossed the shoulder holster on my bed. "We'll go with that."

I opened my mouth, hoping something supportive would fall out. "She…" Nothing followed. "I'm sorry."

He shrugged. "I'm used to it. You ready?"

16

"What do you think?" Cooper sat back, but nothing about him appeared relaxed, even after a lengthy, gluttonous brunch. I had to give him credit, though. This time, he'd waited until we were ensconced in the relative privacy of the rectory to start the business talk.

I leaned forward, shifting some of the papers in front of me to see the pictures again. The guy from the airport. The monster in its overaged frat-boy guise. Only one full-frame picture of his face made it into the file to identify him, but Cooper had shown us a video, and a series of digital stills pulled from it. It tracked him from the moment he emerged from a men's bathroom until he fled through the baggage claim doors. No records from before. No indication when he landed or images of him from any gate or terminal. Nothing could keep the dread and foreboding out of my voice. "I think this is going to be far more complicated than any of us are prepared for."

"There's no record of him disembarking a plane? Or of crossing security?" Sister Betty asked, laying the report back in the file folder.

Cooper shook his head and crossed his arms. "Nothing. We had techs go back forty-eight hours, and there's nothing, not even using facial recognition or behavioral analysis."

"How is that possible?" Marty even abandoned his tablets to pore over the documentation in front of us.

"What about coming in through the baggage claim doors?" I asked.

"Nada," Cooper said. "When the techs didn't find record through security, that was the first place they looked. They can't even find record of him going into the bathroom. "It's as if he materialized in the bathroom and walked out."

"Maybe he did," I said, thinking out loud.

"IFM," Marty muttered.

"Yeah," I agreed. If Cooper and DEMON's hypothesis about this creature's supernatural pedigree was right, Marty's *It's Fucking Magic* would be a plausible explanation for anything we might encounter.

"What are your thoughts on how to proceed, Hunter?" Cooper asked, his voice lacking the irony and sarcasm I'd have anticipated hours earlier.

"We do it the old-fashioned way," I said, pushing my chair back from the table. "We'll split up and investigate."

W hether you're Joe Average or have the dubious blessing of being associated with law enforcement, dealing with the TSA sucks. If I didn't know better, I'd say the federal government had done a job fair targeting wraiths and slapped uniforms into the ones that passed for human. But I knew better. DEMON had tight control over the various species that could and could not hold jobs interacting with humans, even if no other government branch was aware of it. Besides, not even the government would be dumb enough to allow literal soul-sucking creatures to interact with humans.

Human or not, the TSA agents at Louis Armstrong airport provided nothing Cooper hadn't already shared with us. Even with the additional access and conversational lubrication hastily-procured federal IDs provided, no one we interviewed remembered the frat-boy man in any security line. With as many travelers as the airport handled on an average day, I'd expected as much. The gate agents we talked to provided even less detail, but Marty's digital wizardry captured every word they said as I asked questions and probed for more.

The only bright spot of the trip happened when I stumbled into my favorite New England coffee and donut chain and procured a cold brew and a chocolate-glazed donut. And that happened a very long nine hours after a sour-faced man hustled Marty and I into claustrophobic offices off the terminal proper in the furthest approximation of southern hospitality possible.

Leaning against the high-top table in the coffee shop, I scarfed the last bite of my donut, watching my partner. With a yawn, he cracked his knuckles and stretched, asking the question I'd been asking myself for the last couple of hours. "What now?"

I sighed and shook the ice in the almost empty cup to get the last of the coffee lurking in the bottom. "We figure out which supernats can materialize in our world. With and without assistance. 'With' gives us the long list, and 'without,' the short. Then we keep hacking away at it until we've got the most likely suspects."

"Done and done." He tapped his tablet to life and slid it across the table. "The biggest culprit is likely to be a nightmare."

I swore under my breath. Something I knew how to fight would have been ideal. "I was hoping for something a little more corporeal. Goblins, minor devils. Hell, I'd even go for taking down a herd of manticores."

"I hate manticores," Marty mumbled and shuddered, probably recalling the last skirmish we had with them in Nepal. A week stalking the haunted forest for a leathery-winged beast with the body of a lion, a scorpion's stinger while dreading a not-quite-human face emerging from the shadows leaves a lasting—and negative—impression. Worse when it took three days after the first fight to finally kill the damned thing.

Longest three days of my life.

I shuddered, too, remembering the stitches I'd needed after the final battle. My thigh twinged with phantom pain, and I pressed it with the heel of my hand. "Yeah, me too, but it would be a straight forward job. Hunt, capture or kill, move on."

He scoffed. "Since when is anything we do 'straight forward'?"

As much as I hated to admit it, he had a point. Instead of saying anything, I picked up the tablet and skimmed the text. I sucked the last of the coffee from my cup and hoped for a monster easier than a nightmare.

A girl could dream, after all.

My heart thumped against my ribs as I tried to slow my breathing. I shivered, though I wasn't cold. Every nerve buzzed with the aftermath of the nightmare, every sound amplified, every twitching shadow making me jump. I blinked against the light and tried to focus on the details of the hotel room to ground myself. My bed. Marty's bed. The unbalanced ceiling fan.

This was real. Despite what happened in the dream, everything was fine. None of it had actually happened.

I looked around.

Or had it?

The pen trembled in my hand, poised over my notebook, but the words to describe what I'd seen wouldn't come.

Marty rubbed his eyes, squinting. "Did you get it?"

"No." I dropped the pen into the open binding and lay the notebook in my lap. "Before I can get it down," I shrugged, "it's gone." Not that my body noticed. I needed another run through the French Quarter to burn off all the energy jangling my nerves. It'd probably be enjoyable without a hellhound at my heels.

Marty yawned and nodded. "What now?"

Sweat ran down my back like a spider across my hot skin. I rolled my shoulders and tried to ignore the sensation by focusing on my notebook. The few words I'd scribbled made little sense. Banquet. Blood bisque. Sparkly dress. Key. Illegible squiggles between them should have been words, but weren't. At least not words I could read.

"Try to sleep?"

My body trembled, and my brain whirred, flashing images that made no sense. "Not an option."

"Guided meditation?" He already sounded half asleep. Lucky bastard.

Sister Betty taught me not long after I started training with her. She'd refused to let me leave training sessions before I'd used it to bring myself down. It'd probably saved my life by making sure I didn't do something stupid and get killed. Fighting the things that had eaten my baby sister in front of me did little to dissipate the anger that threatened to consume me back then. Meditation helped. Sometimes, when things got bad, it still did.

But not tonight.

"I need to get up and move."

"'Kay." He yawned and buried himself under the fluffy blankets so deep, only the top of his brown curls peeked out. "Turn out the light."

"Yup." I put my notebook on the nightstand and threw back my blankets. At four in the morning, surely there'd be something to do in New Orleans. Maybe even make a misbehaving monster regret its life choices.

I slid out of bed and dressed quietly, strapping on my new belly band holster for "every day" concealed wear. The light switch made a soft snap, and Marty, cocooned in blankets, mumbled, "Take a weapon."

"Already packing." I patted the Glock banded to me under my loose tank top as I left.

Adrenaline and nerves conspired to make the silent hallway, ominous instead of the mundane, abandoned space it should be this early. Something felt familiar, like déjà vu, but I couldn't remember what should happen next. The harder I tried to remember, the more the thought evaded me. All I had to do was walk down the hallway and take the elevator to the lobby to find other people, but I couldn't move. Instead, I scanned both directions, my back pressed against my door, alert for whatever might try to kill me next.

Crystal chandeliers glittered. Ugly paisley carpet patterns wove a drunken path between rows of closed doors.

I waited.

Nothing happened.

My hand slid under my tank to release the strap securing my Glock.

Silence.

"This is stupid," I whispered, fear sweat cutting a path down my spine. Of course it felt familiar. It should. I'd been living here for days. The last time the hallway felt like this, I'd caught up to the Black Dog and chased it. Then, there'd been a reason why my heart raced, why the atmosphere felt heavy and dangerous. But not now.

I willed my feet to move. They reluctantly obeyed.

Every instinct urged me in the opposite direction my feet took. Instead of heading to the elevator, instead of seeking the comfort of other people, I followed the path I'd used to stalk the Black Dog. Scorched paw prints marked the carpet, if you knew where to look.

Before I peeked around the corner, my Glock pointed at the floor in my two-handed grip.

Empty.

I stepped into the branching hallway, relaxing my shoulders, but not re-holstering the gun. Whether a bullet would work against the creature I'd been tasked to find was unknown, but I preferred useless to empty-handed.

The hallway couldn't be more normal. Nothing seemed out of the ordinary. The same ugly carpet, the same too fancy chandeliers, and silent doors. At the end stood the table with the flowers and mirror I'd seen before.

That I'd hallucinated in before.

But had it been a hallucination?

When I'd stalked the Black Dog, I'd had that horror movie experience of walking down the "hallway that doesn't end." In that mirror, I'd glimpsed the hellhound I couldn't see with my own eyes. But, in that vision, I'd been wearing a sleek, sparkling evening gown instead of my black denim, tank and—

The dress.

My reflection had worn a dress. The same dress from my nightmare.

My stomach cramped. I turned slowly, aiming my Glock low down the empty hallway.

What the hell was I going to shoot? A mirror? The wall?

Though none of my possible targets made sense rationally or tactically, I couldn't force myself to holster the Glock.

Investigation made sense.

I approached the mirror cautiously.

My reflection in the splotchy, silvered glass remained true. Faded, ripped jeans, a loose black tank top, and black Doc Martens. Blue-streaked black hair uncombed and bed head wild. Nothing behind me. Only me, armed and foolishly stalking a mirror, perilously close to endangering the first civilian to leave their room. They'd regret the urge to go for an early run, that's for sure.

The reflection didn't change and nothing new appeared. I watched to be sure, nerves and bewilderment eventually giving way to pride. At least I could hold proper stance half asleep.

"Don't mind me." I reluctantly holstered my Glock, eyes not leaving the mirror. "Just losing my mind."

This time, the hallways didn't lengthen as I approached the antique mirror. I leaned as close as I could without disturbing the flower arrangement in front of it. Interrupted, erratic sleep shadowed my pale face, but everything else appeared normal.

"Hallucinations," I confirmed, readjusting my tank top to cover the lump in the belly band holster.

My reflection mimicked, but for a moment, it felt mocking. I chided myself for paranoia and shook my head. Nothing supernatural. Only me, half asleep in a deserted hotel hallway obsessing over nightmares.

I turned away, determined to burn off nervous energy and go back to sleep.

Before I turned the corner, I glanced back and caught my reflection wearing a long, black sparkling evening gown, hand raised in a teasing wave.

———

"I don't see anything, Cee," Marty grumbled.

"I don't either," I said, "but that doesn't mean something screwy isn't happening with this mirror."

Sister Betty stepped back and contemplated it from a distance, arms crossed over her faded t-shirt. "There's lore about haunted mirrors, especially silver-backed antiques. Given the hotel's history and location, a few haunted items would be fairly normal. I'll speak with Father Callahan about it."

"Are you sure it was your reflection?" Marty gestured to the hallway branching back to our room, his oversized black, gray, white, and purple striped tank top swaying around him like a dress. "That's a long way to see a clear image in a damaged mirror."

"I know what I saw," I insisted. "My reflection waved at me, and it was wearing a dress. The same dress I first saw with the Black Dog and again in my nightmare." Marty and I locked eyes. "My reflection waved, Marty. I didn't."

"It's not unprecedented," Sister Betty stifled a yawn, "but certainly unusual."

"That's kind of our forte, isn't it?" I said.

"Indeed, my dear." She smiled.

Marty didn't speak as he side-stepped the table and flowers we'd moved to get closer to the mirror. His breath fogged the glass as he leaned close. With one finger, he pushed the mirror, but it didn't move. He stepped back, joining Sister Betty.

Neither of them took their sleepy gaze off the mirror.

"Any idea what we do now?" I asked. I'd already had one nightmare come true. When Marty and I hunted the Black Dog, we'd been attacked by a man or, rather, a supernatural creature disguised as a man. The dream showed the attack almost play by play. In another, the creature exacted revenge. I shoved away the mental image of his bloody knife. That one hadn't happened. Yet. I hoped it wouldn't.

"Now? At," Marty pulled out his phone, "four-thirty? We go back to bed."

"We don't know what this is, so until we figure it out—"

"It's part of my nightmare," I said, interrupting Sister Betty. "Part of what started when I hunted the Black Dog. And if Hardin's right—"

"Do you think he is?" Marty asked

Both of them stared at me.

"Dunno," I said, the sudden, thready rasp in my own voice disturbing. Whether I remembered the details or not, the prospect of my nightmares coming true terrified me. Especially the recent ones. I hoped Agent Hardin's information was wrong.

"Are we willing to risk it?" Sister Betty turned back to the mirror.

"No." I rubbed the goosebumps on my arms before running my fingers through my hair. "No, we're not."

The rectory office smelled like stale coffee and old incense. Father Callahan sat behind Father Robicheau's old desk, stacks of books flanking his laptop. Marty sat across from him, typing on a laptop as Father Callahan spoke. Sister Betty paced, a book open in her hand. I sat on the floor sipping coffee, back against the wall, a book propped on my thighs. Discarded remnants from our early breakfast and mid-morning snacks haunted the desk and even the floor beside me. The clutter softened the otherwise stark room, or maybe the absence of a homicidal priest determined to rid the world of monster hunters just made the ambiance a whole lot less icky.

"So," Father Callahan leaned back and folded his hands behind his head, "the only conclusion we can draw is that it's unlikely the mirror is haunted."

I put the mug on the carpeted floor beside me.

"Unlikely, but not impossible." Sister Betty folded her book around her thumb.

"Yes, unlikely, but the best we can do without a complete history," Father Callahan said.

"Even in a haunted hotel?" Marty's fingers slowed on the keyboard.

"Yes," Father Callahan said. "Age or relative spiritual activity of a location doesn't correlate with mirror activity."

"The huge mirror at Tujague's is well over a hundred years old, and none of the known activity has anything to do with it," I said, briefly lifting the book from my lap. "If any mirror's going to be haunted, I'd wager on that one."

"Exactly the example that came to mind." Father Callahan nodded and sat up straight again. "Since its founding, the diocese has monitored reports of spiritual activity, especially businesses that profit from it, explicitly or implicitly. And though your hotel has a reputation for activity, none is mirror-related nor similar to the hallway distortion Caitlin experienced."

Marty nodded, though I wondered how much he already knew. The way he'd raided the Catholic Church's servers over the past week, he might have discovered the Holy Grail's location.

"As much as there is here, I haven't found any connection between mirrors and dreams in this." I tapped the book in my lap.

"Same." Sister Betty closed the volume in her hand. "I'm hoping the Order will have something."

Sister Betty's Order, the Holy Order of the Sisters of Mercy of Saint Brendan, had an extensive library covering the entire human spiritual experience from terrestrial culture to supernatural lore at their base in Ireland. Though I'd yet to discover how, Father Callahan's impressive knowledge of lore and access to restricted Vatican information related to his connections with her Order. Neither of them discussed it, and when I asked, they deflected the conversation so skillfully, it took several minutes to realize what happened. I made a mental note to ask Marty what he could find out.

"What do we do until they call?" Marty asked.

"Well," I groaned as I got to my feet, "there's plenty of magic in this city, and where there's magic, there's practitioners. I think I'll go see who I can find. Anyone want to come?"

17

S ome days, you hunt. Some days, you're hunted.

The last time I hunted in New Orleans, my quarry found me. I shouldn't have been surprised when it happened again, but with the jovial afternoon chaos of Chartres Street and Jackson Square, I didn't notice I'd been targeted.

Scarves and flowy textiles draping the fortune teller tables and chairs fluttered in the reluctant breeze. Signs swayed and one with a series of hand-painted tarot cards fell flat on the stone paving. One tasseled umbrella lifted enough to rattle the rigging securing it to a young woman's folding chair, the sound all but lost in the corner jazz band's music and the conversations between artists and tourists. From the long rows of art to the tiny tables and the river of tourists flowing between it all, I took it all in, too tired to focus on anything except whether the woman dancing in front of the band was Stevie Nicks, or just dressed like her.

"Hunter," said a wizened voice laced with impatience and emphasis indicating this wasn't the first time.

I turned, curious.

A woman waved me over to her table. The sign propped against it featured a purple and green hand on a black background, gold lines etching the palms. She raised her voice again, a croak of noise over the music, talk, and laughter. "Hunter, come here."

How had she known? I pointed to myself with a questioning look and tightened my stomach muscles, hoping the Glock banded to me didn't show or that the wind hadn't exposed it.

"Yes, yes," she said, her impatience growing, "you are the only active hunter in the city today."

"What's going on?" Marty asked from behind me.

"Dunno, but I think we're about to find out." I walked toward the woman shaded by her sun-bleached rainbow-colored golf umbrella.

"For a hunter, you pay little attention to the dangers around you," she chided, gesturing at the stool across from her.

"I'm sorry." I studied her to figure out why she looked so familiar. "I didn't hear you."

"Then there may be much you don't hear, and that, *cherie*," she pointed a crooked finger at me, "could be detrimental."

That one word triggered the memory. "I've seen you before. At Jazz Musicians Park." That might not have been the name, but it was tourist-close. She'd caught me trying to clean some unfortunate powdered sugar out of my black shirt after my first experience with beignets. Side note: no matter how careful you are, powdered sugar blows *everywhere* with that first bite. You might think you're slick, but you're not, and you're going to look like a coke fiend. There's no delicate way to eat them properly without all the sugar, and then, what's the point?

She cackled. "She remembers. Please," she insisted, another gesture toward the stool made the offer a command, "sit."

Marty and I exchanged a glance that said everything we didn't.

Another breeze blew through, more a ponderous motion of air than relief from the heat and humidity. I shrugged and sat. "Why do you call me 'hunter'?"

Sunlight filtered through the faded fabric overhead, and her dark eyes sparkled with mischief. "That's what you are, isn't it? A hunter of monsters? A knight of the Church?"

A shudder ran through me. No one had ever identified me as a monster hunter unless I'd told them, worked with them, or killed a monster in front of them. Most of the time it was the "decapitated something that tried to eat you" experience. Or work. But mostly decapitation.

She waited for my answer, her crone hands on the black velour table covering.

"I... Yes. No one's ever called me a knight before."

A dismissive shrug. "Titles change with time."

"How did you know? Did you," my left hand lay on the table, my right crossed under it, hovering over the holster, "see something?"

"Not the way you think, or expect, but," she tapped her head, "I see plenty."

Unsure what she meant, though knowing it could have multiple meanings, I nodded. "If you're looking for help—"

"You are."

Her simple declarative stopped my words, and my hands fell into my lap. "What do you mean?"

"You seek monsters you cannot hunt, cannot kill." The umbrella bobbed as she sat back. Her clothes seemed as wrinkled as the day I saw her in the park, but the strange light through the umbrella made her look older. Without the animation of expression or talking, deep cracks scarred her face. I wondered how old she must be, how many years she'd spent in the sun.

"What's your name?"

Her hands disappeared into her big sleeves. "Names are shadows that take shape when you focus and change when you stop." She produced a deck of cards from inside her sleeve and placed them on the velour cloth. I recognized the oversized stack by the blue, white, and black plaid pattern and regretted sitting at her table. The Rider-Waite Tarot deck. "Shuffle," she commanded.

"This isn't a good idea." Marty bit off my nickname at the first sibilant hint.

Smart. Names held power.

"I think I agree," I said, already reaching for the deck. I'd had my cards read before. Nothing bad had happened, except losing twenty bucks. I hadn't learned more than I might have gleaned from a horoscope or prescient fortune cookie. In fact, I'd had more illuminating experiences high on caffeine and no sleep. Though I had no burning desire for this woman to read my cards in the middle of Chartres Street on a sticky Louisiana day, I suspected declining wouldn't be an option.

The old woman nodded in approval as I shuffled.

"Will you tell me your name?" I asked.

"No," she said and closed her eyes. "Focus. Shuffle."

I obeyed. The Louisiana humidity seemed to evaporate from the weak shadows encircling me. After I finished, I stacked them neatly on the table.

Without opening her eyes, she picked them up and pressed the deck between her palms.

My stomach cramped with nerves and something I couldn't identify.

She opened her eyes, now glowing bluish-white.

"Holy—"

The old woman's head lolled. For a moment, her glamour flickered, her craggy, wrinkled features superimposed over an ageless face.

"Shut up," I whispered at Marty. I'd heard about the transformation of half-fae creatures delivering prophecy. A disturbance could disrupt the prophecy or turn the will of the person—

Creature?

—offering it.

Her skin took on a bluish cast, though I couldn't tell how much distortion came from the light burning out of what had been her eyes.

A surge of magic poured off her as she smiled, my own body reacting with euphoric relaxation. I bit my lip to restrain a giddy laugh.

"You are more powerful than you know, hunter." She sounded nothing like before. Thousands of voices layered to become hers, male and female, from very young to very old.

I winced, the complexity of the sound hurt my ears, but my heavy limbs refused to move.

The first card to hit the table wasn't a card I knew. Unfamiliar runes decorated the upper right and lower left corners. In the center, an emerald green, open-mouthed dragon writhed, spewing spiraling gouts of orange-red flame.

The old woman didn't incline her head to the card, but her hand hovered over it. Blue-white light emanated from where her eyes should have been, the glare aimed at me and strong enough to make me squint. "The Dragon," she said, as if I would understand.

I knew better than to ask questions, but I certainly had them. This card had not come from the traditional deck. Behind me, Marty tapped notes on his cell phone. At least we'd have a record to review later.

She withdrew her hand to pull a second card, laying another unfamiliar card to the left of the dragon. This one a gold-foiled bird of flame rising from a pile of ash. Different runes decorated the corners of the card. Her hand hovered over it, palm fractions of an inch from the card's glossy face. "Oooh," she crooned. "I should have expected you to manifest The Phoenix."

A little girl laughed, the beat of musician's hand drums whipping her into a wild frenzy. Her shrill voice became a squeal, and though I worried the sound would break the old woman's trance, I couldn't stop the girl, too busy trying to catch every shift, every nuance of the fortune teller's behavior.

The old woman didn't seem to notice her, only pulled another card, laying it to the right of the dragon. A hollow-eyed skull stared back as she withdrew her hand. Long, curving fangs protruded from both jaws, glistening with wet, fresh red drops in stark contrast to the matte blank voids where the eyes should have been.

In my line of work, you reach for extremes. You reach for the super-holy, saint-like lifestyle, or you cultivate a sense of humor about the dark. You learn to laugh at what scares the shit out of you. Grinning skulls are funny, cute even, with heart-shaped eye holes emblazoned on a t-shirt. When a skeleton assembles out of a pile of bones and runs at you in a dark sewer, singing helps, especially the song about which bones connect. Silly as it is, it removes fear from the equation as you sight-in a Mossberg loaded with explosive rounds packed with blessed Jerusalem dirt. When I say I giggled so hard I almost missed the shot, I'm not being modest.

My affinity skewed dark, but this was different.

Humor could not survive against the card on the table. Not even the blackest gallows humor could thrive. Those empty eyes stared through me, woke something within and made it resonate. Staring into the matte, colorless holes felt like standing on the edge of a cliff and wanting, even for a heartbeat, to jump.

That void called me.

And something within me responded.

The old woman whimpered as her hand hovered over the card. She blinked rapidly, her eyes returning to normal. Wrenching coughs doubled her over. Both Marty and I rushed to her side. The fabric-draped camp table toppled, and cards spilled across the stone-paved square.

"Are you okay?" Marty held her in the chair as she slumped forward, hacking into a wrinkled, yellowed handkerchief cupped in her hand.

She nodded, but the coughing didn't allow her the breath to answer.

The little girl skipped by, the lilt of laughter ringing in her voice as she sang, "Three blind mice, three blind mice." She locked eyes with me. Her bright, lightweight dress spun around her as she twirled. "See how they run." With determination I'd never have expected from a child, she looked from me to Marty, then to the old woman. Fear warbled its way down my spine. "See how they run." With another eerie laugh, she ran across the square and disappeared into the crowd around the corner.

Marty looked at me. "What the fu—" he glanced at the old woman, "um, hell was that?"

"Such language," she wheezed, "around a lady."

"Yes, ma'am, my apologies." He squatted at her side, balancing on his toes. "I didn't mean to offend you."

"Or your lady friend." She waved the discolored handkerchief at me.

"I love her to death, ma'am," Marty's lips quirked in a teasing grin, "but she's no lady."

I rolled my eyes and gathered spilled cards while Marty righted the table. The old woman murmured grateful things the way only a Southern matriarch can—simultaneously gracious yet without any doubt her words constituted an order. "Yes, *cher*, thank you. Set it right here." She gestured at one of the two pieces of fabric Marty held. "That goes over top. You are so kind, *merci*, ah, *merci*."

Straightening the cards in my hand, I noticed only familiar Rider-Waite Tarot images. I flipped through them, one at a time while her attention remained on Marty.

"You won't find them," she said, her voice rough from her coughing fit.

Startled, I placed the cards on the table. "I'm sorry. I should've asked permission."

She stared. "Yes, you should have, *cherie*, but that's not what I said." When I didn't respond, she nodded at the chair and waved Marty to the other. "Sit. We have much to discuss."

18

The patter of a late afternoon shower forced us closer to the table for shelter under the old umbrella. Fat, sporadic raindrops failed to deter the musicians, though the tourists took little notice as they hurried by, heads covered with shopping bags, arms, and colorful umbrellas. Artists covered their work with sheets of clear plastic and blue tarps and waited for the rain to pass. I scooted my seat forward to avoid the worst of the drips off the edge of the umbrella.

The fortune teller who'd called out to me in the square, Madame Sabine, didn't seem affected by the weather. She reached into the folds of wrinkled fabric in her lap, then pressed a copper-wrapped stone amulet into my palm, staring at the chips of silvered glass on the surface. "The things you seek are not part of this world but are in it. They gather and wait." Cold rain rolled into the waistband of my jeans, but the stone transfixed me. "What waits? And how will I know when to use this? Or how to use it?" I still wasn't certain what my target was, never mind what to do once I found it. The stone in my hand warmed since she'd first put it in my hand, but neither the weight nor the warmth provided what I really needed—answers.

"You need not look." She stroked the gray stone. "What you seek, *cherie*, seeks you. Be patient, be vigilant. You will know."

The leather cord softened as I twisted it around my thumb. "And this will help?"

"Every door has a key," Madame Sabine said.

"What about the tarot cards?"

She turned to Marty, one eyebrow arched with regal censure.

He stuttered the first syllable before he regained his composure. "T-they weren't traditional cards you pulled."

Her wrinkled hand caressed the cards stacked in the center of the small table with remarkable care. "There are times," she said, barely louder than the musicians and intermittent rain, "when worlds mix, but not as they should, especially here. In these moments of power, we can do nothing but give it space."

I nodded, but the unusual Tarot card images wouldn't leave me.

Madame Sabine looked down at the deck still on the table in front of her, the whites of her eyes too bright. "We can only say *c'est la vie* and rely on the protectors of this world."

Responsibility, my old friend. "Is the mixing of worlds...malevolent?" I asked.

She shook her head and tapped the deck. "There is no bad. No good. Only our interpretation. Is a cat bad because it hunts and eats a bird? Or the rain bad if it falls when we wish it wouldn't?" With her other hand, she gestured to the sky. The rain stopped, the umbrella fabric brightening, the sun breaking through the clouds.

"Did you do that?" Marty asked, a tremor in his voice.

Madame Sabine only smiled, her eyes glowing around her dark irises. "There's power here, Hunter, more than you can contain or control. Remind your partners, before the power lashes back and takes more than they're willing to give."

———

The amulet hung heavy against my chest, and I stroked it absently. "I don't know why you put it on," Marty said from across the book-cluttered desk, without glancing up from his tablet. "Never mess with unknown magical objects. That's basic self-preservation."

"You've said that already," I said.

"Normally, I'd agree," Sister Betty said, finishing the glass of sweet tea Deacon Paul delivered after Marty and I returned to the rectory from our encounter with Madame Sabine. "But not this time."

Marty opened his mouth, then what she said sunk in. His jaw snapped shut, eyes wide.

I wished I had it on video.

"I'm okay with you wearing it." She wiped the condensation from her glass with her thumb. "For now. Madame Sabine's never been known to practice malicious magic. She's helped previous hunters, including Sister Evangeline." Her voice dropped as she mentioned the fallen hunter, a fierce, motorcycle-riding, shotgun-wielding force responsible for the territory between Tallahassee and San Antonio. I didn't think Sister Betty and Sister Evangeline knew each other well, but Sister Betty seemed profoundly affected by her death.

Murder. Her murder.

Father Robicheau, her Church-designated partner, masterminded an "accident" where Sister Evangeline fell from a helicopter in mid-flight. The one person responsible for supporting her mission murdered her. She relied on the same support I did, that Sister Betty depended on. The trusted relationship she never should have had to question killed her.

Nothing like a fundamental shift in your worldview to fuck with your head.

Thoughts of my little sister, Shannon, dressed in pink ruffles threatened, but I shoved them down hard.

This wasn't the time.

"We, that is, the Church, have commissioned her in the past. I trust her." Sister Betty gestured at the amulet. "I'm guessing that's native stone."

I pressed it against my chest. Instead of an irritating, unfamiliar weight, the stone felt as if it belonged there.

Marty huffed, perturbed. "I don't think it's a good idea if we don't know what it'll do."

"It hasn't done anything," I said.

"Yet," he countered. "She called it a key. It could open anything from a door to Pandora's box. And God knows," he said with a sour little smile, "with you, things go south at the worst possible time."

"South's a great destination." I raised my water glass. "Fabulous, even."

"And we've been in a hot mess since arrived." He snorted.

"Include that in your Yelp review." Sister Betty smirked behind the rim of her glass.

"I can see the title now: *New Orleans, Vacationing Monster Hunters, Beware.*" The stone swung like a pendulum as I released it. He had a point, but admitting it might swell his head. "Let's focus on what we can handle." Shuffling through the papers on the desk, I pulled out one. "The creature from the airport—"

"Which DEMON conveniently lost," Marty griped.

"Jesus, do we need to feed you or something?"

He scowled, then stuck out his tongue. The laugh that followed signaled, at least, a temporary reprieve from his stormy mood. "I learned it by watching you."

Shaking my head, I pointed at the paper again. "The creature from the airport causes humans to collapse at its touch."

"Death." Marty tapped his tablet to life. "It causes death."

"What?" Sister Betty asked.

I closed my eyes.

"The guy in the airport, Benito Hernandez, died after the creature touched him." Marty passed the tablet to Sister Betty, and I leaned over her shoulder. "Massive coronary event. He never regained consciousness."

I skimmed the details, stomach too sour to read closely. Another death I should have prevented. Another name on the list in my head. The creature looked like some overgrown frat boy, and though I knew he was a monster, I did nothing until too late. When I should have acted, I waited. That man, Benito Rodriguez, died on my watch.

What the hell was I doing in this job if I couldn't do it when it mattered most?

I didn't have an answer.

"Seems to rule out a nightmare," she sighed. "There's no record of creatures killing humans with touch except Death."

"Could it have been Death?" I asked, hopeful.

She shook her head and returned Marty's tablet. "Death taking a humanoid form isn't unheard of, of course, but it usually takes a female form. Besides, in a densely populated place, Death wouldn't have taken just one soul."

"We're like potato chips?" Marty said. "Can't have just one?"

"You're salty, for sure," I retorted. "Why wouldn't Death be content with one?"

"It's not that," she said. "Humans are inordinately attracted to Death, especially in humanoid form. It's not that Death wouldn't have restraint, but humans can't resist Death."

"That's grim," Marty muttered.

"I saw it once," Sister Betty said. "Death, that is, in human form. She was the most beautiful person I'd ever seen, though I knew what she was..." Her voice trailed off. "No, we struck that theory early. With the evidence at hand, the Lore Keeper had no information."

That she'd contacted the Lore Keeper shouldn't have surprised me, but as a barometer for the level of crap awaiting us, contacting the Vatican's highest-ranking occult specialist never failed to catch my attention. None of the monster hunters I'd met ever mentioned the Lore Keeper, and Marty's technically illegal research never turned up more than oblique references. Whoever the Lore Keeper was or where their knowledge came from, only the uppermost Vatican hierarchy knew.

"That's...disturbing." Marty looked down at the report. "We're working blind."

"No more than usual," I said. "We've fought things we didn't understand before. We'll do it again."

"No," Marty said, so pale that even the greenish-yellowish bruise on his forehead drained of color. "We've always had back up. We've always had some idea of what we're dealing with and how to eliminate it, and in the most obscure cases, the Lore Keeper found answers."

"But we don't know what to research," I said, my words tentative and faltering. "We've got one direct observation of this creature's effect on people, which could be bad or misleading." I glanced from Marty to Sister Betty. "What if it does something else, and death was the result in this case? What if it affects people differently?"

"We could be looking at it wrong," Sister Betty agreed, taking the paper I'd picked up.

"Did Hernandez have a history of heart trouble?" I asked.

Marty tapped, swiped, and tapped again. "None on record, though he had high cholesterol at his last physical. Seven years ago."

"A lot can happen in seven years," Sister Betty said. "Health issues could have contributed to his death."

"But what triggered it?" I leaned back and stared at the spill of light across rectory ceiling. "Something had to activate it, to cause... What'd they call it?"

"Massive coronary event," Marty replied, turning to his laptop, fingers rapid-firing across the keyboard.

"Right." I draped an arm across my eyes. A slow, resonant headache throbbed deep inside my skull. After a full night's sleep, it might go away.

"What else could it cause?" Marty chewed the side of his thumbnail.

"I have no idea," Sister Betty and I said at the same time.

Hours later and still trapped in the rectory, we hadn't gotten much further, though we'd all grown much crabbier, despite the delivery of refreshments by a nervous Deacon Paul.

I tore a candy wrapper into thin strips and folded it into origami stars. Sister Betty watched me launch another tiny star at my empty coffee cup. "Seriously?"

"What?" I asked.

She waved a hand at the tiny pieces of poorly folded paper littering the desk.

"They're paper and tiny. Not the best aerodynamics."

Her right eyebrow arched, her lips puckered.

I sat up, sighed, and scooped the paper scraps into my hand. "Sitting around's killing me."

"The Order will call soon," she said as if the words tried her already thin patience.

"We're wasting time," I said again. "I could be out looking for this thing while we wait. You could call me on my—"

"Knock, knock." We both turned at Father Callahan's familiar greeting, though neither of our faces must have reflected our appreciation for the arrival of another person. "Have I interrupted something?"

"Just them antagonizing each other," Marty said dryly. "I told them to get a room. Even offered to vacate mine, but no such luck. For any of us."

"Marty!" Sister Betty scowled at him. "That's enough."

He held both hands up and pretended to be chastised. "Okay, I give up. Sorry." The significant look he gave Father Callahan lacked subtlety and any attempt at being covert.

"Right." Father Callahan held up his phone and a paper file folder. "Well, maybe this will lift everyone's spirits."

"What's that?" Sister Betty asked.

"The Lore Keeper's report on strange deaths from a creature's touch. Seems they happen all over the world, but in cycles. At one point, your hotel experienced quite a rash of them." He put the folder on the table, and Sister Betty opened it eagerly. I hovered over her shoulder, skimming the text as she turned the pages. "A legend formed around the deaths and, in human lore, it was considered the suicide hotel."

"Why hadn't we discovered that already?" I asked as Sister Betty flipped through grainy, old photos.

"I would have caught that," Marty said, confused and somewhat defensive.

"No, probably not. So much was done to erase the legend, it's only preserved in the most obscure libraries."

"Why? Haunted hotels thrive here." I looked up from the pages Sister Betty studied.

"Haunted hotels, yes," he said, "but this isn't a haunting. No hotel, even in a city renown for the paranormal, could survive if their reputation involved customers who had nightmares and committed suicide during their stay."

Marty and I looked at each other, neither mentioning the nightmares we'd both experienced.

"True." Marty looked back down at his tablet. "But Hernandez didn't commit suicide. He dropped dead in the middle of a public space."

I shook my head. Nightmares. Death, even if by suicide. More puzzle pieces, but still, not enough. "We're still missing something."

"But what?" Sister Betty asked.

The harder I tried to focus on the idea, the vaguer it became. "I don't know. Whether it's a nightmare or something else, we've got to draw it out, watch it, then stop it before it kills."

"How do you propose to do that?"

"Bait," I said, looking at my three partners.

19

"Credible bait isn't armed." Sister Betty stepped back, surveyed me, then reached to straighten a seam. "You'll blend in like this. Besides, 'bait' was your idea, so stop complaining."

"I'm not complaining." I swatted her hand away and adjusted the form-fitting fabric encasing the smooth curve of my hip. Every inch of this egregiously pink ensemble was her fault. From the boob-smashing, low-cut halter top to the perilously short skirt. I resisted the urge to tug at the matching, skimpy thong underneath and raised my hands for her inspection. "I'm voicing my concerns about being unarmed, especially given our recent experiences."

"Legs are the most important weapons you've got in that getup," Marty said from his bed, now transformed into a reclining fortress of tech and pillows.

With a laugh, Sister Betty patted my bare thigh. "He has a point. And you've got better stems for this than anyone else." The heat of a fierce blush rushed up my neck and burned the tips of my ears. Conflicting waves of emotion made me want to flee, strip, and jump her. Not in that order, but maybe all at once.

Marty snickered from his nest, an evil cackle of perverse glee at my humiliation.

Note to self: *retaliate*.

He pressed a finger to his ear and muttered to Father Callahan, en route, somewhere between the hotel and Saint Louis Cathedral.

"You look good." Sister Betty handed me a glittery clutch too small to hold more than a tube of lipstick, ID, and maybe a little cash.

"What the hell am I supposed to pack in that?"

She shoved the purse at me. "You act like you've never dressed up before, Caitlin."

The warning in her voice made me bite back the sarcasm that yearned to be free. I took the sorry excuse for a purse and sighed.

She eyed me, her hands on her hips. Far from being glitzed up like some Bourbon Street Barbie, she wore workout sweats, a t-shirt so thin a hint of skin color showed through, and her hair in a ponytail. "You done?"

I grunted a response and tried not to roll my eyes. Push too hard and I'd regret it. Maybe not today, but she'd remember the next time we hit the gym. She always remembered in the gym.

"Good." Her tone brooked no resistance. "I'm not in the mood to kick your ass, no matter how much you deserve it."

"Yeah, yeah."

"Don't make me change my mind," she warned.

But whether she wanted to or not, she couldn't. She'd been shot on my watch. "You're not kicking anyone's ass."

"I still could."

"Not with stitches in your side."

"Don't test me." She turned and unearthed a pair of shoes from a shroud of tissue paper.

"Oh, hell no." I retreated a few steps. "I will not wear those."

The shoes dangled from her fingers, though "shoes" might have been a generous euphemism for the configuration of straps attached a thin, steeply sloped silver sole, and a dangerous spiked heel.

Sister Betty raised her eyebrow, stepped forward, and thrust them at me.

I shook my head. "I'm bait, I'm unarmed, and now you're hobbling me."

She cleared her throat, raising her hand, the dangling straps, soles, and spikes wobbling in my face.

Neither of us moved.

From the far side of the room, the *Jeopardy* theme song crescendoed out of the silence.

"Ugh," I snatched the shoes, "fine, I'll wear the damned things. But if I break my neck and die, I'm coming back to haunt your ass."

"As long as it's just my ass," she said sweetly, turning away.

And now, instead of doing something useful or mood-improving, like hunting the nightmare and kicking any misbehaving monster ass that might get in my way, Sister Betty stationed me outside the bar. In a dress. Perched in a chair looking pretty and watching the world go by like I had nothing better to do.

The murmur of conversation from the bar split on a woman's sharp laugh, crashed together with a cheer from a chorus of voices, then resumed its low buzz.

If ever I needed a drink, this was it, and yet...

I sighed and shifted, careful not to flash the lobby. No one remotely suspicious walked by, but since I'd encountered the frat boy-man from the airport here, recon made sense.

A woman in a sumptuous, yet conservative, dress gave me side-eye and turned up her nose as she passed. The patina on her pearls suggested old money, and her sneer of disdain confirmed it. I pretended not to hear her harrumph of contempt.

"And then she had this whip," said the leader of a tribe of twenty-something guys crossing the lobby, "and fucking six inch heels, man." In shorts and a polo, he walked backward directing his words at his similarly-dressed companions. "Just wait, you'll see. I'm telling you, it's incredible."

I bit the inside of my cheek as he stumbled down the short stairs to the door.

"Everybody hates working," a man in a well-tailored suit said as he stomped by on his way into the bar, a designer leather computer case bumping his hip. The corners of his mouth flicked down in distaste as his eyes glided over me. A younger man with a less expensive case followed, furiously typing on his phone with both thumbs. Pretending he didn't see me, the older man continued as they disappeared into the carousel bar. "When it comes down to it, though, I hate being broke a hell of a lot more than I hate working."

I yawned and pressed my fingers against the inner corner of my burning eyes to avoid ruining my makeup. This job couldn't be over fast enough. At this point, I'd sacrifice my theoretical vacation for a few days of sleep. Well, part of my vacation, at least.

After the mirror incident, I hadn't slept. I lay in bed, staring up at the ceiling trying to figure it out. The couple of times my eyes drifted closed, details from the nightmare jerked me awake. Remembering the disturbingly dark and reflective bowl of viscous blood bisque made my stomach roil, and the way the liquid clung and glittered on a silver spoon made goosebumps riot across my skin. I dreaded sleep as much as I craved it, but if struggling to stay awake meant I didn't have to see that nightmare, or watch the death of the woman in Rome again, or to hear Shannon's terror—

Out of habit, I scanned the lobby for something, anything of interest to distract me. It took a few seconds before my brain reacted to what I saw.

To whom I saw.

Across the lobby, near the left end of the front desk, he emerged from one of the ballroom spaces.

I unlocked my phone without looking, subtly aiming the camera at frat-boy man, the nightmare, crossing the lobby. Without taking my eyes off him, I started the video feed.

He never looked to either side, but headed for the front door, nose raised as if following a scent. People parted around him like water around rocks. Neither his day-dreamy pace nor his vague smile faltered.

My Bluetooth headset rang, and I tapped it, still tracking the man with my phone as I stood and took a couple of hesitant steps. "She hobbled me with these heels."

"S'okay." The staccato clicking of Marty's keyboard betrayed his reaction to the streaming video. "I'll monitor where he goes."

"Which does nothing." I followed my target, tugging my skirt with my free hand and trying not to wobble.

"Easy, killer. This is recon, remember? Information over capture."

"And if we lose him?" My shoes cracked like gunfire on the marble floor. I muttered curses under my breath and tried to walk softer.

"Got him," Marty said, then directed another comment to someone else. Maybe Father Callahan, maybe Agent Cooper. "We've got eyes on him."

I wove through the people at the door and stepped into the street, my legs aching with the tension of trying not to trip or break an ankle. Or both. "Where is he?"

"Around the corner. Bistro side."

I swore again. "I'm coming up. I can't chase anything in these shoes."

"Come on up, hoochie. I got beads and you won't even have to show me your boobs."

I hung up on him.

Bastard.

Retaliation, for sure.

S ister Betty convinced me to keep the dress on, but only because arguing wasted time. I pulled on my Docs over my custom ankle holster and slid in a Derringer before running out. I'd have preferred a bigger gun or even the gas-powered "stinger" Marty bought me for my birthday, but weapon-hiding real-estate didn't exist in the violently pink skintight fabric.

"Which way am I going?" The phantom clicks of Marty's typing echoed through the headset like some alien heartbeat as I waited, impatiently, for the elevator's slow descent.

"Left out of the lobby. Hard right around the bistro."

The elevator dinged at the first floor, but the doors didn't immediately open.

"You've still got eyes on him?"

"And a tail."

"Cooper?"

"One and the same." Marty muttered a curse. "He's good. I can't pick him out."

"The mark?"

"No, Cooper."

"I find that hard to believe." I pressed the headset into my right ear. Agent Cooper wasn't exactly the type of person you'd expect to find in New Orleans. Except at an accountants' convention. Even then, he'd only blend in among people who looked like him. Short, stocky, stodgy, even. Completely ordinary and remarkably unremarkable.

"I wouldn't have bet on it, either."

I rounded the corner of the bistro, only to run straight in to a dark-haired man a little taller than me and stronger than he looked. He grinned, one arm clamped around me, pulling me into the downdraft of stale beer breath. A sweep of hair flipped back as he tossed his head only to fall across his forehead again. "Where you goin', baby girl?"

"Dude, tonight is not the night." I pushed against his chest. He resisted and swayed. Fantastic. I wouldn't have to break a sweat taking this grabby bastard down.

"Aww, come on, baby, you don't know what kind of night it could be." His grin turned into a leer as he stared into my cleavage. He ground himself against me, his interest undeniable. Small, but undeniable.

"This will not turn out well for you," I warned. "You've got one more chance to let go before you regret it."

He tried to jam his leg between mine as he rubbed his crotch against me. "You don't know what *you* might regret, beautiful." His tongue ran across his scaly, chapped lips, and I recoiled, reminded of a certain giant space slug and how much my dress suddenly felt like a metal bikini.

But I didn't need a chain.

Instead, I stomped his instep. Hard.

Nothing crunches better than foot bones under Docs. Might not have broken anything, but I sure as hell popped a few joints. Either way, he howled and lost his balance trying to cradle his injured foot against his meaty thigh. I stood out of the way before he could trample or trap me, my hands on my hips. The way he carried on, some of those satisfying fireworks in his foot might have been broken bones.

I failed to feel guilt. "Told you."

"You bitch!" Spittle flew as he screamed, awkwardly cradling his foot against his knee, his ass propped against the wall.

"Right. You assault me, and I'm the bitch." I shook my head.

"Are you really going to argue with him?" Marty had a point, even if he sounded bored.

"Right." I jogged, clomping and splashing along the wet street. "Call the police. Let them chat with him."

"You're pressing charges?" Marty sounded shocked.

"How about you send me in the right direction and dial up NOLA PD?" A sea of milling tourists filled the neon-lit streets, a cacophony of music in the air. Another night in the party city.

New Orleans, a vacation disaster for monster hunters. Zero stars.

Despite being distracted by mentally writing my review for fellow hunters, Marty's directions sounded familiar, and I realized I'd be passing Helen's house. Or Hel. Or however the Norse goddess who'd taken up residence in the French Quarter wanted to be known. The last time I'd passed her place, I'd been running, though last time, I'd been chased by an otherworldly portent of death, a border collie of the dead. This seemed almost relaxing in comparison.

I skirted a car, sucking in my side to avoid it as I passed Helen's door. For a brief instant, I wondered if she'd let me enlist the help of her brother, Fenrir, a massive wolf. Or dog. But a god of sorts. Or son of a god. Something like that. I hadn't read that chapter of the Norse mythology book yet.

"Before you ask, the answer's no," Marty said.

"What?"

"You are not getting Fenrir to chase down this creature." He gave the next round of directions.

"You don't know what I'm thinking."

"Yeah, I do. You slowed down and stared so hard at the door, you almost ran into a car."

"That's creepy."

"That I know what you're thinking?"

"That you stalk me with cameras." I turned the corner. "And it was a pothole, smartass."

"If you say so," he chuckled.

He must not have been watching his monitor while he teased me, or he'd have warned me about the gorilla in the middle of the road.

A no-shit, real-life gorilla.

Great.

I skidded to a stop. "Uhh, Marty?"

"What the fuck is that?"

"I planned to ask you the same thing."

The gorilla stood on its hind legs, its eyes flashing brilliant gold.

Even better. A goddamned supernat. Maybe the same one that attacked us before.

"We've got a problem," I said.

"You have no idea," Marty said, awe dropping his voice into a whisper.

20

I stepped back, scanning the street with my peripheral vision for anything that might become a weapon without taking my eyes off the gorilla in the middle of the street. "I need good news, Marty."

"Wish I had some." He swore with ferocity. "Cee, I have to call Cooper. There are flying monkeys pouring out of Café Lafitte in Exile."

"What?"

"Literal. Flying. Monkeys."

"You're kidding." Flying monkeys didn't exist outside the movie that scarred my young psyche. To my knowledge, or the Church's—or at least Sister Betty's Order—supernats hadn't evolved into creatures of modern mythology. At least not yet. "There's no such thing."

"Wish I was," he said, dry and curt. His other phone chirped. "Lemme call you back."

"Not a good time, I've got a sit—"

The headset beeped as he ended the call.

"—uation here."

The gorilla took up half the street, staring at me and brandishing huge teeth.

Great.

I'm gonna die wearing a dress and a thong.

Scandalous as they were, at least my panties were clean. That had to count for something.

How the hell did you deal with gorillas? Especially gorillas that weren't gorillas and were some kind of supernat? If Sister Betty covered this in any of our lessons or training sessions, I sure as hell didn't remember it.

Derringers would convince most humans that messing with someone else might be a better use of their time. Fae and smaller supernats would get the hint with the right ammo. But this? Even with cold iron blessed hollow points filled with a proprietary blend of pixie dust and silver filaments, the piece in my ankle holster would only annoy this creature.

"Hello," I said with a wave. Nothing too big, too fast, or too threatening. I hoped.

It grunted and stood up, its massive fists lifting fractionally off the ground.

"What, or who, are you?"

Another grunt and it flailed its arms, gnashing big teeth.

"Right. Brilliant conversation." I ignored the sudden chill in my blood. What supernatural creatures might take gorilla form and what could I do about it? I hated these encounters where my weapons didn't matter either because they were out of reach, like now, or ineffectual against the target, also like now. If I didn't come up with some miraculous idea, I might die. I pulled the skirt of the tight, fluorescent pink dress higher up my thighs. If we had to fight, I needed as much mobility as possible, though I dreaded the atomic, no, apocalyptic wedgie a roundhouse would give me.

I considered slipping off the thong, debating the merits of the fabric's epic internal intrusion not only up my butt, but deep into...well, more delicate areas versus flashing the beast in front of me. Thin as it was, breaking the elastic would require effort and conspicuous movement, and might not work. Next time Sister Betty made me wear a dress, I'd insist on combat-friendly panties, lines be damned.

The gorilla leaned forward and charged a few loping steps, making a noise something like a combined grunt, laugh, and challenge.

Very slowly, I shimmied the back of the dress up, slid my hands over my butt and hooked the elastic of the thong with my thumbs. "I don't know what you are, but I'm not here to ruin your day. I'm chasing something else—"

The rumble it emitted dropped an octave before rising in an animalistic scream of challenge. Arms raised over its silver-black chest, the beast flailed its massive arms again.

I froze, hands on my outer thighs, the thong's elastic stretched taut between my thumbs and against the curve of my butt. Why did no else ever find themselves in this kind of situation? And why the hell did Sister Betty not consider the fighting merits of my panties when shopping? Surely, there had to be other options. Did they make tear-away thongs? I made a mental note to ask a stripper later.

"Easy," I said, my voice low and soothing. Or, an attempt at low and soothing. Since the gorilla didn't charge, I assumed I got close.

It walked closer, a rumbling hoot echoing in its thick chest.

Wriggling my butt, I worked my hands down my thighs. "That's right. Easy." Unless there was some kind of zoo jailbreak, this gorilla had to be supernat, though I didn't know what kind. That, of course, meant problems. The lack of information created a minefield of any possible interaction. One wrong assumption—especially without backup—and this escalated in a bad way. As if I needed help making things harder for myself. Transformed human or not, I decided to assume the beast had higher cognitive function and understood non-threatening moves.

The thong's elastic fell off my thumbs. Silky fabric the same egregiously pink color as my dress slid down my legs and promptly snagged on my boot lace hooks.

"Of course," I said, staring at the beast as I lifted one foot and tried to kick free of the fancy death trap of satin and elastic.

No matter how much I wiggled, the loathsome excuse for a garment clung to the metal hook, the elastic caught in the tread of my shoe.

I swore.

The gorilla cocked its head.

"Not you," I muttered, leaning forward to free myself.

Everything would have been fine if I didn't lose my balance at that precise moment.

To be fair, the ringing scream of terror behind me more than contributed to the way I wobbled and fell against a car, my underwear tangled around my ankle.

Of course, the woman behind me, the screamer, ran, and the gorilla lunged after her in a crashing, swinging charge.

Human or not, predators chase.

I swore, shoving against the car to launch myself into the gorilla's path. Or, at least, to distract it. Making myself the more appealing option might be my only chance to save her and, perhaps, a large contingent of the city's nightlife. I might not be Faye Ray, but I'd have to do.

With an extra totter thanks to the thong, I nearly collided with the oncoming gorilla.

It stopped.

I considered my options, and my precarious balance.

It snarled.

"Nice gorilla." I wondered what the hell to do next. "Are you...?"

Words failed. How did you ask a creature, especially one capable of tearing your joints apart, a question that might piss them off? Or at least annoy them enough to make breaking limbs appealing? Would asking if it was human be...insulting?

I couldn't risk finding out.

"Can you understand me?"

One grunt and it settled on its haunches.

I'd take that as a yes.

If I could have taken a moment to enjoy the relief rushing through me, I would have. But if this went bad, I was so screwed. Without Marty in my ear, the likelihood of it going bad increased exponentially.

"I mean no harm." I held up my empty hands.

Another single grunt. It approached tentatively, making a strange rumbling sound. Its gold eyes flashed, and suddenly, I couldn't remember if I *should* hold its gaze.

I hoped it understood I intended no challenge.

Its nostrils flared as it leaned forward and sniffed me. Standing still, I submitted to the inspection. Maybe this opened negotiation. If nothing else, it bought me time.

The gorilla's teeth appeared between snarling lips.

All the better to eat you with, my dear.

We both tensed when it leaned down, gesturing at my ankle with its thick black finger.

It must smell gun oil.

I looked at my Docs, garlanded with the obnoxiously pink thong, one side still tangled on my boot lace hook, the other dangling like a perverse anklet. Think. Some magic combination of words had to get me out of this unmauled and unmaimed. "I can explain."

The gorilla and I locked eyes. It cocked its head like some gigantic dog.

Nothing came to mind. At least nothing that would keep me alive. "Hi, I'm a monster hunter and trying to kill things like you," kinda made me a target. So, we stared at each other. "Okay, maybe I can't explain."

The gorilla moved slowly, cautious, and hooked a finger in the elastic dangling around my left ankle. Looking up at me, it tugged.

"Yeah, they aren't mine." The implications made me squeamish. "Well, they *are* mine, but they aren't *mine*. I'm only wearing them because of the dress. Not that I normally dress like this." My mouth snapped shut so hard, I bit my tongue. Why the hell did I need to explain myself to a supernatural gorilla? And one possibly up to no good? One I might end up hunting? *Get it together, Caitlin.*

It tugged the underwear again.

Maybe it had some innate sense of justice and thought removing obstacles made for a fair fight. Or maybe it was just pervy and wanted my panties. Either way, I lifted my ankle.

With unusual delicacy, the gorilla pulled the underwear off my raised left. Once free, I put my foot down, and lifted the other when it tapped my right ankle.

What the hell is my life that some supernatural primate is removing my underwear in the middle of the street? In broad…well, twilight?

My sleepy brain protested that regardless of hour, it was all weird. It took real effort to shut down the imaginary debate.

I blinked as the pink elastic came free from the metal hook and the gorilla pulled the panties off my shoe. I held out my hand, but the massive paw retreated, the flimsy garment folded in it.

Right.

Pervy.

I dropped my hand, overwhelmingly aware that I no longer had anything on under the dress. There'd certainly be no lines now, though I couldn't imagine Sister Betty approving of this particular solution once she learned of their absence. Giant supernatural gorilla might pale in comparison to flying monkeys, even when you add in panty theft.

What the hell was my life?

I shook my head.

Focus.

"I'm not sure where we go from here. I know you're supernatural, and that—"

"You hunt the nightmare."

Startled, I blinked at the massive creature. "I'm sorry, I didn't realize you speak."

"I don't," it said, its diction far more erudite and educated than I anticipated. "At least, not usually in this form, but what's happening in the city makes the impossible possible."

Fan-freaking-tastic. "Right. That's why I'm here. To help with..." my gesture turned into an awkward flail, "the strangeness."

It nodded. "You are a hunter."

"Yes," I said. Lying would create more trouble than admitting the truth. Another question gnawed at me, and I weighed the repercussions of asking. Fleet-fingered Marty would have found an answer, or at least kept me from sounding like an awkward teenager asking for a first date. I shifted my weight from foot to foot wishing for pockets, a holster, or anything to occupy my hands. "I'm sorry, I'm not sure what kind of super-natural cre—um, entity you are."

Its primal grin made me supremely uncomfortable. "You needn't concern yourself with that. My kind does no harm to yours. There are more important things to address."

Surviving awkward and perhaps stupid question number one? Check. Next topic. "Do you know what I'm chasing?"

"Yes, and you only have three days to catch it."

Why the hell was it always three days? Couldn't a girl get a week? Ten days? Maybe a couple of weeks to research thoroughly, enjoy the week-end, and still get regular sleep? Abbreviated gigs weren't a big deal, until they happened back to back with no down time between them to recover and think.

I pinched the bridge of my nose and took a deep breath. "Why three days?"

Believe it or not, a gorilla's smile can be as patronizing as the most condescending human. I braced for some inter-species mansplaining. "Have you not paid attention?"

My back stiffened. "I've been a little busy."

"Too busy to see the world around you?"

"What do you mean?" I resisted the urge to examine my memories for anything odd or unusual. That would keep me busy for days since almost everything I experienced qualified as unusual or odd. Sometimes, both. Like standing in the middle of the street having a conversation with a supernatural gorilla who had removed and kept my panties.

He sat, settling in for a lecture, it seemed. "I presume you've heard of the nexus?"

"Yes." Bless Marty and Sister Betty.

"Good. And you know it's a source of power?"

"Yes, one of the reasons so many supernats are drawn to it. And, I presume, why my team's battling flying monkeys at Lafitte's?"

He snorted. "They are not unrelated. Do you know of the Compact?"

It didn't even sound familiar. I shook my head.

"The Compact keeps the peace between dimensions and within the city though it's crowded with, as you crudely put it, 'supernats.'"

Great. I'd insulted a primate strong enough to rip my arms off. Go me.

He perked at the sound of sirens screaming past on a parallel street. "The Compact regulates places where the veil's thin. It keeps the borders intact, at least where it's respected."

"Wait, what?" Sister Betty had mentioned the veil between worlds before, but in the most abstract terms. As in, not-anything-I-would-have-to-deal-with abstract. "How is that possible?"

"How is it possible, Hunter, that you don't know?"

Embarrassment surged, immediate and hot. Had I come to New Orleans to work, I'd have prepared. I'd have extensive information on the inhabitants, the nexus, and the veil. But that's not what I'd come for, and now a supernatural gorilla in the middle of Burgundy Street was making me feel inadequate. "I tend to deal more with the corporeal."

It sounded lame, even to me.

He grinned in an ape-y way that felt more like a threat than an expression of humor. "Are you sure you're a hunter?"

"Last time I checked." I reminded myself of my lack of firepower and back up.

As if anticipating a challenge, he didn't speak immediately. "The Compact is reaffirmed every twelve years. Last time, there were..." his leathery paw swept through the air in a graceful gesture, "disagreements."

"Disagreements?"

"Disturbing the nexus with inter-dimensional conflict causes...problems."

I did the math. "Katrina?"

After a moment, he nodded. "An unfortunate side effect."

"These 'disagreements' caused the most devastating hurricane in decades?"

"Negative energy has to go somewhere. This time it spanned multiple worlds." He shrugged. "In the end, it worked out."

"Not for the thousands who lost their homes, their livelihoods." He didn't react, but I pressed on. "Their lives." Repercussions still reverberated through the community and not just for the lost souls of the most vulnerable who hadn't been evacuated in time. Katrina changed everything, and survivors still bore the trauma, like Officer LaFontaine's acerbic reaction to federal government credentials.

"That's not my concern."

"Must be nice."

With a grunt, he stood. "We're wasting time."

"No shit. How about you finish your story about the Compact and how all this affects New Orleans, me, and my job?"

21

Sister Betty braced her arms against her knees, panting, a rough circle of gray, malformed monkey corpses strewn around her, their feathered wings askew.

"I'm empty." I slid my Derringer into my ankle holster and flicked monkey brains off my shoe. Another expensive leather cleaning. If these weren't so damned cute off duty, I'd cave and buy regular combat boots. Combat boots just didn't have the same flair, so I kept buying—and cleaning—Docs. If the pope knew about my shoe vice, and the associated costs, it might be the proverbial straw to break the excommunication camel's back.

Agent Cooper Hardin handed me a Glock as he toed one the dead primates to check for signs of life. "One in the chamber, should be three more in the mag. Extras in my pocket."

We turned, back to back, and I reached into his pocket for ammo.

"See anything else?" Sister Betty asked, a hand on her side as she straightened. She shouldn't have been in this fight, not with unhealed stitches, and had I not encountered the gorilla, she wouldn't have been. Yet another protective responsibility I'd failed to uphold.

Pushing the thought away, I scanned the sky and snapped the new magazine into place. "Nothing in the air. Ground?"

"Nothing," Cooper said, holstering his weapon. "We're clear."

"How's your side?" I asked Sister Betty. "Do we need to get you to a doctor?"

"No. Busted stitch. Nothing serious." Sister Betty sounded strained. "Glad you showed up when you did."

"What kept you?" Cooper nudged a feathered wing out of his way and revealed another dead monkey.

In the midst of battle, I hadn't noticed, but these things were uglier and scarier than those that terrorized my dreams as a kid. Like some brainchild of Jim Henson, Stephen King, Clive Barker, and Ridley Scott, their grayish teeth looked vicious but didn't compare to the ferocity of their black talons. It was a wonder any of us hadn't been shredded during the fight.

"I got delayed by a gorilla." I stepped around one fallen flying monkey and stepped to the next, the distant music of a second line reaching us. Whether a funeral, a wedding, or just a spectacle for the tourists, I hoped it wasn't headed this way. Keeping spectators away posed enough of a challenge without the garish little parades drawing them closer, never mind all the inevitable videos, live streams, and other recordings people posted. When all else failed, concocting stories of a movie shoot worked, but the fewer exposed, the better.

Both Cooper and Sister Betty turned to look at me. Cooper, bent over another primate corpse, found his words first. "A...gorilla? An actual, living, breathing gorilla? In the middle of the French Quarter?"

"Yes, that's what I said. A giant gorilla on Burgundy Street." I ignored his incredulous look. "We had a little chat about the Compact."

Cooper straightened, rigid and staring at me. "What did you say?"

Bingo. Cooper's big secret.

"You've heard of it, Agent Hardin?" I asked, gratified and trying to restrain my amusement.

"It's classified information—"

"I should have known," Sister Betty muttered. "It makes so much sense."

My jaw clenched. "You knew?"

Her shrug ended in a wince. "We thought they'd fallen out of favor."

"How do you know that?" Cooper demanded. "Where did you get that information?"

For the first time since Marty hung up on me, my headset beeped. I pushed the button, drowning out whatever Cooper said next. "DEMON's records indicate they've been actively involved in Compacts since the late sixties," Marty said. "The first agent delegate attended in 1981, but no records after that. Can't find a reason."

"You know, it's creepy that you know what we're talking about," I said.

"You're welcome. I'm on the way via Uncle Sam's black SUV taxi service."

"How'd you swing that?"

"Don't you have an argument to interrupt?"

"Yeah, but you're answering me later, buddy." I tapped the headset button to end the call.

Sister Betty scowled, hands on her hips, obviously at the end of rant. "We're on the same team, remember? Your words."

"Seems DEMON's known about these Compacts since the sixties. And has participated." They forgot their argument.

Cooper gaped, unfazed by Sister Betty glowering at him. "That's classified. How—?"

"And at least one agent attended in 1981, but none since." I stared at him. "Why?"

"This isn't the place to discuss it." An alarming flush crept up his neck. "If your partner's hacking the federal government—"

"Don't get your panties in a knot, Cooper." I forgot what I intended to say, immediately distracted by another voice.

"Why, Miss Kelley, we meet again."

My eyes rolled of their own volition, and a headache instantly bloomed behind my eyes. "Officer LaFontaine. How delightful." I turned to face the rotund, red-faced police officer.

"Not a sentiment I share." His accent gave the venom-laced words a pleasant cadence. "Every time I see you, you're mucking up my city."

His partner, Officer Boudreaux stood behind him, slightly shorter, but infinitely more pleasant. And attractive. He didn't speak, but nodded, a restrained smile playing at the corner of his lips. My heart fluttered, and I looked at his superior officer's shining pate, wishing for underwear as I tried to stifle my reaction.

Officer Beau LaFontaine hitched up his utility belt and stepped over one of the dead winged primates without noticing my momentary distraction. "And today," he continued, one hand hovering over to the unsecured Glock on his belt, "you're holding the gun and not, allegedly, a member of the clergy."

I ignored the barb about our last encounter. "I'm armed, but," I gestured to the carnage, "not without reason."

Cooper side-stepped a pair of entangled wings, his Glock holstered and hand out to Officer LaFontaine. "I'm Agent Cooper Hardin—"

"I remember you, Federal Agent Hardin." LaFontaine sneered, enunciating Cooper's title an epithet. "One of them no-such-agencies Miss Kelley claimed to work for."

"I gave you contacts and credentials—"

"Photoshop." He interrupted me with a self-satisfied smirk. "Easy to fake." He rocked on his heels. "I hope you all can take time out of your busy monkey-slaying schedule to come to the station because even *federal* agencies need clearance to operate in this city."

"Miss Kelley." The new voice cooled my fiery rebuttal before it had a chance to escape. Officer Boudreau smiled at me.

A shiver. "Hi." The word came out without thought, immediately followed by the burn and irritation of instant embarrassment.

"Looks like you've had an interesting evening," Boudreaux said, still smiling. His hands rested on his belt, but in a far less threatening way. Naturally in control, a direct contrast to his partner's bluster. And, my God, those eyes.

"You could say that." Sister Betty holstered and secured her Glock before approaching, her hand out. "I don't think we've officially met."

"There's no time now, either." LaFontaine stomped through the bloodied street to stand between Boudreaux and Sister Betty. "What in blazes happened here, Miss Kelley, and who gave you authorization—"

His words stopped, as if snapped off. When I looked, he stood eye to eye with Agent Hardin and neither moved.

Sister Betty shrugged.

"Officer LaFontaine," Cooper said, vaguely amused. "May I call you Beau?"

The dumbstruck officer gave a rigid nod, his mouth gaping.

"Good," Cooper purred. "As a fellow officer of the law, I realize the strain you're under to keep this city safe can lead to a certain...sensitivity."

Another robotic nod.

Officer Boudreaux approached, and I avoided eye contact. His hand drifted back to his weapon. "What's he doing?" He stepped closer, focused on Cooper and LaFontaine ringed by flying monkey corpses.

I shook my head in response, catching the echo of my thoughts in Sister Betty's eyes. There might be more to Agent Cooper Hardin than we thought.

"You're going to cut Miss Kelley some slack, respect her credentials and mine, and let us do our jobs."

"I don't know what you're doing—"

Hardin's hand flew up in Boudreaux's direction, his open palm seeming to freeze and silence the younger officer.

Right. Note to self, don't piss off Hardin.

Also, determine what kind of juju this dude had before our "partnership" went much further.

"Did you hear me, Beau?"

Officer LaFontaine's head bobbed again, but the movement seemed beyond his control.

"You can do better than that," Cooper chided.

Sister Betty stepped closer. Cooper flicked a hand in her direction. She stopped and tilted her head as if listening to a distant sound.

Boudreaux shook his head, frowning in confusion. I touched his arm. His muscles tensed under my touch, and our eyes met, his an unfathomable brown speckled with green.

I swallowed hard and fought the urge to rub the tingle of electricity racing up my arm. "Don't," I said.

"He's my partner." His voice sounded distant but determined as he released his weapon. "He's doing something to my partner."

Disagreeing would have been a lie, but I couldn't defend Hardin either. Sister Betty took another step toward Cooper, despite the warning gesture still aimed her way.

"Officer LaFontaine." The cadence of Cooper's voice made my muscles heavy and softened Boudreaux's tension. "Beau, you're going to go easy on Miss Kelley and her team, aren't you?"

LaFontaine nodded again, a more natural, fluid motion accompanied by a soft "uh huh."

"Good." Cooper patted LaFontaine's shoulder. "When we finish this conversation, you'll feel relaxed. In control. Confident. Appreciative of the beneficial partnership you've found. Won't that be nice?"

"Yes," LaFontaine said, his voice dreamy and distant.

"Why's he hypnotizing my partner?" Boudreaux pulled away, quickly navigating the dead monkey obstacle course between him and LaFontaine.

Before Boudreaux reached them, LaFontaine blinked, shook his head, and smiled. "I believe we met th'other day, Agent Hardin."

Sister Betty answered my wordless question with a shrug and a shake of her head. Whatever Cooper was, or what he'd done, wasn't something she was familiar with.

LaFontaine clapped Boudreaux on the back, the thunderous sound an ominous preamble to his jovial laugh. "Relax, son, will you? You've met Agent Cooper Hardin, haven't you?"

Gorillas. Flying monkeys. And Beau LaFontaine yukking it up with a federal agent.

Things get weird in New Orleans.

"What do you think Cooper is?" I asked, trying to find a comfortable position in the back of the government SUV that didn't gunk up the seats too much. Cooper arranged for a ride to the hotel and conduct through service entrances so we didn't disturb the normals with our bloody, brain-splattered clothes. Still, I couldn't relax into making a mess. Getting brains out of leather, even black leather, sucked. I didn't envy whoever had to clean after Sister Betty and I got out.

"Not sure." She leaned her head back on the seat and sighed, her arms folded across her stomach. "Logically, he's probably a human with magic."

I nodded, though I doubted it. Not only because I would have sensed something magical about him, but because not much in my world followed logic. Occam's razor wasn't my go-to tool. "What he did back there..."

"Yeah," she said when I didn't finish the thought. "I'm not sure what to think about it."

"Marty'll have his work cut out for him." I wondered how much he'd seen en route. We hadn't found an opportunity to discuss between his arrival and departure.

"True," she said.

The car turned down Canal Street and stopped. I leaned my head against the tinted glass and watched the red street car rattle down the road beside us.

"So..." Sister Betty's words dissolved into awkward silence as we stared out opposite windows.

"Hmm?"

"What's with you and Boudreaux?"

"What?" I didn't look at her. The shift in her tone said it all. She'd never admit it, but furtive jealousy colored her cautious question.

"You and Boudreaux. The spark between you."

From her reflection in the window, I knew she studied me. I concentrated on the bustling foot traffic taking advantage of our red light. "I don't even know him." Something happened, though I wouldn't have characterized it as a spark. Maybe a rush of post-fight adrenaline, or a surge of hormones because I needed to get laid, or the misfiring of my sleep-deprived brain, but not a spark. Only one spark mattered in my life, and my gut told me I'd be the one to get burned.

"Okay," she said, and her reflection turned away.

I turned to her, hoping she'd finally say what she really felt for once. "What's that supposed to mean?" We'd danced this dance for years, and it always ended with her stepping back.

"Nothing." She reached for the handle over the door as the car turned through the intersection before making a quick right down a side street.

"No, it means something. What are you saying?"

"Caitlin," she said softly, "I only asked a question."

One long look into her slate blue eyes, and I yielded, knowing it was an escape. If she didn't want to go there, we wouldn't. I could wait, but I wouldn't be idle while I waited for jealousy to spur her to action. "I hate it when you do this."

"Do what?"

"This."

The orange glow of the parking deck lights made my eyes ache, but I stared into them. It was easier than looking at her.

Neither of us spoke, even when the car stopped and we got out. A hotel staff member waited by a door marked "Service Entry." In silence, we followed him down long, narrow hallways to a service elevator. He ushered us in, turned a key, and the doors closed. When they opened on our floor, he gave brief directions to orient us, then disappeared behind the closing elevator doors.

Sister Betty followed me to my room. "Be careful, Caitlin," she said as I fumbled with my keycard. "That's all I'm saying."

"That's all you ever say." I stepped in, closing the door and leaving her in the hall.

I only had time to strip before my cellphone rang. Thumbing it to speaker phone, I dropped the device on the bed and stepped into the marble bathroom. "Yeah, Marty, what's up?"

"I'm at the cathedral. You and Sister Betty need to get here. Now."

"What's happening?"

"We're under attack."

22

I'd never seen an attack quite like the one on the St. Louis Cathedral. From the second we jumped out of the car on Royal Street, we heard it. A clicking, buzzing swarm shrouded the building's white stone edifice in a greenish-gray living insect shell.

"What are they?" Sister Betty raised her voice over the gnawing insects.

I didn't need an entomologist to know. "Locusts."

Locusts, but not your average locusts. We ran down Pirate Alley, noticing only that the bugs ignored St. Anthony's garden behind the church and, from the crowd of gawkers around its iron fence, the lush expanse of Jackson Square Park seemed untouched.

"Locusts," Sister Betty repeated.

We shared a significant look.

"Got any Raid?" I asked.

She rolled her eyes and pulled out her phone. "I'll see what our options are."

Onlookers approached the cathedral as if stunned. Most stood in awed silence watching fine white powder drift from the stone like snow. Fortune tellers scrambled to fold tables and umbrellas, though because of the humming insect drone or the ominous clouds scudding across the darkening sky, I couldn't tell.

One of the artists at the corner of St. Ann Street abandoned his paintings, sketching madly as he walked closer. Only the children seemed undisturbed. The cluster of squealing, laughing dervishes darted around the adults, playing, oblivious to the strange happenings. The little girl I'd seen the day before stopped when she saw me. Still wearing her white dress, her hair hung in wet strings, the fabric of her dress rendered transparent with water. Instead of taking in the spectacle of the bug-ensconced cathedral, she stared at me. Her companion, a boy roughly the same age, stopped when she did. The bright green plastic squirt gun dangling from his hand dripped water.

I elbowed Sister Betty and gestured to the kids. "There."

"What?" She unplugged the ear not pressed to her phone and looked where I pointed. "I don't see—"

I walked away, trying not to look like some child-abducting criminal as I hurried toward them.

The little girl didn't move. With unnatural gravity, she lifted her own squirt gun and aimed it at me. Closing one eye, she whispered "bang."

At my hesitation, she lowered the squirt gun, covered her mouth, and giggled.

No wonder people made movies like *Children of the Corn*. Yesterday's creepy nursery rhyme had been less unnerving.

Her companion retreated a couple of steps and looked around, his light brown hair swishing across his forehead. He ran, his squirt gun clattering to the ground in his wake. She followed, glancing over her shoulder once before I lost sight of her.

I scooped up the abandoned toy and returned to Sister Betty.

"I don't understand." Her brow furrowed as she stared at the plastic gun in my hand. "What do you intend to do with that?"

"Bless it."

"What?"

"It's a water gun." I gave it a shake to slosh the water inside. "Bless it."

"Caitlin, I don't see what you think a squirt gun is going to do against this." She waved a hand toward the bug-encrusted church.

"Don't you see? This is someone's nightmare. Someone feared the plague of locusts. Someone religious. They're hidden in the church, and the bugs are trying to get at THEM." I held up the water gun. "And if it's a religious fear, a religious symbol like holy water will help protect them."

Her scowl of confusion bloomed into understanding, then wilted. "I've never done it before, and I don't have blessed salt, or the—"

"But you have belief." I thrust the gun at her. "You believe in God. You believe God will protect all His children. Invoking that protection should be enough."

"That's not how this works. I don't have—"

"You have to try." I caught her wrist and pressed the water gun into her hand. "You have faith. You have belief. We need to get inside."

Her eyes searched mine, and I read her doubt.

I held her hand between both of mine. "Please. Believe."

With a soft sigh of defeat and a resigned nod, she closed her eyes and bowed her head.

An approaching siren jolted the bystanders to action. Tourists raised cameras and phones for a final look, one final picture for social media, then fled. Even the artist tucked his sketchbook under his arm and scurried back to pack his canvases and painted panels onto his ancient cart while casting cautious looks over his shoulder.

A pair of young men in khaki shorts and pastel polos stopped in front of a shop door on St. Ann Street, paper shopping bags dangling from the crook of their elbows. As people fled, they crossed the narrow pedestrian street, mouths open in comic shock.

"Here." Sister Betty pressed the water gun into my hand and pushed it toward me.

Before I tore my eyes away from the two frozen men, I saw him. The nightmare emerged from the store behind the shopping couple, looking the same as when I encountered him in the airport and again in the hotel lobby.

We locked eyes.

A scream preceded the crash of stone on stone.

My eyes snapped to the cathedral as the living sheath of locusts closed over the gap where the clock's lintel once formed a perfect peak. Chunks of broken masonry cracked the gray stone paver next to the cathedral door. Smaller pieces fell and rolled away, cutting lines through the fine, powdery dust that haloed the building.

"They're devouring the church," Sister Betty said, awestruck. "They'll tear it apart."

Biting back a curse, I took the water gun and ran to where the door of St. Louis Cathedral should be under the crawling, scaly skin of bugs. Bracing myself, I aimed and pulled the trigger.

The first spray of water blew back in my face.

I recoiled in surprise and wiped my arm across my face. Muttering about wind, I turned, changed the angle of the gun, and squeezed the plastic trigger again.

And got much the same result.

Not exactly what I'd expected.

Only the incessant shriek of the siren drowned out the incessant hum of the bugs. If I hadn't glanced up to wipe water out of my face again, the next hunk of the façade would have killed me. Instead, I dodged. It crashed to the ground and shattered, spraying me with dust and stone shrapnel.

Sister Betty grabbed my arm, but I pulled free, raising the plastic gun to fire again. The splintering crack and crash behind the cathedral heralded the death of one of the low palms in the garden. She jerked my arm again, the stream of water going wild as she diverted my aim. "You're going to get killed. We can find another way."

I yanked my arm back again, the muffled thunder of boots on the stone behind me announcing the arrival of the firefighters. Taking less care, I squirted the bugs swarming the door. Water splashed several with a hiss, and as they dropped to the stone pavement, others poured into the vacancy, blanketing the handle with chittering greenish-gray bugs.

A wisp of smoke rose from the pile of blackened bugs on the ground.

Sister Betty looped an arm around me, leveraging her body weight to knock me down. We rolled across the square as a heavy block of column fell where we'd stood. She curled up, clutching her side as firemen dragged a hose past us and sprayed the building with water, showering us with kickback.

Nothing happened.

Torrents of runoff poured into the stone square, but the bugs only parted around the point of impact and splash zone. Everywhere else, they continued gnawing, powdered stone making the air silty.

"There's got to be some other way of getting them off the walls," Sister Betty said, pale and breathless as she sat up.

"Bless the water." I stood and pulled out my phone. The screen must have taken the impact when I fell. Spidery cracks webbed the glass, but it still responded as I called Marty.

"What?"

"The water. They died when I hit them with the water you blessed. Bless the water coming out of the hose. Make it a giant holy water squirt gun."

"I can't, Caitlin. It doesn't work that way."

"But it did," I insisted over Marty's answer in my ear. "You did it with the water gun. Those bugs burned when holy water hit them. They were smoking. You have to bless the water."

"Holy water?" Marty must have covered the mouthpiece of his phone, muffling his voice.

Sister Betty stared at me, ready to protest again.

I held out a hand to her. "You did it before. You can do it again."

She squared her shoulders, pursing her lips as she took my hand. "This is crazy."

"I know." I pulled her to her feet. "Sometimes, crazy's our only option."

She held her side for a moment, and I waited. Shaking her head, she walked to the fire truck, stopping short to avoid colliding with a running firefighter.

"They're demon bugs?" Marty asked.

"No." I turned away from the noise to make it easier for him to hear me. "I think they're someone's nightmare. If they're attacking the church, whoever conjured them must be inside. Find the person who's afraid of locusts. Convince them it's a nightmare."

"And how am I supposed to do that?"

"I don't know." I scanned St. Ann Street. The two fashionable guys with their boutique bags looked flustered and stared down the street toward the river. The nightmare was gone, but I could guess where he went. "I've got to chase the nightmare. I saw him on St. Ann Street." Before he answered, I ended the call and shoved my phone in my pocket. Sister Betty laid hands on the heavy canvas hose and closed her eyes as I ran past.

I had only turned the corner when the sound started.

Under the roar of the water, the hiss, sizzle, and pop of locusts sounded like microwave popcorn. What I didn't expect was the scream of the dying bugs. The sound drilled through my skull and stabbed at my brain. People emerged from shops and ran, hands over their ears as they tried to escape the sound.

By the time I got to the corner of St. Ann and Decatur Streets, it was too late. Too many people thronged the street to see where the nightmare had gone.

S ister Betty sat in the pew, her arm around the androgynous young African-American person with a tight cap of curls, long eyelashes, and a strong jaw. The young person curled against Sister Betty as if under a protective wing, drinking in her murmured words of comfort. Father Callahan and I stood a respectful distance away with Marty, our backs mostly to them to provide more privacy.

"How'd it happen?" I asked my two partners.

"I asked Riley," Marty nodded at the young person in the pew, "about the nightmares and whether they remembered being touched while walking around the city."

I snorted at the immense challenge the question posed. Pinpointing one unexpected touch in any city, much less one with such a robust night-time scene, would be virtually impossible. They could have been touched anywhere with deliberation, or like the man in the airport, by accident. "I can imagine how that went."

Marty nodded, his lips a grim line. "About as well as you'd expect. The locust nightmare is one they've had all their lives, but two nights ago, it became more vivid than before."

"Does that correlate to being out in crowds at all?"

"Only with a day of travel and their arrival in the city." Marty shrugged. "How exactly are we supposed to track this thing, and if we find it—"

"When we find it," I corrected.

"—what are we supposed to do with it?"

"Where's..." I stopped. "Where's Riley staying?"

"The Wyndham. About a block away from us."

I nodded, thinking. The nightmare might be contained to the French Quarter, since all the disturbances had happened within its boundaries. Eight, maybe ten, blocks total.

"Are you going to answer me?" Marty asked, more out of exasperation than real frustration. He hadn't turned pink or bug-eyed yet.

"I'm thinking."

"Oh. That's what I smell. I thought it was barbequed bugs," he quipped.

I walked to the back of the church toward the rails of votives and stared down into the flickering candle flames. The solution felt close. As if the pieces were there, but not in the right order. Maybe some still upside down. As much as I'd learned about the nightmares, I didn't have the full picture. But I still had Cooper and Madame Sabine.

I spun back to Marty and Father Callahan, who stopped their conversation in surprise. "I have an idea."

23

The last time I knocked on Helen's door, I hadn't known she was the Norse goddess of the underworld, nor what job waited for me. Sister Betty and I still needed to discuss the way it all went down, especially about why the Vatican sent the mission directly and with restrictions. But, I'd fight that battle later.

This time, as I approached on the goddess's door, I felt better prepared.

"Helen isn't a nightmare, Cee, so how would she be connected to what we're chasing?" Marty asked.

"I'm not sure she is, exactly, but—"

"Woah, woah, woah." Sister Betty grabbed my arm just above my elbow, jerking me back before my knuckles made contact with the door. "We are *not* knocking on her door with some half-baked accusation—"

"I never said I was going to accuse her of anything," I said and aimed a pointed look at Sister Betty's fingers curled around my arm. "Mind?"

"Nope." Sister Betty shook her head. "Not until you tell me whatever's going on in that head of yours."

Begrudgingly, I admitted she had a point. My recent plans hadn't been as well scripted as she taught me. More than once, I'd violated her Scooby Doo rule by heading off alone to do things that might get me injured or killed. But, in my defense, I'd only done it when the risk of inaction outweighed the potential harm. "She's a powerful supernatural creature—"

"Goddess," Marty corrected.

"Right, goddess."

"Of the underworld," Marty continued, pointedly, "as in 'dead,' as in 'how you could end up if you do something reckless or run off at the mouth.'"

"O-*kay*, I get it." I rolled my eyes. "Can I finish now?"

He made a nonchalant gesture for me to continue. "Sure."

"Without interruption?"

"Depends on what you say."

"Knock it off." Sister Betty's scowl darkened with irritation. "Caitlin, get to the point."

"Assuming Helen is due some degree of respect," I said, "it would make sense that she would attend this Compact. Possibly even wield some authority, even if only ceremonial."

"We don't know that," Sister Betty warned, though with hesitation.

"No, we don't, but she's powerful. Maybe enough to be considered to be a delegate. I mean, if the thing we're chasing is, how could they exclude her?"

"Representing who?" Sister Betty asked.

I shrugged. "I haven't figured that out yet. I'm just assuming she's got," I gestured with my free hand, looking for the word, "supernatural street cred, I guess."

Sister Betty's face relaxed some, and her grip slackened. "That makes sense. But it doesn't tell me what you're planning to do."

"It's not quite a plan." I winced as her fingers squeezed my arm. "That hurts, you know."

"We can't alienate her," Sister Betty warned.

"You're assuming we have a partnership with her to begin with," Marty said. "Or that her presence in the city isn't part of her own agenda."

My heart swelled, grateful he understood. "Exactly."

"What do you mean?"

"Her dealings in New Orleans have her returning regularly, making her a semi-permanent resident, right?" I said.

Sister Betty paused, as if trying to determine how much she should admit knowing. "Sure, we'll say that."

"And since you sent me to her for the Black Dog job and she took guardianship of the dog once I captured it, I'm assuming the Church knows about these dealings."

"I wouldn't say you captured it, but go on." Sister Betty released me and crossed her arms.

"Well, what if she returned to New Orleans to attend the Compact and not in response to the Church's request for help?" I risked a glance at Marty, hoping I played dumb well enough to protect his "research."

"No," Sister Betty said after a long pause. "We had to convince her to come back."

Relieved she'd offered the information without revealing what Marty had already discovered, I pressed on. "But how hard was it to convince her?"

She thought, then put her hands on her hips, her fingers in her back pockets. "Not as difficult as working with other pantheon members," she admitted.

Marty's shoulders dropped, and he winked at me. Mischief managed, his secret database delving safe.

I watched Sister Betty hopefully, waiting for her to relent.

With an exasperated sigh, she said, "Maybe you're right. Maybe she already had plans to be here, but that doesn't mean she's attending the Compact."

"What else would it be?"

"Any number of things!" She threw her hands up. "We can't assume we know anything about her business."

"Until we go in, we know nothing. It's a gamble, but we only have a couple days before it starts. That's plenty of time for nightmares to tear this city apart."

She rubbed her eyes. "I must be tired because this crazy plan makes sense."

"We're all tired," I said, looking at Marty. With the discolored bruise on his head and the dark rings under his eyes, he looked worse than the rest of us. His weary nod only completed a dismal picture.

"Fine," she said, "but be *nice*. Keep that tongue of yours in check."

"That's what she said," Marty snickered.

Sister Betty swatted Marty as I stepped up to the door and knocked. Behind me, Marty feigned injury, and the two of them traded barbs. I took a deep breath and waited.

After a few minutes, Guillaume, Helen's stately, silver-haired butler answered the door. He stood in the open doorway, gave us a quick glance up and down. "How may I help you?"

"Hi, Guillaume," I said. "Could we speak with Helen, please?"

"The mistress isn't accepting visitors today."

I opened my mouth in anticipation of saying thank you, then closed it. "I'm sorry?"

"Mistress Helen isn't accepting visitors today."

Great. Now I'd get crap from the peanut gallery for not calling. "This is kind of urgent. There's something going on that's beyond our purview, and her expertise—"

"I'm sorry, Miss Kelley. Good day." He pushed the door closed, only to have it thump against my toe.

"I know this is rude, but I really must insist."

The old man's eyes narrowed, creating a spectacular starburst of wrinkles in the corner of each eye. "Yes, it's exceedingly rude."

"Please? This is for the good of the city, and maybe even our world. Tell her it's about the Compact because I think she'll agree to see us."

His lips puckered in an angry knot, and I expected him to force the door closed despite my blocking foot. "Wait here," he said finally, "and I will present your request."

"Thank you," I said, removing my foot.

He gave a brief bow then closed the door with a snap of the latch.

We waited, not speaking.

"He's not coming back," Marty said.

"Give it time," Sister Betty said.

The three of us stood silent at the door, waiting. A few cars drove by, and between their passage, we listened to the distant sounds of music and voices.

"What do we do now?" Marty asked.

Before I could answer, I heard footsteps behind the door. A chill rushed through me. The gamble had worked. I tried to restrain my goofy, gleeful grin as the door opened.

Guillaume had recovered his cool, aloof professionalism. "This way, please."

We followed him upstairs to the same parlor where we'd met Helen a few days before. This time, she wasn't waiting for us.

"The mistress will be right with you," Guillaume said, and although he remained professional, I caught the hint of a sneer.

Right. Noted. I pissed you off. And maybe Helen. This meeting would certainly go well.

"I hope this works, Cee." Marty echoed my thoughts and fidgeted with his phone after Guillaume left the room.

Sister Betty sat in the overly delicate and probably expensive antique chair I'd loathed when I last visited. Neither the unnecessarily thin legs nor age of the piece phased her, though they'd tormented me into forced stillness. Maybe she weighed less. Or maybe, she sat still better than me. I sat beside her in a sturdier chair, free to wiggle as I questioned my own wisdom and hoped I could pull this off.

The air in the room seemed to shiver as the door opened and Helen walked in. Like some kind of Forties silver screen star, she wore a long satin dressing gown in the palest pink, trimmed in marabou. She didn't deign to look at us until she settled in the wingback chair, surreptitiously covering her left leg and tucking her satin-gloved left hand under her right. Even around people who knew, she took pains to conceal the skeletal half of her body. I wondered how many living people had seen her without her camouflage.

"Helen—"

Her glare silenced me. In the stifling room, silence filled the space between us. I bit my lip and waited. She stared a moment longer, then glanced at each of us in turn.

Sister Betty cleared her throat only to receive the full heat of the Norse goddess's stare. Instantly, my mentor reverted to the parochial student she must have been at one time. Sister Betty bowed her head, concentrating on her primly clasped hands.

The infantile silent treatment grated my nerves raw. When I couldn't stand another second, Helen finally spoke. "I hope," she said, "this visit ends more respectfully than it began."

None of us said anything, but Sister Betty looked up, marginally less chastised than before. "On behalf of all of us," she said, cautiously, "please allow me to apologize for the sudden intrusion."

"I'm not interested in your groveling," Helen snapped with cool indifference, her eyes fierce. "Instead of wasting my time, tell me why you're here."

I took a slow breath and reminded myself that we started this, that I led us into this mess. "We've learned about the Compact and wanted to know if you could help us gain access to it."

Her delicately arched brow rose in undisguised shock. "Excuse me?" "The Compact," I said, "the gathering—" "I know what the Compact is. Why do you want to attend? And why do you think I would help you?" Her clipped words conveyed irritation despite her deceptively relaxed pose. At least her demi-god brother, Fenrir, wasn't growling at her feet.

"Well..." I swallowed hard and looked at Sister Betty.

"Given your contact with other realms and your experience—"

Helen laughed, her whole body shaking. "You have no one else to ask."

I glanced at Sister Betty, then Marty. Both of them shrugged. "No, we don't," I said, finally. "You're the most powerful being in New Orleans, and if anyone could pull a diplomatic string, it would be you."

As her laughter abated, Helen dabbed the corner of her right eye, then the tissue disappeared under her hair to dab at the dead half of her face. "And why would I do that?"

"Because," I said, "if we can't stop the nightmares from causing chaos, there won't be a city left."

She raised her eyebrow and listened as I told her about the nightmares, including the locusts and other attacks we knew about. When I finished, she drummed her fingers on the chair. "You assume that I, as you humans say, give a shit."

I recoiled, taken aback by her profanity. "I...well, yes. If your realm—"

"The underworld," she corrected with disinterest.

"If the underworld," I repeated, "is replenished by the death of humans and grows as they proliferate and die, maintaining the equilibrium of this world should be of paramount importance to you."

Her face revealed no indication that she heard or considered my words. "Not only do you incorrectly assume my interest, you also incorrectly assume I can procure access to the Compact."

"Your influence—"

"The hosting realm controls access." She interrupted Sister Betty. "To gain access, seek the nightmare council." She rose, finishing the graceful movement with a wave. "Good luck," she added with a grin that would be mocking in any other context.

We watched her leave, Sister Betty's jaw clenched, and Marty sat, silent.

The door latched with a click behind her.

Frustration welled within me, my muscles shaking as my fists clenched. I sprang from the chair and paced, whirling on Guillaume as he entered to usher us out.

The second we were outside, I looked around, wild, eager for something to punch, something to kick.

"Cee." Marty gestured down the street. "This way."

"No," I said, rolling my neck, "I'm going for a walk or something."

"We need to come up with a strategy," Sister Betty said.

"How? We learned nothing! We're back where we started, chasing spooks we don't know how to deal with." I paced the street. "I've got to burn off some energy."

"Come back to the hotel. We'll change, go for a run," Sister Betty said. "There's gym space in the cathedral basement with equipment and mats. We can train."

If Helen wouldn't help and we didn't know where to find the nightmare, hiding in the cathedral basement wouldn't dissipate the static buzzing under my skin. I needed to patrol, to hunt. At least in the streets, I had a chance to track it, find it, chase it down, and demand answers.

"We need to be smart," she said, gently.

Despite my burning desire to run through the city, I gave a tight nod. She held out her hand.

My anger melted as I stared at it. The problem I'd been ignoring reasserted itself. Even if I took her hand, it didn't mean what I wanted it to mean. She cared, and I knew it. She might even be as attracted to me as I was to her, but...

But.

Regardless what she thought, what she felt, and in spite of her jealousy when she asked about Officer Boudreaux, she'd never take it further. We had an intimacy more intense than anything I'd known. We casually held hands and hugged. The kisses we'd shared practically melted my panties, but that was it. She'd refuse to go further, despite the temptation. Her hand didn't mean what I wanted, but here she was, offering the one thing we both knew I wanted.

An eternity stretched between heartbeats as I stared at her open palm with the tiny calluses at the base of each finger.

It wasn't enough, but it was enough for now. The torture I put myself through to keep my friend and mentor had to be enough. For now.

I took her hand.

She pulled me into a tight hug, as if trying to squeeze the rage and frustration out of me. I tried to pull back, but she resisted, her heart pounding against me when I finally relented and hugged her back just as fiercely.

My Scarlet Witch might not have the power to warp my reality, but my god, she'd mastered manipulating my heart.

24

"Are you done?"

I answered with a grunt and kicked the bag harder, fighting the taunt in her words.

"No," she said, pacing. "You twist when you kick like that and you'll blow out your knee in the middle of a fight."

I gritted my teeth, adjusted my form, and kicked again with more focus. My leg flew up and around, the reverberation of contact a familiar sensation. It felt better, connected the way I expected, but I refused to show satisfaction.

"Better. Again." She circled me, checking every angle.

Sweat dripped in my eyes. I glared at the bag, imagining the nightmare, imagining taking down Helen for not giving a damn, and imagining kicking Cooper in the teeth for not telling us about the Compact in the first place. I kicked again, my muscles burning, a growl of effort accompanying the movement.

"Good." For the first time since we started, she sounded happy. "Now, on to boxing."

I shook my head and stepped back, leaning over, breathing hard. Sweat dripped on the blue mats. "No," I panted. "I'm done."

She checked her watch. "Shorter than usual."

"I haven't slept well in days." I dropped to the mat, leaning back to look up at her.

"Then shower and head back to the hotel. Get some sleep." She crossed the mat and opened a small refrigerator, pulling out a water bottle. "I've got extra clothes you can borrow."

I nodded, wondering if I'd make it through a shower before sleep ninja'd me. The mat felt ridiculously comfortable, a sure sign I would sink into dreamless sleep as soon as I crawled into bed. I could only hope "dreamless" included "without nightmares."

"Do you feel better, at least?" She offered me the water, which I immediately uncapped.

I nodded, taking a long swig of water that ended in a cough. "Yes, thank you."

Sister Betty sat beside me on the mat and crossed her arms. "You did well, but you've got to watch those twists. Have you been practicing?"

"Not as much as you want me to, but I don't do much of this kind of fighting," I re-capped the bottle. "It's more the *pew-pew* kind of fighting."

She laughed at my finger guns and shook her head as I lay back on the mat. "Not an excuse for neglecting the basics. Practice your forms. You never know when—"

"Am I interrupting?"

I rolled my head on the mat. Sideways, Cooper looked taller and a little less like an accountant. It didn't fix the way his suit didn't quite fit, or his vaguely confused expression, but an improvement was an improvement.

"Welcome to the gym, Agent Hardin," Sister Betty said, drawing her knees up to her chest and wrapping her arms around them.

"Cooper, please." He gestured to the mat. "Mind if I join you?"

"Feel free."

I scooted myself around to see him but didn't get up. "What's up, Cooper?"

He sank to the mat more gracefully than I expected. "You look...comfortable."

Knowing I looked like I'd stepped out of a fully-clothed shower and probably reeked, I grinned. "Thanks." My tired muscles relished the post-exertion release. If I closed my eyes, I might even drift off to sleep right here in the middle of the floor.

"Glad to see you're staying in shape," he said, "because we're not done yet."

I sighed and sat up. "Obviously, but we don't know what the hell to do once I find the nightmare. Or how to deal with the Compact."

"That's why I'm here," he said. "But first, we need to discuss the victims."

I sat on the edge of the bed, staring at my Docs, trying to summon the energy to lean over and pick them up. Beside the antique-looking nightstand, they looked huge and heavy. Cumbersome. Inelegant. They looked the way my heart felt.

Tears pricked my eyes.

"Cooper's sending a car to take us—what's wrong?" Marty asked.

I sniffed and dashed a hand across my face. "Nothing, just zoned out, I guess. Thinking about what Cooper said last night." That not only did the nightmare's touch manifest a human's worst fears, it stole a piece of their soul, and necrotized whatever remained. Anyone touched by a nightmare touched would die, even if not immediately. Each victim would lose themselves until their living spark extinguished and their body stopped functioning.

And I still hadn't managed to locate or stop it.

I rubbed my face. One night of uninterrupted sleep hadn't made much of a difference. Reality felt like a bad dream.

If I couldn't stop people from being touched, from dying from what Cooper called "soul ablation" after being touched, what was the point of me doing the job? Why not step aside for someone who could actually protect others?

Even with Marty watching, I couldn't reach for my battle-scarred boots. History made them heavy. I hadn't owned them long, but they'd been through a lot, and not just the monkey brain stains. Most of the scratches had been buffed into ghostly color variations in the leather. I knew each one came from, from the first scratches across the top when I kicked a monster with spikes growing out of its legs, to the abrasions on the toes where I climbed an ancient Roman column for better line of sight. Cleanings handled the blood, but even so, history made them impossible to touch.

"No, there's something wrong." He sat beside me, leaning down to try to look into my eyes. "What's up?"

I managed to conjure a mask of a smile, an all-too-familiar sensation. "Nah, I'm just tired. Didn't sleep well." The lie came out too easily, but I still felt the need to prop it up to make sure he believed it. "Before that, too many nights not sleeping. Trying to figure this out." I shook my head, not sure what else to say. Under the tired, where I should have felt something, there was nothing. Not dread, or fear, or anticipation. Only a void and bone-deep weariness.

He stared for longer than comfortable before asking, "You sure?"

Lying without words felt less difficult, so I nodded.

Marty took my hand and squeezed it. "If you're not, I'm here. We can talk."

My throat closed, and tears threatened, but I squeezed his hand in return, jerking up the corners of my mouth a little farther. "It's not serious. Once we catch the nightmare and handle this Compact thing, I'll sleep for a week and be back to normal."

The skeptical quirk of his eyebrows said volumes though he said nothing.

"I promise." Guilt reverberated within me. I doubted sleep could do anything to fill the yawning blackness, though I might escape it for a while.

Replies crossed Marty's face in tiny flashes of expression until I looked away. Mustering every iota of energy I had, I leaned down and picked up my boots. "What did Cooper say about Riley's status?"

"Stable, but catatonic. Unresponsive to stimuli." Marty stood, watching me. "The hospital downgraded them from good to fair about a half hour ago."

"I thought you said Riley was stable?"

Marty shrugged. "They are, but I suppose it has to do with the catatonia."

"When did it start?"

"Not sure. Someone found Riley sitting on a bench last night outside Café du Monde. Called 911 when they didn't respond. They've been in the hospital since." He checked his phone. "Cooper's vehicle's here. You ready?"

"As I'll ever be." I slid off the bed, picked up my Glock off the nightstand, and tucked it into my belly band holster. Hospital rules or not, something told me New Orleans and I would just never get along unless I carried some kind of weapon.

Our second trip to Tulane Medical Center should have been less distressing since my team wasn't being treated for battle-sustained wounds. Seeing Riley in bed, sprouting a hydra of wires and tubes, made it equally difficult.

Madame Sabine, dressed in her old, colorless clothes, sat in the chair beside the bed. An expression of peace stripped years from her face. She hummed some tuneless melody I couldn't recognize, her eyes closed, head back.

I nodded in her direction and Sister Betty whispered, "She's evaluating Riley."

"How?"

"I don't know. When I reported Riley's experience and condition, the Order referred me to her." She shrugged, and her gaze drifted back to the old woman. "There are things I've learned to accept on faith."

Typically, Sister Betty's Order, the Holy Order of the Sisters of Saint Brendan, passed along hunting jobs, or information about threats, or provided arcane monster research, but recently, things had changed. The last job with the Black Dog hadn't come through the normal chain of command and lacked the typical exit clause. Though the message bore the Order's familiar stamp, it closed with Vatican staff signatures instead of the Reverend Mother's arthritic scrawl. And now, the Order referred Sister Betty to a fortune teller for a consult on a soul in jeopardy?

Not knowing what to make of it, I nodded and reaffirmed my intent to talk to have a long, detailed discussion about the Order with Sister Betty later. "Has she said anything about Riley, yet?"

"To say something about the patient, I would have to finish, which I could do if you would stop yammering," the old woman muttered, one eye open a sliver. "Both of you, sit and be quiet, or leave."

Sister Betty and I sat in the hard plastic chairs in the corner.

Madame Sabine, satisfied, closed her eye and resumed her humming.

I closed my eyes to listen. That indistinct sound drained away tension. My muscles relaxed, and I floated. On the edge of perception, a bad dream built on a sound, *the* sound that haunted my entire life—a sick, wet crunch and never-ending, echoing scream. The last sound my sister, Shannon, would ever make.

"Cee?"

I jerked upright again. "Yeah?"

"You fell asleep." Sister Betty patted my hand. "Were you dreaming?"

"I don't think so. Not really." Another effortless lie. I rubbed my eyes to avoid meeting hers. "What did I miss?"

"Not much. Madame Sabine's waiting."

The old woman leaned forward in the chair. "Hunter, are you wearing the amulet?"

With a nod, I pulled the amulet out of my shirt, light catching the glass. "Yes, ma'am."

"Good." She sat back in the chair. "You'll need it soon."

"What does it do, Madame Sabine?" I asked.

She shrugged. "I don't know. I only sense it will be important and you must have it when the time's right."

"But how will—"

"You will know," she said. "We're here to talk about your friend."

Sister Betty crossed the room to sit on the edge of Riley's bed. Even when she took their hand, Riley didn't move, didn't react. I hoped it meant peace, and their sleep remained undisturbed until I could free them.

I had to find a way.

"How do we heal them?" I asked.

Madame Sabine blinked. "There's nothing we can do."

"Wait, what?" I said, rising and joining Sister Betty at Riley's side. "I thought the Order recommended you because you could help reverse this."

"No, *cherie*," she said softly. "I cannot reverse this. There's nothing we can do but make them comfortable until the end."

"Are you saying they're going to die?"

"We all die," she said.

"Caitlin," Sister Betty said.

"What can we do to stop it?" I asked, gesturing at Riley and ignoring Sister Betty. "To save them?"

"Nothing." She stared at the young person in the hospital bed, her wrinkled lips downturned and sad. "The touch of nightmares outside of normal sleep disturbs the natural order. Sleep bridges the realms and protects against the touch of nightmares. When our worlds mix in such an unnatural way, they cross into our realm where the veil is thin."

"Because the power draws their attention?" I demanded. "What is the purpose of them crossing over and touching humans?"

"I don't know," she said, stroking Riley's cheek with tender compassion. "Even I only know what I know."

"And because the veil is thin and a nightmare crossed over, Riley's going to die."

"So it seems," she said. "Awake, we lack protection. The touch of nightmares is too much and consumes our divine spark. Without it, we die."

Biting back the urge to rail against fairness, I stared down at Riley's face, marred by a few minor blemishes, but otherwise perfect and relaxed in sleep. A stark contrast to the way they trembled while they talked about the fear of locusts spurred by traumatizing bad dreams from childhood after vacation Bible school. They had stared up at Sister Betty with the innocent eyes of a terrified child and had only truly relaxed once Father Callahan sat and put his arm around them. I'd stopped the locusts, but it hadn't been enough. The nightmare could still be out there, could do this to someone else, and all because I hadn't acted fast enough. "How do I stop the nightmare?"

Madame Sabine looked up at me.

"Knock, knock." Father Callahan opened the door slowly. "How are things in here?"

"Someone else is dying on my watch," I said. "Seems to be the new trend."

"Now, Caitlin, you can't—"

"It's the truth, but I won't let it happen again." Not when it meant another name on my list. I directed my next question at Madame Sabine. "How do I stop it?"

"There's no simple answer," Father Callahan said.

"He's right." Cooper stepped into the room, followed by Marty. "There are things in play we don't understand—"

"But it's not an excuse for not acting."

"She's right," Sister Betty said. "The threat isn't only with regard to the manifestations of fears or the physical harm that befalls those touched, but also to the affected's spiritual well-being. We have to act, Daniel."

I blinked and tried to remember when I'd last heard Sister Betty address Father Callahan by his first name. If I'd heard it, I couldn't pin it to an exact event.

Father Callahan pressed his lips together and nodded. "Yes, I know. I didn't advocate doing nothing, and neither did Cooper, only a common sense approach." He continued in a hurry as I opened my mouth. "This has happened before."

25

"What?" Sister Betty, Marty and I all asked the same question at the same time.

Father Callahan held up his hands in a placating gesture, but Cooper spoke first. "Before DEMON became an agency in the federal government, it existed as a fringe group. I won't go into all the details, mostly because they aren't relevant," Cooper said, "but we observed similar incidents and reported them to the Church years ago."

"How many years ago?" Sister Betty's shoulders stiffened.

"That's not—"

"Two hundred and four." Father Callahan leaned against the wall.

"That was classified." Cooper glared at the taller man.

"They deserve to know." Father Callahan gestured for Cooper to continue.

"DEMON's existed since," Marty's eyes twitched as he calculated, "1814?"

"Longer, in some capacity," Cooper said. "But the point is, we've seen this touch-induced soul ablation before, and it's not impossible to reverse."

"Then we can save Riley."

"Yes, Caitlin, but it won't be easy."

"Is anything?" I leaned forward, bracing my arms on my thighs. "What do we do?"

Cooper actually shuffled his feet, his hands in his pockets. Had he bit his lip, he'd have looked like a child playing dress up.

"What?" I asked. "What's so terrible you don't want to tell me?"

"We don't know. The manifestations stopped before the agents could figure out what happened. The soul-ablated weren't discovered until after."

"Then how can you say it can be reversed if you don't know how?" I demanded.

"We know what's causing the problem," Marty said.

"But not how to stop it," I replied, "so we're exactly where we started. Nowhere."

"The members of the Compact will know," Cooper said.

"Which members?" I asked.

"We're not sure," Cooper said, shuffling again, "but we do know it's possible."

"Again, we're back at nothing."

"Caitlin, it's not nothing. It's a start," Father Callahan said with unusual confidence, as if a positive outlook would make the impossible possible. "First, you need to access."

"Right." I let my head drop and tried to reign in my irritation. "Any suggestions?"

"Helen?" Cooper offered.

"Oh, right, like I didn't start with her." I might have rolled my eyes, but in my defense, involuntary reactions to stupid suggestions are out of my control. "She refused."

"Why?"

"Doesn't matter. She's not helping. Next suggestion."

Cooper turned to Father Callahan again. "Does the Church have other contacts with supernatural beings?"

Madame Sabine's laughter made us all turn as she slid out of her chair and crossed the room. She stopped in front of me, her hand lighting on my shoulder. I looked into her eyes, eyes that once transformed into glowing blue-white orbs as she pulled non-existent tarot cards from a normal deck. The electric buzz of magic radiated across my skin as she patted me. "*Cherie*, you're wasting time. Instead of debating, go. Let the Compact find you."

Without another word, she left, humming to herself as the door closed behind her.

Taking advice from others typically gets me in trouble, which is why I avoid even the most sensible tidbits of wisdom. Madame Sabine's advice, I discovered, was no different.

"I think this is the first time I'm glad to see you, Miss Kelley," Officer LaFontaine said, peering over the door of his cruiser, the front sight of his Mossberg 12-gauge service weapon shaking despite bracing it as he trained it on the twelve-foot-wide coil of writhing snake filling most of the street.

I glanced at him from where I stood, amused. "Why? Animal control busy?"

"I hope you're joking," he said. Drops of sweat rolled down his bald, sunburned head. "This is more than a snake, and I only say that because I've seen it with my own eyes."

I glanced across the front seat of the car to where Boudreaux crouched behind the other open door, aiming another shotgun at the eight-foot-high pile of snake. He looked marginally more composed but refused to take his eyes off the creature. Probably best. The last thing I needed was those beautiful eyes rendering me stupid.

Crouching beside LaFontaine, I asked for a rundown as Marty leaned in to listen.

"You'll think I'm crazy," LaFontaine said.

"There's a fair chance I already think that."

He didn't react, but Marty poked my kidney.

"For the sake of getting this situation under control," I said, "let's pretend I won't."

LaFontaine glanced at me out of the corner of his eye. "It has nine heads."

"A hydra." Marty sounded impressed. "No shit."

Great. Know what's worse than a massive supernatural snake roughly ninety feet long? A massive supernatural snake roughly ninety feet long with nine regenerating heads. Any head I managed to remove would grow back—with an extra one for good measure. "Have you shot it or wounded it yet?"

He licked his lips, his usual jackass swagger and bluster gone, though I couldn't be sure how much fear neutralized or how much related to Cooper's little hypnotism session. Engaging the supernatural in battle obviously rattled LaFontaine's worldview more than witnessing the aftermath. Compared to his rather blasé reaction to dead flying monkeys, this felt extreme. But then again, a lot of people get squeamish when it comes to snakes. Regardless the reason, I felt a little bad for him as I waited for him to respond. "Yes," he said reluctantly after a long pause. "You wouldn't believe what happened."

I glanced to Boudreaux. "Was it a headshot?"

"Yes," they both said, the radio in the cruiser crackling and interrupting us.

"Let me guess," I said, "you blew off a head and two grew back."

LaFontaine's shotgun rattled against the door. "How the hell did you know that?"

With a grin, I patted the officer's shoulder. "This isn't my first rodeo." I turned to Marty. "There's a sword in the arsenal."

Marty nodded, already texting. "Father C's en route with blades, additional firepower, and flamethrowers."

"Ooh, new toys? Where'd he find them?"

"Flame throwers?" LaFontaine's concentration broke, and he looked at me, his hands still braced against the car door. "What the hell are you going to do with a flamethrower?"

"Prevent heads from growing back after we cut them off," I said, barely sparing a glance his way before continuing my conversation with Marty. "Get Sister Betty to canvas for the victim. If possible, we need to figure out where they encountered the nightmare."

Marty nodded, his thumbs coordinating our response. "Backup plan?"

With a shrug, I said, "If shit goes south, you and Sister Betty gear up and jump in."

He grinned, looking up from his phone.

"Only," I stressed, "if it goes FUBAR. Neither of you should be fighting until you're fully healed."

"Okay." His grin dimmed, though not by much. All I could do was hope they'd listen.

"Shit," Boudreaux said. "Beau, you seeing this?"

I turned at the same time as Officer LaFontaine. The thick rope of coiled muscle rolled against itself, the snake rolling into a tighter knot, its blue-black scales glinting in the Louisiana sun. Two heads rose out of the center, followed by two more, then three more after that. Over the top of the snake's body squirmed several, much smaller, multi-headed hydra. One of the smallest opened three of its mouths and hissed, issuing a tiny burst of mist.

Not just a hydra, but a hydra with babies that had already gotten their acid. Fantastic.

"I need a riot shield, helmet, and machete," I said.

"On it," Marty said, stashing his phone and kneeling, his backpack already at his feet.

"Riot gear? What for?" Officer Boudreaux glanced up at me in quick bursts, unwilling to stop watching the snake ball.

"They spit more acid than housewife reality shows, and I'm too damned cute to have my face melted." I passed my Glock to Marty and unstrapped the belly band holster for the two sheathed machetes he pulled out of his backpack. The sixteen-inch blades wouldn't deliver killing blows to the snake, but with a little creativity, I could do some incapacitating damage until reinforcements arrived with bigger, badder toys. I tucked my shirt in, strapped on one sheath. I wouldn't always need both blades in hand, but I knew better than to go into the fight with just one. Testing my range of movement, I twisted and wind-milled my arms, thrusting my chin at Boudreaux. "You got gear, or not?"

He shared a look with Officer LaFontaine, holstered his weapon and scrambled to the trunk. A moment later, a helmet wobbled on my head. "It's too big."

"That's a first," Marty said. "Usually, her head is way too big."

"Yeah, yeah." I ignored his snark, pulled the black helmet off and handed it back to Boudreaux. "Got anything smaller?"

He shook his head. "It's the smallest one we carry."

Anything smaller probably wouldn't fit either officer. "I'll skip it. Hand me that shield."

Despite the doubt on his face, he handed the black shield to me. "What about Callahan? Aren't you going to wait?"

Marty held up five fingers.

"Nope," I said, sliding my arm through the straps and hefting the three-quarter length black shield, testing the weight. I swung the shield over me in a few practice moves to test my balance. Shorter than the two cops, this would cover more of me, especially during what I liked to call "tactical ducking." Full-length clear riot shields provided superior visual advantages, but the small window and heavier shield were better suited to an encounter with a fanged, acid-spitting mama snake. "He should get here right when I need him."

"For what?"

"Father C's on flamethrower duty." I stretched and planted a kiss on

Boudreaux's cheek. "Don't shoot me, okay? And don't land any headshots on those wigglers until I tell you."

Boudreaux didn't answer, but his blush said plenty.

Marty and I fist bumped. "Don't get dead," he said.

"Don't plan on it." I took the machete he offered and stepped around the open cruiser door.

The bigger hydra heads bobbed low over its coils as I entered the dead zone between the cruiser and the squirming reptile pile towering over me. "Nice wormies," I said, circling, the shield in front of me as I peered through the window.

Little hydras swarmed over the top loop of the snake coil, hundreds of tiny heads opening and hissing at me, the bigger heads hovering protectively over them.

Did snakes have maternal instincts?

I stepped closer, brandishing the machete.

One of the big heads darted forward, the forked tongue stabbing at the clear window in the riot shield. The head retreated, but others swarmed forward, tongues scenting the air.

The whoosh and rush of heat signaled Father Callahan's arrival.

Glancing back, Father Callahan stood between me and the cruiser. He grinned under broad goggles, his teeth almost as white as his clerical collar. The apparatus strapped to his back made him look like some kind of mad scientist. After a quick thumbs up, he aimed the wand's igniter at the beasts.

"Let's dance."

I angled the shield low as I approached, ready to use it as cover. Through the window, I watched some of the smaller hydra slither off coil mountain and fall to the ground with a smack, their heads awkwardly swinging and bobbing after landing. I sidestepped the overgrown, multi-headed mudworms and swung the machete at the creepy crawlies studying me from on high.

The impact of a striking head smashing into the shield almost knocked me off my feet. I stayed low, and a stream of flame shot over my shield. Waddling backward in a crouch, I looked through the shield's window at the hissing chorus. Charred stalks missing baby snake heads drooped between the open, acid-spitting live ones.

Strike one, a success.

Another mama hydra head struck, a fang sticking in the thick plexiglass window. Acid dripped down the shield, scarring the window's clear surface a milky white. I yanked against the retreating head to avoid losing my shield and darted my other arm around to hack at the snake's exposed body. But, being my luck, I only managed a deep, anger-inducing cut instead of the near-decapitating strike I'd wanted. Pulling the shield close, I crouched as three more heads struck at once, crushing me into the ground. As they retreated, another pounded the shield, making my arm numb. Moving fast, I leapt and spun, managing to almost sever one head and duck beneath the shield before Father Callahan's flame cauterized the wriggling stump and burned away the scrap of flesh attaching the head.

One down, at least a hundred more to go.

Piece of cake.

T he last three heads of the hydra loomed over me, striking my cracked shield from different directions. I prayed it would hold, watching the tip of a lone fang wedge deeper into the starburst impact point in the clouded plexiglass. A stream of fire arced over me long enough to scramble to my feet and dart across the snake-littered ground. Sweat poured into my face, and my muscles ached, but I rattled my remaining machete against the shield to draw the hydra's attention.

Sister Betty yelled from the other side of the reptile knot, and Father Callahan shot another burst of flame directly at the three heads. As intended, the heads each turned in a different direction. I lunged at the one aiming for me, twisting the shield at the last second to deflect an incoming stream of acid, my machete severing the waving stalk of flesh. I smelled burning plastic as I slammed into the ground, the severed head landing on top of my shield.

When the ability to breathe returned, I almost regretted the first lungful of air, thick with the reek of burned meat. The stench of burning flesh intensified me as Father Callahan's flame cauterized the cut I'd made. I clenched my jaw against the urge to vomit.

As the flame guttered to a stop, I rolled to my feet, raised the battered shield over my head, and ran to Father Callahan's side. A second before I got there, one of the remaining hydra heads attacked, striking at him so hard, it dragged the dead weight of the snake's body across the pavement. The gunshot that blinded one of its eyes seemed to have irritated it. Father Callahan backtracked, but with each lunge, the snake got closer despite its missing eye. I screamed a battle cry and jumped, the machete cutting the snake deep. A shotgun blast finished the decapitation as I fell through the space between Father C and the snake. He landed on his rear and scrambled to get the flame thrower nozzle up to burn the stump before the heads grew back.

Exhausted, but not done, I struggled to my feet in time to see Sister Betty lop off the last injured snake head with her machete and yell in triumph, a gout of flame from Marty's flamethrower arcing over her riot shield to burn the severed neck.

The hydra shuddered once and fell with a ground-shaking thump.

Panting, I collapsed against the hood of the cruiser, surveying the gory wreckage.

"Well done, Cee." Father Callahan patted my shoulder before slumping onto the metal hood beside me.

"Thanks." I wiped my forearm across my forehead, though it felt wetter afterward. "Not too shabby yourself."

"That was…"

I looked up into the stunned face of Officer Boudreaux and shaded my eyes to see him against the sun. "Kinda gross, right?"

"Amazing," he said, breathless.

Laughter bubbled up from deep inside, and I leaned back on my elbows, though the hood of the car burned from the sunlight. "Thanks." I poked my chin at Sister Betty behind him. "But I'm sure my mentor has fifty ways I could have done better."

She winced, handing me the machete hilt first. "Nah. Only ten."

"Slacker," I teased.

"Forgive me," she said with a wry grin. "Chopping off heads distracted me from monitoring your form."

"Sister Hot—um—Betty and I make a pretty good team." Marty stretched to plant an elbow on her shoulder.

She raised an eyebrow. "I'm retired from the monster hunter business."

"But isn't it easier than wrangling deviants like our dear Caitlin?"

"Probably." She eyed me thoughtfully. "But I think I'll stick with that a little longer."

"I'd rather you have not had to jump in." I watched her for signs of injury or pain.

"Well, I've invested too much time in you to watch you die." Sister Betty put her hands on her hips, standing tall. "And Marty's not bad."

He grinned.

"Not a hunter, but not bad." The corner of her mouth twitched.

I laughed as his expression evaporated. "The trainer giveth, and the trainer taketh away."

"Is this something you handle often?" Boudreaux glanced over his shoulder at his partner talking with Cooper. I hadn't noticed when Cooper arrived. Maybe we could leave clean-up and debrief detail to him since he hadn't been around for the really messy stuff.

Beside me, Father Callahan, Marty, and Betty started planning how to locate the victim.

"More or less." I sat up and slid down the goo-covered hood. My team would be fine without me for a minute.

Boudreaux looked at me, and electricity raced across my skin. "You know, I was thinking, maybe we should go out for dinner while you're here. I can, I don't know, show you things tourists don't get to see."

"I, uh—"

"Caitlin!"

My head snapped around at the sound of Cooper's voice only to see him sprint past, dodging the slippery debris of dead hydra with inhuman accuracy and grace. Whatever he saw, this couldn't be good. Without thinking, I ran after him, leaving the rest of my team, and Boudreaux's unanswered invitation, behind.

26

My muscles burned as I raced through the streets, dodging cars and pedestrians, jumping potholes, and splashing through the ever-present puddles. Each thudding step made me ache for sleep, to stop, to rest. With every breath, I heaved fire, but I fought to keep going, my eyes on the nightmare mere paces ahead of Cooper. If I could get there...

Cooper yelled, but approaching sirens drowned him out.

I pushed harder, unwilling to let the bastard escape.

LaFontaine and Boudreaux's cruiser skidded to a stop at the end of the street, blocking it with no space between the tight corridor of houses. I slowed, reaching for the gun I hadn't remembered to strap on once the hydra fight ended, and cursed.

"Stop where you are! Put your hands up!" Cooper's command echoed in the street.

The nightmare froze, then slowly turned to face the agent and his gun. He raised his hands, the hem of his shirt lifted to expose his pale belly.

Four heads peered over the top of the cruiser. Officer LaFontaine, Officer Boudreaux, Sister Betty, and Father Callahan all aimed weapons at the nightmare's back.

Cooper adjusted his stance to avoid aiming his Glock at the cruiser and barked orders the creature didn't follow. It shook its head, eyes wide with terror.

I jogged the last few steps to Cooper, staying behind him. "I don't think it understands."

"Yeah, I got that impression," he muttered, then yelled again, but in a language I couldn't identify.

It nodded for the first time.

"That makes things easier."

"What language was that?"

"Elvish," he said before yelling again in the same language.

Sister Betty rounded the trunk of the car, lowering her weapon. She said something that sounded like what Cooper said. When had she learned Elvish?

The creature turned to Sister Betty and spoke, voice shaking in terror. She nodded.

"What did it say?" I asked Cooper.

He ignored me, shouting what could only be a command. The nightmare whipped around, its hands thrusting higher into the air.

"Are you going to tell me what's going on?"

"I'm not a translator. When it's over, we'll debrief."

I bristled, but before some acidic reply fell out of my mouth, Sister Betty called to him. "Agent Hardin, stand down. Gyleeto agrees to come peacefully and safely."

"He can agree all he wants, but I won't trust him until he's on the ground and contained."

"This isn't necessary," Sister Betty insisted, holstering her weapon, her hands palm out and at chest height. "We have to show good faith. And trust."

The nightmare's head swiveled between Cooper and Sister Betty.

I stepped where Cooper could see me. "She's right. This might be key to accessing the Compact."

"Down!" Cooper screamed. I dove for the ground, hands protecting my head as he fired.

When I looked up, Sister Betty sat on the ground cupping her arm. The thunder of dented metal resounded through the street as the nightmare landed on the trunk of the cruiser and jumped off the other side.

Cooper pursued the nightmare, and I scrambled over the dirty pavement to Sister Betty. She stared at me, eyes wide, her face deathly white.

"What happened?" I asked. "Are you hurt? Did you get shot?"

She blinked then looked down at her hand covering her arm as Marty knelt beside her. Tears welled in her eyes. Her lower lip trembled. She said nothing.

I reached for her hand, to coax it away. "Let me see."

She twisted away from me and shook her head.

"He touched her, Cee," Marty said, so softly, I almost missed it.

Ice coursed through me. "What?" Ice and rage.

"The nightmare." A tear ran down his cheek. "I saw it. He shoved her to get away. Both hands. He touched her."

"No." I tried to make eye contact with Sister Betty, but she looked at the ground, her shoulders shaking. "That can't be right."

A single sob broke out of her. She shook her head and folded forward, drawing her knees up, shaking with the force of her tears.

My jaw clenched as I rocked back on my heels. I hadn't watched them. I distracted Cooper. I neglected my team, my responsibilities.

"Father Callahan's gone after him." Marty's arm curled around Sister Betty as she sobbed. "Let's take her back to the hotel."

To wait. For the manifestation of her fears. To wait until catatonia took her, too.

"Caitlin?"

I failed the woman I loved. My carelessness sentenced her to death.

"Come on, Cee. Let's go."

But I couldn't. I jumped to my feet and ran after the nightmare.

"What the hell is wrong with you, Caitlin?" Sister Betty slammed the rectory door behind her. "This," she fumbled for words, "stunt was far more reckless than any of the crap you pulled in training as a teenager."

I crossed the room to the armory door, unable to look at her. Yes, I'd pursued the nightmare that touched her and damned her to have her worst fears manifest. Yes, I'd chased the thing that would eventually destroy the divine spark within that kept her alive. Did I regret it? Fuck, no. "Nothing's wrong with me. My job is to save people. The nightmare escaped. I chased it to prevent it from touching anyone else."

The implication hung between us. It touched her while I wasn't looking. While I distracted the agent covering her. She'd been touched, and it was my fault. The ramifications made me sick. I imagined her catatonic in a hospital bed like Riley, or worse, losing her altogether.

Our eyes met. The redness around hers and the tiny red veins criss-crossing the whites made my chest ache. They telegraphed her fear, her awareness of her fate. First the nightmare feeding on her fear, then, death from the inside out.

I might as well have murdered her myself.

I paced the room, my back to her so I wouldn't have to look at her any longer. "Why's this an issue? You've taken bigger risks to catch a monster."

"This isn't the same thing," she said, her voice rising, her words becoming brittle. "What if it touched you, Caitlin? There are sensible times to put yourself in harm's way, and there's," she grunted in frustration, "stupid ways of doing it. This was stupid. Do you get that? Running off alone to chase a monster is stupid. If it touched you—"

"Like it touched you?"

Her jaw clenched, but it didn't stop her lip from trembling. She said nothing.

"Cooper and Father C were already in pursuit. I joined to even up the odds of us catching it." I swallowed hard around the lump in my throat as I lied. The guys had chased as soon as the nightmare ran. I followed because I needed to kill it, whatever it took. I ran four blocks before I heard Cooper yelling. When I got there, the nightmare had disappeared into a club. We'd searched but found nothing.

"You're reckless." She followed me as I paced the small room, her pink rosary beads dangling from her clenched fist.

"I'm doing my job," I insisted.

When we'd returned to the scene, Sister Betty'd sat in the back of Officer LaFontaine and Officer Boudreaux's cruiser praying and running a rosary through her fingers. She'd refused to tell us her nightmare, shaking her head as tears rolled down her cheeks. Seeing the same beads in her hand now choked me up, but I refused to cry. I couldn't let on how scared I was, too.

With nowhere to hide in the rectory, I kept my back to her.

"It's not just today, either. You let the Black Dog chase you. Do you know what might have happened if it caught you? Do you understand the risk you took? Even if you managed to keep its focus off the thousands of people you endangered on Bourbon and all the side streets, it could have killed *you*. Then what would have happened?"

"It didn't."

"That's not the point!"

"And if it got me, so what?" I whirled, yelling at her, though I didn't want to. "There are other monster hunters. Sister Evangeline died, and now I'm here. Even if something happens to me, there are others. And that's worst-case scenario. Maybe I'd manage to mortally wound whatever tries to eat me before I died. Maybe I'd trigger some kind of allergic reaction to whatever gets me. It doesn't matter. I'm not special. I'm just doing the work someone else would do if I wasn't here. I protect people, but if I couldn't, someone else would." My eyes fell on the beads in her hand, and a ripple in her tight shirt indicating the newly re-bandaged stitches in her side. "Maybe someone else should."

She threw her arms up, exasperated. "Either you're not listening, or you don't care whether you live or die."

"I didn't say that." I fought the sting of tears.

"You don't have to," she said softly, her faltering words cracking. "Your carelessness is like a death wish."

"If I was careless, I'd say 'fuck it,' take my vacation, and let the world fend for itself. Instead, I'm risking my life to save everyone else. Everyone." I wrestled to contain what crawled under my skin, my hands balled into fists as I resisted picking up something, anything, to throw. Instead, I whipped around. "Yet no matter what I do, someone bitches because it's never enough. It's not enough for Hardin who wants me some kind of robot that does nothing but fight monsters. It's not enough for you because God forbid I don't account for every minute risk. It's not enough for the Pope, for Giulietta Perricone, or Benito Hernandez, or Shannon because none of them survived when I should have saved them. They were *all* my fault! And now, you."

Her shoulders dropped, and her anger melted.

The first tear dripped off my nose.

"Is...that what this is about? People you weren't able to save?"

My jaw ached as I clenched my teeth, my nails cutting into my palm.

"Caitlin, you can't save everyone."

"Yes, I can. I can get better, I can get stronger, I can—"

"No." Sister Betty reached out and touched my shoulder, and I shivered. "There will always be someone, something bigger and badder than you and bent on destruction or murder. All you can do—"

"Not good enough." I swatted her hand away, my heart aching at the hurt in her eyes. "I will do my job. If that means I die doing it, so be it, but if there's even the smallest chance I can save someone, I will. If there's some way I can save you—" I bit off the rest and turned, wild, needing to flee. I snatched my key and my Glock off the table and darted around her.

"Where are you going?" she called after me.

"To do my fucking job."

Humidity made the air thick. Walking back to the hotel felt like wading through swamp water, and tourists further slowed my progress to a crawl, especially around jazz bands playing in the street for change. None of it did much to ease my frustration, but I tried to be patient.

A blast of cool air poured over me as I entered my hotel. I shivered and calmed a little. As I crossed the lobby, the sheen of perspiration finally drying on my exposed skin, I realized maybe Sister Betty had a point. Letting the Black Dog chase me like prey had been one of my craziest, and most impulsive, ideas. The improvisation led to its capture, but maybe I'd risked too much. Whether I could have had a smarter or safer idea in the moment didn't matter, but I hadn't taken time to consider the possible encounters, and maybe that was her point.

Maybe running after the nightmare under the pretense of backing up Cooper and Father Callahan was equally dumb. Two of my team had the matter in hand, two more needed me, and I'd run off, helping neither. I'd had time to think and pick the best solution but chose not to. My emotions won out over reason, and I'd been lucky. Next time...

A lump of dread rose from deep in my gut and lodged in my throat as I crossed the lobby.

If Sister Betty did die—

No. None of that. Not now. Not yet.

There had to be a solution, a way of stopping the nightmare without risking everything. I clutched the amulet between my breasts. Whatever its purpose, the weight felt grounding as I entered the empty elevator, pressed the button for my floor, leaned against the railing, and closed my eyes.

I had to find a way of stopping it.

Sister Betty would die if I didn't, and time was running out.

My reflection stared back at me, sweaty, dried hydra goo crusting my shirt. I needed a shower and, from the bags under my eyes, a nap. Cleaning up and getting some shut eye, hopefully nightmare-free, should clear up my perspective, then I'd come up with a plan, bring it to the team, and we'd try again

The elevator dinged, and I stepped out onto my floor, distracted by my thoughts.

By the time I looked up, I'd passed my door and stood in the hallway with the mirror, still clutching the amulet. I shook my head and turned around with a snort.

Then, I heard my name.

I leaned back to look down the hall. Faint strains of music seemed to come from one of the rooms, and from the opposite end of the hallway, a cellphone rang. The mirror caught my eye again. Something about it never failed to draw my attention, maybe because I expected something unusual from it again. As far away as I was, my reflection looked normal.

Until it waved.

"Shit."

A monster hunter's work is never done.

With one last longing glance at my hotel room door, I turned on my heel and stalked the mirror. As I approached, the sparkling darkness surrounding my reflection swirled into a long, sparkling evening gown. I still gripped the amulet, but my reflection held a clutch that glinted in the overhead lights. Something in my reflection's expression seemed... concerned, as if my reflection felt some kind of urgency to reach me.

My reflection and I ran at each other.

Just as I approached the table with the flowers and prepared to stop, reality bent, and I ran through what felt like an icy waterfall.

27

C rashing a party's way more fun when you intend to do it. And when your arrival doesn't instantly provoke an armed response. Welcome to my life.

It happened so fast, I thought I'd finally crossed some threshold of sleep deprivation and landed in a hallucination. One minute, I was dirty, tired, and running down a hallway toward some alternate reality image of me in a magic or enchanted mirror, then I stepped into the middle of a hotel ballroom surrounded by a spectacle of impeccably dressed supernatural creatures. Less than a heartbeat later, cold, iron-strong fingers gripped my arms, tangled in my hair, and exposed my throat to the threatening prick of fangs over my jugular. A killing bite.

Believe it or not, I've had worse receptions.

Being zapped into a party by magical mirror portal only to be set upon by vampires isn't the worst way I've spent a Friday night. Doesn't crack my top ten, either. But that doesn't mean I was immediately prepared. It took almost a full minute to figure out what the hell had happened, including being restrained by not just the one vamp with his teeth at my throat, but by two. They must have heard of me before.

The gathering seemed to get the gist of the situation before me, though probably because they had a bigger-picture view and could turn their heads without puncturing their throats. A hushed silence settled around me, then swelled to an angry uproar.

"These are supposed to be closed proceedings!"

"If this is the security being offered, I'm leaving."

"What's the meaning of this?" I couldn't see who owned the angriest approaching voice. All motion, including turning or normal breathing, was out of the question, so I waited.

"George, Lafayette, stand down." This voice sounded less flustered and far more amused.

The snick of retracting teeth shook me with a primal chill. Though the vampires didn't release me, the imminent danger of becoming an unwilling blood donor had passed. I addressed the vampires holding me and straightened as much as their imprisoning grip would allow. "Not exactly the welcome I'd show my guests, but hey, you do you, boo."

Silence fell on the crowd, and hundreds of eyes stared at me from all over the dimly lit room. Not that there was anything remotely intimidating about standing in a pool of light in front of a ballroom filled with creatures, most of which had at least a passing interest in killing me. Or at least "playing" with me to the maiming point.

The vampires held me immobile, on display for the creatures clustered around tables, whispering and pointing. Some creatures I recognized, like the sasquatch pair in the back sporting only bowties, the golden glow of were-creature eyes in the heaviest shadows, and the iridescent aura of a beautiful woman who had to be fae. Others I felt glad I didn't recognize, like the scaled beast with six eyes and rows of hideous teeth, or short, tumbling creatures that might be goblins, or kobolds, or even gremlins. The most disturbing ones looked as human as me, though something wasn't quite right about them.

That's when I understood.

"This is the Compact."

"Of course it is," said the offended, exasperated voice from behind me. "What else did you think you were interrupting?" The creature walked around me, a skeleton in a tuxedo. The black jacket and white shirt hung loose on its frame everywhere except the collar bones. "Exactly what do you intend to accomplish with this unforgiveable intrusion?"

One creature, a hair-covered thing with a long, split tongue flicking between viciously sharp teeth made me think about some chimerical combination of a snake, shark and…Afghan hound. I tried not to stare at any of them, but each time I paused to take in the next creature, I met some other implausible image. Instead, I met the black void of the skeleton's eye sockets in front of me. "I didn't intentionally intrude."

The skeleton scoffed, though how it spoke without a voice box baffled me. It crossed its arms, and I swear I heard the rattle and scrape of bones. "Well, how'd you get here?"

"You know." I shifted as much as I could, immediately losing my train of thought, stunned into silence. My battle-dirty jeans and tank top had transformed into the same black, sequined dress I'd seen on my reflection. Sparkly fabric glided provocatively over my skin and spilled to the floor, a round, glittery clutch only slightly larger than the amulet, in my hand.

"I'm waiting," the skeleton prompted.

I looked up at the clutch, mouth open. Crossing through the mirror, I'd become my reflection. "The amulet must have let me pass," I muttered before realizing I'd said it aloud.

"What?" When I didn't answer, the skeleton stepped closer, and the vampires tightened their grip. "What did you say?"

"Can I have my arms back, please?" I glared at the blond vampire holding my left arm and preventing it from reaching the clutch in my right hand. Whether the surly, scowling bloodsucker was Lafayette or George, I didn't care. "It's not like you couldn't catch me whenever you wanted."

The vampire's hair gleamed almost as pale as his ghastly skin as he tossed it over his shoulder and looked to the skeleton.

Great. Rattlin' Bones-y must be the emcee of this shindig.

I gave the skeleton the full extent of The Look, expecting it to work as well as it did on humans and human-like supernats. On this…creature, it didn't do much.

Bones-y waited for me to answer.

"Fine." I sighed. "If you'll let me look in my purse, I think I've got whatever passes as an invitation around here."

If skeletons could have eyebrows, I'm pretty sure one of his would have jumped off his bony forehead. And as much as you could expect a walking pile of bones to express emotion, this one looked curious. He crossed his arms and stared at me a moment longer, then nodded.

The blond vampire released my hand.

I repressed the urge to scowl at my former captive. No need to earn the next problem. It would come just fine on its own. "I'm going to open my purse now." I wiggled the bag in my right hand. "It's too small for weapons, so let's not get frisky, okay?" That wasn't quite true, but I didn't know what was in it, and too much truth might be hazardous to my health.

Opening the clutch, I prayed nothing inside would alarm the supernaturals within striking distance. Laying on the plush black satin lining was a tube of lipstick, a plastic key card from my hotel room, and a golden coin.

I pulled out the coin, angling it in the light. One side was embossed with an image of a paddlewheel river boat, a fleur-de-lis, and a half mask, an engraving of the city name and date around the outer edge. The other side caught the light as I flipped it over, and someone at a nearby table gasped. Conversation rippled through the room, too low to understand.

"How did you get that?" demanded the skeleton in the tuxedo, its arms akimbo.

Before I could read the flip side of the coin, the frowning blond vampire re-captured my hand, and his dark-haired partner plucked it from my fingers. "Hey!"

The skeleton took the coin from the vampire. "Remove her."

"Wait," I protested.

"Stop." The word resonated through the ballroom, silencing all conversation.

The skeleton stiffened.

I looked around and followed the gaze of the creatures in the room until I saw him. My gut fluttered with hope as a silverback gorilla loped across the room.

It couldn't be...

The skeleton shivered as the creature approached, the coin clutched in its fingers, unconcealed by lack of flesh. "Lushiku, this is highly irregular. A simple matter of security—"

"She has a ticket, does she not?" The gorilla, Lushiku, pointed a thick, black, leathery finger at the coin peeking between the bones of the skeleton's hand.

"A forgery."

"You have not tested it." The gorilla settled on its haunches, knuckles on the ground, his posture wrinkling the red sash draped across his massive chest. He winked at me. I wondered what he did with my panties. And why he wanted them in the first place. Maybe he'd consider it prepayment for helping me.

"I don't need to," the skeleton said, defensive. "She's not on the member rolls. She's an intruder, and I refuse to imperil the proceedings—"

"A forgery is simple enough to prove, but you have neither checked the rolls for Miss Kelley's name, nor have you tested her ticket. Is it integrity that concerns you, or are you and your faction still trying to discriminate against the humans?"

The skeleton bristled, his bones scraping against the coin. "Your accusations are unfounded."

"They're mere observations, Gideon. If you perceive them as accusations, perhaps they have merit."

Murmurs rippled through the crowd behind Lushiku. Creatures from across the room rose, drawing closer to see.

Gideon crossed his arms. "This is highly improper, an obstruction of procedure, and I'll have you know—"

With a low, menacing growl, Lushiku leaned forward and said, "Test the ticket. Or explain why your contingent has blocked human admission to the Compact for decades."

I recoiled as a worm-like creature with tentacles wriggled up to us and arched like a king cobra. Smaller tentacles around the mouth squirmed in our direction as it leaned forward to chirp at Gideon.

The skeleton scowled as much as a fleshless creature can and snapped at the wormlike creature. "That's not true. The nightmare council has never prevented humans from attending."

"Bullshit," a delicate voice said with a European accent I couldn't identify. "The nightmare council didn't even attempt contact prior to the Compact, as outlined in the bylaws."

Gideon stared at the female speaker behind me but didn't retort.

"Milagros is ready." Lushiku gestured to the wormlike creature and its extended tentacle. "Test the ticket."

"You endanger the spirit of diplomacy," Gideon stammered, his bones grinding the coin.

"Test the ticket," said a humanoid female at the table nearest us.

"Test the ticket," echoed a winged, androgynous creature who hovered over us.

Other voices repeated the phrase until it became a chant. The vampires' grips loosened on my arms as they murmured to each other, unsure what to do.

As the crowd grew closer, Gideon looked from one creature to the next before reluctantly handing the coin to Milagros, the worm-like creature. "It's a forgery, you'll see. Humans haven't attended our Compact in decades. Her ticket is fake."

"Which is the problem," Lushiku said as the worm-like creature flipped the coin into its mouth. "Humans have as much right to attend as any other being, yet you and your boss omitted them from the proceedings. Did you think we hadn't noticed?"

"When do I get a say?"

The vampires remembered their purpose and jerked me back, the dark-haired one clamping a hand over my mouth. "Shut up," he said. "Until we know you're supposed to be here, you say nothing."

I tried biting his fingers, but he squeezed my face and crushed my lips against my teeth.

Between the shoulders and heads of the crowd, I saw him. The frat boy-man, Gyleeto, his hair still shabby-chic though he wore a tuxedo. When he saw me, his eyes widened. With a panicked glance around, he disappeared behind other creatures.

I struggled to free myself from the vampires as Lushiku argued with Gideon.

"—exposing the human population to predators and poachers will only unbalance the realm. You cannot expect to advance your agenda without repercussions."

I grunted and struggled, only fractionally moving the guards who gripped me.

The wormlike creature ejected the coin onto a waiting tentacle and offered it to Lushiku. "The ticket is legitimate and not a forgery," Milagros said in a shockingly human and delicately accented voice. "It is issued to Caitlin Kelley, hunter of monsters, designated representatives of mundane humans."

I had never heard of anything like this creature and wondered if Sister Betty had. Fear about her condition surged, but I pushed it away. To get out of this, I had to focus. Maybe I could find a solution for saving her here.

They all looked at me.

"Hunter," Lushiku, prompted. "What is your name?"

I twisted to look at the vampire with his hand over my mouth. Though close to my height and eerily slender, his preternatural strength made up for any advantage I might have exploited. His dark eyebrows rose, as if in question.

I rolled my eyes, waiting for him to release me.

"You're no fun, intruder," he murmured. "Let me into your mind, and we'll have fun."

I tried to bite him again, though his hand on my mouth made it impossible.

"This is the first time a human has ever tried to eat me. You know," he laughed, "I could give you fangs of your own if you really want to play vampire."

"Lafayette," Lushiku said, exasperated. "Release the hunter and allow her to answer."

"You're no fun either, monkey." Lafayette removed his hand.

"I'm going to kick your—"

"Answer the question, Hunter." Lushiku interrupted my threat.

"Yes." I ignored the saliva smeared around my mouth. "I'm Caitlin Kelley, a monster hunter for the Holy Roman Catholic Church."

Distrust radiated from the monsters nearest me, their eyes not leaving me, even as they murmured to each other.

"But I have never been a, what was it? Representative of humans?"

My admission prompted another ripple of conversation and gasps through the assembly.

"The ticket's a forgery," exclaimed Gideon, his skeletal grin triumphant. "Remove her."

"She may not see herself as a representative," said a gray-faced man in elegant, but tattered clothing, "but perhaps she was so designated without her knowledge."

"Where did you get this?" Lushiku plucked the coin from the tentacle Milagros offered.

"Before I ended up here, it wasn't a coin. It was a copper-wrapped stone, and when I passed through the mirror in my hotel—"

"Which hotel?"

"Who gave you the stone?"

"—it became a purse and the coin was inside."

More overlapping voices, but I caught words like "collectors," "amulet," and "carousel."

Lushiku gestured for silence, then nodded at the vampires. "Release her."

"But the list—" Gideon interrupted, shaking his head.

The vampires did not move.

"Bring the list," commanded Lushiku, anger compressing his face and baring his fangs. He rose to his full height, arms lifted in a regal gesture.

Voices repeated the call across the ballroom, the sound swelling until the crowd parted in silence to reveal a familiar form bearing a clipboard.

2 8

F rat boy-man, Gyleeto, hurried, though his steps still seemed hesitant. He glanced from me to Lushiku, clutching the clipboard like armor.

"You," was all I could say.

His mincing steps veered toward Lushiku, offering him the clipboard.

"Thank you." Lushiku glanced at me. "Do you know him?"

"He's the one causing trouble. The one I've been chasing. He touches people, their worst nightmares manifest, cause havoc, and then the humans die, their souls destroyed by some kind of mystical infection."

"I can't help it." Gyleeto cowered at Lushiku's elbow.

I jerked against the restraining hands of the vampires. "You speak English? Then you knew what we were saying!"

The frat boy man cringed. "I'm sorry."

"Sorry isn't good enough." I lunged forward so hard the vampires moved to catch their balance. "My partner's to going to die because you touched her."

"Miss Kelley," Gideon said.

"No." I struggled against the imprisoning hands. "Let me go, damnit."

"Miss Kelley is on the list," Lushiku announced, pointing to the clipboard.

"What?" Gideon stepped to the gorilla's side to look at the list. "No, that says 'human delegate.' That could be anyone."

"Exactly," said Lushiku. "She's human and has a ticket in her name. She's the defacto delegate." He looked at the vampires, flashing his teeth again. "I said release her."

This time, they complied. I rushed to grab the nightmare, only to be stopped short. Again.

"Now, now, you should know better." Lafayette crushed me against his chest, arms around me like iron bands. "Like you said, you touch him, you die. This is for your own protection. Besides," he leaned in and sniffed deeply, "you smell fantastic."

Replying with colorful invectives made one old-fashioned looking creature at a nearby table stare at me with horror. I didn't care.

Lafayette laughed, unmoving as I squirmed.

"Let me go," I demanded through clenched teeth.

"I rather enjoy this, actually," Lafayette said, pulling me against him. "It's a little like holding a fish, if I remember my human days accurately."

"I'll remind you what gutting a fish looks like as soon as you let me go."

"Enough," said Lushiku. "Lafayette's right to protect you, Miss Kelley, though his methods are...objectionable." The gorilla stared at the vampire, raising half of his imposing brow. "But, if you've sufficiently regained control, he will release you."

"I'm in control, but he," I pointed at the elusive nightmare, "will not get away again. I've been chasing him all over this goddamned city, and I will get my answers."

Lushiku put one heavy hand on the nightmare's shoulders. "You will get your answers. Will you agree to a truce if we guarantee this?"

Answers within reach, I relaxed as much as Lafayette would allow. "Yes," I said.

With Lushiku's gesture, Lafayette dropped me to my feet.

"Miss Kelley, please take your place at the table, and we'll continue. Gideon," Lushiku continued, "I believe we can call a brief recess so Miss Kelley can get her bearings."

"We have a tight schedule," the skeleton said.

"There's contingency time built in," Lushiku insisted, a thinly veiled warning in his tone. "I entreat the hosting council to spend some in honor of our new arrival. And," he leaned forward, his knuckles pressing against the ground as if preparing to attack the walking pile of bones, "I do not anticipate denial of such a reasonable request."

If Gideon had lips, the uptight skeleton would have pursed them.

Instead, he answered with a curt nod, pivoted on one heel, and walked to a podium several feet away.

Though the vampires didn't touch me again, they guided me to a table near the podium where humanoid servants prepared a place for me with a beautiful table setting. I sat, allowing one of the creatures to push in my chair for me.

Gyleeto stood off to one side, clutching his clipboard. As I took my seat, he tried to escape, but Lushiku stepped in front of him, personally pulling out a seat for the nightmare. The jittery creature evaluated his options, then sat out of my arm's reach.

Lushiku nodded, satisfied, and gestured to the seated nightmare. "As a show of good faith, Miss Kelley, we will join your table for the rest of the event."

The nightmare looked up, alarmed, lips trembling with protest. "But I have duties—"

"I will take responsibility," Lushiku interrupted. "I'm sure Zikros will understand."

The nightmare bowed his head and sat still, as if hoping to go unnoticed until dismissed.

Gideon stood behind the podium, his bony hand over the microphone as he conferred with another skeleton.

"Why'd you do it?" I asked the nightmare. "Why'd you hurt people?"

He winced, watching me out of the corner of his eye. "I'm sorry," he muttered.

"That's not what I asked." I leaned closer, and he retreated, but didn't leave the chair. "Why'd you do it? Why'd you touch those people? You killed the man in the airport. Riley's dying in the hospital. My friend's going to die because of you. Why'd you do it?"

The nightmare cowered, a tear glinting on his cheek. "I was hungry," he said, miserable.

"What?"

"Gentle creatures," Gideon tapped the microphone for attention, "our apologies for the interruption. We'll be getting back on track in a few minutes."

"What did you say?" I pressed.

Gyleeto looked up at me, his eyes shining with unshed tears. "I said I was hungry."

"You feed on people?"

"No," he said, "but it doesn't matter. I'll be destroyed for this."

"Why destroyed?"

"As an example," he snorted. "For causing an inter-dimensional incident."

"What is the meaning of this?"

I turned toward the source of the imperious voice. A red-skinned, horned creature wearing a tuxedo stormed into the room. Apart from the stylish, well-fitted suit, tailored black shirt, and satin bow tie, he looked like a demon stereotype.

Gyleeto slunk down in his seat, muttering, and I realized who the creature must be. The head of the nightmare council. "Your boss?" I asked.

The trembling nightmare nodded, hiding his eyes behind his hand.

"Master Zikros, so glad you were able rejoin us," Lushiku said, rising from his seat. "Allow me to introduce—"

Zikros scowled at him and sneered at me. "I'm not wasting my time meeting some human. What I care about is that you've circumvented my direct orders to my staff." The heated glare he leveled at Gyleeto made me as uncomfortable as the cringing nightmare.

Lushiku straightened, his words crisp, his tone sharpening. "I assure you, your associate's in service of the Compact."

"We're hosting the Compact. That's service enough." Zikros snapped his fingers. Gyleeto sprang to his feet, nearly toppling the chair to scurry behind the demon creature. "Over-reaching self-importance like this is why movements like ours gain momentum across all dimensions. You are nothing yet assume yourself of greater standing than you deserve. No creature from the earthly plane can stand up for itself—even against creatures from their own realm." Zikros towered over Lushiku, sneering. "A worthless plane of livestock with delusions of grandeur."

"Each dimension serves a purpose, and none can exist without the others. Even your dimension cannot exist on its own."

"No," Zikros said, grinning, "but it would thrive without the restrictions imposed on it by this Compact. My people are condemned to starve while this lot," he gestured at me, "overburden their planet and endanger not only themselves, but every other realm. If humans were the superior beings they believe themselves to be, maybe they should start keeping their numbers manageable and lifestyles sustainable. Maybe then we, the more responsible realms, wouldn't be forced to seek alternative measures of control."

Hesitant applause started in the back of the room, paused, and resumed, gaining support before rising conversation drowned it out.

"This is not the time to debate your agenda," Lushiku said calmly.

"Of course it is," Zikros said. "Because even the presence of this human and her essence is unnecessary torture for all of my kind." His nostrils flared as if to prove the point. "There's a reason they weren't invited and that you've chosen to undermine the choices of the host council is a personal insult."

"She was invited, Master Zikros," Gideon said.

I hadn't heard him approach, but the skeleton stood behind Lushiku, wringing his bony hands and almost bowing.

"What. Did. You. Say?"

Even I shivered.

"She's on the list," Gideon whispered. "She has a ticket."

Zikros turned his burning eyes on me. "Let me see it."

"Nice to meet you, too. My name's Caitlin Kelley." I leaned back in the chair. "I assume from the conversation you've had around me that yours is Zikros, so that's what I'll call you."

The crunch of his grinding teeth broke the silence with chilling dissonance.

Maybe someday I'd recognize those line-crossing moments before they happened.

"I don't give a damn what your name is. Show me your ticket."

"Hospitality, much?" I reached for my purse. "Haven't traveled beyond my plane before, but I bet this'll be my least favorite." A second later, I popped the clasp and tossed him the coin.

He inspected it, his sneer deepening into a disgusted frown. The roaring, inarticulate sound he made didn't make much sense, but it made the elegantly dressed creatures around me cringe and cover listening orifices.

Gyleeto came at a run, clipboard in hand. Zikros snatched it and compared the text on the coin to the list. Then, turned on me. "Where did you get this? Who put you up to this?"

Lushiku inserted himself between us. "Master Zikros, I must insist—"

"I am head of the hosting council, and I dictate how this goes. Sit down and shut up, monkey."

In a terrifying sneer, Lushiku bared his fangs and growled.

"Boys, boys, put them away." An elegant, soothing, yet amused voice joined the chaos.

My head ached. All I wanted was a nap, and the longer this went on, the more complicated it got. I rubbed my temples and tried to see around the vampires.

The voice belonged to a woman in a stylized, fitted tuxedo. A top hat perched on her wild mane of dark curls, a long, thin cigarette holder balanced between the index and middle finger of her left hand. "There's no need for a pissing contest in polite company."

Neither Lushiku nor Zikros moved. Lafayette and George stepped back to flank her.

I stood, offering my hand. "Caitlin Kelley, unwelcome human addition to the Compact."

She smiled, glanced at my hand without taking it, and smiled. "Be careful who you offer your hand to, Hunter." With an elegant gesture, she indicated Zikros and his cowering associate, "Especially in mixed company." ₁

Recognizing the wisdom in her words, I retracted my hand in the least awkward way I could. "Right," I said. "I'm sorry, I didn't catch your name."

"Because I didn't give it." With a turn of her head, she dismissed me and focused on Zikros. "Zeke, you needn't be such a dick. You're giving us a bad name."

He gritted his teeth. "Your indelicacies do not amuse me, succubus. Learn your place."

She laughed, throwing her head back in delight. The top hat never budged, even when she straightened and dabbed at her eyes with a silken handkerchief. "You say that like I have some subordinate place. It's cute." Tucking the handkerchief in her breast pocket and arranging the point artfully, she continued, "Looking like the big guy doesn't make you the big guy." She patted his chest and addressed the cowering nightmare. "What did I miss?"

"Who are you?" I asked, disregarding propriety and manners in an attempt to follow what the hell was going on.

The elegant woman Zikros called a succubus raised one eyebrow and stared me down. "Are all hunters so rude?"

"I don't speak for all hunters. I'm trying to figure out what's going on."

She couldn't disguise her smirk as she sat and took a drag off her cigarette. "A little late for that, don't you think?"

"Mistress," Gyleeto's voice barely registered as a whisper, "may I be excused?"

"Have you eaten?"

He hung his head, as if in shame. "Yes, Mistress."

"Then, yes, you may go."

"I dismiss my people, not you, succubus," growled Zikros.

"And, my dearest, hot-headed, Zeke, I outrank you." She didn't deign to look at him. "I can, and will, dismiss who I choose, as I choose, so kindly fuck off."

Gyleeto waited beside her, looking between the two figures.

"Go." She shooed him away with a flick of her fingers. "Your assignment's in my room on the desk. I expect it done by dawn."

I glanced at my wrist out of habit, only to discover my watch had been replaced by a gemstone-encrusted bangle roughly the same size. If everything transformed when I stepped between the worlds, I hoped the transition gave me good fighting underwear, though I wasn't in any hurry to find out.

"Yes, ma'am," the nightmare said, hurrying off into the crowd.

"Excuse me," Gideon said, suddenly far less confident addressing the elegant woman, "may we resume the schedule?"

"I suppose that's why we're here, so let's get it over with."

"You will not derail my objectives," Zikros threatened, standing over her.

"Your objectives are stupid." The woman flipped open a portfolio placed in front of her by a humanoid servant. "And, as such, I'm not letting them proceed. As I mentioned, I outrank you, and when I object to your idiot policies, which I do, they won't be implemented."

Zikros sputtered, but words didn't manifest out of the sound.

"You might see the earthly realm as a hunting ground where you can glut your basest desires, but the fact of the matter is that we need them as much as they need us."

"Still right here," I said, trying to learn as much as possible from her double talk.

She glanced at me out of the corner of her eye but kept talking to Zikros. "Give me trouble, and I'll remove you from the council. Permanently. Understood?"

"Okay, look, I'm sure your in-fighting is delightful and entertaining for you, but I'm losing time here," I said. Sister Betty needed me to find an answer for healing soul ablation from a nightmare's touch and get back, plus we needed to stop the nightmare incursion from affecting more humans.

Zikros, Lushiku, and the woman looked at me. Gideon shuffled his feet. The flush I saw across his cheekbones had to be a trick of the lighting.

"My friend's dying because she got touched—"

"You'd have us starve, then?" Zikros demanded.

The succubus rolled her eyes. "Really, you are so dramatic, Zeke. No one's starving. There's plenty to feed our entire realm. It's the Collectors we need to worry about."

Zikros scoffed.

"Again, still here." I stood to get attention this time.

It didn't work.

"My realm will not be destroyed to preserve human livestock." Zikros addressed the gathering. "Any who deny my people access to the human realm for feeding will share their fate."

Anger and arguments swelled around us.

"And you, Miss Kelley," Zikros whispered, leaning so close, I felt heat radiating off his red skin, "if you interfere, I'll make sure you're last to die."

29

Hot-headed. Reactionary. Impulsive. Reckless.

These words have all been used to describe me at one point or another. Individually, they don't paint a flattering picture, but they explain why I often get in trouble. They also explain how I manage to get out of fights alive, especially when shit gets weird.

And shit got weird in the ballroom.

Whether I saw or felt the vampires move to capture me is irrelevant, but somehow, I dodged the right way. They overcorrected and tackled Zikros instead. The demon-looking nightmare howled with rage as the two bloodsuckers scrambled off him. He popped up like an evil jack-in-the-box into the face of a hissing succubus who kneed him in the junk.

Weaponless yet again—though neither by choice nor oversight—I ducked under the table and crawled to the other side.

"What is the meaning of this nonsense?"

I jumped and knocked my head on the table before I emerged through the trailing tablecloths. First, I saw Lushiku's hairy legs, but beyond him stood Helen, swathed in cream-colored silk slightly lighter than her hair. Fists perched on her slender hips, a shimmery pink ribbon trailed from her right, pulled taut by a snarling Fenrir.

The vampires, Lafayette and George, disappeared.

Zikros seemed to forget the translucent opal-colored stone knife the succubus held at his throat as he faced the massive, growling wolf-dog. "Lady Helen."

"I'm waiting," she prompted, then looked at his captor. "Violetta?"

Violetta smiled. Neither her grip on Zikros or her knife faltered. "Lady Helen. I heard you were in town. So glad you were able to join us."

Helen crossed her arms, more of Gleipnir sliding through her fingers to give her demi-god brother, Fenrir, a little more leash. She flicked a lazy gesture at Zikros. "What's this about?"

"A disagreement, my lady, nothing more." Violetta pulled Zikros closer. "My colleague threatened an honored guest, and—"

"I see no guest," Helen said with such affected boredom, I expected her to yawn.

Violetta glanced at the table, holding Zikros. "She must have, um, stepped out."

"You lost her?" Amusement, this time from Helen.

A black, leathery hand appeared in front of my face. Lushiku helped me to my feet before drawing attention to me. "Miss Kelley is right here, Lady Violetta."

"Great." She pressed the knife against his throat. "Zeke wanted to apologize for being inappropriate."

Zikros sneered in defiance and glared at me. "I don't apologize to livestock."

The iridescent blade drew a trickle of blood that looked black as it ran down his red throat. "You are so rude, Zeke, and I've had it with your impertinence." She wiggled the blade, and he winced. "My apologies, Lady Helen, Miss Kelly. Neither Zeke's agenda nor his behavior represent our dimension."

"If I'd known this was going to be such a savage event, I wouldn't have worn white." Helen tugged Gleipnir, and Fenrir took a reluctant step backward.

"I assure you, my lady," Violetta struggled to restrain Zikros as he fought her grip, "this isn't the tone we wish to set. As soon as Zeke *calms the fuck down*, this will all be over."

Fenrir sat at Helen's feet, his ears flicking, eyes wide and alert.

Helen glanced down at the massive wolf with the raised fur. "If Fenrir can be controlled, I don't understand why you cannot control Zikros. Then again," she turned to me so slowly, it gave me chills, "Miss Kelley's quite the polarizing figure. Especially when driving her agenda."

I managed a smile and half-bow in her direction. "Nice to see you again, too, Helen. You look lovely."

She scanned me with indifference and turned to Violetta. "How long before we resume business? I have other, more important, engagements to attend."

"But this affects your world, too, Helen." I stepped forward, restrained by Lushiku's extended arm in front of me. "He's trying to exploit our realm."

Helen raised an eyebrow and laughed delicately. "*Our* realm, Miss Kelley?"

"Well, yes," I said. "Earth."

"That is hardly 'my' realm."

"But you live there. You have businesses there."

"I spend time and conduct business in many dimensions. Earth isn't particularly special."

"But it should be." Lushiku's arm allowed me one step forward as she turned away. Fenrir lunged to his feet, teeth exposed, his growl so low, I felt it more than heard it.

"And why is that?"

Whether right or wrong, I spit out the only answer that came to mind. "Human souls populate the underworld. Without them, you'd have no kingdom to rule."

Her thin eyebrow arched. "You think Earth's the only realm feeding my kingdom?"

A stone dropped into my gut from somewhere inside. I had nothing else to offer.

She tugged Gleipnir and turned away. "I've had enough."

"What about the nexus?"

A murmur rippled through the crowd. Helen stopped and turned. "What about it?"

"The New Orleans nexus is important to you. To all of you." I addressed the creatures in the ballroom. Even Zikros paid attention.

If only I had more to say.

"It's not the only one," Helen said, when I didn't go on. "Good night."

"Good night, Lady Helen," Violetta said, disappointment coloring her voice.

"Are you so bored with life you're willing to permit a massacre?" I demanded.

Helen's eyes flashed as she glared at me despite her eerie control. "Excuse me?"

Lushiku's arm pressed against my abdomen but didn't yield as I leaned forward. "You're deliberately ignoring a threat to humanity because it doesn't interest you. You're willing to sacrifice an entire planet—"

She laughed. Helen actually laughed. "Humans are so theatrical and dramatic. When will you and your kind learn, Miss Kelley, that you are not the top of the so-called food chain? That your existence is insignificant? That the pantheon hasn't considered you once since you made your passion for self-destruction abundantly clear? Why bother delaying the inevitable?"

"There's more to humanity than a self-destructive minority. Some people work for the good of others, to protect others, and to save them when they're in danger."

"And you see yourself as one of these people?" she asked.

"Sure." I made eye contact with Zikros. "I fight things that snack on humans."

"Then why are you ignoring the threat of the Collectors?"

I'd heard the name before, several times, yet knew nothing about them. "What do you mean?"

"That self-sacrificing, 'save the world' drive only extends to personal causes, then?" She cocked her head, a waterfall of hair cascading over the left side of her face. "Only for saving the woman you love?"

"That's not what I—"

"You didn't have to, my dear," she said. "If you're content to ignore the bigger threat to pursue the one affecting you personally, that's your choice. But don't plead for philanthropic assistance."

Of course, that's when it happened.

Helen turned her back, Fenrir leading her away. Lushiku turned to address Gideon. Violetta looked at me and opened her mouth to speak.

Zikros seized his opportunity.

In her moment of distraction, Violetta's hold slackened enough to relieve the pressure of the blade on Zikros's throat. He folded in half, jammed his fist in Violetta's stomach, then slammed his head into her face.

The knife clattered to the floor.

Violetta collapsed, her air gone. Zikros and I dove for the iridescent stone knife, the beads and sequins of my dress catching as I scrambled across the carpet. I cursed and pushed harder, my fingers folding around the bone handle an instant before his. Zikros screamed for Lafayette and George, though neither appeared. I rolled as he lunged, dress sticking like Velcro to the carpet as I ducked under the table again.

My arms wrapped around the table's center support a heartbeat before his fingers caught the hem of the dress and yanked. Threads popped, and the straps dug into my shoulders, threatening to break. Unable to pull me out completely, he crawled toward me, only to have his attack interrupted by an angry silverback gorilla pummeling his back.

I scrambled from under the table, kicking off my shoes and retreating a few steps to watch the beating, knife in hand.

Violetta knelt on all fours, her top hat askew as she retched and fought to reclaim her air.

Helen watched with feigned boredom, her slightly narrowed eyes betraying her interest.

Lushiku pounded on Zikros with animal fury, and I wondered if Zikros would survive.

"STOP!" Gideon screamed.

Everything fell silent.

The skeleton twisted his fingers nervously, but he stood with more poise than I would have expected amidst such chaos. "This is highly irregular." His voice jangled with nerves. "Guests of the Compact should not behave in such a manner."

Zikros roared and thrashed, and Lushiku pinned him to the ground, though it required his entire body weight and all his focus.

I crouched at Zikros's side, careful to avoid his touch. The blade flashed as I lowered it to his throat. "You know livestock stampede and kill ranchers, right, Zeke?"

He spat, though most of it splashed right back in his face. "I will hunt you down, then your family, your friends, and feed them to my people while you watch. When you have watched me exterminate the entire human race, then, I will savor your death slowly. You—"

The knife literally cut off his words.

His mouth moved, finishing the sentence before surprise washed over him and the blood ran out of him.

"You killed him." Violetta bent over me, sounding pained as she held her stomach.

"I'm a hunter. He threatened my family. My world. And me." I handed her back her knife and stood. "No matter what you did, he wouldn't have changed. It was in his eyes."

She nodded and took the blade. "I'd have done the same."

I looked at her. "How do I save the people who are dying from this?"

"I'll dispatch healers to those who have been touched."

A rock lifted off my heart. "They'll survive? Return to normal, soul restored and all?"

She smiled the way adults smile at worried children. "Yes, they'll be fully restored. It's typically an accidental affliction, and when reported, reversed as quickly as possible."

I thanked her and provided the information they'd need to reach Riley, Sister Betty, and scribbled a quick note of introduction and instruction. "There's at least one more we haven't found yet."

"Once you find them, we'll heal them as well." She beckoned a humanoid runner, gave instructions in a language I couldn't identify along with the note.

"Now what?" I asked.

Violetta shrugged and gestured to Gideon. "We recess for body removal and a quick cleaning, then get back to work."

"Another day at the office?"

"Something like that," she said with a smile.

"Do you, Hunter, consent to represent the humans in this Compact unless death prevents you from doing so?"

Staring into Gideon's dark eye sockets reminded me of Madame Sabine's tarot card. I suppressed a shiver and turned to Lushiku. "Isn't there a better representative for the human world than me?"

Low conversation rippled through the room. Creatures turned to at each other. Some with waving eyestalks looked at many creatures at once. Tentacles, teeth, fur, wings, and scales stood out against elegant evening wear, yet everywhere I looked, I saw disapproval, doubt, and fear.

Lushiku's eyes flashed amber, and he bowed to Gideon. "If I may speak to the Compact."

With a graceful nod and a sweep of his tuxedoed arm, the skeleton master of ceremonies yielded the floor.

"Gathered members of the Compact," Lushiku's deep voice boomed through the speakers, "I represent the Hidden Earth clans of the Indo-African region." I repeated the name to myself to try to remember. "The Hunter is here not by designation of the humans, nor by members of the

Compact." Another scattering of whispers. "To their ways, and many of ours, this isn't considered fair representation, but the events that brought her to us make her the representation humans need."

A few claps from the back. Though I strained to see into the shadows, I couldn't make out where they came from.

"This Hunter pursued a threat to her people through a foreign city, defended the vulnerable, and seeks to save those affected by unsanctioned feedings by nightmares."

"She'll kill us if she stays," cried a voice from somewhere in the middle of the room.

Noises and murmurs of assent followed.

"She killed Zikros. What else will she do, if given a chance?" Another voice from the back corner of the room.

Lushiku waited for the whispers to stop. "Zikros threatened her tribe, her world, and her person. How would you react?" Applause peppered the low hum of conversation. "The human realm is vulnerable to almost every other realm, and where the barrier becomes too thin to ignore, the humans need hunters to protect them against rogue elements."

"Why should we?" asked an angry growl of a voice.

"Like any ecosystem, when one realm fails, we all fail." Violetta managed to sound indifferent, even bored, though her words spawned cries of alarm. One creature sobbed dramatically.

Lushiku waited, but only for a moment before raising his voice to reclaim his audience's attention. "Additionally, the former representative of the nightmare council betrayed the agreements established by this very Compact and overpowered his superior who tried to control him, thus subjecting the realm to censure under the rules of failed, attempted coup until such time as stability can be re-established and proven."

Violetta sat up straight, rigid in her chair as she stared up at Lushiku, her lips tightening into a knot. A flush of color darkened her pale chest, neck, and flamed at the tips of her ears. As I watched the muscles in her jaw twitch, I had no doubt she'd have words with Lushiku after this speech.

"This hunter protected us, though some of us depend on her realm for sustenance."

Lounging against back into her chair, Violetta studied her manicure as the murmuring continued. The tight clench of her jaw hinted at the lie in her posture.

"Imagine she wasn't here," Lushiku continued, "and we were vulnerable to their feeding. Would you still deny the need for a protector?"

A gasp. Horrified whispers. Reluctant assent.

Violetta cast a dour glance at Lushiku, eyebrows raised, arms crossed over her chest, the corner of her mouth twisted in a sour pucker.

Definitely would be words. Maybe projectiles.

Lushiku noticed and changed tactics. "What if vampires threatened us the way the nightmares threatened humans?"

A wave of motion parted the crowd, revealing the vampire's table at its center. Another beautiful woman looked up askance, Lafayette and George standing behind her. George made a nearly imperceptible shift toward a jewel-encrusted ceremonial blade on his hip, which I hadn't seen earlier. If I hadn't been concerned another fight might break out, I'd have laughed at the absurdity of a vampire carrying a weapon.

"But," Lushiku quickly added with a slight bow for the vampires and another for Violetta, "they abide by the laws and agreements that preserve the balance between worlds."

George relaxed, and the preternatural stillness seeped out of the woman in front of him. Violetta nodded, her eyes closing briefly in acknowledgement. My relief turned to revulsion when I caught Lafayette's rakish grin, the tip of his tongue sliding across his lips.

A green-skinned creature with a massive, slicked blue-black pompadour stood, and I couldn't help but wonder if the mile-high hair hid horns. "You're asking us to permit a hunter to stalk us while we struggle to survive and punish us for sating our needs."

"No," Lushiku said. "I'm asking for a new accord, for new negotiations to govern the Compact and the business that crosses worlds."

Hesitant applause grew louder as creatures voiced their approval.

"As appointee to the council representing the humans of the Earth realm, Caitlin Kelley, Hunter, has the support of the Hidden Earth clans of the Indo-African region."

I tried to memorize what he said to tell Marty and Sister Betty later, but my brain hiccupped trying to digest the meaning. "Wait, I'm supposed to speak for all humans?"

Even in the primate's face, I read irritation. "Are you not a protector of humans? Do you not already speak for them in matters concerning higher beings?"

Higher beings.

I held my tongue.

Another day, another miracle.

To be the sole voice for the humans in this Compact "until death prevented" me from doing so? Anyone from DEMON or even the Church would be better prepared to take on this role. It required a certain diplomatic flair, of which I had a demonstrable lack. I hadn't been in this room more than an hour before I killed someone. An important someone. Well, formerly important. Still, what kind of credibility could I have after that? "There are more—"

"She speaks for the humans."

Helen's crisp, aristocratic pronunciation rang through the ballroom.

The crowd didn't exactly part, but people turned in their seats toward her shadow-swaddled table. Guillaume stood behind her, offering his hand as she rose. Her hair swept across half her face. "She transacts on their behalf and has the vote of the pantheon."

Maybe things got interesting for her after all. I wished for my headset, for Marty's nimble, detail-capturing fingers. I dug my fingernails into my palm, forcing my sleep-deprived brain to remember the conversation.

Lushiku nodded, his black and gray fur gleaming.

"And the vote of the queen," the female vampire said from her spot in front of the vampire thugs. The queen? Queen of the vampires? Catherine? Sister Betty mentioned her in a briefing, but I only knew her reputation. Queen Catherine couldn't know me. How could she vote for me? Part of me wondered what these leaders knew.

"With three votes of support, the referendum is presented to the floor." Gideon returned to the podium.

Within moments, I heard my name across the room. Dozens of... appendages rose until the room filled with a sea of human hands, paws and claws, a few tentacles, and even a flipper or two, if the light wasn't playing tricks on me. When the master of ceremonies called for dissent, the only hesitant hand in the air belonged to Gyleeto, the frat-boy man/nightmare I'd been chasing since I landed in New Orleans.

Gideon turned toward me, and I looked into the black void where his eyes should be. "Congratulations, Caitlin Kelley, Hunter, and Human Representative of the Compact." With a sweeping gesture, he indicated the table in front of the podium where a humanoid servant placed a leather portfolio. "Please join us, and we'll continue."

I sat, thanking the tuxedoed shade who pulled out my chair and helped me slide it in.

"Congratulations." Lushiku leaned over to whisper in my ear.

"Thanks, I think." Before he stepped away, I touched his arm. "I have a question."

He nodded with a quiet grunt.

I beckoned him closer, leaning in to whisper. "What did you do with my panties?"

His chortling animal laughter drew the room's attention. He shook his head and returned to his table with long, swinging strides that alternated between feet and fists.

Definitely pervy.

I opened the leather portfolio in front of me as Gideon called the Compact to order. Cooper was gonna be so pissed when he found out.

30

Sleep transformed our entire team as much as Deacon Paul and Father Callahan transformed the old office in St. Louis Cathedral. Only the old green carpet and the tiny door to the arsenal of weapons remained from its previous inhabitant. In place of Father Robicheau's imposing wooden monstrosity of a desk stood a smaller, modern, modular workspace with cabinets, shelves, and plenty of space for multiple chairs. Behind the desk, a new bookcase, already filled with Father Callahan's most important reference books. Comfortable chairs, couches and small tables made it welcoming.

Father Callahan put his book on the desk and stood as we entered. "Glad to see the two of you well rested."

"A little sleep works wonders." I handed him the bag of beignets we'd bought on the way. Sister Betty put the paper tray of coffee cups on the table. "A few more nights like that, and I might feel partially human."

Father Callahan hugged Sister Betty, asked about her stitches, and offered her a chair.

She dismissed his comments with a half-smile and removed the five cups from the tray.

Watching them, emotion clotted in my throat. I'd come close to losing Sister Betty twice in less than a week. Marty'd been hurt. Father Callahan only narrowly missed being bitten by a hydra. The longer they stayed close to me, the more they got hurt, the closer they got to dead.

And yet, they endured it. They volunteered to stay. Not even my parents did that.

"I'm glad you both decided to stay." I tried not to sound as awkward as I felt.

"Where else would we be, Caitlin?" Father Callahan took his seat, leaning as far back as his ergonomic chair would allow. "Regional monster hunter's a complicated, difficult job, and you'll need help keeping such a massive territory in line."

I nodded and claimed a coffee cup before I slid into a chair. Cooper leveraged my new role with the Compact to convince me to accept the regional monster hunter position covering the south from the Tallahassee to San Antonio and everything in between. A massive territory indeed. Riding a motorcycle like Sister Evangeline didn't seem so eccentric when you saw the lines on the map.

"Someone has to keep an eye on you, wild child." Something in Sister Betty's teasing tone belied the seriousness of the sentiment, or maybe something in her steel-blue eyes. Either way, she meant it. She intended to keep me safe, even if only from my own bad decisions. It wasn't the reason I wanted her to stay, but I'd take it.

"Really, we owe it to Father Robicheau for so conveniently vacating his position for me," Father Callahan said with humorless smirk.

Sister Betty hung her head. She had to be thinking about Sister Evangeline, the hunter Father Callahan murdered for his twisted beliefs. "At least some good will come of his crimes," she said, softly.

Father Callahan cleared his throat. "Marty stepped out with Cooper, but they'll be right back." He picked up the grease-spotted paper bag, rolling the edges back, and sniffed inside. "I thank God for beignets."

"Until you eat them with that on." I gestured at his black frock shirt.

"Rumor has it you'd know." He winked at me.

"That might or might not be true," I admitted with a laugh.

They smiled at me, and I felt an inkling of confidence return. With them here while I took on Sister Evangeline's old territory, maybe I wouldn't screw this up. Maybe I had a shot at keeping the list in my head short, never adding another innocent victim's name to it.

When I shook off the thought, they were both staring at me. Sister Betty looked expectant and concerned, but Father Callahan beamed with pride.

They looked at me the way I wanted my parents to look at me. Like they had before Shannon's death ripped a hole in my family.

I picked at the paper coffee cup, trying to swallow the sudden lump in my throat. "Seriously, thank you for staying."

Cooper and Marty's conversation about the relative merits of Marvel over DC preceded their entrance, and not even juggling plastic bags and Styrofoam containers interrupted it.

"Yeah, but Marvel has Black Widow and Scarlet Witch, and you can't say they aren't badass. Ask Cee." Marty deposited his load of breakfast containers on the table. "She 'ships them and, if you think about it, they're a more dynamic duo than DC has dreamed up." He shot me a look. "They're the perfect match."

A hot blush raced to the tips of my ears so fast, I thought I might pass out.

"There's so much wrong with that, I don't even know where to start." Cooper placed his stack of Styrofoam containers on the table. "Breakfast is served."

Marty sat beside me. I elbowed him hard as I reached for plastic utensils. "How about you let me fly my nerd flag, instead of flying it for me."

He rubbed his side. "Sure, beat up a friend trying to help."

"Uh huh." I pulled the lid off my coffee and set it aside.

"Hello?"

We all turned, but I knew the voice. An earthquake of nerves started in my heart and radiated through the rest of me.

"Officer Boudreaux," Father Callahan said in his most genial, pleasant voice, "how can we help you this morning?"

Boudreaux filled the doorway, smiling at each of us in turn. The expression widened when he locked eyes with me. "Deacon Paul said you'd be in here. I hope I'm not interrupting." He lifted a brown paper bag. "I brought beignets. The good ones."

"Please, join us," Father Callahan said. I reached back and dragged the nearest chair to where we clustered around the table. "We just sat down for breakfast."

Boudreaux smiled and strode across the room, handing Marty the grease-spotted bag before sitting beside me. Under the shuffle of the others passing plastic utensils, food containers, and coffee, he leaned close and whispered, "How about that date?"

"Are you asking me out, Officer Boudreaux?" I bit the inside of my cheek to control the grin and avoided looking at him.

"What if I am?"

"Then, officer, I'd be afraid you'd arrest me if I said no." I popped the plastic fork out of its sealed package, glancing at him out of the corner of my eye.

"Then how about I ask you as Rene Boudreaux?" He grinned, a devilish glint in his eye.

Curse him for such pretty eyes and nerve-wrangling smile.

I hurried to answer before the quiet settled around us. "Then I'd say yes."

"Good." He peeled foil off some kind of breakfast burrito. "That's the way I like to start my mornings."

"How's that?" Sister Betty asked, leaning around Marty.

"With coffee," I said before he could answer.

He sipped from his cup, almost spilling it as he tried to nod.

Sister Betty frowned, skeptical as Marty, Father Callahan, and Cooper shared confused glances.

"So," I pulled a notebook across the table, starting the meeting, "what do we know about the Collectors?"

THE END

III

TROUBLE IN MIND

3 1

I am not a diplomat. If asked, Sister Betty, my friend and badass mentor, would laud my general combat skills then argue that anyone else on the planet would be better suited to handle conflicts requiring tact, level-headedness, or verbal restraint.

She did, in fact, make that exact argument.

Multiple times.

With Father Callahan as they argued behind closed doors in the rectory of the St. Louis Cathedral.

After my accidental and dramatic entrance into supernatural politics via literally stumbling into the trans-dimensional conclave of creatures known as the Compact two weeks ago, the dynamic pair that guided my monster hunting argued passionately (and regularly). The rectory doors muffled little of what they said, especially at their peak volume. More than once I caught Sister Betty emphasizing my "increasingly reckless behavior" only to be countered by Father Callahan's overstatement of my strengths.

Their "discussions" centered on one question: whether or not I should lead another meeting of supernatural community leaders. A smaller scale Compact, but more informal. A get-to-know-and-trust-me kind of meeting, an "I'm from the Church and here to *help*," kind of introduction. I don't know if they came to an agreement or if Sister Betty yielded to the inevitable. Either way, instead of lounging poolside with a book or sucking down a voodoo daiquiri at Lafitte's Blacksmith Shop with my current distraction, Officer Rene Boudreaux, I ended up at the head of a massive oval table in a nondescript hotel conference room attempting to call an unruly gathering of cryptids to order.

Again.

Not for the first time today, I wished for a hammer or some other melee weapon. Instead, I tapped my water glass with a pen. "I need everyone's attention, please."

Spoiler alert: I didn't get it.

The raucous assembly included familiar creatures from the diminutive sprite sitting cross-legged on the edge of the table, his wings fluttering with irritation, to the impressively muscled were in human form, her eyes glowing gold with barely contained aggression. Others, I couldn't identify, like Ibekta, who resembled some unholy mix of an afghan hound, snake, and shark. I'd never encountered a being like him before seeing him at the Compact, but if his kind lived in my territory, I needed to know why he jabbed a finger at a bored elf plucking split ends from her (or his?) long, butter-blond locks, and hopefully before I discovered what damage his jaws could do.

I raised my voice and tried again. "Please end the side conversations."

No one seemed to hear, though a few deigned to glare my direction because variety, I guess. Sister Betty's inscrutable expression revealed nothing when our eyes locked.

This was going exactly as anticipated, like every public speaking nightmare I'd ever had.

The meeting might have been a success had the conversation not inevitably returned to the missing supernats or the diminishing powers affecting all their communities. I'd redirected the conversation the first time, but as soon as I asked one question to determine how the Collectors infiltrated their respective realms, the proverbial shit hit the fan for the second time. Rational conversations devolved into micro-arguments between neighbors. Larger ones sucked in multiple participants, some across the length of the table. Accusations flew, starting with the human shaman accusing the dwarf of undermining his power. Literally. Something about mining some special kind of rock from under the shaman's house, but he didn't finish before the part-stone creature let loose a torrent of heavily accented words and jumped in his chair, walking in quick precarious circles in the slowly spinning office chair to continue slinging insults. I envied the chair's ability to swivel away from the madness.

If I hadn't already been questioning my life decisions that brought me here, I would be now.

A giant television at the end of the room displayed a grid of faces staring back at me. Creatures who couldn't physically attend the afternoon meeting filled the screen. The only friendly face staring back at me from among them belonged to Lushiku, the leader of the Hidden Earth clans from somewhere in the African jungle. In his gorilla form, the warmth of his smile triggered some kind of uncanny valley reaction, but I ignored it for the support he intended it to convey. I had plenty of detractors to deal with without alienating an ally. A member of the Sasquatch tribe who identified himself as the "sheeran," scowled in front of a thick copse of trees. I couldn't tell if he had resting Bigfoot face or some personal beef with me. In another square, a vampire studied me, his upper lip curled in distaste. Either was easier to watch than the mer-creature floating in a tank at the Audubon Aquarium a few miles away. Something about the light and the way the creature's distorted face drifted made me queasy.

"I need everyone's attention," I said, struggling to maintain ownership of my lunch. Even giving them a moment to settle, nothing around the table changed. The assault on my ears continued.

Enough.

I whistled through my fingers, a shrill dagger of sound cutting through the noise. The room fell silent; all eyes turned to me.

Faint forest noises from the TV and the whirr of computer fans filled the sudden silence. The human shaman sat. Even the elf lost interest in picking at their hair. With a protesting crunch of metal, the dwarf dropped into the chair, the sound of yet another charge for the Church's Visa.

Beside the tower of technology providing electronic access to this dumpster fire of a meeting, Marty, my partner and friend, winked encouragement, his curls bouncing with his tight nod.

"Thank you." I shifted from one pained foot to the other and surveyed the table. Only Ibekta remained standing. "Ibekta, let's table this. I'll schedule time on our next agenda."

Ibekta's scaled jaws snapped shut with a click. His long hair, or fur, swayed as he spun in my direction, one fist on his hip. His indrawn breath caught as I leveled the kind of authoritarian glare at him that Sister Betty used in the gym. Reluctantly, he slumped into his chair. Though I'd never seen a crocodile pout, I recognized the sour, if toothy, expression.

Everyone stared at me. The dress shoes Sister Betty insisted I wear pinched my toes and blistered my heels, but I didn't sit. I didn't dare. Bad things happened when I sat, namely a loss of crowd control. "It's been a long afternoon, and I appreciate everyone's patience."

Sister Betty nodded at the edge of my peripheral vision. Given her arguments against my role in this whole affair and the awkwardness between us lately, her approval felt good. Better than it probably should have, yet nothing lessened the pain of standing in these godawful shoes. My Doc Marten combat boots might never be appropriate for anything besides kicking monster ass, but they put me in a less stabby-punchy-kicky mood. We needed to have a serious discussion about functional fashion, especially after the toxic pink dress and non-combat-ready panties. Maybe I didn't mind her dressing me up as much as I said, but my patience, and pain tolerance, had limits.

Focus.

I glanced at the tablet on the table in front of me. "We've only got a couple items left."

A murmur rippled through the room again. On screen, a vampire I didn't recognize rolled his eyes and crossed his arms. Protruding fang tips dimpled his lower lip. Impatience betrayed his undead youth as much as his still-too-human fidgeting. Why had Queen Catherine sent an immature vamp as clan representative? I could only imagine what the baby bloodsucker would report. Another call to look forward to.

"This is ridiculous," grumbled the were-creature, her skin-tight polo sleeves straining against her muscular arms. "We will not share pack secrets with any hunter. It's insulting enough to attend pointless meetings like, like…humans." She spat the last word like a curse.

Given her oversized, albeit human, teeth, she'd likely transform into something predatory and bigger than I'd rather deal with in a confined space full of anxious supernats.

The presence of the sixteen-inch silver-edged Bowie knife secured under the table eased my anxiety. Relaxing my shoulders, I visualized drawing the blade, sliding across the table, and sinking the point into something squishy. I wouldn't provoke her transformation, or allow anyone else to, but if it happened, I'd be ready.

If I got a shot, that is.

Two seats closer and heavily armed under her black tunic, Sister Betty would get first crack. As fast as I could be, she usually beat me.

"Meetings aren't uniquely human communication tools," teased Violetta, the leader of the nightmare council as she swiveled toward the snarling were-woman. With an almost flirtatious smile, Violetta flicked a stray curl out of her face. "At least amongst the civilized."

Though it had little effect on the were, that smile had me wondering if Violetta's lineage actually included succubi. Her boss had called her a succubus, but I hadn't found out if he intended to insult or call her out before I'd killed him. And since the focus of my hunt had shifted away from the nightmare that had caused so much havoc, I hadn't had time to learn more about them or their culture. Asking outright might be considered rude, so I hadn't asked. Vampires got touchy about that kind of thing, especially if they considered your tone smug, but then again, bloodsuckers got bitchy about hierarchy.

With a menacing growl, the were-whatever rose and leaned across the table, shoulders hunched, the fabric of her shirt straining as her muscles swelled.

Violetta laughed and waved an elegant, thin-fingered hand. "Down, girl."

"Enough." Irritation sharpened my words.

All eyes snapped to me again.

"Squabbling won't stop the Collectors from hurting your communities."

Around the table, heads bowed. The sprite shuddered. Something sparkly fell from his wings but disappeared before it hit the table.

"You may have your," I floundered for the word, "disagreements, but set them aside. For your survival."

Creatures glanced at each other, animosities and arguments temporarily forgotten. The were-creature turned to the gnome beside her, leaning down to speak as privately as possible in the crowded room. Even the deceptively human representative of the Heavenly Host chatted with Ibekta. On screen, almost all the participants typed, some at inhuman speed.

Nothing fosters solidarity like shared dissent.

Whatever it took, I had to get them to cooperate. Everything depended on it, and probably more than they realized. We'd run out of other options, and as long as the disappearances continued, as long as the loss of powers among them destabilized the divisions between dimensions and worlds, the Collectors threatened us all.

Since I'd crashed the massive gathering of the supernatural community known as the Compact and taken the position of Regional Monster Hunter left vacant by the death of Sister Evangeline, my team and I had tapped every available resource. I'd approached the local but reclusive Ursuline Convent. They promised cooperation and support, yet provided little of either, which sent Marty and I library delving and ransacking online databases. Sister Betty tapped her Order, the Holy Order of the Sisters of Mercy of Saint Brendan, for their extensive arcane archive. Father Callahan reached out to his contacts, including the Sisters of the Sword, Sister Evangeline's order. As far as our net stretched, we only turned up a handful of tangential references, none of them substantial or actionable. Not even the Lore Keeper, the most mysterious and knowledgeable member of the Catholic Church, had anything useful.

Attempts to talk with individual supernat leaders only heightened their distrust, and really, I didn't blame them. My questions exposed weaknesses, and no one could ignore who asked. The Monster Hunter. The one who killed a hostile nightmare clan leader in the middle of the Compact. The one with the reputation for quietly taking down the biggest, baddest creatures around. The hired gun (and fists) of the Holy Roman Catholic Church.

Suffice to say I got nowhere fast. That these leaders even agreed to meet with me could be classified a miracle. But as we struggled to find some way to work together, more members of their communities got sick or lost their powers. Others simply disappeared. One vampire, a werewolf, a human magic user and his pet ghoul in the last four days alone. Some communities blamed me or my employer, but most simply closed ranks and shut up.

Every missing supernatural creature from my territory felt like a personal affront. Every report of sickness or lost abilities, an accusation. I'd memorized names of the inexplicably missing, of those ill or debilitated the loss of their powers. No matter how I ordered the list, no pattern emerged. And while I yearned for something tangible to fight, communities suffered, rendered vulnerable to everything from reduced fertility to the threat of human discovery because of their diminished ability to hide.

And now, those frustrated, scared dissenters stared at me and waited for me to say something brilliant. I had to find some way to convince them to open up, to trust me, the boogeyman of the stories they used to scare their kids into good behavior. If I didn't, I at least needed to get them to come back to the table next time to try again. Not that I wanted to spend another afternoon embroiled in political wrangling, but I didn't see any other option. If the supernats cooperated at the Compact to keep their dimension-spanning territories stable, they could do the same to help me save them from the Collectors.

Or at least, I hoped they could. If they couldn't, I didn't know what to do next.

"Why haven't you stopped them?" A small voice cut through the noise.

There it was. The question I'd been asking myself for two weeks.

I fought the urge to cringe as I looked around the room. It took a moment to identify the speaker as the slender boy across from Marty. The waifish creature looked at me with wide, haunting eyes, his skin faintly green under the fluorescent lights. "Why haven't you stopped the Collectors?"

This boy wanted an answer I hadn't been able to give myself. Why the hell hadn't I caught whatever hunted these supernatural creatures? Why couldn't I find the threat to the safety and integrity of the city? My city. My territory. My responsibility.

Now that this inexpressibly sad child stared at me, the question weighed more. This child represented an entire clan of reclusive dryads that had taken refuge in the swamps of the Mississippi delta. Was he orphaned? The only one strong enough to attend? The magical drain affected supernats differently. How many in his community lay dying?

Guilt over my lack of answers plagued my sleepless nights, and now, his haunted eyes spurred it to new depths. There had to be a logic behind all of this, so why hadn't I figured it out? Shiny new job title or not, could I really consider myself a protector of the vulnerable if I couldn't deliver?

And how the hell would I live with myself if I failed?

My feet hurt; my legs ached. The bickering made my head throb. I wanted to sit, but I couldn't, especially not after that question. Instead, I looked at him. "I'm working on it," I said, the response lame even to me. "I know that's not a satisfying answer, but that's why I'm asking for information on your communities, your realms—"

"Why should we tell you anything?" A beautiful silver-haired woman wearing a crown of daisies stood. Her blue cheeks tinged purple as she flushed. "They," her hand whipped through the air at the were-creature, "will exploit it. What if they attack while your focus is elsewhere? How will you defend my people from the risk your questions expose them to?"

Muted agreement ricocheted through the room. The imperious woman stared me down. "What guarantee can you provide that you, or your kind, Hunter, will not use what you learn against us?"

I held up my hands to quell the rising voices. "I understand your concern." As often as I'd used it, the phrase felt hollow. "You have the assurance of the Church—"

An explosion of snorts and groans of frustration only confirmed I'd said the wrong thing.

"That's not good enough." The daisy-crowned woman's voice rose above the chaos. "You cannot protect us, Hunter, not even from your own kind."

———

"That was fun." I collapsed into a chair as the door shut behind the last departing supernatural creature. The small, electronic sounds from Marty's technology tower filled the empty room. "I get why the Compact only happens once every twelve years." Though this meeting hadn't come close to the same size, I had a new appreciation for the skills required to foster cooperation from such an assembly. Skills I most certainly did not possess.

"You did well." Sister Betty drew a leg up into her seat and leaned against the arm.

I propped my head on my hands and peered through my fingers. "Yeah. Okay."

"No, really, you did a good job."

I snorted and pressed my thumbs against the inner corner of my eye sockets. "By potentially starting an inter-species war? Sure, top notch."

Sister Betty patted my shoulder, but when I shifted away, she withdrew her hand. "Without the stringent bindings of an agreement like the Compact, all these factions walking out without missing appendages is remarkable."

My confusion pushed me upright to see her clearly. "You told Father Callahan I'd make a mess of this, and now that I've screwed it up, you're complimenting me?" I looked at her. "I'm dreaming, right? If you're part of my dream, you have to tell me."

"You're so dramatic, my padawan," she laughed.

Marty rolled his eyes, typing on his phone. "Learn to take a compliment."

Turning back to Sister Betty, our eyes locked, though I wanted to look anywhere else. "You said I couldn't manage a group of disparate, temperamental, and disagreeable creatures."

"That's not what I said," she said, exasperation eclipsing her patience. "You're capable. But for a first attempt, the stakes are an unfair burden."

I leaned back as far as the chair allowed. Everything hurt. From my head to my feet. Then, there was the exhaustion. Or weariness. Whatever. It gnawed my spine, and no amount of caffeine, sugar, exercise, or sleep dissipated it. No matter what I tried, it persisted and made everything harder.

"I'm proud of you, Caitlin."

Her words twisted my gut. She'd only said it twice before. The first time after narrowly defeating a bloodthirsty swarm of gremlins we'd flushed out of the British Royal Air Force base in Buckinghamshire. The second in Rome, me curled in her lap sobbing my heart out.

Until now, it had been easy, despite all we'd been through. Now, every day seemed more confusing than the one before. Her praise felt like another change in the rules of conduct. I didn't know how to act anymore. As much as I craved her touch, I couldn't bear it. Outside the gym, it made me flinch, but not out of fear or repulsion. More like self-defense. My internal organs twisted in nervous knots as our eyes tried to communicate while avoiding the landmines buried in our silence.

Our wordless struggle had to look batshit crazy to anyone else.

My phone rescued me with a buzz. I pulled it out of my pocket. "Sorry," I pushed away from the table, "this'll just take a second."

Sister Betty nodded, but Marty made kissing noises.

I flipped him off and walked away to answer it.

H i, beautiful."

My body flushed in response to the smile in Officer Rene Boudreaux's voice. Despite my responding smile, I ran a hand through my hair and huffed. "You wouldn't say that if you could see me."

"Doubt it." His accent made music of his words. "We still on for dinner?"

"Yeah, but let's say later and closer to the Quarter. Is that okay?"

"If it means spending time with you, sure."

"You're sweet." I glanced over my shoulder. At the paper-littered conference room table, Marty and Sister Betty seemed engrossed in conversation, but her posture told me otherwise. She might not hear every word, but she'd catch the gist. "I'll text you later."

"Sounds good. I'm at Royal Street Station. Traffic willing, I can be there in under ten."

"Barring any parades." They sprang up like unexpected summer storms and caused just as much traffic disruption.

"You're thinking second line," he said with a laugh. He'd explained the jazz processions celebrating everything from funerals to weddings, but the difference seemed a matter of semantics. Any time a procession of people and musicians filled the streets and choked traffic to a halt, it qualified as a parade. "But yes, traffic and second line willing."

"Alright. I'll text as soon as I can."

"Looking forward to it. Stay out of trouble," he teased.

"Not in this line of work." I said goodbye and returned to the table where my team stared at me. "What?"

"It's weird that you have a boyfriend," Marty said.

I rolled my eyes, ignoring the wriggle of embarrassment in my gut. "He's not my boyfriend. We've been on a few dates. That's all."

"And tonight?" Marty teased.

"Dinner." I busied myself straightening the papers in front of me.

"Hate to break it to you, Cee," he propped his chin on his hand and batted his eyelashes, "but you've caught a case of boyfriend."

"Enough." Sister Betty's jaw clenched. "You two taunt each other like twelve year olds."

"It amuses you." Marty closed his laptop with an impish grin. "Admit it." When Sister Betty looked away, he mouthed the words "she's jealous."

Without considering what he meant, I changed the subject. "Let's head back to the rectory and see if Father Callahan's made any progress."

Sister Betty agreed and swept the papers in front of her into a stack without regard to their direction. Seeing some upside down or even face down in the pile told me more about her state of mind than I wanted to acknowledge.

So, I didn't.

Marty broke down his tech tower, packing everything into padded cases. I walked around the table, pushed in chairs, and tried to clear my head. No matter how hard I worked, the Collectors remained elusive. In fact, the deeper I dug, the less I seemed to learn. We had rumors that conflicted about gangs of magic users roving the streets trying to take over the city, and others suggesting rogue operatives trying to start a supernatural war for fun and profit. Clans accused each other of being behind the disappearances, but the numbers didn't seem to support the claims. Maybe if I didn't chase an answer, the solution would appear. But the more I tried to not think, the more the image of Sister Betty's chaotic stack of papers intruded, underscored by Marty's silent comment.

W hat can I offer them?" I directed the question at both Father Callahan and Sister Betty as I paced his rectory office. "They don't trust me one on one yet refuse to designate anyone they do trust." I dug my fingers into my hair, pulling fistfuls to relieve my intensifying headache. "To make progress on the Collectors, I need info, but I can't get it without their trust, and I can't get their trust until I make progress. It's an infinite loop."

"There's got to be a way around it." Sister Betty gnawed her thumbnail.

"If there is, I don't see it," I said, exasperated and exhausted.

Father Callahan leaned back in his desk chair, hands behind his head as he stared at the ceiling. "Magical intervention can preserve secrecy."

Sister Betty's hand fell away from her mouth as she shook her head. "Not for a group, and Caitlin's not doing this alone."

Not only did I hate dealing with something as nebulous and fickle as magic, I'd already considered and dismissed magical secrecy. Magic, in general, had its uses, but I didn't trust it. Or magic users. Once, I'd infiltrated a guild of wizards trying to gain control of a state government and gotten burned by magic's limitations. Our contacts provided passwords, plans, and locations, and though we'd negotiated Sister Betty as my backup, when I attempted to share the information, the magic prohibited repetition. I'd managed to take down the guild on my own but scooped up our informants as co-conspirators under the auspices of protecting their cover. They might have been detained an extra day or two by the federal government's Department of Extradimensional Magical and Occult Nuisances, or DEMON for short, while a trusted coven evaluated their handiwork. Once the coven confirmed the magic acted as it should have, we released our informants, but I justified their extended stay as a penalty for not disclosing the limitations of our agreement.

"Let's keep looking," Sister Betty said. "Either we'll figure it out, or their people will demand action."

"I don't want to wait for that." I dropped into a chair.

"It's not our choice," she said.

Father Callahan sat up. "We have to accept their decision, even if it's doing nothing."

I didn't like it. Inaction endangered innocents. Innocents who lived in my territory. The people I swore to shield from predators. Every one of them was as much my responsibility as my team. Maybe more. Knowing I hadn't stopped the Collectors hunting in my territory was exquisite torture. If I could figure out how they got in, how they stole powers, how they abducted victims, I'd—

"Caitlin," Sister Betty said softly.

"What?" The interruption annoyed me, though I'd gain nothing from chasing the thought.

"If they choose to do nothing, you have to accept it."

"Doing nothing is stupid."

"I know. I agree." Her compassionate, patronizing smile infuriated me. "Even Cooper agrees, but—"

"Cooper agrees?" I disagreed with Sister Betty and Father Callahan on occasion, but not often. Agreeing with Agent Cooper Hardin from DEMON never happened. Since we'd met, he'd challenged nearly every decision I made, second-guessed every plan I presented. "Isn't that a sign of the impending apocalypse?"

"There are six other seals to worry about," Father Callahan said.

Sister Betty's expression didn't change, and she didn't acknowledge him. "It's not our place to impose. We support, we protect, we don't control."

"It's not enough," I said pushing back from the table so hard that my chair wobbled.

"Caitlin—"

"If what you're about to say has anything to do with accepting risk—"

"It wasn't," Sister Betty interrupted.

"Good, because I'm getting tired of making excuses for people getting hurt, or worse."

"What are you talking about?" Sister Betty stood, pushing her chair back. "Who's making excuses for people getting hurt?"

"We are." I pressed my hands against my skull to appease my throbbing headache. "We all are."

She argued, but I didn't listen. Nothing I said would change this argument. I could only nod and wait until she deemed the conversation over. If she sensed resistance, she'd persist until I yielded. My jaw muscles clenched as I waited her out.

I'd find another way to convince this community to let me save it.

I had to.

My list of the dead had too many names. I refused to add more.

Sister Betty followed me out of St. Louis Cathedral. "Where are you going for dinner?"

"Not sure." I glanced at her. "Rene picked somewhere."

"That's good." She nodded, but said nothing else as we walked through the nave. Before we stepped outside, she put her hand on my shoulder. "I'm happy you've found someone, Caitlin. You deserve a boyfriend."

"He's not my boyfriend." I resisted the urge to wriggle away. Rene provided a delightful distraction and some necessary, and rather athletic, stress relief, but little more than that. As much fun as we had in and out of bed, nothing we had would last. My heart wanted one person, but she'd set limits I had to respect. And until she decided to change that—

No. Daydreams wasted precious energy.

Besides, with everything out to kill me, denying myself those moments didn't make sense, even if I couldn't share them with the one I really wanted.

"This job..." She didn't look at me. "It wears you down in ways you won't expect. Seize happiness. Don't leave room for regret."

We'd had opportunities. Sparks when our eyes met. Innocent touches infused with enough electricity to light up a city. A kiss that nearly became more. A kiss I couldn't forget.

Then came her restraint. The threat of losing her soul and dying without it had shaken her, made her re-evaluate things. Her actions. Her commitments. Her vows and the demands of her faith.

And she created distance between us.

She'd found me venting my frustration on a punching bag, but instead of stepping in to give direction, she'd taken away my balance. No matter our relationship, no matter her feelings, she'd married the Church. Her vows didn't leave space for anyone else beyond her trainees. After she said what she needed to, she walked out of the gym, taking my heart with her and leaving me sitting on the mats alone.

But why bring up regrets now? Was bestowing her blessing some kind of peace offering? What did it mean?

I opened my mouth, but words failed.

She waited, but when I said nothing, she nodded. Her eyes darted away before they revealed anything. "You're going to be late," she said softly, and stepped into the stream of people leaving the church.

Was I happiness she'd seized, or a regret?

T ough crowd?" Rene Boudreaux asked as I slumped into the front seat of his car.

"You have no idea." Cool air poured over me as I latched the seatbelt and sank back.

"Your meeting or your team?"

I rested my hand on his thigh and closed my eyes. "Yes."

He covered my hand with his briefly before putting the car in gear and easing into traffic. "That kind of day."

"Yeah." I kept my eyes closed. "How was yours?"

"Fine."

The turn signal's tick didn't drown out my thoughts. Once they ground past the Collectors and rehashed Sister Betty's comments, I noticed his silence. Did he have little to say, or was he letting me process? Was he protecting me, or did he think me uninterested in his life?

I couldn't decide which felt worse.

The push and pull of navigating traffic lulled me, and I tried to set aside the million little crises taking up space in my head until after dinner. Or until after whatever followed dinner, if anything. There'd be time tomorrow to figure out how to fix things, starting with Sister Betty. She'd called me reckless more than once, and whether I agreed, her perception affected her trust in me. Gaining it had been hard enough the first time. I couldn't lose it. Proving I deserved it yet again would be nearly impossible and make finding the Collectors harder.

But no more. Not tonight, at least. Maybe if I stopped obsessing for a while, I'd have some epiphany. Stranger things had happened. In my life, I relied on stranger things happening.

Rene's fingers slid between mine. "Want to reschedule?"

"Nah, I just need a minute." A couple minutes wouldn't do much, but I could get it together enough to fake being okay, at least for him. He wouldn't be able to tell real okay from fake okay.

It should have bothered me that my first instinct involved faking something I couldn't feel. I didn't have the energy to explore it further. There'd be time to think about it later. After the Collectors. Until then, I could fake okay well enough to fool the people closest to me.

We crawled through traffic in silence. Not even the radio played. As if a bubble swallowed me whole, numbness enveloped me. The buzzy feeling in my nerves subsided to...nothing. Only the heat of Rene's hand in mine registered. My mind continued to spin, but on mute, a vortex of restless motion without sound.

If only it could stay like this.

The car rolled to a stop. I reluctantly opened my eyes.

A familiar yet not unpleasant knot clenched my gut as Rene smiled. "Hey, pretty lady."

Guilt ate at me, but I smiled back. I didn't deserve this break, not when so many suffered. Not when I should be working the damned problem. And he deserved someone…more. More available. More…whole. "Hey."

He lifted our joined hands and kissed the back of mine. "It's nice to see you smile."

"Thanks." Awkwardness replaced the retreating numbness. I focused on our hands.

Rene didn't seem to notice. "Have you been to Port St. Peter yet?" When I told him I hadn't, he said, "We could have walked, but I thought you might need time to decompress."

"You're sweet."

With that, we got out of the car and walked out of the concealed private parking lot. We turned down the street, weaving between pedestrians. His hand lighted on the small of my back as he stepped behind me to avoid a pack of women, one wearing a plastic tiara and glittery satin sash.

Drunken voices raised in song greeted us before we got close to the bar. Johnny Cash, Ring of Fire. Maybe it was the familiarity with the song, or maybe it was a bar tradition, but they sounded better than they should have.

"Hey, Sherrie." Rene greeted the tall bartender in a silver studded golf hat before she noticed him.

Grinning, she threw both arms up with a welcome cheer, her silver bracer-like bangles reflecting the strings of purple and white fairy lights over the bar. Her long, dark straight hair cascaded over her shoulders as she moved. "My favorite officer of the law. How you doin', baby? How's my favorite quarterican?"

He stepped up to an open space at the massive wooden bar to give her a one-armed hug and a kiss on the cheek. After, he swept an arm around me and pulled me beside him. "I'd like you to meet Caitlin. She's going to be here for a while, and I intend to get her addicted to your peanut butter and bacon burger."

I looked up at him in horror. The monstrous combination made me shudder, but Sherrie's boisterous laugh distracted me. "Don't worry, honey," she said. "It only sounds terrible." She leaned over the bar to hug me, too, then rested her hand on a wooden pull decorated with a dragon. "What you kids drinkin'?"

Rene ordered two fruity wheat beers that sounded as awful as the burger, then escorted me into one of the narrow booths along the opposite wall, carrying both bottles.

"I hope you know what you're doing." I put my phone on the table as I got comfortable. "Because peanut butter and bacon on a burger—"

"Trust me." He held up a defensive hand as the drunken crowd broke into the chorus of a Willie Nelson song. "You won't forget it, and you won't find anything else like it."

"There might be a reason for that." I glanced over my shoulder. Sherrie flitted from one end of the bar to the other, each nimble movement precise, each interaction personal, yet professional and allowing her time to sing along. "She must have worked here a long time."

"I think so," Rene said. "She's the first friend I made when I moved here."

"What's a 'quarterican'?"

He laughed. "Something like an endearment for those who live and work in the French Quarter."

"Kinda racist, isn't it?"

A scowl flickered across his face. "I hadn't considered that." A moment passed, and he said, "I don't think 'quarter rat' is any better."

"Y'all need to work on your endearments." I took a swig of my beer.

He covered his mouth to contain the mouthful of beer that almost showered me when he laughed.

"I never considered that people lived around here." I'd chased the Black Dog through the streets in another part of the Quarter, heedless of the houses on either side. Then there'd been the nightmare. It touched Sister Betty, putting her soul at risk of ablation, and I'd chased it through the city without considering how that act endangered more innocent humans. Maybe I was as reckless as Sister Betty thought.

"Few would," he said, interrupting my thoughts. "A couple thousand people live here." At my raised eyebrow, he said, "Someone's got to keep these places alive between tourist seasons. Who else will convince them of the glory of peanut butter and bacon on burgers?"

We talked, without saying anything important until our food arrived, and I admitted how wrong I'd been about the burger, especially when paired with the strawberry wheat beer.

My phone buzzed. The Scarlet Witch avatar gave me a sultry side eye as I read enough of Sister Betty's text to know it contained nothing urgent.

"Work?" Rene asked around a mouthful of decadence.

I nodded. "I'll get it later."

"Did you," he wiped his mouth and took a quick swallow of beer. "Did you ever think about, you know, doing something different?"

I poked at the potato salad on my plate. "I guess everyone does at some point."

"Nope, I've always wanted to be a cop." He took a massive bite and chewed.

"Can't relate." I smirked and took another bite.

He waited for me to finish before he asked, "What would you be doing, if not this?"

I'd wondered the same thing. More often in the past few weeks. Who was I, if not a Hunter? But could I call myself a Hunter if I couldn't find what I'd been hunting? My most recent jobs ended with a stroke of serendipity. The Black Dog found me before wreaking havoc on the living and unliving populations of New Orleans. Stopping the nightmares happened almost by accident. Neither required the skills I'd developed, and those successes felt like cheating. Chasing the Collectors should have been an easy return to normal, yet I had squat. If I couldn't take them down with such an extensive intellectual and physical arsenal, would I be able to end them at all? "I don't know," I said.

"How'd you start fighting monsters?"

Shannon.

Her name wouldn't answer his question. How could it? How could anything convey the experience of seeing your baby sister murdered while you're helpless to fight back? My stomach cramped with the memory of the night monsters crept out of our closet, and the way one had snatched her in its jaws, tossed her in the air, and devoured her in two massive bites.

"Are you okay?"

"Yup." I laid my napkin across the plate, covering the last few bites that would never make it down my throat now. "Just don't like to talk about it."

"Hey." He reached across the table and grabbed my hand. "I'm sorry. I didn't know."

"You couldn't have."

"I wish I could make it better," he said. "I'd save you from all of it, if I could."

When I glanced up, my response died before I gave it voice. He meant it. Whatever he thought needed repair, he wanted to fix it. I didn't know what to say, especially to the idea of being saved, so I said the only thing that might make sense. "Thank you."

A half smile materialized before he spoke. "I also wish I hadn't brought it up."

"It doesn't matter." I shrugged. "There's nothing anyone can do, so there's no point—"

"There is a point." He squeezed my hand. "If I hadn't brought it up, we could go back to enjoying the evening."

My phone clattered against my mostly empty beer bottle as it vibrated. I turned it over to hide the avatar of the Scarlet Witch on the incoming text. "We can still do that."

33

When Sister Betty called instead of texting, I answered.

"Why are you ignoring my texts?"

"Hello to you, too." Marty mouthing the words "she's jealous" came to mind again. "I'm not ignoring anything. I'm eating dinner. What's up?"

Her irritation diminished, though I doubted she believed me. "Father Callahan arranged a meeting with the Carter brothers, but they're only available tonight."

My blood ran cold. "You're kidding."

Rene looked up, his eyebrows raised as he chewed.

"I'm sorry to interrupt your date," she said. "The thing is, the Carter brothers are—"

"Is it really them? They exist?" I slid my plate aside. The legend of the Carter brothers had fascinated me for a long time and had been part of the reason I chose New Orleans for my vacation that hadn't happened. Rumored to be the first vampires in the city, none of my resources could confirm it, nor would any vampire answer direct questions about any other vampire with the surname Carter. Did I dare hope this heralded the beginning of something going right?

"It sounds legitimate," Sister Betty said cautiously.

My heart lodged in my throat. Rene stared at me, questioning without words. I shook my head. "Where's the meeting?"

"The apartment."

All at once, my heart stopped, fell to my feet, then raced. "I'll be there."

———

B ut the Carter brothers are a ghost story." Rene kept pace with every step I took down Royal Street no matter how many people or sidewalk signs I dodged.

"Maybe not." I side-stepped another person more interested in taking a selfie than paying attention to the NPCs populating his world. Annoying obstacles and all, I'd insisted on leaving the car behind. Navigating the Quarter by car at this hour would have taken far longer than walking the few blocks to the apartment, even without trying to find parking. "If these are Wayne and John Carter, they might know something about the Collectors."

Rene caught my elbow. "We're chasing vampires?"

"Yes."

He didn't react, just stood there, holding me in place as a cluster of pedestrians broke around us.

"You should know they exist. You got the briefings." My irritation flared, and I took another half step, pulling against his restraining grip.

"But I never thought I'd actually..." He let go as his words failed. The more sheepish his expression, the more adorable he looked. I tried really, really hard not to notice. "They're not supposed to exist. They're legends," he insisted.

"And so are hydra, yet you helped me fight one. Welcome to my world." Those damned puppy dog eyes melted me, though I resented the delay. "I don't know if they're who they say they are, but it's worth a shot." I gestured down Royal. "Can we go now?"

After a moment, his shoulders lifted in the suggestion of a shrug. I took it for acceptance and scanned street signs before walking even faster, almost running, toward the sign for St. Ann Street. Rene fell behind, but he'd catch up.

Halfway down the block, I stopped in front of the red building, drinking in the yellowish light filtering through the green shutters and black porch latticework.

Rene's arm grazed my back as he stepped closer. "Need a moment?"

Scowling, I looked up at him. "Hilarious."

"I try."

"Do you know the story?"

"It changes, depending on who you ask." He glanced up at the apartment. "What's consistent through all the versions is that the apartment's been empty for almost fifty years. Locals refuse to rent it. When rented, tenants rarely stay more than six months. Every new one calls about a break-in, though nothing's ever stolen." At my bemused smirk, he said, "I've taken the tours."

"No judgment." I held up my hands.

He continued. "Sometime in the thirties, two guys said to be twins and alleged perpetrators of the most gruesome events known to any New Orleans private residence lived there. They evaded police, allegedly with supernatural strength. I don't know if I believe it, but it's said that it took six officers two hours to subdue them."

"'Gruesome events' is the best euphemism for a bathtub lasagna of human remains and quicklime I've ever heard." I started for the door that looked like an entrance to the residences.

"They were executed," Rene said as he followed. "Electrocuted."

"Allegedly," I said. "Three years later, authorities exhumed them, but the bodies were gone."

His surprise morphed into bemusement. "You believe that?"

I put my hands on my hips, tilting my head. "You know what? I do. You know the Norse goddess of the underworld is a diplomatic resident in this city. Why is this so hard to believe?"

"It seems...crazy."

"You've got to be a lot more open minded to roll with me and mine."

He couldn't hide his smile. "Next you'll invite me to dinner with Jacques St. Germaine."

"Nah. He only comes out once a year. Besides, last I heard, he's feuding with Queen Catherine." I jerked my head at the door. "You coming?"

"I think I love you, Caitlin Kelley." He grinned and took my hand.

Nodding, I turned on my heel, a sick feeling in the pit of my stomach sapping any pleasure from his words. There'd be time to deal with the yucky love stuff later.

The small apartment parlor was well-appointed and poorly lit. Where shadows hadn't claimed corners, sickly yellow light soured the color of things. The ochre-tinged walls might have been white or cream. I tried not to focus on it and watch the thin, red-headed man stroll around the room instead. He touched everything he passed. His fingertips slid lovingly across the back of a velvet chaise, then straightened a milk-glass lampshade. As if assuring himself everything still existed, he made another lap, touching, adjusting, even caressing a gilt frame, but always moving. He'd stopped talking, but I could be patient.

Rene could not. "There are many rumors about you and your brother, Mr. Carter."

I wished we sat close enough to jam my elbow into his ribs.

Wayne Carter blinked as if waking from a dream. "New Orleans is built on nothing if not rumors and reputations." He rubbed his fingertips together, considering them. "That does not make either true."

"Your home is lovely, Mr. Carter," I said, trying to change the subject.

He nodded, absentmindedly. "Wherever I am in the world, my thoughts return here."

Rene and I shared a glance. I wished Marty was here. As much as I knew about the Carter brothers, Marty would know more. I missed his guidance for steering the conversation through treacherous terrain. I cleared my throat. "Do you return often?"

"When I can," he said mildly, his accent not exactly Southern, but more like something out of an old black and white movie.

"My mentor, Sister Bet—Sister Brigit of the Holy Order of the Sisters of Mercy of Saint Brendan, said you might have information about the threat to the supernatural communities."

He glanced at me, his lips pursed in a coquettish pucker. "And Sister Brigit thought I'd help communities that offered no assistance when my brother and I were exposed?"

My words dried up. Had we considered that possibility?

"One might argue the supernatural communities, as you call them, exposed us to begin with."

"I thought a woman escaped the apartment." Rene's voice trailed off, as if he realized he sat in that same apartment now. He flashed an apologetic grimace and, mercifully, shut up.

Wayne Carter didn't seem to notice. He rounded the velvet chair and perched on the seat cushion. Awkward silence swelled to fill the room until Wayne slid back and crossed his legs. "You think a mere woman could be clever enough to escape the clutches of two," he paused and grinned, his perfectly white teeth gleaming, "vampires?"

"Since you're a throwback from another time, I'll be nice and ask you to keep the woman-bashing to a minimum." I tried to smile, though I'm sure it more closely resembled a teeth-baring warning rictus. "Consider it a courtesy that I spare you my typical response."

Wayne Carter's average face flattened into an indifferent mask. With a genteel gesture, he said, "As is today's custom to say, 'whatever.'"

Had I not been tempted to adjust his misogyny with my fists, I might have laughed. Then again, one doesn't fight vampires one isn't prepared to stake, and those inclined to help deserved an extra helping of restraint. "Please continue. Did the supernatural communities expose you?"

He examined his nails. "My brother and I had done and were doing nothing of any concern to anyone when this wild thing ran to the police, claimed we abducted her and drank her blood. Suddenly, my brother and I were wanted men."

"If you did nothing wrong," I said, "why run?"

Carter chuckled. "Ask your pretty beau why innocent men run from the police, my dear."

Rene's eyes hardened, his neck rigid. A muscle flexed in his jaw. "We're not here to discuss the police."

Carter's amusement gave me chills. "You're right. That's not why you're imposing upon me. You mentioned these so-called Collectors."

"That's right."

Wayne Carter's pale lips pressed together as he considered a distant point. "The missing and those whose magic has been..." he swirled his hand in a vague gesture, "compromised."

I'd already opened my mouth to explain what we knew, but astonishment kept it open after words failed to materialize. A quick mental shake restored my senses. "Yes."

"When one considers the name," the ghost of an enigmatic smile haunted the corners of his lips, "one is halfway to understanding."

Nothing irked me more than interview subjects talking like shitty fortune cookies.

Fine. I could play this game.

"The Collectors," I said slowly, as if enunciating the words would resolve the riddle.

Wayne stared at me, expectant.

Father Callahan, Sister Betty, Marty, and I'd pored over the details without finding any discernible pattern. I stared at my hands hanging between my knees and ran through the litany again. Abducted supernat-

ural creatures, stripped powers. The resulting imbalance of magic destabilizing the division between dimensions. Possible exposure of the
supernatural world. We even considered the old man who'd attacked me
during the hunt for the Black Dog and his comment about adding me to
the collection. But why? To what purpose? Who would benefit? Now,
sitting in front of someone who seemed to know what was going on, the
dots didn't connect any faster. "We've looked at—"

"Perhaps it's not looking, but what's there to perceive."

More fortune cookie bullshit. My jaw clenched, teeth grinding
together.

"Come, now, *concentrate*." The mockery in Carter's words further
grated my nerves. "I'd have expected a woman of your intellect to put this
together long ago."

The fierce crunch of my teeth grinding made Rene jump, but perhaps
thanks to Sister Betty's prayers on my behalf, I didn't say anything. Maybe
the benefits of living in the nexus of leylines had strengthened my
restraint. A dose of my own frustration and the judgmental bullshit from
a complete (and arrogant) stranger concentrated—

"They're concentrating magic." The words sounded more astonished
than I felt. "They're using the nexus to concentrate the power they steal."

Carter's soft clap gave me chills. "Brava, though I expected you to
reach that conclusion much sooner, given their name."

My patience evaporated. "Cut the crap, Carter. What's the magic being
used for?"

He leaned forward on his crossed knees as if confessing some deep
secret. "What do you know about dragons, Miss Kelley?"

He said dragon?" Through the phone, I couldn't determine whether
Sister Betty sounded more confused or disturbed, though I could
hear her pacing.

"Massive winged lizard with big, chompy teeth and a habit of belching
flame," I confirmed. Though no expert, I knew enough to be uncomfortable with the idea of a dragon in the Crescent City. Dragons rarely
crossed into the human realm, but when they did, it never ended well.
Pompeii. The same beast started both the Great Chicago fire in 1871 and
the Cuyahoga River fire in 1969. Rumor had it that some of the worst of

the California wildfires in 2017 and 2018 might have been sparked by a hatchling. More rumors linked the massive fires in Australia to at least one crossing.

Her teeth clicked. Chewing a pen cap or something. "Humans and dragons don't fare well in the same space, which is part of the reason they were relocated to Faerie."

"I thought that's where they originated?"

"Yes, but since they're one of the few species that can move between worlds with few repercussions, at least once you get past the initial demands of crossing, they've got a history of living here, too." Her voice dropped, as if she talked to herself instead of me. "It's harder for them to thrive since they can't generate the kind of magical energy to sustain them the way Faerie does."

"How much more?"

"Magicians invented alchemy in an effort to save the species before the Compact agreed to relocation as preservation."

"How does changing base metals to gold keep dragons alive?"

Rene raised his eyebrow as he glanced at me.

She made a soft sound that might have been a half laugh. "There's a reason why dragons collect gold and gems, Caitlin, and why they also attract humans. Gold may be a soft metal, and a diamond might be a shiny rock, but they have a magical resonance. If someone has found a way to use that resonance to unnaturally accelerate a hatchling's growth like Carter implied..."

"Not only are we dealing with a dragon, but one not tempered by age or wisdom."

"Yes."

Could this day get any better?

Something itched my brain. Why now? There had to be some significance or some connection. Should I be investigating jewelry heists or plundered estates? Rene used my shoulders to steer me down a side street, breaking my focus.

"If it is an uncontrollable juvenile, do we know how to kill it?"

"Yes, but we don't have what we need. No magic strong enough, no artifacts of power." She sighed. "I don't know what we're going to do."

"If it's not from here, can't we just...relocate it?" Rene steered me around another corner.

"What?"

"Why don't we send it back to Faerie?"

After a long pause, she said, "That's not the worst idea."

"I'll take that as a compliment. I'm on my way to meet Marty. Meet you at the hotel?"

"No," she said over shuffling noises on her side. "You're closer to the Cathedral. I'll meet you there. Where is he?"

"Having a drink with Father Callahan—"

She swore. "He's on that damned pub crawl with the Bishop of South Carolina."

"What?" I skidded to a stop, and Rene barreled into me, grabbing my shoulders to prevent both of us toppling over.

"You heard me. They'll be hammered, especially if the Bishop brought Jim." She grunted and I heard a crash. "I'll get to the rectory and make coffee. Plan on a 'wrangling cats' strategy, especially if Jim's there."

"Got it." I took Rene's hand and continued walking.

"Be careful, Caitlin. If Carter's right, this city's far more dangerous than we thought."

Goody. Exactly what I needed.

I ended the call, and Rene and I hustled along another block without talking. The almost meditative dodge-and-weave around pedestrians allowed me the unusual luxury of organizing what I knew about dragons. Their size, life cycle, diet. The more I thought, the more I hurried. Few places in New Orleans would accommodate a dragon, even a juvenile, and since we'd found no evidence of it hunting, someone had to be caring for it.

Though I knew little about how it could be used or concentrated with the nexus, the amount of magic collected in lost abilities and abducted supernats concerned me. If a big, impulsive, magically enhanced baby dragon threw a tantrum or rebelled against its handlers—

"Did they say where they were?" Rene's question jostled me out of my head.

Checking my phone's GPS, I shook my head. "Marty's sharing his location. Nav Bitch will get us there."

"Nav Bitch?"

"GPS." I gestured with my chin and pocketed my phone. "We should meet at the end of this block."

That's when I noticed the emptiness of the street.

This close to Bourbon at this time of night, the street should have been filled with the press of under-inhibited people in varying states of inebriation, celebration, and awe. The air should have been alive with raucous, glorious noise of laughter and revelry spilling out of clubs and bars, rattling beads, loud music, and the conversations of people clustered around restaurant doors.

Instead, Rene and I stood alone.

Not good.

Empty New Orleans streets and I had a bad track record. Last time, I lost my panties to a gorilla. That episode absolutely needed to remain my career low point for encounters. If nothing else, I had pants on, so no matter how bad this went, my odds of keeping my underwear had already improved. Besides, this time I'd come armed with a Glock 43 tucked against the curve of my back in my belly band holster. Easier to get to. Less obvious. Still, nothing about this felt good, even by comparison.

"Stop right there." Three cloaked figures stepped into the next intersection.

Awesome.

Rene shifted into a defensive stance but didn't draw his gun.

Ambient light didn't penetrate the shadowy void under the strangers' hoods. Long sleeves hid their hands and any potential weapons. I did a quick mental run down. No awkward bumps, so unless they concealed rifles vertically at their sides, at best they had small arms, like pistols. Not fun to work around, but one shot wouldn't hit both Rene and I as long as we stayed far enough apart. Another point of advantage for Team Panty Defender. I swallowed the urge to giggle.

Right. Potentially magical bad guys at one o'clock. Focus.

I took a half step forward and to the side, not in front of Rene, but not beside him either. My hands in front of me, palms out, I said, "Look, I don't have time for games. I've got more important things to do."

"And I'm a cop," Rene said.

Their obscured faces made it impossible to tell which of them spoke. "Your interference will not be tolerated, conduit."

Conduit? That was new. If intended as an insult, I didn't get it. I decided to play it off instead. "You've got me confused with someone else. Or maybe you've got the wrong word?"

"There's no mistake, witch," said another of the hooded figures, deeper and definitely male. Maybe the one on the right?

"Not a witch, either," I took another step forward, "though I've been called something that rhymes with it."

All three raised their hands in cheesy, eerie unison.

It should have given me pause, but I rolled my eyes and put my hands on my hips. One hand snaked behind me as I spoke loud enough to cover the sound of releasing the safety strap over the grip of the pistol concealed at my back. "Hokey theatrics won't impress me, I promise. I've seen some shit."

Hands raised to the sky, the three overlapping voices muttered something incomprehensible that might have been Latin. Or gibberish. Legitimate magic involved more than goofy incantations and hand-wavium, so if this trio expected to accomplish something with chanting and gesticulations, maybe I could resolve this without firing a shot.

Time to find out.

"As it happens," I said, bringing both hands out to my sides again, "I know a few tricks."

Their cloaks rustled, their litany crumbling into uneven words as they looked at each other.

Keeping them in my peripheral, I lifted my chin and shouted, "Azerath!"

The cloaked trio resumed muttering but faster, frantic.

"Metrion!" My fingers curled into claws as I brought them together overhead with effort.

"Zin—"

Before I could shout the last word or complete the gesture, the three turned and ran in the direction from which they'd come.

I lowered my hands and chuckled at Rene's baffled expression. "Nerd education is seriously lacking these days. Do kids not watch cartoons anymore?"

Rene's answer drowned in the flood of sound as people poured into the streets. Under it all, the chorus of a Meatloaf song announced the arrival of our cohorts. Marty, Father Callahan, and two others emerged from a side street on my left, swaying in an uneven line and scream-singing what they'd do for love.

My skin prickled, and I ignored whatever Rene said.

The cloaked trio stepped into the street again, a pulsing ball of purple hovering between their outstretched hands. The unearthly light cast hideous shadows on their faces, but I didn't stop focusing on them.

I didn't think.

I just ran, shoving aside a pedestrian.

The glow pulsed. Grew. Warped. Elongated.

Marty turned toward it, mouth opening in either surprise or the next verse as purple lightning flew at him. I launched myself into the bolt's path.

Someone screamed.

Everything went black.

34

E asy." Marty pressed my shoulder against the lumpy ground, his other hand applying pressure to my forehead. "You're still bleeding."

My head pounded as much from the outside as from the inside. I groaned.

Marty's face hovered over me, too shadowed by background glare for me to see his expression. "Welcome back," he said.

I lay still. Every muscle and joint throbbed in unison. Closing my eyes, I waited for the worst to pass. Only when it stopped did I notice the absence of the silent scream echoing in my head. The silence hurt more than the unending sound. "What happened?"

"Let me explain." Marty refused to let me rise. "There is too much. I will sum up."

"Prince Humperdink or the iocaine powder?"

"Neither this time, but good to know getting knocked out hasn't affected your sense of humor."

"One of these days, it might." I tried to shift off the rock poking into my back, but Marty wouldn't allow it. He slid a hand under me to remove it, careful not to shift me in any way. My head ached, which tracked with hitting it on the ground. "I guess I did my thing, huh?"

"The usual." Marty nodded. "Something deadly appears, you taunt it, piss it off, then jump in front of its nasty tricks."

"Sounds like me." I peeked through a squint and lifted my arm. Blood glistened on my hand. "I remember most of that."

"Good," he said over the wail of sirens.

"What knocked me on my ass?"

"A magic projectile to the chest. Incidentally," he gestured at someone I couldn't see, "that's why you're staying put until you get checked out." Gently, but firmly, my partner pushed my hand down.

I tried not to wince.

"She okay?" Rene knelt at my side. His unsteady grin flickered, but I didn't miss the fear and panic in his eyes. "Nothing like waking up in a pool of your own blood, huh?"

"Not the first time," I said, wiping a hand on my shirt. "Probably not the last, either."

"Especially in this line of work." He took my hand, holding it tenderly.

"Sure. At work, too." I struggled against Marty's hand but lacked the strength to budge it. "Scalp wounds bleed like crazy. I'm fine."

"There could be more." Rene let go of my hand to help Marty pin me. "The paramedics will check you out."

"Where's Sister Betty? She'll tell you—"

"You're not going anywhere, Caitlin," Marty said, his voice soft.

A nother deep breath, another attempt to quell my rising irritation. Instead of growling at the nurse taking my blood pressure, I sat back and endured his ministrations. He murmured my reading with a note of approval.

I tried to smile. "Any idea when I'll be released?"

"Depends on how you keep doing." His smile, though kind, held more professional courtesy than anything.

All the better to dodge your question. Pressing my lips together, I smothered a sigh.

"When will Dr. Canterbury arrive?" Sister Betty asked.

"Could be hours." The nurse tucked his hands into the pockets of his blue scrubs. "Last I heard, his flight was delayed."

Emergency room sounds obliterated any awkward silence. I retreated behind closed eyes and willed myself to be anywhere but stuck in bed. The rattle of the privacy curtain and the click of the door marked the nurse's departure.

Sister Betty said, "You don't have to pretend to sleep."

"I'm not," I said, without moving. Everything ached from slamming into the ground and stillness kept it manageable.

Monitors beeped, some of them mine. Outside, raised voices rushed to another emergency. If nothing else, being the one in bed beat sitting beside it and waiting to find out if someone would wake up. Being stuck here meant my people were safe and that I'd finally done my job.

"It's a precaution to make sure you're okay."

I rolled my head on the pillow to look at her. "I told you, I'm fine. The X-rays came back fine. Every doctor has said I'm fine. What more do you need?"

She watched me with frustrating calm. "These doctors can't deal with magic. Most don't know it exists." Not once did she look away. "We're waiting for Doctor Canterbury."

And so we did.

I drifted off, only to be awakened by another nurse checking the dilation of my eyes. "Good," she murmured after her litany of questions. "Oriented, alert. No signs of head trauma." She tucked her pen light into her breast pocket. "You're good to go."

"Great!" I twisted in the bed, ready to climb out.

"No." Sister Betty sounded half asleep as she bolted out of the chair at my bedside. Even in her "casual" nun garb, a prim skirt and cardigan, she moved fast. "We have a specialist inbound. A diocese physician."

The nurse's eyes narrowed. "There's really no need—"

"The diocese insists." Sister Betty inclined her head over clasped hands, a few rosary beads escaping between her palms.

After a moment, the nurse said, "I'll see what I can find out. We'll need that bed before the night's over."

Sister Betty thanked her, waiting until the door closed before continuing. "Don't you understand that this is to protect you? To keep you doing what you do? So you can protect those that cannot protect themselves?"

"Because I've got such a great track record with that." I gave up trying to swing my legs over the side of the bed while she stood there. Too many machines blocked the other side. "I'm not afraid of dying."

She recoiled as if I'd slapped her. "Maybe you should be."

"Why?"

Her brow furrowed in confused frustration. "Don't you understand that having to explain this to you isn't normal? That you should have some sense of self-preservation?"

"I don't care about that." Maybe the numbness insulated me from caring. Maybe the weight on my chest suffocated it. Whatever caused it, I meant it. I didn't care. When it came to protecting others or self-preservation, I knew where my loyalty lay.

"Then what do you care about?"

Whether I've done enough. When I looked back, when someone else looked at everything I'd done, was it enough? Was it worth it? Was I? But I couldn't tell her that.

"It might not be so bad," I said, "if it was worth it."

She stared at me, then shook her head. "You're a danger to yourself, which threatens everyone around you. Including those you love." Her words cut deep, then twisted and shredded my heart.

A million things came to mind, and I could say none of them. No matter how hard I tried, no matter how hard I pushed, I couldn't make any of it better. If I focused harder, if I kept going, maybe I'd figure out a way to be enough at some point. "Okay, I get it. I suck. My instincts suck. Can I get back to hunting monsters, now? I've got a dragon to find, and I'm useless like this." I hit the bed with a fist.

"That's not it at all, and you know it."

"If I'm here, and those magic users got away, things are only going to get worse. It's my responsibility to stop it. This city, this region is my responsibility and I'll be damned if it goes to hell while I'm in bed."

"You're only here until we're sure you're okay," she said, her expression tired and pained.

"I am," I insisted.

"How about I determine that?" A new voice resonated through the room, then the curtain whisked aside, revealing a burly man with a big white beard. His round stomach protruded through his open lab coat and preceded him by a full second. Exertion tinged his cheeks jolly red, and it might have been the lighting, but I swear his eyes twinkled.

"Am I hallucinating, or is that Santa Claus?" I asked Sister Betty without looking at her.

Before she could answer, the man laughed in hooting peals that shook his belly and brought to mind tiny reindeer on snow-covered houses.

Sister Betty and I looked at each other.

When Dr. Canterbury recovered, he said, "No, no, though my cousin and I are regularly mistaken for each other."

"You're...Santa's cousin?" I shook my head and turned to Sister Betty. "Maybe I do belong here."

"So do I," she said, incredulous.

"Ladies, don't make me have Kris put you on the naughty list." He settled glasses onto his pink nose and squinted at a small tablet. "Now, let's see if we can get you on your way."

We returned to the St. Louis Cathedral a little before sunrise, the one concession Sister Betty made as we left the hospital. Our arrival should have been without fanfare, and might have been if Rene, Marty, Father Callahan, and his inebriated entourage weren't camped out in the rectory office waiting for us. The reek of burnt coffee permeating the room suggested they'd been nursing the same pot for hours, yet it didn't cover the tang of alcohol in the air. As soon as I crossed the threshold, Rene launched out of his seat and rushed to my side.

"I'm fine," I said, gently removing his hand from my elbow. "I've got this."

Father Callahan sat at his desk and nodded as our eyes met. A stiff man with steel gray hair and forced smile sat in the chair across from him beside Marty. The stranger gripped the chair arm rests, as if prepared to stand. His eyes darted from me to Sister Betty to another stranger, a kilt-clad man lounging in the chair against the wall. The man wearing the green tartan grinned at me with drunken good nature, cradling a coffee cup against his chest.

Marty shifted the empty chair at his other side a little closer and patted the seat. He didn't stand. We had a rule about the walking wounded, especially when that meant me.

Ignoring Rene hovering beside me, solicitous and awkward, I crossed the room with confidence. And without betraying the ache in my hips.

"You took a bolt of magic for me," Marty said as I sat.

"Any time, partner." I tried to look relaxed.

"You know you're crazy." Marty laid his hand on mine, slipping his fingers between mine. "Thank you, crazy girl."

A lump formed in my throat. Not trusting my voice, I nodded.

"Caitlin," Father Callahan didn't stand or make a fuss, "glad to see you're okay."

"Thank you." I acknowledged both his words and the coffee Rene handed me. "I'd have been here sooner, but Santa's cousin's flight was delayed."

Marty muttered something, but I only caught, "what?"

Father Callahan smiled. "Dr. Canterbury has been traveling. The magical expulsions from the northern US led to an influx of magical injuries along Canada's southern border."

"Right." The sentence intensified my headache. I made a mental note to ask Marty about it later. "I appreciate you being here. You shouldn't have—"

"I'd like you to meet our guests," Father Callahan interrupted. He gestured to the older, nervous gentleman blinking at me with glassy eyes. "This is Bishop Robert from South Carolina."

"Nice to meet you." I stood, shaking his hand.

"Caitlin's the regional hunter replacing Sister Evangeline," Father Callahan explained.

The man paled, dropped my hand, and though his smile didn't move, he turned a disturbing shade of green. Either he was about to hurl or Hulk out. "Terrible shame, that." He rose and hurried to the door. "You'll excuse me, please."

"Turn right. Second door on the left," Father Callahan called after him.

Our other visitor giggled and drank from his mug as the Bishop disappeared.

"You must be Jim." I walked over, hand out.

"That's me," he said, offering me a flask with a devilish grin. "Unlike the Bishop, I can hold my liquor. Care to catch up?"

By the time the debriefing ended, strong sunlight poured through the rectory window. I regretted turning down Jim's flask before he and the Bishop left. I leaned on Father Callahan's desk, head in my hands. Despite Dr. Canterbury's assurance that the ballistic magic had no lingering effects, each throb in my skull reverberated throughout my entire body. I knew that the more I moved, the faster I'd feel better, but that didn't motivate me out of the chair.

"I'm tapped out." Marty lay his head on his folded arms and closed his eyes.

"We all need rest." Sister Betty yawned. "Especially Caitlin."

Too tired to argue, I sat up. "Let's regroup at noon. We'll chase the leads on the three weirdos you found while I..." My hand flailed but failed to conjure a word.

"Let's not plan." Marty stood, offering me his hand. "Sleep now. Plan later."

"We can't let the leads go cold. The sooner we start, the better our chances of finding and stopping them," I said. "Or at least stopping them from snatching anyone else." Despite what they'd uncovered in the hours I wasted in the hospital, our information remained thin. Suggestion. Rumor. All of it qualified with words like *possible* and *potential*. We had three suspects but couldn't identify them or confirm their role in the overall problem. They'd run from a fake spell from a cartoon character, yet they'd thrown real magic at Marty. If not them, then who did they work for? How many were out there? How many other supernats would disappear before I figured it out? How could I stop when I knew so little? The enormity of it all sunk in and lodged in my gut.

Ruminating on it wouldn't get me anywhere. Action, however small, might. Taking a deep breath, I straightened and reached for Marty's tablet.

He slid the tablet away and offered his hand again. "Sleep first." He wiggled his fingers in invitation. "We can't work miracles if we're dead."

"You don't know that," I grumbled, but let him pull me up. My balance wavered as I looked from him to Sister Betty to Father Callahan. Sudden emotion welled up in my chest and stole my breath. Whatever success I claimed wouldn't have been possible without them. They believed in me, even when I didn't deserve it. And their faith in me got them hurt. They suffered because they believed in my ability to overcome the obstacles we faced. How do you make up for that? How do you pay those debts? I owed them so much. "Thanks, everyone. For everything." I stared at my pale hand in Marty's darker one. "Things haven't been easy, and I haven't—"

"Don't." Father Callahan walked around his desk to wrap an arm around me. "Go rest."

I blinked away tears, hanging my head to hide what I couldn't hold back. No matter what happened, I owed them. Whatever it took, I had to find a way to take down the Collectors and earn their faith. "Okay."

Father Callahan squeezed me again before Marty led me out the door.

Neither of us spoke as we crossed the cathedral nave. I squinted in the blinding sunlight, and it made coronas around everything, including the tuba player perched on a three-legged stool outside the Cabildo. He almost looked angelic as he nodded at me, not missing a note.

Instead of cutting through the park, Marty led me to the shaded side street. I wanted to apologize for...everything. He'd gotten hurt when we'd been hunting the Black Dog and would have on this one, if luck hadn't intervened on his behalf. How close had he come to getting hurt this time? How many more superhuman moves could I pull off? What if I had reacted a second later? How close had I come to losing him?

His body language gave away nothing. Not even awareness of being studied. A splash of reflected sunlight from a car passing on Decatur Street emphasized the dark hollows under his eyes.

I'd gotten lucky. Damned lucky. How long could I protect him with luck? Or Sister Betty? Or anyone else?

"What will it take for you to see me as an equal?" His tone wrenched something inside me, his words laden with weariness, disappointment. Sadness?

"What do you mean?"

He shoved his hands into his pockets, his jerky movements hinting at his distress. "When will you at least pretend I can defend myself?"

Each step took effort. Words were almost impossible. "I know you can."

"Yet you intervene like I'm some rando off the street. Like I'm incapable, or untrained." His eyes fixed on the uneven stone pavers. "I'm not. You know that. We did some of the same training. We learned the same things, and though I might not be as good a shot as you, I *am* capable of defending myself."

"I know."

"Then when will you treat me like an equal?"

Whatever energy I had left drained out of me. I leaned against the bollard at the end of the alley. "I..."

"What?"

I shook my head, staring at his feet in front of mine. "I'm sorry."

His voice softened, but none of his tension abated. "I'm not your responsibility."

"You're wrong," I said. Whenever I gave the direction to walk into any situation or how to handle a mission, I asked them to accept the consequences for all of my mistakes. In exchange, I shouldered responsibility for each of their lives, and had to make sure everyone walked away in one piece.

"No, *you* are." He squatted and took my hands. "Me, Sister Betty, Father Callahan, Agent Cooper, Rene. We're a team. Officially or unofficially. We work together. We support each other. None of us is helpless—"

"But you're *all* my responsibility." The oppressive weight bearing down on my shoulders underscored the reality of my words. "Everything that happens to you, to any of you, is my responsibility. From the knock on the head you took in St. Louis #1 when hunting the Black Dog, to the nightmare touching Sister Betty, to—" I gestured back toward the Cathedral, "magic lightning bolts. Protecting you is my job—"

"No." He laid a finger across my lips. "*We* are a team. *We* work together to defend those who cannot defend themselves. *We* assume the risks and responsibilities of our own free will. You may lead us, but *we* are equal."

Tears threatened, but I coughed them back. He didn't understand. He couldn't.

"You have to let us help, Cee. You can't do this alone."

But I could, and I had to before any of them got hurt again.

"Are you hearing me?" Another squeeze. "Really hearing me?"

I nodded. Arguing required energy I didn't have. What energy I had needed to be spent on figuring out how to deal with the Collectors and ending the threat they posed to the supernaturals, to the city at large, and especially to my team. I could pull it together that long. I had to. Or at least I could pretend to.

"But you don't agree."

Our eyes met. Resignation softened the lines creasing his forehead.

One tear streamed down my cheek. I dashed it away, annoyed it fell, annoyed he'd seen it, and shook my head. "Doesn't matter. There's a job to do."

He sighed and looked down. "You're a damned fool, Caitlin Kelley, you know that?"

"Tell me something I don't know," I croaked.

"That's probably impossible." He winked when our eyes met. "How about we Uber back to the hotel?"

I could have cried with relief. "Oh god, yes."

"I got you, boo." He pulled out his phone. "I'll always have your back."

After sleeping far later than I intended, I dragged myself through the motions of getting ready and hauling myself out the door. Once in the big black SUV courtesy of Agent Cooper and his pull at DEMON, Sister Betty plied me with coffee to dull the crankiness and Marty shoved a chocolate pastry under my nose to ward off hangry. They knew me well.

Sister Betty and Marty couldn't have gotten much sleep, but neither of them showed it as they explained what they'd accomplished while I slept, including the plan to review a map of the city at a local library branch. I had to admit, I probably wouldn't have come up with that even with a solid eight hours of sleep. Guilt writhed through my barely functional brain. If they could manage, why couldn't I?

The driver stopped at the library on Loyola where a smiling woman waited, hands folded in front of her. Everything about her screamed stereotypical librarian from the respectable and modest clothing, to the thick rims of her glasses to the silver streaks in her corona of tight, natural curls. Obviously, I suspected a trap.

"This is…cool," I said, confused by such a personal welcome.

"Me and Liberty are tight." Marty winked and slid out to greet the smiling woman, who pulled him into a hug like some long-lost relative.

With his charm at max capacity, Marty made introductions, and Liberty led us through the library. Her unceasing murmured narrative detailed the history and available resources, and only stopped at the open door of a private room. Inside, a map covered several tables pushed together. "This is the best we had on short notice." She gestured to the tight space with an apologetic grimace. "Our academic rooms are booked well in advance."

"This will be fine, thank you," Sister Betty said.

"You're the best, Liberty," Marty cooed. For someone who didn't know much about "yucky love stuff," Marty had mastered the kind of flirting that made Liberty blush.

I stepped into the room, pushing aside a chair to get closer. Leaning over the yellowing map made me dizzy. With the city spread out before me, this felt personal. My new home, the place I'd sworn to protect. In it hid something, many somethings, I had to find. The Collectors. The dragon. The dragon's handlers. The missing supernats. In a place with so many possibilities, where did I start? Did Batman feel like this? Maybe that's what made him such a grumpy bastard.

The librarian, Liberty, hesitated, as if unwilling to leave. "This is the only map on site using the scale you requested." She directed her question at Marty. "Book research?"

"More like a game," I muttered. Dungeons and Dragons with actual dragons.

"We get a lot of writers. Historians, too, though this map is too modern for most."

"It's perfect, thank you," Sister Betty said, her dismissal polite but unmistakable.

Liberty didn't seem inclined to leave. "If you take notes, please use a separate table. No notebooks or pens on the map, regardless of padding. And absolutely no food or drink."

Marty flashed a brilliant smile and a quick salute. "Scout's honor."

Her smile intensified, and with a nod, she left.

"Look at you flirting," I teased. "Since when were you a Boy Scout?"

"I haven't told you everything about me."

I raised an eyebrow.

"Okay, never." He blushed. "Flirting's fun; it's the rest that doesn't work for me." He pulled a plastic dragon out of his pocket and leaned over the map. "See anything big enough?"

Starting with the biggest (or, at least, the toothiest) puzzle piece as Sister Betty and Marty proposed made sense, though it seemed no less daunting. We studied the shapes and lines before us, dismissing the most obvious and impossible spaces, like the Superdome, Loyola and Tulane University campuses, and Audubon and City Parks. I squinted enough to blur the words and searched for space where the figurine would fit with room to spare.

"They'll need relative seclusion," I traced I-10 from the airport through the city, "with access to transportation."

Sister Betty glanced over her shoulder, then pulled out a tube of mini M&M's. Checking her notes, she placed one tiny candy wherever a supernatural creature disappeared. A broad, misshapen circle of candy formed around the library, a few outliers breaking the pattern.

"There's the rough perimeter," I said, examining the spaces within. "What's big enough to be their base?"

"This." Marty placed the plastic dragon on the map, his voice grave and hesitant. "If the scale's right, this should be it."

Sister Betty leaned over to read the label. "Charity Hospital."

"The one shut down during Katrina." Shivers coursed up my spine.

Marty nodded.

"Let's check it out," I said.

35

"ny luck?"

Sister Betty's expression provided all the answer I needed as she paced her hotel room in a worn pair of gray sweatpants and black tank top. No one seemed willing to grant more than an external tour of Charity Hospital, but she refused to give up. She pulled the phone away from her ear, tapped the screen twice, and said, "If one more person puts me on hold, I'm crawling through the phone."

"Ready to do this my way?" I asked with a devilish grin.

Her sneer intensified.

"All right." I placed the bags of food on the table in front of Marty.

Two more taps to her phone and she held it to her ear with a sigh.

"We'd be done if you'd let me do my thing yesterday." I helped Marty unpack the bags.

"You're supposed to be resting," she said.

I had tried. Last night, I'd gotten a few hours, but as much as I craved sleep, the moment I lay down, my eyes popped open and my muscles jumped with the *need* to move. Getting breakfast seemed a reasonable alternative. In answer to her questioning stare, I flopped across her bed. "Happy?"

She rolled her eyes, then perked up and spoke into her phone.

"Don't antagonize her." Marty snagged a chip from an open Styrofoam container. "She's worried about you."

"I'm fine." I rearranged the pillows, taking the box he offered.

"I know when you're fine and when you're not better than you," he said without levity or sarcasm. "You're not, by the way."

"What's that supposed to mean?" I scowled at him.

"Exactly what I said." The amusement in his eyes died. "Why are you getting defensive?"

"I'm not," I snapped. "I'm just—" I rubbed my face. "Tired. Frustrated. Annoyed."

"Then go rest."

"I tried," I said. "I can't. The Collectors are out there, and if those magic users who attacked us are with them, or *are* them, that makes us all vulnerable. We don't have the resources to deal with magic. Or the dragon. And NOPD has been less than forthcoming with assistance to find missing supernats, now that they know what they are. How am I supposed to sleep with all that going on?"

His expression didn't change.

"And instead of moving this whole thing forward," I gestured at Sister Betty still talking to some functionary on the phone, "we're wasting time asking for permission."

"You can take an hour to sleep. It'll be here when you wake up."

"But they'll be further along—"

He popped another chip in his mouth. "Maybe, but you'll be sharper after some sleep."

"I can't." I stared at the open containers of food I didn't want. "I'm meeting with Helen, then Violetta."

"Let's combine them." He had his phone in hand before he finished. "I'll handle the logistics." He typed with both thumbs, then glanced up. "Next?"

"Charity Hospital."

"We need clearance," Sister Betty said, making me jump. I hadn't heard her approach. Her free hand flicked up at the phone. "On hold. Again."

"We don't need permission," I said.

"We're going to do everything we can to get it," she insisted.

Marty's phone made an electronic whoosh as he put it down. "What else?"

"Rene," I sighed. The longing and dread evoked by thoughts of him confused me. Though I'd seen little of him since the hospital, whenever he was around, he hovered and fussed, making me feel fragile and weak and I resented it. And then, there was the whole thing where he kept directly and indirectly confessing he loved me. He couldn't know me, so how could he love me? Didn't he know what love was? Hell, did *I*?

Sister Betty paced, her ponytail swinging.

There ought to be a limit on how many conflicting things you could feel for any one person at any one time.

"I sent Rene to talk to Cooper," Father Callahan said as he entered the room from the bathroom. "Since Cooper isn't able to work, Rene can absorb some of his responsibilities." He smirked. "Besides, those two should bond."

"What's wrong with Cooper?" I ignored the heat in my reddening face. As much as the agent existed to be a righteous pain in my ass, his absence disturbed me.

Father Callahan shook his head. "Nothing worth discussing."

The lack of reaction from the others suggested they already knew.

My excuses eliminated, I didn't know what to say. "So, is this a coup or something?" My attempt at humor fell so flat, I sounded petulant.

"Nah," Marty said. "You're cute, but violent. None of us want to deal with that."

"If I need to take you down," Sister Betty teased, "I can."

"I'll hold your phone," Father Callahan offered.

"I'll record it for YouTube." Marty held up his.

"Y'all are so helpful." I rolled my eyes, hoping the tears remained a threat until I returned to my room.

"We've got you covered, Cee," Marty said gently, lowering his phone. "Even if means defending you against yourself."

A s soon as I closed my eyes, Marty shook me awake.

"Dude," I grumbled, "you told me to rest."

"Yeah," he nudged me again, "six hours ago."

I sat up, flinging blankets aside, dizzy with a sudden head rush. "Why didn't you wake me?"

"I did." He stepped aside as I clambered out of bed. "Twice. You didn't get up."

I didn't remember, but he wouldn't lie. Sleeping that hard didn't necessarily mean anything bad, but what if I started sleeping through calls? What if someone died because I didn't wake up? What if my team got hurt because I missed a fight? I shuddered.

"Cee, are you okay?"

Pulling on pants made it easy to avoid his gaze. "Just annoyed I slept so long."

"You needed it." His words sounded more like a question.

I zipped my jeans, noticing the darkness outside. "When am I supposed to meet with Helen and Violetta?"

He glanced at his phone. "You've got time."

Turning my back, I tugged off my t-shirt, pulled on a bra, then grabbed a cleaner shirt. I refused to dress up. Whatever I wore in their presence would feel inadequate. Better to be comfortable. And armed. The velcro rip of the bellyband holster made me shiver as I opened it.

"All this sleeping," Marty said, shaking his head, "it's not like you."

"Maybe I needed it, like you said. It's been a crazy couple of months." I leaned down to grab the socks I kicked off before my nap. "Taking a magic blast to the chest and face-planting into pavement probably contributed."

"Except this isn't the first time."

Though I tried not to react, I felt unintentional hesitation in my movements. I sat on the edge of the bed and pulled on my socks, willing a response to emerge.

Nothing came.

Marty took his opportunity. "When you're on a job, you attack it. You don't sleep. You drive yourself to exhaustion. Remember North Carolina?"

I didn't answer. Spending a couple days in the hospital after the job for dehydration and exhaustion hadn't been a high point, but arguing about it wouldn't get me anywhere. I could get ready to meet with Helen and Violetta and maybe, if I got lucky, learn something. I pulled on my Docs and cinched the laces until the leather hugged my foot and ankle.

Marty didn't say anything as he sat beside me.

I tensed, expecting him to put an arm around me. If he did, I'd fall apart, and that would be the end.

He didn't. What he said was worse.

"If there's something wrong, let's work on making it better."

The alien sound I made wasn't a laugh, but I didn't know what else to call it. "That's the thing," I rubbed the riot of goosebumps pebbling my arms, "nothing's wrong."

"Something is," he said softly. "This isn't like you."

Who could say what was "like me" anymore? Not me. What I was supposed to be contradicted my reality. A hunter who couldn't find her prey, a protector whose team and charges kept getting hurt. I couldn't even claim victory over the last couple of missions without giving dumb luck due credit.

"What's up?"

Tangled thoughts crashed through me, mangled by a contradictory mix of too much and not enough sleep. How could I explain the all-consuming emptiness I couldn't fill? Or the vacuum of emotion lurking behind every cloudburst of joy or despair? That even in those moments of feeling something, I didn't feel anything? How could I explain craving numbness when I couldn't deal? None of it made sense. Everything felt... wrong, yet for no reason. How do you explain being broken when nothing's broken?

With a shake of my head, I searched for words. It wasn't that anything was wrong. Or right. It just...was. The black hole inside me had pulled everything in and left nothing behind. Anything intense enough to break through only did for a moment before the void took over and things got still again. How could I explain preferring feeling nothing? That I needed those moments of oblivion? That I wanted to step out and sink into the relief of nothingness?

Escaping might be as easy as not being.

Time froze.

Never had the thought asserted itself like that before. Dying had never scared me. I knew darkness in all its permutations from my baby sister becoming a two-bite snack for a monster to a panoply of grim ends ever since. Death came for us all, regardless. My own death didn't bother me, but the sense of relief accompanying the thought of it did. The tantalizing comfort that *not existing* offered shifted the earth beneath me.

The void had called. And something within me responded.

Marty took my hand, his thumbs rubbing the calluses at the base of my fingers. I usually complained about my mannish hands, but right now, they didn't seem so burly or awkward.

I slid my fingers between his and held on.

"I won't think less of you if you tell me what's wrong. You know that, right?"

I nodded, not trusting my constricted throat.

"I won't give you shit for being vulnerable."

My gaze dropped to our joined hands. I nodded and squeezed his. It felt like holding on for dear life, and maybe it was. My lifeline. I couldn't explain the temptation to dive into that void, but even if my strength failed, he'd hold on until his gave out.

"What's wrong?"

I forced a smile. "Nothing," I said. "Really."

"That's bullshit," he said, his smirk only lasting a second. "You're not okay. I can see that. I might be the only one other than Sister Betty to see it, and I don't know what's going on between you that prevents her from saying anything. Whatever it is, you have to know that I won't let you go through it alone."

"But nothing's wrong." The words came out on their own, like some kind of defense mechanism. Everything felt wrong, everything inside me screamed for help, but I couldn't admit it, couldn't say anything. The words stopped before they ever got to my mouth.

I felt the heat of his gaze, but couldn't face him.

"I don't know why you're lying, but I know you are. You can't fake this with me. I've seen you at your worst, remember? I've held you up in the shower when you were too broken to stand on your own. I've hauled your drunk and disorderly ass out of the dirt after an all-day concert. You're the only person I've ever known to cry to heavy metal."

I couldn't fight the smile accompanying the memory. Marty and I went to Carolina Rebellion whenever work brought us close enough to Charlotte to spend the weekend at the outdoor concert. We drank Jack Daniels, sang, danced, and giggled our way through people watching. And I remembered the night I cried. Standing well behind the crowd, singing a mournful ballad along with one of my favorite bands, and before I knew it, tears. Then, the tears became sobs. Sobs dropped me to my knees on the trash-littered ground. Maybe the three days of relentless sun, or the plethora of beer and whiskey caught up to me. Or maybe the lyrics reminded me of Shannon too much. Whatever caused it, he helped me through a truly messy moment, and I didn't deserve him.

"You're strong and you'll get through this, Cee." He took my hand. "But maybe, and don't get pissed off, but maybe this time, you need help."

I expected a surge of anger, but it didn't come. He'd suggested it before, that I get help, that I talk to someone who could help, and every other time, I'd gotten furious. But not now. Everything remained completely numb.

"I want you to be safe," he said.

"Safe's not exactly a side effect of hunting monsters, you know."

"Maybe not, but the monsters inside you are more dangerous than anything we fight."

He wasn't wrong and I knew it, but I couldn't admit it, either.

"You have professional backup when you hunt monsters. You need the same when you're fighting your own."

Tears threatened. My throat worked to swallow them.

He opened his mouth, but closed it. Instead, he lifted my hand and kissed my scarred knuckles.

I understood.

"I love you, Cee."

Keeping eye contact became impossible, so I looked down at my hand in Marty's, my skin deathly white against his.

"I know." And I did, but I couldn't say more, not even to tell him I loved him. Not without everything crashing down and taking me with it. I could only hope he understood, too.

From somewhere, I found the strength to stand when he did. He handed me the Glock and I slid it into the holster in the curve of my lower back. We left together, but I avoided my reflection in the mirror when I passed.

The recipe for my personal hell will undoubtedly include fragile antique furniture, delicate teacups, bitter tea, and small talk. Thanks to the old-world tastes of my hostess, Helen, a.k.a. Hel, the Norse goddess of the underworld, I've logged plenty of time precariously balanced on spindly-legged chairs while trying not to fidget. Every minute locked in one position while keeping my weight off the chair counted as both a workout and torture. Definitely skipping squats this week, whether Sister Betty approved or not.

"I certainly understand your preference for neutrality," I said, my teacup rattling on its saucer, "but this goes beyond political abstinence. I've been attacked twice—"

"Are all hunters so dramatic?" Violetta asked with a coquettish flutter of her lashes.

"Dramatic?" I tried not to rise to her bait.

"Yes, dear. You're familiar with the concept?" The beguiling leader of the nightmare clan put her fingers to her lips, her almost black curls bouncing. "It's one of my favorite qualities. My question is mere curiosity because if all hunters are like you, I'll have to," her hungry grin sent chills down my spine, "pay more attention."

My stuttered tumble of words amused her and frustrated me. "That," I said when I finally recovered, "isn't what we were talking about."

"No, but it's far more amusing." Violetta leaned forward and lifted the teapot, glancing at Helen. "A refresh, Lady Helen?"

The two women exuded casual elegance. Despite the informal conversation and their ostensibly relaxed postures, they moved with an awareness I aspired to achieve, surpassing Sister Betty's enviable skills. Outsiders might have assumed them harmless, but I saw them for what they were. Dangerous. Formidable. Downright terrifying. No matter what I wanted, I'd get nothing without their full knowledge, and they'd probably screw me over in the process.

"Oh my," Violetta sighed, disappointed. "I think I broke her."

Glancing around the room, I realized she meant me.

"Others came before her," Helen said. "Others will come after."

"But I like this one." Violetta's prissy pout still managed to be endearing. "Zeke always said I played too rough."

"He wasn't wrong." Helen took a bird-like sip of tea.

The mention of her former colleague and clan council member, Zikros, made me stiffen in anticipation of reprimand or retribution. I'd killed him at the Compact where I'd met Violetta and been dubbed representative for the human realm. Or, as I'd come to think of it, my "through the looking glass" moment. I'd known other dimensions existed, of course, but hadn't been aware of the conclave of supernats, or how it kept the balance between realms in places where the border thinned. The last Compact hadn't known the source of disturbances that allowed nightmares to move freely into the human realm, only that Zikros, emboldened by them, pushed for its unrestricted use as a feeding ground. And after he promised to kill off the entire planet while making me watch, if he considered Violetta's play rough, I couldn't imagine what it might include.

Violetta's intense scrutiny made me feel naked.

"What?" I asked, paranoia taking over.

"You, my dear." Her stare didn't waver. "You've lost that interesting spark."

"I haven't lost anything," I said, but it felt like a lie.

Neither woman spoke for what felt like an eternity. I reminded myself not to squirm.

Helen broke the silence first. "What you've lost won't hinder you." She slid her glove-covered left hand across the surface of the tea table between us before setting her cup down. "Not yet, at least. When it becomes evident, you won't be able to ignore it."

"What does that mean?"

The look she leveled at me reminded me that goddesses feel no obligation to explain their cryptic pronouncements. Rather than shrivel, I stared back, patient and implacable until she deigned to reply. "What do you want, Hunter? I grow tired of this."

As if responding to her mood, Fenrir, her massive wolf-dog demi-god brother rounded a low couch with a warning grumble, teeth bared in a snarl.

"'S'up, Fen," I said, trying to quell my rush of nerves. "Good to see you, too."

Helen's irritation drew my attention. "My patience is not infinite, Miss Kelley."

"You'd think—" I started, but her stern glare inspired me to shut up. "Right. The point." I cleared my throat. "The Collectors are destabilizing the realms by draining magic from supernatural creatures in order to accelerate the growth of a dragon in this one." I explained the attack on Bourbon, the missing supernats and the ill that remained in their communities. "I need help figuring out how they're accessing other realms, the source of the magic, which may involve alchemy, help finding the magic users that attacked us, and access to a magical implement we can use to destroy the dragon."

"You presume much," muttered Helen.

Violetta laughed. "That, my dear, is why humans will never be a dominant life form." She glanced at Helen, who looked bored. "So short sighted."

Rather than respond, I sipped my tea. My skin crawled in the silence. My heart pounded as thoughts clambered over each other. Anything could be happening while I sat here, waiting for a literal nightmare to deliver her judgment of humans. Who would disappear next? Some high ranking supernatural? Or would my team be attacked again? Whatever happened here, Charity Hospital would be my next stop.

My neck ached. I resisted the urge to stretch it while the Norse goddess of the underworld and the ranking head of the nightmare clan stared at me like some alien specimen. Though, to be fair, I kind of was. To them, at least.

When Violetta realized I intended to remain silent, she said, "You work so hard over such short life spans," she tilted her head, considering me, "yet you waste so much time and energy doing things the most difficult way possible."

"Call it a hobby," I said. "Or blame it on a lack of an army."

"Why would you need an army?" Violetta asked with a patronizing smile.

"Until we figure out how to be in multiple places at once, or evolve the skill, we can only chase as many monsters as we have Hunters." I shrugged. "Right now, New Orleans has more bad guys than I can chase."

She rolled her eyes and tossed her head, curls bouncing around her face. "For such a creative species, you suck at energy conservation."

"Then, please," I spread my hands in invitation, "enlighten me."

"What are you hunting?"

This crap again. I waited for the punchline, then said, "The Collectors. They're the key to the rest."

"But what are the Collectors?" Helen interrupted, more frustrated than me.

I looked at her one vibrant eye and tried not to imagine the other hidden behind her silken fall of blond hair. "That's what I'd hoped you'd tell me. We don't know who—"

"That's what I mean about wasting energy," Violetta laughed. "Your kind is so primitive, it's like watching evolutionary forces fail over and over again. Quite the little puzzle for Darwin. I'm sure he's gnashing his teeth over it."

I gritted mine and waited. How many names would be added to my list before teasing me ceased to amuse her? Between Carter and these two, we could have been done with the whole thing if they'd only cooperate and share what they knew without games.

Hel stared into the distance and sipped her tea.

"Primitive? Because we lack superpowers or—"

Violetta's laugh interrupted.

"At least we're polite." I set my cup down.

When she regained her composure, she dabbed at tissue at the corner of her eyes. "My dear, you simply must spend some time with me in my realm. You are a delight."

"Well, when I opt for a slow death by soul ablation, I'll do that."

"I never said anything about touching you," she murmured over the rim of her cup. "Unless you're ready for some to-die-for touching."

"You call me primitive and now you're hitting on me?"

"Oh, no, my dear, not you." She set her cup aside and arranged herself artfully in the delicate armchair. "Your species."

I rolled my eyes. "Well, that makes me feel better."

"Your stories make a third of your population out to be weak, even calling them 'the gentler sex,' or the 'fairer' sex. Your mythologies, even your modern ones, portray them as helpless, but any fool with eyes can see their raw power."

"A...third?" Either she'd done the math wrong, or we had some fundamental misunderstanding.

"The women, love, do keep up." She shook her head "Not to mention that, as a species, you're quite obsessed with genitalia. Pathologically so. It's," she gestured with a sneer of disgust, "disturbing."

I shook my head. "Can we get back to what we were talking about?"

Violetta and Helen exchanged a look.

"If there's something going on, as the Compact's human representative, I have a right to know." I shifted, wincing as the old wood creaked. Whether it meant anything or not, reminding them of the title bestowed on me couldn't hurt.

Helen gave an elegant shrug and wandered to the window, her gloved left hand opening the sheer curtains.

I couldn't take any more. I sprang to my feet. "Either tell me or tell me to fuck off, because people, people like you, will die if we keep wasting time playing games."

Helen didn't turn, despite my ragged breathing.

The tick of Helen's clock filled the silence. Its hollow chime rang the hour. Fenrir snorted, a mutt's wry amusement, perhaps. Before my sanity snapped and let loose the scream raging inside my head, Violetta spoke. "What you chase is worthless. Disposable."

"What?" What was it with immortals sounding like shitty fortune cookies?

"You chase appendages."

"What do you mean?"

"Appendages are only as valuable as the brain directing them." Violetta watched me, her eyes wide as if urging me to understand. "Why bother with minor functionaries?"

I stared into her eyes, confused, and then, it clicked. I should have realized, I should have made the connection before, long before now.

"They all have the same purpose, growing the dragon, and if we find the dragon—"

Violetta's hand shot out in front of me before I'd taken two full steps toward the door, though she avoided touching me. "Brava, little Hunter. One more question before you go."

"Yes?" I rocked on the balls of my feet, my brain sizzling, my fingers twitching. Even if we didn't know the source, if we got to the dragon, the other pieces would turn up.

"Your ticket to the Compact."

The shift in conversation confused me. "Yes?"

"Do you still have it?"

"Of course." Then, I doubted whether I should have admitted it.

"Do you carry it with you?"

"No," I said, more confused. The Compact only happened once every twelve years. Why should I carry it? I'd hidden it in the armory at the St. Louis Cathedral where it would remain for a little more than a decade until I required it again.

"You should," Violetta said.

36

W e've got access to Charity Hospital," Sister Betty said, her voice slightly tinny in my Bluetooth earbud.

"Awesome," I said, hand up, signaling Marty not to move.

After the briefest pause, she asked, "You're already there, aren't you?"

To my own credit, I didn't laugh. My Scarlet Witch knew me well. "For recon, but yay, I'm legal!"

She sighed. "That's not how this works, Caitlin."

"Right. Signal's crap. We'll be out in an hour. Call you then, bye!" After the rush of words, I ended the call and put my dust mask back on. My lungs already felt dirty from breathing the thick air without it. All the windows we glimpsed through open doors were dirty and, broken or unbroken, covered with wire mesh. From what we'd seen, birds and animals still managed to get in, just not enough breeze to stir the oppressive heat.

"This might not be a good idea." Marty adjusted his mask and aimed his flashlight at a wall covered with either mold or poorly removed graffiti. Silver letters above the mess glittered in the beam. *Welcome to the Medical Center of Louisiana. Where the Unusual Occurs & Miracles Happen.*

"It's not like we're here for karaoke," I said. "Once we get the lay of the land, we leave. Now, double time before our favorite nun shows up to beat my ass."

"I'd pay to watch that," he muttered.

"Until she kicks *yours* for following me." I scanned the ground.

"True." His flashlight beam landed on an IV bag filled with cloudy liquid, its dangling tubing waiting for a patient.

"Besides," I flicked my light at him, "I didn't think you got into that."

"What?" He shaded his eyes. "Violence? A well-deserved beating? Sister Hotpants is poetry in motion when she fights. You should study her."

"Funny." I sidestepped a pile of junk that might have been a wheelchair in a past life.

Marty consulted his phone. "These maps don't have much detail."

I glanced over his shoulder. "Weren't there better ones?"

"This is the best I could find on the way over." He expanded the image with his finger and thumb. "I mean, I'm good, but even I need time to work magic. The easy finds have probably been hidden to discourage thrill seekers."

"Thrill seekers?" Nothing interesting remained in the building. Nothing worth breaking in to steal, at least. And if a dragon had taken up residence, anyone foolhardy enough to invade would regret it for the rest of their short and painful life. "What's thrilling about this?"

"For someone who plumbs the mysteries of spooky places, you lack the urban adventurer spirit." Marty nudged a pile of unidentifiable matter with his toe. "People like exploring abandoned buildings." He gestured at the IV pole with his flashlight. "Especially hastily abandoned ones. Then, there's the rumors."

"What rumors?" I passed an open door, glancing at the mattress and pile of newspapers in the room beyond. Like the tent city under I-10 on the way over, this place meant shelter, and for more than wildlife. Something we'd need to consider for our return trip.

"If you believe the tours, weird shit goes on around here."

I stepped over a flattened plastic vodka bottle. "Like?"

"Lights go on and off though there's no power. And the hauntings. Any abandoned building gets that reputation after a while, of course, especially when people died there." He stepped and a pebble skittered down the hall. "The rumors seem to be just that. None of the details are credible, but they're alluring to the average person."

I'd seen too much to find mysteries casually appealing. "I'll take your word for it."

Each footstep crunched as we explored. Occasionally, birds took flight or unseen animals scrambled, but even when they scared the bejesus out of us, we found nothing unexpected. No dragons. No signs of nefarious habitation. Charity Hospital was exactly what we expected: an abandoned medical facility.

"What is that smell?" I resisted the urge to cover my nose. With a flashlight in one hand, my other had to stay open. Just in case.

"I don't know, but it reeks like moldy ass."

I bit the inside of my cheek to contain my laugh. "Never tell me why you know what 'moldy ass' smells like."

He shined his light on the heavy metal door at the end of the hall. "High school locker rooms."

"Gross, dude." I walked to the door, hauling it open and holding it with my foot as I leaned through the doorway into a windowless stairwell. Profound silence roared at me from above and below. The size of the building registered and, for the first time, gave me pause. Maybe we should have brought backup. We didn't know what waited for us above, or below. Anything could happen. Other than knowing we'd entered the building, no one knew where we were. If anything happened, Marty and I might simply disappear. If anything happened, could I get him out safely?

Maybe this is what Sister Betty meant when she called me reckless.

I pushed the thought away. We were here. I had a job to do. One way or another, it had to get done or the city would suffer. Marty and I could handle this and get out in one piece. Of that much, I was confident. Mostly. Enough to go on with it, at least.

Leaning back, I asked, "Ready to go spelunking into the bowels?"

Marty's mask muffled his fake gagging. "Nasty."

"What? The basement *is* the most likely place for a lair."

He swiped his arm across his forehead. "I could've done without the metaphor."

"I have to amuse myself somehow." Propping the door open with my hip, I checked my weapons, secured my phone in my pocket, and brushed hair out of my eyes. The stairway's mustiness penetrated the mask, and I tried not to choke as I breathed. "Let's get this over with."

But before I stepped over the threshold, animal eyes glinted in the flashlight beam.

I froze.

A rat the size of a Chihuahua popped up over a pair of beach ball-sized spheres in the corner. Paws spread wide, the rat chittered a warning. "Ugh." The sound escaped before I realized I'd intended to make one.

"What's up?" Marty whispered and leaned close.

Without warning, the massive rat stumbled, and its hind legs disappeared into the ball. Its claws dug into the shimmery surface as the rat scrambled for purchase. It emitted a short, sharp sound, a scream, before the sparkly sac devoured it and closed, seamless.

I backpedaled into Marty, shoving him back.

The timoredax.

"What?" Marty asked as I whipped around. "What did you see?"

Despite my rising panic, I remembered to close the door quietly and checked the seals around it. How small could juveniles compress themselves? Even flexible exoskeletons had to have limitations. How many sacs had been in the corner? Two? Three? Any of the creepy bastards on the walls?

"Fuck, fuck, fuckity fuck." Restraining myself to that little profanity took effort. I fumbled my phone out of my pocket. "They're eating the fucking rats."

"Easy there, F-bomb queen." Marty raised an eyebrow, torn between being disturbed and amused. "Don't hurt yourself cussing over dead rats."

No matter how much I liked the title, we didn't have time to screw around. He might not recognize the gravity of our predicament, but I did. Worse, I had no answer. Had someone left a door open to Faerie, or had the border between here and there gotten that weak?

This was going to get ugly.

"Marty." I flashed my light around looking for more eggs. I intended to give him some kind of instruction, but what the hell could I say?

"Yes, your Majesty?" he quipped.

I'd relinquish my profane kingdom for a single can of magical, mystical Raid. "You're lucky I don't have time to smack you."

A re you sure?" Sister Betty demanded, staring through me. A too-bright overhead light would have completed the stereotypical interrogation atmosphere. The rectory office walls encroached by inches under the intensity of her questions and the vigilant audience Father Callahan, Marty, Rene, and Madame Sabine provided. "Are you sure it wasn't the lighting? Or something else that caught the rat?"

"I know what I saw," I repeated and slid the tablet to her. "It was one of these."

The egg sac in the photo was more evenly rounded, maybe from lack of a rat crouching on it, but the photo captured the sheen. A crawly sensation rippled my skin, but I resisted the urge to flee to the bathroom to strip and hunt for tiny spiders lurking in my clothes. I hadn't found any during either of my previous inspections, and a third check would amount to a paranoid waste of time.

"If there's one, there are hundreds," Father Callahan said, distant and contemplative. "Maybe thousands. The timoredax may be solitary hunters, but they spawn massive colonies."

Sister Betty muttered a curse, then glanced at Madame Sabine at the end of the table. The older woman sat so still, I thought she might be asleep. Sister Betty recovered her bravery, muttering, "Who the hell smuggled them in?"

"At least they're not those Harry Potter spiders." Rene laughed nervously.

"Where do you think Rowling got the idea?" I asked.

"Tolkien, too," Father Callahan added.

Rene's confidence evaporated. "I was kidding."

"They weren't," Marty said.

"But they're just stories," Rene protested.

"They're no story." Marty took the tablet from Sister Betty and passed it to Rene.

Rene paled as his eyes progressed down the page. "Legs up to eight feet long."

"That's an eighteen-foot leg span, assuming two-foot body girth," Marty said. "And that's average. Allowed to hunt and amass size without natural predators…" His voice trailed off and he gave a suggestive shrug.

I'd only dealt with a baby timoredax before. Bigger than a Rottweiler and a bitch to bring down. Thankfully, the babies didn't spit acid. Attempting to skewer me with their horrifying fangs and leg spikes was plenty, thank you very much. With any luck, we'd only have to deal with babies. I didn't trust our luck, however.

"You didn't say anything about spiderwebs, though," Rene said, confused.

"Timoredax are ambush hunters, like huntsman spiders," Sister Betty said, her voice flat.

"They don't build webs," Marty said when Rene didn't seem to understand the implications. "They chase prey."

"But what are they doing here?" Sister Betty asked herself.

Marty didn't seem to hear her as he struggled to contain his amusement at Rene's growing horror. I wondered if Rene would pass out before I figured out when to stop my partner's playful, if terrifying, hazing.

"That's just the opening act," I said, perhaps taking a bit too much enjoyment watching him squirm. "If we survive, there's the dragon."

"If?" Rene choked.

"They're sentinels," Sister Betty muttered, crossing her arms.

We all looked at her.

"They're the front guard," she said, standing up straighter and talking faster. "They're intended to be the first line of defense, the thing that takes down intruders. The fae train them as a kind of guard, and whoever brought them here knows that. They're using them the same way."

Marty made a sound of disgust. "That's..."

"Maniacal?" I suggested. "Brilliant?"

Everyone looked at me.

"What? I'm a realist," I said. "Before we can confirm what we're facing in the basement, whether it's a dragon or some magic user bent on destroying anything supernatural, we'll have to face hungry creepy crawlies ready to eat our faces. It's brilliant." I shrugged. "Whoever we're up against, this isn't their first diabolical plot."

"I hate it when you're right," Marty said and reclaimed his tablet.

"They aren't invulnerable," Father Callahan said. "Let's work on that strategy first."

"We have to assume there will be adults," Sister Betty said, scribbling a note on a pad of paper, "so we have to prepare for acid."

I nodded. "Then we plan for dragon."

"We'll need it if we survive the spiders," Marty agreed.

"Right," Rene mumbled. "If."

"Don't worry," Marty said. "Stick around long enough, and near-death experiences won't feel so overwhelming."

"We'll need to spend the most time planning for the dragon," Sister Betty said. "The last dragon hunters died eons ago, and there isn't much information on how to take them down without magical weapons, other than beheading."

"That's where I help." Madame Sabine's voice creaked with her long silence. She held up the amulet she'd given me during our first encounter. The smoked glass chips glittered as the unremarkable stone twisted on its cord. It had admitted me to the Compact. If Madame Sabine offered it as a solution to dragon slaying and Violetta wanted me to wear it, what else was it capable of?

Hours later, Rene looked up from the open book in front of him on Father Callahan's desk and asked, "Is it possible—"

"Yes," I said in unison with Sister Betty, Father Callahan, and Marty.

"I haven't asked my question," Rene protested.

"Doesn't matter," Sister Betty put her pen down. "Whether it's super-human acts of bravery and stupidity, or divine intervention, if it involves Caitlin, it's possible, and we account for it. What did you have in mind?"

Rene stared at Sister Betty. I could sense his whirring thoughts, but he gathered himself and continued. "If Caitlin wears the amulet, would it interact with a cross? Or other symbol of faith?"

Sister Betty and Father Callahan exchanged a look.

"It's worth considering." Sister Betty turned to me.

Declining to discuss the state of my faith, I addressed Rene's question. "Things get weird when mixing the inherent magics of religion."

"Especially Catholicism." The old book Father Callahan flipped through smeared dust on his black shirt.

"Which is why I don't wear symbols of faith unless they're proven to provide reliable advantage against...whatever I'm fighting." I avoided Sister Betty's gaze, grateful that lying in church didn't invoke immediate divine retribution. We'd been avoiding the discussion for so long, I'd started to believe I might never have to discuss it. Knowing her, though, she'd crack me sooner or later. Until then, though, me and my on-going religious crisis stayed between me and the divine being upstairs.

"You're getting quite the indoctrination into Caitlin's world." Father Callahan chuckled.

"Yessir," Rene said. "I didn't realize it involved more than hunting and shooting monsters."

Marty coughed, his head bowed and hand covering his mouth.

"*Much* more." Sister Betty restrained her admonition to an emphasized word and gestured to Father Callahan's book. "Find anything?"

"Other than damage from a multitude of environmental sins," he turned a delicate, water-warped page, "no. It goes back to the city's founding, but no historical activity suggests a history of alchemists or any of the known dragon cults. At least, not yet."

"If it doesn't fall apart before you get to that part," Marty grumbled. "They need to be digitized."

"They will be." Father Callahan considered the book in his hand, his voice full of something like reverence. "They've seen a lot, especially in this city. We're fortunate they've lasted this long."

"Like Sister Betty said, divine intervention." I picked up another from the stack in front of Father Callahan, carefully opened it, and winced as the paper crackled. "There must be something here we need."

Rene leaned close, brushing against me. "You don't strike me as the superstitious type."

Despite the little jolt of contact, that weird aversion crept back in, like when he told me he loved me. He couldn't. Worse, I hadn't decided if I wanted him to.

"You've known me a month. Less actually," I reminded him, eyebrow raised. "You don't have me figured out."

"That's something I look forward to," Rene said with a wistful smile.

"Can we get back to work, please?" I gestured to the books we had and trying to ignore the vague nausea battling the heat of attraction in my veins. "We might have a strategy for the timoredax already here, but these things aren't native to our realm. How are they getting here? And maybe more importantly, how do we shut that door?"

Madame Sabine cleared her throat with a rattling cough, and I jumped. She'd been sitting quietly on the couch for so long, I'd forgotten she was here. "There is much you should learn," she waved at the books, "but what you need is not there."

More fortune cookie BS? Or had we graduated to Yoda? Glowy-eye trances and deciphering Tarot cards that didn't exist in the traditional arcanas fell near the bottom of my list of things I wanted to deal with, just above the disaster of my personal relationships. So, of course, dealing with them is exactly what I prepared to do.

I stood and perched on the far edge of Father Callahan's desk, closer to her and out of Rene's immediate reach. "What do you mean?"

Madame Sabine shifted, then smiled. Age and wrinkles hid her magic, but her eyes hinted at what lay beneath. "There are other paths through these obstacles. The way through is not always behind the door you expect."

Awesome. The last time she'd said something that cryptic, I'd taken the Alice in Wonderland express route into the middle of an interdimensional political convention. "Am I going to fall into the dragon's lair?" I sat, hoping I didn't sound as impertinent as I felt.

"The nexus is a place of doors." She shrugged. "We cannot know all."

"Comforting." I chewed my bottom lip, thinking. If she knew something, anything, that might help save the city from a threat I hadn't antici-pated, I needed to know. "What should we expect to happen?"

The old woman adjusted her layered skirt and folded her hands in her lap. "I cannot say."

My shoulders slumped. Back to the beginning.

Her laugh caught me off guard. "So glum," she chided, clucking.

"We've made no progress." The acid frustration surprised even me, but I couldn't stop the question before it fell out. "Am I supposed to be happy?"

She considered me, silencing Sister Betty with a gesture. "Hunters are pillars of hope, defenders against the horrors of the dark. Where will we be if they lose faith because the path forward is not clear?"

Before I could respond, Marty's phone beeped. We all turned to him.

"What is it?" I asked.

He shook his head and put his phone face down on the desk. "Another disappearance."

A fist squeezed my internal organs. Had I not been sitting, my knees might have buckled. My head felt too heavy to hold up, so I stared at the floor. I should have been able to stop this, to change it. And I hadn't. We didn't know the scope of what waited for us, and only had a plan for half the threats we knew about. Worst of all, we had no answers for the biggest one. There were too many holes, too many pitfalls, and while I spent precious time researching, another innocent paid the price. Another victim for my list. Another failure. How could anyone, supernat-ural or not, trust me? How could I hold on to hope when I couldn't look innocent people in the eyes and explain why I hadn't stopped what threatened them? How could I call myself a Hunter? What the hell was I doing?

"Hunter."

Chills ran the length of my spine, but I didn't look up. I didn't deserve the title.

"Hunter." Steel infused Madame Sabine's voice.

"I'm no Hunter." The truth made my chest ache.

"Caitlin," Sister Betty gasped.

"I've failed." The words hurt, but they were the truest words I'd ever spoken. I looked up. Father Callahan's face showed nothing, but Sister Betty's contorted with pain. "In every possible way, no matter where we look, I've failed to discover who these Collectors are or how they're operating. I should have found something. I'm supposed to stop it and I'm failing. I'm failing at everything."

"That's not true," Sister Betty insisted. Father Callahan's hand on her shoulder prevented her from approaching. "And you're working on the next step."

"Not fast enough." I shook my head. "It's not enough."

"You only fail if you give up," Madame Sabine said.

They all stared at me. I couldn't look at Rene or Sister Betty. Or anyone else. I focused on the floor, the strange industrial carpet pattern. The weight in my chest pulling me down. I wished I could crawl under the desk and sleep. To let everything disappear until the storm passed. Or until I didn't wake up anymore. Either would be fine. However it came, I wanted the numbness. I wanted the peace it offered. I needed the relief it promised.

"Caitlin."

The tenderness in Marty's voice made me look up. When our eyes met, I couldn't help but recall our conversation. The way he'd seen how not fine I was even when I couldn't put it in to words. He'd called me on the excuses and lies I couldn't avoid telling. He'd suggested I'd need help. I could see he was right, and I knew all I had to do was say so. All I had to do was say I needed help, and maybe I wouldn't need words. Maybe he'd understand if I reached a hand across the gulf between us.

But I couldn't do it.

In his eyes, I saw the supernatural and human worlds depending on me. That needed me to stand against the dark. Without a defender, the monsters would win. Without a champion, the humans and supernaturals didn't stand a chance.

As much as I didn't want to exist anymore, as much as I wanted the numbness to stay, I couldn't leave anyone else to Shannon's fate. As much as I yearned to escape it all, her memory weighed on me.

"This is your choice, Cee. No one else's," Marty said. "What do you want to do?"

I covered my face with my hands. His infernal compassion burned me alive. There was only one answer I could give, so I gave it.

Even a half-assed plan counted as a plan, after all.

"Gather up whatever armor we can scrounge. We roll as soon as we're geared up. I've got an idea I need to...follow up on." I turned and left the room before we made eye contact again.

37

I stared at the weapons lined up on Father Callahan's desk. The lump of the amulet pressed against my ribs beneath my crossed arms. We couldn't count on any of it working on the timoredax, at least not permanently. Blunt force, maybe. Blades, yes, but with limited effect. The same went for the dragon. We'd be lucky to do more than annoy with what we had on hand, and being actually effective would require a miracle. Every option felt impossible, but we had to try. Or rather, *I* had to try. This couldn't be another gig where I expected some *deus ex machina* win delivered by the hands of fate. Whatever the risk, whatever the outcome, this win had to be my win.

"I don't like it," Sister Betty said, finally.

"It makes the most sense," I said, calculating how to implement my own plan despite her objections. As much as I trusted her strategic experience, I couldn't agree with her insistence on taking the entire team into Charity Hospital. We'd risk too much getting through the gauntlet of predatory acid-spitting fae spiders, never mind the dragon. I wouldn't lose anyone to either threat, and if she wouldn't listen, I'd have to do what she taught me. Improvise and overcome. Scooby Doo rule be damned.

"You're not going alone." Sister Betty turned to glare at me, hands on her hips.

"We are barely prepared to deal with the timoredax," I said like I hadn't been hammering the same handful of points for the last hour. "*If* we manage to get the whole team through them without injury, and *if* we don't encounter anything else that wants to eat, maim, or murder us on the way, we've still got to fight a goddamned dragon." I held up my hand when her lips moved. "The only trick we've got in the arsenal to kill a dragon is beheading it. Why risk the whole team when the odds are so demonstrably against us?"

"Facing a dragon alone is suicide. For anyone," Sister Betty insisted. "The odds improve when we go together."

"No, they don't. *You* taught me that. The risk multiplies by each person we have to ninja past the creepy crawlies and anything else in there." When she didn't say anything, I pressed on. "I'm going alone."

"I'll go with you. I may not have your expertise," Rene said, "but I can do more than—"

"Your lack of expertise is your primary vulnerability," interrupted Sister Betty. She squared her shoulders, arms crossed and eyes flinty. "We're all going and adhering to the roles I've outlined, and that's final."

"Those of us not trained as Hunters," Father Callahan said, attempting to placate Rene's obvious pique, "will provide support."

"I've hunted plenty," Rene argued.

"Not like this," I said. "Experienced as my team is, I don't want them fighting this."

"Which is exactly why you shouldn't go alone," Sister Betty said.

"Remember the hydra?" Marty asked Rene.

"Of course."

Marty shrugged. "This will be harder."

Rene leaned forward in his chair, his fists knotting between his knees. "I want to do more."

"Dude, we all do," Marty snapped, then recovered. "Our assignment is support."

"Caitlin and Sister Betty are the most experienced with challenges of this magnitude," Father Callahan said. "Regardless of any experience the rest of us have, they are the most qualified to handle whatever we encounter."

"And, if things get bad," I said, "bad with no possibility of recovery, you all cut and run."

Hard faces stared back at me as I scanned the room.

"No," Rene stood, hand hovering at his side as if over the service weapon he usually wore, "I'm not abandoning you."

"No one's asking you to," Sister Betty said, "but you will follow orders."

The longer the silence lingered, the more the room shrank.

"The order is," I locked eyes with Sister Betty before turning to Rene, "if Sister Betty and I can't fight our way out, everyone else evacuates."

"No." Rene crossed his arms. "I'm not leaving you behind to die."

Sister Betty turned to confront him. "Officer Boudreaux, if the situation becomes untenable, the civilians, including you, evacuate. Your objective is survival. You must relay information to the next team. If that doesn't happen, things get infinitely worse for the citizens you swore to protect."

A muscle flexed in Rene's jaw. He turned and glared at me. "Caitlin."

That one word spoke volumes, and some of it I didn't want to hear. "Accept the order or stay behind, Rene," I said softly.

His nostrils flared with each breath. Gone were the bedroom eyes that made my heart flutter. In front of me stood the stolid police officer evaluating the situation to determine how to win the fight. His usual tenderness was consumed by the desire to protect me from the threat. I respected him more, and yeah, I wanted him a little more, but something still recoiled. Maybe he needed me to be the damsel in distress he expected. Or maybe he thought I wanted someone to intervene and take over before the battle. Either way, he hadn't anticipated confrontation or my refusal to yield, and that changed something between us. Relationships with a capital "R" weren't my thing, but if I wanted or needed one, I wanted an equal, a partner to complement my strengths, not a savior.

I stared him down and waited, prepared to remind him of his duty to the city.

He crossed his arms, shoulders tense. "I don't like it," he said, finally.

"You don't have to," I said.

"Are you agreeing to leave if ordered," Sister Betty pushed, studying him, "or will you be bullheaded and jeopardize the city's safety to play hero?"

The tension thickened. I wondered who'd have the upper hand between them.

"I agree to the terms." The words grated out of Rene, his expression indecipherable. His eyes never left Sister Betty, but I could sense him studying me.

"Good." Sister Betty resumed her seat, satisfied.

"As will I," Madame Sabine said from her spot on the couch.

We all stared at her, stunned. Once again, I'd forgotten she was in the room, and I didn't seem to be the only one.

Madame Sabine nodded as if we accepted, rose, and crossed the room to the weapons spread. I still hadn't figured out what she was other than "not entirely human." She didn't fit any of the cryptid types I knew, nor did she move like the elderly human she seemed to be. She surveyed the table, leaning over it, her hands folded behind her back. Her balance didn't falter, but she didn't have preternatural grace either. "I will take," she touched the grip of a 9mm before hefting it to test its weight, "this."

"I can't..." I said, wordlessly seeking Sister Betty's support, "I can't allow that."

Her wrinkled face puckered as she replaced the gun. "You think you can stop me, child?"

Instinctively, I bristled, ready to defend myself and my abilities. "I—"

"You think me some feeble fortune teller? Only capable of swindling tourists?" She stepped closer, hands on her hips, her ferocity driving me back a step despite her age and diminutive height.

"N-no," I said, bracing myself for the moment her piercing eyes glowed or for her voice to resonate with otherworldly layers. "That's not what I meant—"

"What?" She took another step in my direction. "That old women can't fight?"

"N-no, not that." Another step back and I fell into a chair as she advanced. She loomed over me. Though I'd faced bloodthirsty creatures most of my life, none terrified me as much as she did right now. "It's for your safety. Not being trained as a Hunter—"

"And who says I'm not, hmm?" Playfulness made her eyebrows quiver.

I waited, unsure. Sister Betty said Madame Sabine had helped Hunters in the past, but now how. Had she participated in tactical missions? And if she'd been trained in the skills I'd been practicing for over a decade, wouldn't Sister Betty or Father Callahan have said something? Or had Hunters outside the Church's hierarchy taught her? I *hated* having more questions than answers.

The older woman studied me as if reading my thoughts, then finally said, "Time changes titles, Hunter. And in places of power, time is flexible."

"Please don't tell me time travel is an actual thing," I groaned. Other worlds existed, of course, like Faerie and the realm of nightmare, among others, but one temporal layer per world was plenty, thank you very much. The fewer dimensions I had to fight in, the better.

Madame Sabine laughed. "You watch too much TV."

"Told you," Marty mumbled.

I rolled my eyes. "You said it was impossible to disprove."

"Do you two ever quit?" Sister Betty asked, but my mentor bit off her words and stared at the floor like a chastised child when Madame Sabine focused on her.

A rock dropped in my stomach when the old woman turned her craggy face back to mine. I understood what cowed Sister Betty. Two translucent faces floated where Madame Sabine's should be, one superimposed on the other. Her wrinkles floated over an ageless, genderless face like a mask. I tried to concentrate on one, but my focus drifted from one to the other as their alignment shifted. When she spoke, her voice resonated with layers, the united words of thousands. "You think me a husk of a person?"

I opened my mouth with a lie on my tongue, then closed it again. Swallowing hard and bracing for repercussions, I answered honestly. "I don't think you're able to handle this fight. It's too dangerous."

She sighed. "I've been swimming in danger since before you were swimming in your mother's belly."

"But there will be a dragon," I protested.

"And what experience have you with dragons?" she asked.

I shrugged. "I've studied them, their abilities." In the awkward silence, I threw out one last weak answer. "I've hunted a lot of monsters, some bigger than I should have been able to best, but I did. And I have my team to protect. Including you."

After a moment, she nodded. "Things aren't always what they seem. You should know that best, Phoenix," she said in her layered voice.

Another nickname to add to my growing collection. Phoenix. Conduit. Hunter. One more and I'd have a killer punk band name.

Madame Sabine's gnarled fingers snapped in front of my eyes. Her two faces swam over each other, her irises layering, aligning, and then splitting again. Nothing remained still. The random swirling made me queasy. The lips on the ageless face curled into a smile before I gave up and dropped my gaze.

"I don't understand what you want from me or what you expect," I admitted.

"Understanding is not required. Trust. Have faith." The chorus of her layered voices echoed words as slower voices lagged. She reached up to tap my chest, but her gnarled finger thumped the amulet under my shirt. "You need only accept help."

I glanced up.

The ageless face stared back, the aged one drifting over it.

Faith. Trust.

Questions I couldn't ask caught in my throat. What if I didn't have either? What if I couldn't pay the cost of accepting help? What if I failed even with help? What were the consequences of saying no?

Blood thundered in my ears. In the absence of any other sound, the layered voices whispered to each other, though neither of Madame Sabine's mouths moved.

Accept the help offered. Take it on faith. Trust.

Or not.

Either way, there would be a price. I had to decide for my team. My new home city.

Though I wasn't sure if I should, I nodded.

I finally figured you out." Rene caught my gaze in the rearview mirror. His guileless grin prevented my immediate, defensive retort. "You're a paladin."

I blinked, surprised and amused by the implication as well as his hidden nerdiness.

Beside me, Sister Betty groaned and stared out her window.

Marty turned in the passenger seat, scowling. "Not at all."

"Sure she is." Rene steered the black government SUV Agent Cooper had arranged for our use through the congested intersection, sparing a quick glance at him. "She puts herself in harm's way to protect the innocent in the name of the Catholic Church. That makes her a paladin."

"Can we not talk about me like I'm not here, please?" I asked, annoyed. "Besides, I'm more of a knight. My skills don't require or improve with prayer."

"That is so true," Marty agreed with unnecessary enthusiasm.

"Hey!" I smacked the headrest of his seat.

"What I mean is," Marty craned around the seat, "you earn skills physically or intellectually. Without divine intervention."

"Thank you," I said.

"Besides," he continued, "transforming you into a paladin would take more than a miracle."

I reached around the seat to swat at him.

"Lately, you're more a barbarian," Sister Betty muttered loud enough to distract me. "Fueled by rage."

Marty and I confirmed our shared question with a glance, then stared at her. As if sensing the weight of our observation, she looked at us. "What?"

"I'm not saying you're wrong," Marty said, "but where'd you learn RPG classes?"

She smirked. "I've picked up a thing or two hanging out with you nerds."

Marty laughed, and at my other side, Father Callahan chuckled. When the cramp in my heart relaxed enough to breathe, I did too. I couldn't remember how long it had been since we'd all laughed. Since I had.

They debated their own classes and I sat back, listening and holding my breath. The lightness in the car and in my heart confirmed that I couldn't let them follow me into certain death. No matter what happened, they had to survive. They'd be fine without me, but if anything happened to any of them...

Father Callahan nudged my arm and leaned in to whisper, "At least they're getting along."

My snarky retort died when I realized how right he was.

Still, I avoided eye contact with Rene in the rearview mirror. Whatever he and I were, and despite the fun we had, he wasn't Sister Betty, and that mattered more than I wanted to admit.

Secrecy, for a monster hunter, is a dual-edged sword. Keep things too secret, and your untimely demise becomes a question for the ages. Amelia Earhart, for example. Not enough secrecy provokes the rumor mill to spin legends, Area 51 and Bigfoot, among the most notable. Most monster hunting is done at night to control who may stumble upon the truth, or a hungry critter. Daylight risks revealing what lurks at the edge of humanity, but sometimes, the deed has to be done out in the open.

Today was one of those times.

I studied the upper floors of the gray building looming over us. We stood in the shadowed valley between Charity Hospital and Louisiana State University's Gravier Street parking garage, tucked as far out of sight of the street as we could get. Chain-link fences wouldn't provide much cover, and nothing prevented anyone from looking down at us from the

LSU medical building, but it should be enough for our immediate purposes. Once we weaponed up and put on the rest of our protective gear, we'd be headed inside. Anyone indulging in the view into the dismal abyss of the hospital grounds might see us coming and going, but not much else. Unless things got ugly.

Of course, I expected ugly. "I've got a bad feeling about this," I said as my team geared up around me.

"Ditto." Marty snapped his Glock's magazine in place.

"Noted." Sister Betty selected a shotgun from the back of the SUV and handed it to Father Callahan.

"This is too dangerous to bring everyone in," I said, giving the soft armor under my shirt another tug.

"If it's too dangerous for your *team*," Sister Betty stressed the word and scowled at me, "then there's no way you're going in alone. What about that don't you understand?"

"It has nothing to do with understanding." I looked at Marty for support. If he'd had the same bad feeling, he'd be on my side.

"I'm not arguing with her, man." He shrugged and thrust his chin in her direction. "Especially not when she's armed."

Sister Betty held her Mossberg, and one corner of her lips tipped up in a smirk.

Father Callahan didn't immediately respond when I swung my demanding glare his way. "You are incredibly skilled, Caitlin, and whether you admit it or not, you know going in alone is strategically insupportable."

My jaw ached; my teeth clenched. I took a deep breath, collecting my thoughts, structuring my argument. There had to be a way to convince them to stay out of this.

Rene took my wrist, pulling my fist from my hip. "You shouldn't have to do this if you're not comfortable."

Sister Betty glared at him, stopping in the middle of loading her shotgun.

"I—"

"This is your team," Rene insisted. "Your mission. You call the shots. That means you say go or no go, and you can't let someone dictate your instincts."

The shotgun slide clicked, and Sister Betty said, "That's not how this works."

Even in the sticky, humid air, I shivered. Every thought left my head.

Rene straightened in a vaguely military posture that spoke of years of training, years of being obeyed. "The plan shouldn't compromise the leader's—"

"Son," Father Callahan placed a hand on Rene's shoulder, "this isn't the time or place."

Rene glanced at the priest's hand before meeting his eyes. "With all due respect—"

"This ought to be interesting." Marty holstered his Glock and leaned a hip against the back of the SUV, crossing his arms.

"Rene, I know you mean well," I said.

"Yes, I do," he said, eyes still locked on Father Callahan's, "and I won't let you be bullied or ignored by your team."

"You're fighting an imaginary battle." I struggled against irritation, fighting the urge to demand where he got off inserting himself into a dynamic he didn't understand.

"She's undermining your authority, treating you like a puppet," Rene said, his measured tone evaporating with each word as he met Sister Betty's eyes.

"Let's walk, son." Warning rumbled beneath Father Callahan's strict control.

Rene yanked free, but didn't move. He dug in, ready for more. "I'm not going anywhere."

"Rene, stop." My hands shook as I crossed the cracked pavement to step between him and Sister Betty. I looked up at him, waiting until his eyes met mine. Whatever we had didn't compare to my relationships with the rest of my team. Whatever he thought we shared didn't give him license to attack them, even if he intended to protect me. Besides, whatever waited for us beyond the hospital doors would require everything I had, and this unnecessary conflict only drained my limited resources. When he finally looked at me, I said, "No one is undermining me."

"The hell she isn't." He aimed a pointed glare at Sister Betty. "She overrules you on every decision you make, and you never fight back."

"That's not true," I said. "And she would know better than me. She has more experience. She trained me." Even as I said it, the truth of those words sunk deep and I knew my impulse to do this on my own was dead wrong. "Still trains me."

He sneered in horror and stared at me, then swung his gaze around at the others. "The lack of respect you show for your leader is unconscionable. Caitlin risks her life for you, and you have her believing less of herself because of it."

"Stop." I resisted the urge to lay my hand on his chest like I'd done so many times before. I didn't need him to see this as weakness. He had to see strength. "You don't know what you're talking about, and you will not abuse my team."

"Abuse?" Confusion drew his brows together as he stared down at me. "Are you serious?"

"Yes, I am," I said, hands on my hips. "You're berating my team. You've been asked to stop and given an opportunity to let it go. Stop or leave."

Hurt mingled with his confusion. "But—"

"I don't need protection."

"You need backup—"

"On this mission, yes." When Rene opened his mouth, I held up one finger to silence him. "But this bullshit stops here."

The lines around his eyes intensified for a minute, then softened. He laughed a little, his hand compulsively checking his holster's safety strap. "You're quite the challenge, Caitlin."

Not willing to spend any more energy fighting him, I didn't respond.

"You're exactly the woman I've been waiting for." He took both my hands in his, kissing the back of mine, his eyes locked on mine. Emotion I couldn't identify radiated off of him.

Fire burned in my cheeks. My skin crawled. Every nerve twitched, ready to run into the building, guns out and firing at anything that moved. I needed to escape, to hurl myself in front of the threat, come what may. I didn't, though. With everyone watching, I didn't know what to do. He didn't know me, not really, yet he said things like this. As if he only saw what he wanted.

Confronting the dragon single-handedly would be easier than enduring this.

"We don't have time for this." Soon, sooner than I liked, we'd have to have a conversation. A painful, but necessary one where I disabused him of his fantasy version of me.

He pressed his lips to the skinned knuckles of my right hand. As he pulled back, he gently squeezed my hands. "You know this mission is crazy."

"No crazier than any other." I scowled. "What's your point?"

He held my hands against his chest. "Your job is to protect humans, right?"

"As well as the other populations in my territory."

"Isn't it enough to watch over humanity?"

"What are you saying?" I wanted to step back, to remove myself from his grasp and all he implied.

"Your job, your primary purpose as I understand it is to protect humanity from the things that go bump in the night. But instead of sticking to that mission, you're expanding it to other populations who don't need your help, and you're doing it with a skeleton crew." He dropped his hands without releasing mine. "I mean, it takes a police force to protect the city. You're trying to do as much with far less. Why do you have to do more than what you've been tasked to do?"

"It's a huge job," I admitted, ignoring my souring stomach, "and I, *we* may not be able to get it done on our own."

Rene's triumphant smile slowly spread.

The shuffling of my team behind me rankled my nerves and raised the stakes. I couldn't lie with them listening. They'd hear it. They'd know it for a lie, and they deserved better.

Still, I hated the truth. Maybe I'd fail. Maybe I'd die trying to overcome the threat. I'd accepted that reality a long time ago. My team had accepted the same risks for every job we'd taken on and hadn't backed down, no matter how the odds stacked against us. But not him. He didn't have to accept our reality and I wouldn't ask him to.

Ice wriggled under my skin.

Could I really tell him to leave when one person might make the difference between life or death? Between success and failure? My energy drained to nothing just considering the cost. Still, he could not under-mine my team. Or me.

"You don't have to do this," I said. "If you want out, I won't hold it against you."

The team took a collective breath.

"I don't want out. I'm saying you're assuming more responsibility than this job requires." His soft tone didn't make his words sting any less. He could be right, after all. The fight might be too big for us, but could I live with myself if I only concerned myself with protecting humans while supernats suffered? "Think about it, Caitlin. How much can your team really do? How much can you do?" His imploring eyes bored into me until I looked down at my hands still clasped in his. "Will it be worth wasting your time saving creatures you'll have to hunt later?"

The more he said, the less I believed he'd obey any order to leave. If I couldn't trust him in a crisis, could I allow him to follow? And if he really believed what he said, what would happen if he had to make a choice between a human and a supernatural? Between me and someone who actually needed his help?

He kept staring at me as if waiting for an answer, but the questions in my head raged like a preview of the battle I expected once we got inside.

Why did this have to happen now? Why now, right before the biggest fight in my career? Why now when I didn't have the energy to deal with it?

"Caitlin," he said, "the scope of your role—"

"I know my role and the scope of my responsibility, thank you." I jerked my hands out of his and turned to the open SUV, staring at the arsenal laid out in the back. With each constricted breath, I willed the fury to subside. I should have come alone. I should have found some excuse to separate myself from the group and done it alone from the beginning, damn the consequences. If I had, I wouldn't be worried about any of them, and I wouldn't have to deal with this.

"Are…are you mad?"

I turned around, expecting a tentative, apologetic grin. Instead, he blinked, confused. "Did you think I'd be happy?"

Out of the corner of my eye, Sister Betty turned away, pretending not to listen.

"I didn't think you'd be upset." He walked closer and reached for my hand.

I pulled away, glaring at him, my control only temporary. "Why now? Why bring this up now, when you know what we're facing in there?"

He didn't answer immediately, as if considering my reaction. Finally, he said, "Your territory is the entire southern US, right?"

"It doesn't matter," I said, thrown by the shift in the conversation.

"It does matter," he insisted.

"From San Antonio to the panhandle of Florida and everything in between," I said.

"Do you know how many people, human people, live in that area?"

"What does that have to do with it?"

"Everything," he said. "You're trying to save the human world and, as if that's not enough, you've assumed responsibility for the entire supernatural community as well—"

"Only the ones threatened—"

"You can't save them all, Caitlin." His soft, slow words sliced through me.

"Why are you talking to me like a child?" Hot fury burned the tips of my ears. If he expected—

"Because you're acting like one."

I recoiled, the words as violent as a slap. An unnatural calm settled over me. "Excuse me?"

"You believe," he said, his words endlessly patient, despite his angry flush, "you have this superhuman ability to protect anyone and everyone."

I stared at him, refusing to blink, refusing to acknowledge the prickle of tears.

"And as much as I love you for it, you're going to get hurt, or worse," he said, the last word a croak. "You can't be everything to everyone. You should walk away from this fight."

I burned with embarrassment, but shoved it aside in favor of the welling rage. First Sister Betty, now Rene. Who the hell was he to judge? Even with his experience as a police officer, he couldn't understand the complex interactions between the supernatural and human world. I'd been studying it for years and only reached the conclusion that I *still* had a hell of a lot to learn. "You think I should ignore the threat against the supernaturals?"

"No." He ran a hand through his hair. "Not exactly, but if it comes to a choice—"

"A choice of what exactly? Of the value of one life over another? Of the worth of one group over another?"

"Caitlin, honey, that's not what I'm saying."

My short nails cut into my palms at the endearment. With every fiber of my being, I resisted the urge to slap the patronizing concern right the hell off his face. He'd better thank God for my belief that violence only served the purpose of saving lives.

"I'm saying," he continued, "if you have to make a choice—"

"Everything's a choice." Saying it only intensified the gravity of the words. I stood at a crossroads that either jeopardized an innocent, or shrank my team despite knowing what lay beyond the doors of Charity Hospital. I had walked into this expecting one extra fighter. I'd begrudgingly allowed Madame Sabine with the assumption that I'd have another gun to keep her safe, that my team wouldn't have to split their attention more than normal. But, if my team encountered someone who truly needed our help, could I trust Rene to save them?

He'd continued talking and I caught up somewhere in the middle, noting his relief. "But taking on both is impossible. Choose the battles that matter."

My stomach clenched. I couldn't look at him. "Why?"

"What?"

Our eyes met. For the first time, I noticed the rim of green around his blue eyes and I knew how I'd gotten so lost in them. They reminded me of a forest pond, like the place I'd spent so much of my childhood after Shannon's death. My safe space, my retreat from grieving parents and doctors who insisted monsters didn't exist, insisted that I'd created a fantasy stand-in for a gruesome truth I refused to confront. In his eyes, I'd seen what I wanted. A refuge. A place to hide. It all made sense, but it didn't hurt any less. I needed the numbness. I needed to not feel. I called the void to me, bracing myself against what came next. "Why is it enough to protect humans and not supernats?"

"Be—because it is, Caitlin." He stared at me. "You're risking your life—"

"Because these communities aren't like you and me?" I pressed on. "And what if humans victimize them? Aren't I responsible for that harm if I refuse to act?"

"That's not what I said." His words slowed, defensive and hesitant. "I want—"

"I won't stop until the innocent of all species can live without fear."

"I love you for that, but what are you risking—"

"Myself," I said.

He shut up, but only for a moment. "You don't know what I was asking."

"Then ask."

"What are you risking by putting yourself in harm's way? By sacrificing your health, your life—"

"My answer doesn't change." I drew the numbness around me like a shield. With so much at stake, I couldn't afford less. "Doing nothing, I lose myself. If I die fighting to save one life, so be it. If I win, I live to do it again. And again. And again. I will beat back the darkness until I no longer draw breath. I'd rather die fighting than live as a coward."

"I never called you a coward."

"But risking my life for supernatural creatures isn't a worthy pursuit?"

He shook his head. "That's not what I'm saying. I'm saying I don't want to lose you. That I want you to stay. Here. With me."

I laughed. I couldn't help it. "That's the most flattering, selfish, bullshit I've ever heard. But you don't get to make that choice. Not when you risk your life the same way. I have the right to do the same and you don't get to tell me how to do any of this. I'm not *your* property."

"You're my girlfriend," he said.

"Then maybe I shouldn't be."

He didn't say anything. If he had, I might have relented. Might have forgiven him for trying to control me, for trying to impose his will and lay claim to me. But he said nothing. He barely breathed.

And that was it.

That's when I knew.

"If you'll excuse me," I turned, snatching my 1911s out of the SUV, "I have work to do."

He didn't reply. He stood there for a moment, and I waited for the inevitable apology, the continuation of his reasoning, why I hadn't heard what I should have, but it didn't come.

Instead, gravel crunched under his retreating steps as he walked back to the street.

At least he didn't see the tears blurring my vision.

38

"C aitlin."

I checked my ammunition, stripping thoughts out of my head one at a time as my hands went through the motions. Rene and I never would have lasted, despite the tactical advantage he provided to missions. Our respective jobs bred conflict, and we would have imploded over something else, if not this. He was an entertainment, a fling to appease an unscratchable itch. Nothing more. The timing sucked, but it would have happened in a matter of weeks. Or days. Better now than later. Better now than when he got more attached because I didn't feel what he obviously did for me. Later would have been infinitely crueler.

I pulled the numbness closer. Whatever emotion had been there a moment ago compressed into a dull, pulsing irritation. Good. Better. All the better to focus.

"Cee."

Battle plans may never survive contact with the enemy, but the illusion of control they provided usually made it to the battlefield. Not for us, though. Under-prepared and newly short-handed, what little confidence I had remained in the expectation that this mission would fail spectacularly. I hoped, perhaps in vain, that we'd get through those damned timo-redax spiders unscathed. I couldn't afford to lose anyone else, even to injury.

The broken plan demanded immediate attention. Not addressing it meant risking more than I could accept.

"Caitlin."

I reconstructed the strategy in my head, reallocating Rene's responsibilities as I surveyed the grounds. Another chain-link fence stood between us and our entrance into Charity Hospital. Scalable. Marty and I had done it before. But we wouldn't have to this time. Legal access had benefits. Probably something I should pursue in the future.

"Caitlin," Sister Betty repeated, softer this time. Almost a whisper.

"Are you ready?" I slid each of my Colt pistols into a holster and glanced at the one person I expected to be on my side.

The pity, confusion, and hesitation in Marty's expression only pissed me off.

"Are. You. Ready?" The words grated more than the gravel under my feet.

"Caitlin!"

I whirled on Sister Betty. "We don't have time for this. Are you ready?"

She flinched, then squared her shoulders. "You're not going."

"You can't do this without me." I adjusted my stance, ready to grapple.

She grabbed my arm, fingers digging too deep to shake. "You're not fit for this mission."

I gritted my teeth so hard, I swear I heard one crack. "I'm doing my job."

"No, you're not." Her grip relaxed without releasing me. "You're not safe to do this mission. Not with the huge unknowns we face."

"I'm fine." I yanked free, but before I could confront Marty, she jerked me back so hard, I crashed against her and we both stumbled. "Let go."

"No." Her eyes burned, nostrils flaring. "You're not getting yourself or anyone else killed over some reckless impulse you refuse to control."

"Stop calling me reckless—"

"Stop being reckless."

"I'm doing my job." Though I refused to wince, I'd have bruises. At least the outside would match the inside. "That means eliminating this threat."

"Without getting yourself killed."

"That's not a requirement." I smirked, the words pure acid.

She blinked and gave an almost imperceptible shake of her head. "What...what's this about, Caitlin?"

"Saving people." My guts knotted. I'd said too much. She'd make me explain. Iron bands squeezed the air from my lungs. I had to say something to distract her, but I had to fight for the breath to speak. "People depend on us. Humans and supernaturals. We stand between them and…" I gestured at the towering gray building, "whatever's in there. Now, can we go?"

She hesitated. "What about Rene?"

"What do you want me to say?"

Saying nothing, she stared at me. Through me. Reading my thoughts.

I sighed. "It would've happened anyway. I'm annoyed it happened now, but we have work to do." Of course, there was more, but I didn't have time for that shit now.

Sister Betty studied me, her grip relaxing again.

"I'm not incapable of doing this job." I forced myself to keep her gaze.

She released me and looked at Father Callahan. "It's not a good idea. Not now."

"We don't have the luxury of ideal timing." I turned toward Father Callahan. "The longer we wait, the more innocents get hurt and the more power the Collectors amass."

"Becoming a bigger threat," Marty muttered, caution shadowing his eyes.

"I can do this," I told Father Callahan, then Sister Betty. "We can't wait."

"There aren't any other Hunters available, especially with Bubba still MIA." Father Callahan pinched his lower lip. "But the longer we wait…" His words trailed off as he exhaled.

"So, we're doing this." I directed my question at Marty, without venom. "Ready?"

He hesitated. "You're really okay?"

"As okay as ever." I shoved both hands into my back pockets.

Marty looked at Father Callahan. My jaw ached as my teeth clenched. I forced my breath to slow, despite the tightness in my chest from suppressing frustration and rage. Marty had always trusted me before. He'd never sought confirmation from one of the adultier adults before. And now, when I needed his support the most, he looked to someone else. Somewhere beneath the numbness, I felt the bite of betrayal.

Sister Betty and Father Callahan stared at each other so long, they might have been having a telepathic conversation, though if they shared more than significant looks, I missed it.

"I guess we're doing this." Marty shrugged.

"I suppose we are," Father Callahan said, watching me.

Sister Betty tensed. "We shouldn't."

"We wait, people die." I stepped up to the back of the SUV, grabbed extra ammo for Marty's Glock, and held it out to him. He took it without meeting my eyes.

With a step, Sister Betty stood so close, I could feel the heat radiating off of her and smell the faint scent of her shampoo. I tried not to recoil when she touched my shoulder. "You can't do this, Caitlin."

"Stop telling me what I can't do." I gripped the frame of the SUV's open back, funneling everything into keeping calm. If I spun on her again, I'd lose what little support I had, and I couldn't allow any more delays. Regardless of what happened in my personal life, supernats were still disappearing and that took precedence. "You've been training me for this for years and now that I'm doing it, you're trying to stop me. You either want me to succeed or you want me to fail. Decide."

"This isn't—"

"What this isn't," I said, "is a debate." I caught Sister Betty's warped reflection in the blade of a silver-edged steel knife laying in the SUV's cargo compartment. "You're either with me or against me."

"I'm always with you, Caitlin, even when you're wrong." The pain in her voice wrenched my heart. "Like right now."

I picked up a pair of Sigs by the barrel, turned, and handed them to her. "Then let's go."

She took them and walked away to do her checks. I pretended not to notice the absence of her usual grace.

Madame Sabine approached, resting her hand on my arm, murmuring, "Phoenix fire lights your soul, *cherie*."

"That's not the weirdest thing someone's said to me, so thanks, I guess." The Phoenix. One of the three mysterious cards I'd pulled from her Tarot deck that didn't exist in the traditional arcana. Had I followed up on that? My stomach churned as I made a mental note to check with Marty. That dropped ball would undoubtedly thunder through my personal Temple of Doom at exactly the wrong moment.

"Don't burn them with it."

My attention snapped back to her. "What?"

But I knew. I didn't have to see their body language to understand what she meant.

"Your friends." She jutted her chin toward Sister Betty, who adjusted Marty's body armor. "You lash out and burn them with your fire."

I breathed as deep as I could. Though I hardly knew her, the admonishment stung. Maybe because Sister Betty trusted *her* and not me. I'd worked so hard to earn my worth and live up to the person she saw in me, yet after all these years, after all we'd done together, my mentor had chosen a relative stranger over me. Maybe it stung because I knew I'd carry the hurt in Sister Betty's voice with me until…always. Couldn't unhear it, couldn't un-see her disappointment, or the way she turned away.

I glanced at Sister Betty's back as she helped Marty adjust his protective gear.

Maybe it stung because what Madame Sabine said resonated as true. To be so rejected professionally. Personally.

Swallowing took herculean effort. Closing my eyes, I willed down the rising pain. "Sometimes I have to be the bitch." I'd gladly pay for what I'd said once Sister Betty hauled me in the gym. Until then, internalized self-flagellation would have to do.

Madame Sabine teetered on her toes and whispered, "The void bites back."

The numbness recoiled at her words and the hurt rebounded.

"What?" My question came out harsher than I intended, but she'd attacked my last sanctuary, the last place I could release everything weighing me down, avoid the thousand little agonies of getting through what needed to be done. If I couldn't retreat, where could I recharge? Where else could I escape the pressure? Why couldn't I have that much for myself?

"The void comes for us all in time," her craggy enigmatic smile drifted out of focus, "but beware. It lies."

My patience for incomprehensible fortune cookie bullshit vanished and my hands spasmed into fists. "What the hell is that supposed to mean?" At least I didn't yell. I really wanted to yell.

She brushed off my question with a wave, a wink, and a glance at Sister Betty. "You'll surprise us all, *cherie*. It is your destiny."

I sagged against the SUV as my anger burned out. More riddles. It always came down to riddles and whispers of destiny. Ravens and writing desks, and other such nonsense. Midi-chlorians for good measure. And now this. My destiny to surprise.

Frickin' awesome.

And yet, nothing new. Maybe she'd picked up on something Sister Betty said. God knows I'd long ago established my middle name as "Surprise." And "Trouble." And "Smartass." But "Surprise" held seniority.

Madame Sabine walked away, a 9mm secured in her hip holster and a flashlight in hand before I gathered my thoughts enough to answer.

P ermission to access Charity Hospital provided the luxury of keys to the last chain-link fence and door I'd lock-picked last time. It also meant retreat wouldn't require unnecessary feats of agility and strength, and if this went the way I anticipated, that would be important.

"All the better to get you out, my pretties," I muttered to myself as I looped the shackle of the padlock through the chain without snapping it shut.

"What?" Marty asked from behind me.

"Nothing." I turned and scanned their faces. My team, my rag-tag friends, armed and ready to take on whatever waited beyond those doors. Each wore body armor, and dust masks dangled around their necks. Over it all, we'd layered protective gear to shield against adult timoredax acid, including safety glasses. We'd improvised some out of HDPE containers when we'd run out of other suitable options, which made Marty look like an awkward stormtrooper cosplay in poorly crafted gray armor. I felt too proud to laugh or even tease my friend. They all had that look I'd grown accustomed to. Determination and bravado tinged with concern. Following me, they risked their lives. I owed it to them to get them through alive and out in one piece. And untouched by spider acid or anything else we'd encounter.

I owed them that much, however this ended. Shoving a sudden rush of emotion aside, I asked, "Ready?"

This time, they nodded. After one final rundown of the revised plan, one that brokered little chance of me sneaking away, we passed through the final gate, and my motley crew entered Charity Hospital.

39

S tepping into the hospital plunged us into an artificial twilight despite the midday sun outside.

Something I'd failed to consider. Instead of the angled sun of late afternoon Marty and I'd used to navigate, shadows clung to the corners and seeped further into the hall than I liked. Darkness meant cover for the timoredax, or anything else hiding in here. I cursed myself for not leaving everyone outside where they'd be safe.

We clustered together in a loose circle around Madame Sabine which made progress through the hall tedious and slow, but prudence overruled pace. Father Callahan and Madame Sabine's LED flashlights swept through the shadows. We all scanned for the glitter of hidden timoredax eggs, though Sister Betty and I focused more on clearing the space of the fae arachnids or other threats. One of our group would see the eggs with plenty of time to react. Or so we hoped, at least. I halted the group often to parse the sound of our movement from the eerie noises around us.

"We did this twice as fast earlier," Marty grumbled.

I paused, trying to decide if the rustle that followed his words came from us or from something stalking us in the shadows. After a quick check to confirm none of the team had been snatched, I said, "There are more of us now." My gaze lingered on Madame Sabine, and Marty seemed to understand.

The old woman concentrated on moving her flashlight's beam

methodically along the baseboard. Nothing about the inherent danger seemed to bother her. In fact, she seemed...energized and excited. How many times had she accompanied other Hunters like this? Had someone trained her in the art of staying alive while fighting monsters? What had I gotten her into by allowing her to come?

Behind Madame Sabine, Sister Betty guarded against threats from the rear. I'd expected her to argue when I assigned her to the back of the team, but either she saw the logic of her fighting experience protecting our more vulnerable members, or we'd reached a new level of her allowing me my mistakes.

Marty and I crept a few steps ahead of the group, weapons up and sweeping the path. After creating enough distance to get us out of ear shot, he whispered, "Why didn't you tell her to stay put?"

"You gonna tell her that?"

He stifled a laugh, but not the shake of his shoulders. "Fair point." After a few more steps down the deserted hall, he said, "Sorry about Rene."

The sudden constriction in my chest stole my breath. I would have reminded him of our rules if I could have. Instead, I shook my head.

"You—"

As quietly as I could, I cleared my throat to breathe around the lump lodged there. "Don't want to talk about it," I managed.

After this, I'd examine everything. Not just with Rene, but with Sister Betty. There had to be some common thread, some reason they'd both withdrawn, why they both walked away from our relationships. There had to be. A reason, I hoped, other than me. Because if the reason ended up being me—

"Cee," he said.

"I know." I shook my head. "Not now."

"Later, then."

Or not, if I could avoid it. I gathered the team closer, keeping my voice low. "Stairway's at the end of the hall. Tighten ranks, stay alert."

That's when I heard a footstep when there should have been none.

With a hand signal, my team froze. Sister Betty and I locked eyes. Another signal from me and both flashlights went dark. My heart thundered in my ears, but I listened past it. Noises filled the oppressive dark. Scurrying rodents in the ceiling. The rustle of birds. Others defied identification.

Until I heard the scrape of another step.

Chills raced up my spine, and goosebumps rippled across my arms. I knew this feeling. I'd been hunted before.

With the Colt aimed low in a two-handed grip, I strained to detect movement in the deepest shadows. Until it revealed itself, we had to wait.

Sister Betty pointed up toward the tiniest scraping sound, followed by Father Callahan with a similar gesture.

"Upstairs or between floors?" Marty asked, his whisper barely audible.

"Doesn't matter." I holstered my gun, tugged my backpack off over my plastic armor and knelt to dig into it. The team bunched around me, Father Callahan's eyes on the ceiling tiles, Sister Betty guarding our group's perimeter.

"You know most Hunters use guns, right?" Marty murmured.

"Most Hunters aren't dealing with these little fuckers," I retorted, handing him a white bottle with a perforated screw top. Fine white powder drifted off the lid as he gripped it.

He considered the repurposed baby powder bottle and wiped the top. "At least we won't give them diaper rash."

"I don't think baking soda helps that. Then again, chapped spider ass isn't among my top priorities." I grabbed trigger spray bottles full of a cloudy solution from the bag and passed them out as well.

Sister Betty took the one I offered her and hung it on her belt by the trigger. "Use the powder first since we're not sure how effective the liquid solution will be. If you have to use the liquid, shake, then spray."

"I vote for hunting wendigo next," Marty said, twisting the tip of his spray bottle before hanging it on a belt loop. "Bullets work on a wendigo."

"Some bullets," Sister Betty replied.

"Slows them down, at least." Marty twisted his powder bottle open and blew away the dust that puffed out. "Do we know this is going to work?"

I pulled on my pack again and geared up my improvised magical insecticide. Baking soda spiked with pulverized iron filings and a spray bottle of holy water, salt, and baking soda. "If Vikki's right, this should neutralize their acid." Liquid and powdered death, courtesy of our science queen. We'd added iron and salt as insurance since either should be effective on the otherworldly creepers, or anything fae. God bless science, creativity, and the wisdom of Sam and Dean Winchester.

"Shit."

Any farther away and I might have thought Marty's breathy expletive nothing more than a sigh. Kneeling in front of him, I heard him clearly.

My head snapped up. My entire team stared over me, past me, toward the door at the end of the hall. For a heartbeat, I closed my eyes and prayed for spiders, then drew my gun and stood.

Prayer works out in my favor less often than luck. And no matter how much I try to give New Orleans credit for being unpredictable, it still manages to surprise me. Whatever I might have imagined confronting in an abandoned hospital, a little girl in a white dress would not have made my top ten.

Gun in hand, but aimed at the floor, I stepped away from my team. "Hello," I said, inching forward. "How did you get in here?"

She shrugged but didn't respond.

My team shuffled. I trusted Sister Betty to protect them, but I kept myself between them, the child, and the door beyond. She looked too substantial to be a ghost, and that worried me. Insubstantiality would have been a cakewalk.

"I've seen her before," Marty said.

Out of the corner of my eye, I saw the muzzle of his gun pointed at the child.

"Dude." I reached across my body with my left hand to force his gun down without lowering mine. "That's a kid."

"It may look like one, but it's not." Real fear sharpened his words. We'd faced everything from werewolves to witches to hydra and stared down Lovecraftian impossibilities more than once. None of them scared him, not like this kid. She twisted and hummed something tuneless, her stark white dress swirling around her, the dirty tails of her teal ribbon waist-band whipping behind her.

"Don't you feel that?"

I glanced at him, reluctant to take my eyes off the girl. Maybe I sensed something, too, because I felt better with my gun in hand. "We can't risk harming her." I removed my hand from his gun.

"I don't know what the hell she is, but she isn't a child," Marty insisted in a whisper. To his credit, he didn't raise his Glock again. "You know this isn't right, Cee, and we can't treat...it like a human."

"Whatever she is, we have an obligation to help."

"Not if she tries to eat us." He shifted his weight, balancing his shooting stance as his arms trembled.

Behind us, Sister Betty directed her charges with urgent whispers, but the rant in my head drowned out her words. Rene should be here. He should be here to provide cover and protect the rest of the team while I dealt with this kid. His absence put them all at risk, but he had to put his big foot in his big mouth and fuck it all up. If anything, anything at all, happened to them—

"Do you want to play?"

Her voice sent chills up my spine. Unconsciously, my arm rose, barrel aimed at the ethereal child, despite the pit in my stomach.

I remembered her.

The last time I'd seen her, she'd been singing a nursery rhyme. Now, head tilted to one side, her raptor gaze locked on me. Her eyes were... wrong, but not in a way I could identify. They made me want to run.

"What did you say?" My irrational side insisted I should have asked her name, that I should have some kind of human, if not maternal, reaction; that, for the love of God, I shouldn't be pointing a gun at her, but my animal instincts demanded flight. Adrenaline crashed through my veins as time slowed, and a familiar calm settled around me as I prepared for the inevitable fight.

"Do you want to play?" Her baby-toothed smile and the swish of her dress might have been charming anywhere else. Here, in a hot, dark, abandoned hospital, it felt like a taunt, daring me to let down my guard.

Without thinking, I sidestepped to shield Marty, though his gun extended past my arm. Whatever happened, I would not fail to protect him again. "Shoot me," I warned him, "and I'll shoot you back. And it will hurt."

"Deal with the child of the corn and let me worry about my aim," he said. "You can thank me after I keep her from eating your face."

The little girl hummed and swayed, the tune flat and creepy. As the sonorous sound became words, I recognized the rhyme. The same one she'd been singing when we'd encountered her in Jackson Square. "Three blind mice, three blind mice." She stopped and giggled, covering her mouth with both hands, though her eyes remained untouched by her amusement. They looked old, wrong for her face. "There's more of you now." Her baby-plump finger pointed at us as she counted. "Five blind mice," she giggled again, "see how they'll run."

"What are you?" I asked, advancing another step.

She stepped back, eyes widening as if with fear. "You're not my mommy."

"Do you even have one?" Marty asked.

Her eyes hardened, the façade of her fear evaporating as she whipped her head in his direction. Her grin twisted with an evil that curdled my blood. I swore her teeth grew and sharpened. "Time to run, little mice." She lunged at us and snapped her jaws, then turned and ran through the stairway door, her scuffed patent leather shoes sliding on the dirty floor as she disappeared in the dark.

Forgetting myself, I yelled. "No!"

The door crashed behind her and the entire hospital reverberated with the sound. And then, her screech of terror and pain overwhelmed me and I ran.

Sister Betty caught my arm and yanked me back before my hand hit the bar to open the door. "No."

"I can't leave her to the timoredax," I said, raising my voice over the little girl's hysterical screams, "no matter what she is. Maybe she's being controlled—"

"Even if she is," she said, dragging me away from the door, "we need to regroup."

As suddenly as it started, the screaming stopped. Acid roiled my stomach, burned my veins. Only one thing could have stopped her screaming like that.

I didn't even have a name for my list of the dead.

"What's the line? The best laid plans of mice and men?" An unfamiliar voice rang through the hallway.

All of us whirled, guns aimed down the empty corridor. Options raced through my head. Planning would be easier if I knew whatever waited in the dark was actually hostile, but shooting, throwing punches, and subduing the threat had more appeal. Reckless or not, I had my team to worry about, and a civilian elder in our midst that may or may not be able to defend herself. I cut between them to stand in front of my team again. If anything happened, I'd take the heat.

I felt more than saw Sister Betty step between me and the group, the next line of defense. The shuffle behind me caused no alarm. I knew what it meant. Though they had less combat experience, Father Callahan and Marty had followed the plan perfectly, closing ranks behind Madame Sabine and scanning the hallways. If I survived this, I had to remember to tell them how proud they made me.

Somewhere close, a bird took flight, the beat of its wings masking the direction of the approaching footsteps. And they were actual footsteps, not the scratching scrabble of those piercing spider legs. My shoulders relaxed slightly. Unless we'd discovered some mutant strain of were, it couldn't be a timoredax.

A figure emerged from the same room as the little girl, this one taller, stockier, and solid black. What I could see looked human, but outward appearances rarely meant much.

"Who are you?" My shoulders ached with tension, but I didn't let down my guard.

The laugh resounding through the building gave me the chills. Not because it was the mad cackle of a maniac, because it wasn't. And not because it was a menacing Jabba the Hut laugh (because it wasn't that either). This sound, so utterly normal and mundane, had no place here. The voice of a waiter. A cashier. A *have a nice day* kind of voice. Not a creepy stalking-you-through-an-abandoned-building kind of voice. "You invade my home and demand that I identify myself?"

"We have permission to be here," Sister Betty said. "Can you say the same?"

"Permission," the voice scoffed, distinctly male this time. "You grovel at the feet of arbitrary authority for *permission*. I need no authority beyond my own."

"Yeah, that's some interesting bullshit you're spewing and all, but not the point." Maybe I could irritate him to distraction. "Who are you and why are you here?"

"As I said, you're in my domain, and I see no reason to answer your questions."

Right. Cosplaying a douchebag and LARPing as Lord of the Manor. Awesome.

This dumbass had no business here and since a Magic 8 Ball had more juice than him, my limited patience reached its end. I had no desire to find his acid-scarred bones later, so I had to convince him to leave before the spiders appeared. "We," I said, annoyed by the prospect of having to save some moron from their own stupidity, "aren't going anywhere."

"This building isn't safe for urban exploration," Marty said.

"I've never seen anything dangerous." The figure looked up, as if contemplating the ceiling. "If you're scared, maybe you should go."

"Didn't you hear the screaming?" Marty asked, incredulous. "Screaming like that—"

"Means nothing to me." The figure shrugged.

"Whether it does or not..." Sister Betty's words trailed off as the figure shifted, then separated. Three more vaguely humanoid shapes peeled off and flanked the original.

Goddamn it.

Sister Betty subtly shifted her weight forward. Marty muttered behind me. I couldn't understand him and hoped it wasn't important.

Without more light, I couldn't determine whether the three shorter humanoid shapes were the ones we'd encountered on Bourbon. No telltale purple glow or mumbled incantation gave them away. The hooded, cloaked figures might have been Jawas for all the detail I could see. Glowing robotic yellow eyes might have been more comforting than the blankness beneath their hoods.

I couldn't take the chance of getting blasted with another magic fireball, or whatever they hit me with last time. Even without visible wounds, I hadn't felt right since. I decided to try the rational approach. "There's more going on here than you, any of you, probably realize. For your own safety, evacuate the building so my team and I can get to work."

That laugh again. How could something so normal be so disturbing? "Nothing in this building will harm me," he said. He stepped forward, and the three shorter figures followed. "I can't say the same for you, Hunter."

How the hell did everyone immediately identify me as a Hunter? Did I have some kind of sign on my forehead or something? And why did knowing it get them all jazzed to try me? Whatever made me so tempting, if he and his cadre of clones wanted to rumble, I'd oblige. Delivering an ass kicking would make me feel better.

I stepped forward, evading Sister Betty's attempt to hold me back. Raising my gun, I pointed it at the taller figure. "When you say 'nothing,' you didn't take me into consideration."

A rustle and a shift in position told me he pointed a gun at me, too.

I smiled, my own evil chuckle giving me goosebumps.

Game on, motherfucker.

40

This is your one and only warning, Hunter," the taller figure of the four said. "Get out. Get out of this building. Get out of this city. Get out of this state. You have no business here."

If I could have thrown my head back in a laugh without losing sight of him, I would have. The idea of trying to intimidate me with an idle threat was downright hilarious. Instead, I watched him, straining to see his face. "You don't seem to understand how this works."

"I know I have the firepower to eliminate you." It looked like his arm shook, either to emphasize the gun in his hand, or to gesture at his cloaked henchmen. Since I assumed they couldn't see any better than us, I guessed the former.

"I've been shot before and wasn't impressed," I said, trying to figure out how to get a better angle, to get light on his gun and figure out what he had. And I hadn't lied. I had been shot before. It hurt more than a zombie bite and took months to heal, but in the end, I'd survived. Besides, he didn't know about the 3A soft trauma armor under my shirt. Rene explained it wouldn't make me impervious to bullets, but assuming this guy had something less than a .44, it lessened my chances of taking a mortal wound. Yay for being prepared.

Then the murmuring began. A purple glow swelled in front of the cloaked figures.

Well, shit.

As much as I appreciated confirmation of who we dealt with, body armor and improvised acid guards wouldn't do a damned thing against magic.

"Now, I'll repeat my request again, Miss Kelley," he continued, sounding more like a perturbed first-year high school teacher beleaguered by the class idiots than a criminal with magic henchmen. "Get. Out. Of New Orleans."

How is it that every bad guy in town knew my name?

"That's not going to work for me." I shifted my weight, ready to launch myself at the magic wielders, if necessary. In the purple glow, I could see the outline of his face, but also the gun. From the profile, a Smith & Wesson 29 with either the six or six-and-a-half-inch barrel. The Dirty Harry gun. I could barely contain my eye roll. I'd have expected a Glock. This iconic choice could mean he had real strength and the experience to handle the firepower. His grip, however, told another story. He wanted to be a classic movie badass, but he lacked everything it took to be one. Instead of holding the gun straight on either with a second hand to balance the first, this douchenugget pointed the gun at me sideways, the grip parallel to the ground. A modern gangster movie trope. Maybe it looked cool, but it didn't do shit for aim or accuracy. It did tell me he had no idea what he was doing.

"First day with a gun?" I asked, trying to communicate with my team as much as distract him. "Or are you just trying to look as cool as the bad guys in your favorite movies?"

"Cheap tricks won't work on me," he said, though I detected a bit of false bravado.

"Oh, right, me and my Jedi mind tricks. Gotcha. I'll cross that off my list." I stepped back, trying to calculate the distance between us. With that weapon, I needed at least ten feet to maximize the armor's effectiveness. "Let's go back to where we started. There's more in this building than you can imagine."

"I doubt that, Hunter." He stepped forward and out of the glow of the purple magic. But in an attempt to intimidate, or to limit the protective distance, I couldn't be sure. "I'm the most dangerous thing here."

"And I doubt that," I said, sliding back inches as subtly as possible. Much farther and I'd be walking into Marty or whoever stood right behind me. "I'm trying to be real nice but I've had a bad couple of weeks and you pointing that thing at me isn't going to improve my mood any time soon. One last chance before I get real cranky. Get gone, and live to annoy me another day. Consider this your lucky day, punk."

"Ahh." He chuckled. "Another unstable Hunter." His voice changed slightly as he addressed his companions. "How cliché."

I stomped forward, my Docs thumping a heartbeat of echoes down the hall, gun leveled at his chest. Had he not stumbled back a few steps, I could have snatched his gun, or kicked him in the 'nads without much effort. Unfortunately, he had some sense of self-preservation and stepped back, breaking his spell casters' concentration as he collided with one of them. I saw him a little clearer before their magic died. He looked like a kid, eyes wide with fear or shock. How could someone this young be involved with caring for a dragon hatchling? How had he become the mastermind behind this shitshow? Or had this kid stumbled into the wrong place?

"I am not in the mood to deal with your shit, *comprende*? You have exactly two options. Get the fuck out of here and let me deal with things you cannot begin to understand, or I will consider you a threat to the safety of this city and eliminate you. The only bad choice for me involves paperwork."

His teeth rattled for a moment, but his words came out smooth and confident. "This is my territory and woe be unto any who attempt to breach it."

"I've already breached it, asshole, but I haven't decided what I'm going to do with you yet. You've got ten seconds to make your choice." I leaned forward to give the illusion of stepping closer without reducing the distance between us. "Ten."

He stumbled back a step. "You can't do this."

"Nine."

His gun clattered to the floor and he scrambled to pick it up.

"Eight."

Mr. Pissing-His-Pants-With-Fear started babbling, the gun shaking in his hand as he retreated. "You can't just push someone out of their own territory, you know. It's rude and you're going to pay."

"Seven." I took two steps forward to his three back, my gun level and steady.

The magical henchmen turned and ran back through the door they'd emerged from, abandoning their master. From the sounds of their steps, they didn't slow. Either they knew this place well, or they could see in the dark.

"Six."

Then, another scream.

The hooded figure turned, his gun still aimed in my direction, but wobbling frantically. He didn't have the stamina for the standoff or the weight of the gun. But, to be fair, even my arms felt the strain.

"Five."

"What have you done to them?" he shouted, his head whipping back in my direction. "Is this some kind of military operation or something?"

"Four." I stepped forward and caught a glimpse of a barrel at each side of my peripheral vision. Marty and Sister Betty. They advanced with me, but a step behind.

"You're very rude!"

"Three." It came out with almost a giggle. Rude? He'd run out of anything to say and resorted to *rude*? This baby villain had no chops for being a big bad, not any time soon. And his career would end before he ever had the chance.

Except that's when I heard them. The impacts of dozens of tiny feet hitting the ground, scrabbling little steps from either side.

"Two," I said, though my attention no longer centered on the blubbering man backpedaling into the room behind him.

"Caitlin!" Father Callahan yelled, and I saw the puff of dust followed by an inhuman scream.

Then everything went to hell.

Baking soda filled the air like a fine smoke. Father Callahan scrambled back, a protective arm behind him to push Madame Sabine out of the way. Sister Betty sandwiched her from the other side, my mentor releasing the squirt bottle from her belt and spraying the horde of advancing timoredax with the solution.

The spiders reared up, mandibles clacking, some of the larger ones dripping a green acid goo as they stampeded in circles. Alien screams circled us. An acrid, burning smell rose from smoking exoskeletons, but they didn't stop advancing. I fired on one sneaking up on Sister Betty's far side and it exploded, spraying guts, acid, and goo everywhere. Cursing, I swapped out the gun for the less conventional weapons as a stream from Sister Betty's squirt bottle caught one of the little bastards right in the eyeball. Foam boiled out of its multi-faceted eye and all of its legs spasmed, curling up underneath its bulbous body. It rolled toward us, leaking more greenish foam and squealing with a sound that pierced my skull and stabbed at the base of my spine. I reared back my right Doc and punted it down the hall. It bounced, bowling over others, then disappeared.

Before I heard it impact anything, I spun and squeezed the baby powder bottle for all its worth and made an arc of lethal white dust over the closest critters, then switched to spraying the rest with the solution. Sister Betty swung the opposite direction to provide exterminator cover for Marty and Madame Sabine. The absence of the mysterious man registered a second before the shove from behind knocked me so far off balance, I fell to my knees in a pile of baking soda and iron filings.

I landed, of course, face to face with a very angry acid-spitting arachnid the size of a dog. Its front two legs curled back giving the mandibles more space.

My hands and knees slid in the powder on the floor and I couldn't get to my feet. Nothing like staring death in the drippy, acid-spitting, spidery maw.

I closed my eyes.

Marty hauled me to my feet as the first drops of acid sprayed, only splashing the plastic guards strapped around my shins. Someone sprayed a stream of solution in the creature's open mouth and it howled, curled up, and rolled onto its back, legs spasming, foam billowing between its mandibles.

"Thanks," I said to Marty.

"Don't thank me yet." He jutted his chin toward a scene that turned my guts to water.

One of the shadowed man's arms curled around Madame Sabine's neck, his other hand pressing his gun against her temple. No flashy style, just straight on.

Fuck.

"Let her go," Sister Betty demanded, her shotgun aimed at the pair.

Whoever he was, the man wasn't entirely stupid. He twisted, putting Madame Sabine between him and Sister Betty. For the first time, I saw his face clearly. Nothing about him stood out as exceptional. He looked like a young teacher, one untouched by the hardships of overloaded classrooms and years of being underpaid. He gave the impression of...softness. Innocence.

And yet, he held an old woman at gunpoint.

Why did my humanoid foes always look so damned normal? Just once, I'd prefer someone who actually looked like a villain, waxed and curled handlebar mustache and all. Anything but this baby-faced, corn-fed, Midwest-factory-made vanilla bro.

Madame Sabine stood rigid, her chin caught in the crook of his arm, her fingers curled around it trying to pull it away from her throat. They both shook, but his eyes suggested he'd do whatever it took to get free.

"Let her go," I said softly, holding the baking soda bottles in the least threatening way possible. Though, given what they were, I doubted anyone could see them as much of a threat.

Still, he winced. "Whatever those are, drop them."

"Just baking soda, salt and iron," I said. "It won't hurt you."

He sneered. "How do you know I'm not fae?"

Another point in the not-entirely-stupid column. Maybe I'd underestimated him.

"Alright," I said. "I'm going to drop them now." I waited until he gave a curt nod and let both bottles fall at the same time.

"What about the timoredax?" Marty asked.

"I've got perimeter," Father Callahan said. I didn't turn to confirm. If he said he had it, I trusted him.

"I'm going to be cool with you, if you're cool with me," I said, my empty hands up.

He glanced from Sister Betty to me, his movements jerky and uneven. "How am I supposed to be 'cool' with a gun pointed at me?" Then, as if he couldn't restrain it, he grinned. "I might get," he jerked, and Madame Sabine let out a yelp before closing her eyes, "twitchy."

"You'll die half a second after she does," Sister Betty said without inflection. The self-assurance in her voice sent chills up my spine.

"No one's doing anything," I said, "not yet." I could only hope Sister Betty picked up on the word choice. We'd planned for situations like this, we just needed time to figure out the right tactic, then use the right code word.

"The spiders didn't surprise you," Marty said. "Did you bring them here?"

"I'm not telling you anything," the man scoffed, and jerked Madame Sabine, lifting her feet off the floor. She choked, her face turning red.

Rage burned in my veins. I bit the inside of my cheek until I tasted blood.

Not yet.

Not. Yet.

"Because you don't know?" Marty pressed.

"Because that's not what we're talking about," he sneered. "I've got something you want, and you're going to play by my rules. And my first rule is we're not talking about the spiders."

"Probably a good idea," Marty said, "since they probably ate your magic minions. I'm pretty sure exterminators won't deal with this kind of infestation."

As Marty needled the man, his focus stayed off me and, more importantly, off Sister Betty. She lowered her Mossberg too slowly for him to notice.

"Preposterous." The cut-rate mastermind jerked Madame Sabine, dragging her off her toes again. "Nothing in this building would hurt me or anyone I deem worthy of being here."

I didn't have to see Father Callahan's hand behind Sister Betty to know he held the weight of the gun. Her hand encircled the barrel too loosely.

"Not much cuts off terrified screams that completely other than death. And those were screams of pain, bub, like the pain acid causes the average person. You know what that means, right?"

Before he graced us with the blistering retort he'd been brewing, he spun on Sister Betty, aiming the gun at her. "Not. So. Fast."

"That's a movie line if I've ever heard one," I said, hoping my voice didn't betray the panic I felt. "Which one was it, now?"

He didn't turn to me. His full attention, and his aim, remained on Sister Betty. "I don't do sneaky any more than I do rude, lady." The only good news in my world focused on the tremble in his arm as he pointed the gun, sideways again, at Sister Betty's head.

Madame Sabine's eyes widened as his arm tightened under her chin. Her fingers clawed at his arm, and either it didn't hurt, or she didn't have much power in it. No matter how she wiggled, he didn't react.

"Where are you getting your dialogue, dude?" I asked, trying to draw at least his gaze my way. "You should probably watch better movies. Or read. Good books, that is." I reached slowly back to grab the weapon holstered at my back. "I could recommend a few."

"Spiders approaching," warned Father Callahan. "We need to attack before they do."

"Nobody's doing anything," the guy with the gun replied. "Except you, Father. You're going to put down both guns."

"I can't do that without making us all vulnerable to these spiders, including you."

"I told you, nothing in this building will hurt me. Least of all you. Put the guns down." He gestured with his gun. "Hers, too. I know you're holding it."

"Caitlin," Father Callahan said.

"Yeah, put 'em down," I said. I hadn't freed the Glock at my back, but I'd gotten my hand behind me. The rest would happen quick.

Out of the corner of my eye, Father Callahan bent down and lay both weapons inside the rough circle of baking soda. Each movement slow and deliberate, wary. "There's another way to deal with this, son."

The stranger laughed, that weirdly normal sound that gave me the chills. "Call the man 'Father' once and he'll start patronizing." He shook his head. "No, that's not how this is going to go. I've got something you want," he shook Madame Sabine enough to lose her balance and make her scrabble to her feet, "and I've got control of your pet attack dog." He flicked his gun in Sister Betty's direction. "The way I see it, you're going to listen to me, and we're going to do this my way."

"Father C, he's right," Marty said, running attention blocker from me. "We've got to protect the women."

And that was key, wasn't it? My brilliant, cunning friend.

Outside of her attempt to attack him, this guy didn't perceive either me or Sister Betty as a threat. Catching her in the act only reinforced this notion.

"We've got to do whatever we need to do to make sure the women get out okay." Marty continued his campaign.

Father Callahan sighed, though his relief had to be legitimate. "You're right." With contrition I couldn't fathom, he said, "What is it you wish of us?"

If I hadn't known my team well, I'd have assumed every word to be genuine. But I focused my attention on the man pointing a gun at the woman I couldn't help but love.

"You're going to do exactly what I tell you," he said. The gun in his hand had a more pronounced shake. No arm strength. No stamina. I waited until he talked again to release the holster at my back. "You're going to leave the city and never come back. Leave the state. Move your operation, and forget what you've seen here."

"You can't think it's that simple," Marty protested.

The gun remained trained on Sister Betty's head, but she stared at the man, refusing to cower. "Oh," he said with that irritatingly bland laugh. "It is simple. Your refusal makes it complicated. Complicated enough for people to die."

Madame Sabine whimpered, though from pain or because she realized I had a bead on the asshole, I couldn't be sure. If she'd noticed my drawn weapon, I didn't have long before her captor did, too. That he hadn't seen me pull it only kind of surprised me.

"We'll consider moving." Father Callahan floundered as if he couldn't figure out what to say next.

I sighted along the barrel.

Center mass. Three inches below his arm.

"It will take time," Father Callahan continued. "These aren't decisions made locally."

My targets were limited since he had Madame Sabine. If I blew out his knee, or landed a shot in his thigh, his reflexes might make him pull the trigger. He couldn't miss, not at such close range.

"I don't care about your hierarchy. You can make the decision."

My vision tightened, narrowing into a pinpoint.

"And you will forget what you've seen here," he continued.

I visualized the bullet leaving the gun, puncturing his shirt, piercing his flesh, breaking a rib, and blowing out everything in its path.

"You will walk away as if you found nothing here."

No second shot.

I imagined how the tip of the bullet would separate the very threads of his shirt.

This had to count.

As I squeezed the trigger, he turned.

The shot counted.

In the worst way possible.

41

There are times when a well-aimed shot goes miraculously wild. When the divine intervenes and prevents a tragedy. There are times when being a bad shot is a blessing.

This was not one of those times.

I shot true.

I aimed exactly where I should have, the area of greatest body mass.

While the mysterious gunman faced Sister Betty and Father Callahan, I had a clear shot a few inches under his extended arm. A sure thing at this distance. I knew the shot would likely be lethal if it didn't ricochet off a rib, but considering the mortal danger he posed to my team, a fatality would have been a permissible, dismissible offense. Self-defense. Defense of others.

When he turned, the shot remained lethal, but not for my intended target.

Shocked by the sound, the man dropped Madame Sabine, who collapsed in a boneless heap. Father Callahan and Sister Betty rushed forward, him to the woman bleeding on the floor, her to tackle the man who'd caused all this.

I stood there, gun dangling from my hand.

The deafening aftermath of the gunshot dulled the chaos around me. Nothing felt real, nothing felt substantial. Not Sister Betty's diminishing muffled shouts as she gave chase, not Father Callahan's words as he whipped his head between his patient and me, applying pressure to her chest, or Marty's incomprehensible shouts followed by cover fire.

And I stood there, gun in hand, watching the woman I'd shot bleed out.

Not only had I taken them into an unknown situation underprepared and understaffed, I'd fired the shot. I'd caused the most harm when my first priority should have been protection, getting them out in one piece. Healthy and whole.

The old woman stared at me without recrimination, her wrinkled face layered with that flickering ageless, astral image. She held up a shaking hand, and the one word she spoke cut through the din.

"Phoenix."

I crumpled to the floor, crawling through the baking soda and dirt, shoving aside the curled husk of a dead timoredax to get to her.

She reached for me, and I felt the cool, sticky touch of her fingers on my face. "Your fire," she said, her voice strained, "it is enough, but you must learn..." Her words faded into a cough that produced pink bubbles at the corner of her lips.

"No." I took her hands in mine, crying. "Don't talk. I'm sorry. I'm so sorry. I didn't mean—"

"Shh, child." Her eyes closed and opened so slowly, I wasn't sure they'd open all the way. "No time. You must learn about the fire. About the doors." She fumbled at my chest, her hand a fluttering bird at my throat until she pulled the cord of the amulet that hung there free. "There are doors. There are pathways you must learn. Use the fire within." She coughed, and blood poured out of her chest in rhythmic gouts.

"Please don't talk," I whimpered, adding my hand on top of Father Callahan's to help apply pressure, however futile the gesture. "Save your strength."

The gunshots stopped, and I heard Marty on the phone. I heard him say Rene's name, then rapid fire information. Demands for assistance. Backup. An ambulance.

"The doors will open for you." Madame Sabine gasped for breath between her barely audible words. "They will take you to the places of power. To the nest. To the root of it all."

I squeezed her hand, tears burning trails down my cheeks. "Save your strength."

"Open the doors, Phoenix. Use the fire within." The drifting ageless face flickered and disappeared again. "It is enough." Her eyes closed, her rattling breath the only sound between Marty's occasional cover fire.

I looked up at Father Callahan, not sure what to do. He didn't say anything. Fear blazed in his eyes as he pressed his lips together.

Before I could speak again, Madame Sabine opened her eyes and clutched the amulet around my neck, covering it with bloody fingerprints. "Use your fire and open the door."

"Shh, don't talk," I urged, my voice cracking on each syllable. Though it had been forever since I really prayed, prayer filled my mind. I begged God not to let her die, begged Him to listen this time.

"There are other worlds than these," she whispered, smiling despite the pink spittle at the corner of her lips. "Time is a funny thing…"

Her words trailed off and her wrinkled face turned gray. Father Callahan called her by her first name, her real name, as the hot blood flowing over our combined hands slowed and cooled.

"He disappeared," Sister Betty panted as she burst into the hallway. "And there are more spiders. How is—"

She didn't finish her question.

She fell to her knees beside me, checking the vitals we all knew wouldn't be there. The wail of the approaching ambulance finally reached us.

E verything happened fast, but in slow motion.

The police, briefed on the acid-spitting spiders from Faerie, accompanied the medics. They hurried toward us, led by Marty, methodically clearing the hallway. Before they got to us, I had identified the escort. Officers LaFontaine and Boudreaux. Rene, still in the plain clothes he'd been wearing when he stormed off. When he cut our team down by one.

Their haste might have made me feel better a few minutes ago, but not now. It didn't matter. Madame Sabine was dead. I killed her. She was dead and the bad guy got away. Again.

The second Rene's eyes met mine, I turned away. If he'd been here, we'd have had ample cover. We'd have had another good guy with a gun to prevent the worst thing from happening. I would have been able to get them all out.

I felt sick.

Ignoring the cries of my name, I ran down the hall and ducked into a room, vomiting as I turned the corner. Hot bile seared my throat, and the harder I cried, the more came up.

I had killed an innocent woman. A member of my team. Someone who never should have been on scene in the first place.

And what had we salvaged from the loss of her life? Nothing.

"Are you okay?" Marty asked.

I wiped the back of my hand across my mouth, closing my eyes to avoid looking at the puddle in front of my baking soda-dusted boots. It had been years since I'd thrown up like this. After all the bodies, the body *parts*, and lots of retribution against the monsters who made them, my stomach had hardened. Until now. Until I became the monster. "Fine. Dandy."

"You shouldn't run off alone." He put a hand on my back. "Not with timoredax all over the place."

"All the more reason you should be providing cover." I holstered my gun. "I'm fine."

"NOPD and Sister Betty have got it covered."

Silence stretched between us, filled with the tension of all the things he wanted to say. I only hoped he wouldn't.

"Father Callahan is giving her last rites."

"She's dead. They don't give last rites to someone who's already dead."

"No one declared her dead."

I looked up at my friend.

He shrugged. "You know him and technicalities."

Technicalities he discovered had not only saved our lives, but had gotten us information from hostile parties. Exploiting loopholes in doctrine, custom, and the realities behind legends had gotten us out of otherwise unavoidable trouble. Technicalities made his day, and by extension, ours. And now, a technicality allowed Madame Sabine one last sacrament.

"I'm sure it goes back to that Lazarus article he's been tinkering with for years on when death actually happens." He tapped my spine. "Come on, we should get back. When they're ready to move her, we need to clear out."

My head pounded. I couldn't go back out there, couldn't face Sister Betty, Rene, or Father Callahan. Couldn't see Madame Sabine's body on the stretcher, or the puddle of her blood I'd spilled when I shot her. Killed her.

Another name for the list.

Another person I'd failed.

"Caitlin—"

"Don't." I hated the way my voice broke on the world.

"Nobody blames you," Marty continued, his voice low, compassionate.

My throat knotted and I bent over, expecting to be sick again. I leaned on my thighs, my fists clenched to stop my hands from shaking. "Don't do this."

"Come on back. The others are waiting."

I flinched when his hand landed on my shoulder.

"It's not safe here."

"Which is why she shouldn't have been here. Why none of you should be." I stood up, forcing down the rage, swallowing repeatedly to force the acid down my throat. "I should have come alone."

"You said it yourself, we had a job to do, and it's a job too big to do alone."

"Yeah, well, maybe I was wrong. Maybe we shouldn't be doing any of this."

His brow furrowed. "Maybe, but, like you said, if not us, then who?"

I looked at him and considered a thousand responses. He would push back on every single one and find a way to argue me down until I relented. Maybe Rene had a point. Maybe I needed to assert my will more often and make my decisions the ones that mattered. Maybe I needed to trust my gut. This should have been a job I handled on my own as soon as we discovered the spiders. Had I been alone, I could have taken the weirdo in the trench coat and his three stooges. I wouldn't have been caught unawares, and he wouldn't have had a hostage.

"What are you thinking?" His question sounded wary.

"Nothing," I said, preternatural calm taking over. "You're right. We should go."

He stepped in my way, blocking the door. "You're seriously scaring the shit out of me right now."

"Why? Because I'm agreeing with you?" I shrugged. "Isn't that what you wanted?"

"Yes. No." He ran a hand through his sweaty hair. "Fuck, Cee, I don't know. Shouldn't you be freaking out or yelling or crying or something? Anything other than this stone-faced Michael Myers act?"

I knew it should be funny. I knew I should be laughing. But if I started, it would have been the opposite of that eerily normal laugh. It'd sound like a braying hyena, a lunatic cackle, and if I started, I didn't think I'd ever stop. "I'm fine."

"The hell you are."

"We need to go," I said, aware that the calmness in my own voice should have bothered me. "Before anyone else gets hurt."

He stared at me a moment longer. "How about I take your guns?"

I shook my head. "I'm fine."

"No, you're not," he insisted, but didn't argue.

I waited.

He stepped aside and watched me pass.

A tech in tactical police blues fumbled with the rigging for portable battery-operated lights and the cluster of uniforms at the other end of the hall. Medics stood on either end of the yellow metal stretcher outside the perimeter LaFontaine and Rene, no, Officer Boudreaux had created around the body. I looked away. A sheet would have made it easier to be willingly ignorant of what had happened here. To deny that it happened at all. I tried to calm my churning stomach and wrest my thoughts away from the inert form on the dirty floor. The hallway lengthened the way it did in horror movies. The way it had the night I'd fallen into the Compact. Some part of me wondered what that meant now.

As I approached, the medics looked uncomfortable and nervous. LaFontaine, disapproving and sweaty. Father Callahan's expression radiated cool reserve despite the Glock in hand. I saw Sister Betty and Rene, but couldn't look at either. I shifted my gaze to the floor instead. "Alright, let's form up and get out of here. We need point guard and rear guard."

"We've got it taken care of," Sister Betty said.

Gratitude swelled in my chest.

"Caitlin," Rene approached and reached for my hand, "I'm so sorry."

I pulled away. "I'm bloody. I need to get cleaned up."

His hand hovered between us, but I refused to take it.

"Let's go," Sister Betty said, taking the lead.

Rene didn't move.

I walked past him, Marty behind me. Maybe he brought up the rear or maybe Father Callahan did. All I knew for sure was I'd taken Madame Sabine's place as the most vulnerable member of the team, and I hated myself for it.

F ather Callahan drove us to the local police department field office where we were separated and questioned. After hours of paperwork, they released me without a word of recrimination. Like Marty said, no one blamed me. No one even suggested I could have done differently after I'd told, and re-told my account, then again for good measure. I'd expected Officer LaFontaine to barge in and bluster, to give me a hard time, but when I saw him, he'd been professional. He treated me as an equal and with compassion and for whatever reason, his kindness rankled my nerves more than his animosity.

Maybe the lack of blame made it all worse. Maybe it would have been easier to be accused, to be reprimanded and punished, to be locked in a cell instead of standing on the roof of the hotel staring out at the glowing city below me.

Maybe I could have dealt with murder charges better than freedom.

The door at the other side of the pool creaked open and closed, and I counted the seconds for Marty to reach me. Sister Betty must have sent him instead of coming herself.

"You can't make this better," I said, staring out over the city. My knuckles ached from gripping the railing so hard.

"I'm trying not to," he said. "No, that's not what I mean. I mean I know there's nothing I can do, but I'm here."

From below, music reached us in snippets along with the occasional car horn and a drunken chorus of laughter. No one could fix it. Not really. Still, a question tormented me. Would fifteen floors do it? Could I make it to the ground without hurting anyone else?

"No one blames you." His hand squeezed my shoulder as if reading my impulse to climb the railing through touch. "Not me, Cooper, not Father C, Sister Betty. Not even LaFontaine."

He didn't mention Rene.

At the station, I'd been forced to talk with him since he was one of the officers aware of monster hunters, the government's DEMON branch, and the existence of all the crap we fought to keep humans safe. I'd tried not to look at him when I'd recounted what happened, but when you're living through a horror movie, you always end up looking.

And, the fight aside, the changes in his expression killed me on the inside. Confusion. Horror. Puppy dog love. Pity. All rigidly controlled from the thin press of his lips to his distant gaze. He'd never see me the same way. He'd never forgive me. Trouble was, I didn't know if I could, either.

"Please, Caitlin." The desperation in Marty's voice brought tears to my eyes.

I gripped the railing so hard, a spike of red-hot pain shot up my arm, but I couldn't let go. "I killed someone, Marty." Choking back a sob, said it again, forcing the words into reality. "I killed someone because I got lazy. I got sloppy." I saw Madame Sabine's face, her lips a perfect "o" of surprise, bubbles of blood collecting at the corner of her lips. Closing my eyes didn't make the images go away. My whole body shook as I slumped against the railing. "I killed her."

"You were in an impossible situation, Caitlin." He paused. "It's not your fault. Don't be so hard on yourself."

"No." I jerked out of his grip and crossed to the other corner of the rooftop, a fan whipping my hair across my face as I passed. "This is the excuse thing I've been talking about. This isn't something that can be forgiven, this is…" I laughed. "This is a mortal sin. Breaking a commandment. It makes me less than human. I'm just as much a monster as the things I hunt."

Marty didn't say anything, but I heard him approach. After a moment, he wrapped his arms around me, resting his chin on my shoulder.

I stared at the moon, riding low over the New Orleans skyline. A few stars bright enough to burn through the light pollution flickered in the black sky and I stood, a void, bound by Marty's arms. A balloon of flesh surrounding nothing.

Marty squeezed me and whispered, "You didn't do anything wrong."

"What's the point of debating right or wrong?" As much as I wanted to believe him, I couldn't. I'd focused so hard on that one spot below the stranger's armpit, I hadn't seen his intent to move until it was too late. I opened my eyes and stared at the constellations of blood spatter covering both of my arms. "I'm supposed to be one of the defenders. I'm supposed to stand between humanity and the monsters in this world, and I've become what I fight."

He considered me for a moment, then dropped his gaze.

My friend, my companion, my partner couldn't stand to look at me.

I dropped my hands to my side. "I'm supposed to fight shit that goes bump in the night, not *be* the monster."

"You're beating yourself up. You couldn't have—"

I laughed. "Yes, I could have. I should have. That's what I've trained to do since Shannon died. What the hell is the point if I can't do that? What am I doing?"

His hand rested on my shoulder. "You have saved so many lives. Remember Toronto? And that little town in New Hampshire?"

Boscawen. Empusa and her spun copper nest.

I didn't say it. Remembering the name didn't matter. Recounting minor victories didn't bring back the dead or prevent deaths that shouldn't have happened. "And then, there's Rome. And, now, New Orleans."

"Cee—"

"No," I said. "You don't get it. You're there in the middle of things, but you're not responsible for the lives of the people involved. You don't have to account for the living and the dead at the end of the day. You don't remember their names or see them staring back at you whenever you close your eyes."

"Stacy Mills, Seattle. Infatuated by the notion of sparkly vampires in the Pacific northwest, she stumbled into a goblin's lair while we questioned tree guardians a mile away."

I looked at him.

"Joe Tsiang, Cleveland. Chinese foreign national nabbed by that rogue vamp during the Cubs World Series celebration while we tracked the shaman responsible for the win."

My throat tightened.

"Giulietta Perricone, Rome. The Italian anthropology doctoral student with the most remarkable blue eyes I'd ever seen." He swallowed. "We know what happened there."

Pressure in my chest made my ribs ache as I tried to breathe.

He pulled out his phone. "Benito Hernandez, New Orleans. Three kids, Phillipe, Carlotta, Angelo. Massive coronary event resulting from a nightmare's touch."

My throat burned as I struggled to swallow my emotions. "You're not responsible for them." The words spilled out wild and uncontrolled as tears slipped down my cheeks.

"Of course I am," he said, putting his phone away. "I'm supposed to be the one who has your back, or fills in where you can't. Why do you think I light candles in every church we visit?"

Shaking my head, I shrugged, not trusting myself to answer. I'd never considered it, only given him time to do what he needed to do.

"I light one for friends and family I've lost, then one for every person we haven't saved and always a prayer remembering each one by name." He shrugged. "I keep a list."

"Each time I say 'not again,' and it keeps happening. No matter what I do to get better, to be faster, to get stronger, to prepare, it keeps happening," I sobbed. "I'm supposed to stop the monsters, to say 'not today,' and step in front of death."

"And you do," he said softly as he stepped closer, "but you're only human."

Without Marty's support, I would have tumbled to the cement when my knees buckled. He guided us to the ground gently and refused to let go.

I'm not sure how you get through the night after killing someone, even if everyone tells you it's not your fault. Without support, I don't know that I could have done it. After the roof, Marty brought me back down to our room, and he and Sister Betty tag-teamed me through shower and food. When I got tired of pretending to sleep, I got up, got dressed. Either I'd slept some or forgot Sister Betty had traded beds with Marty for the night. As soon as I had clothes on, she stood in front of the room door, fully dressed and blocking my only exit. "You have to talk to me, Caitlin," she said, arms crossed.

"No, I don't." I spun on my heel, or as much as the carpet would let me pivot in my Docs.

"If not me, then talk to someone else. Anyone. You can't bottle this up."

"I don't need to talk," I said, my fists clenched as I tried to control myself as I stalked the short space in relentless circles, trying to deal with the restlessness making my muscles quiver. "I need to find out whoever that asshole was, locate him and figure out if he's part of the Collectors, or if his magic goons are. I need to solve this case and not let anyone else down. I need...need to..." Rage made my skin itch, but I refused to scratch. "I need to punch something."

She stepped into my path. "Then punch me."

"What?" I recoiled. "That's crazy."

"No, it's not." She held out her hands as if wearing the padded mitts from the gym. "You know how to do this. Let it out. You want to punch something? Punch me."

For a heartbeat, the rage wanted to listen. My fists and arms tightened.

I could see the punch, the way my arm would pull back, impact her open palm, how far her arm would recoil, and feel the sting of skin to skin contact. Would it break her hand? I didn't care.

I spun again, pushing away the desire. "No." My voice shook.

"Caitlin," she said, exasperated, "you need to let this go."

"I killed her!" I snatched the hoodie from the end of Marty's bed and flung it into the bathroom. It fell short with an unsatisfying *woosh*. The puddle of fabric reminded me of how Madame Sabine crumpled after I shot her. My legs wobbled as the strength drained out of them, and I fell against the end of Marty's bed. "I killed her," I whispered, the words ragged.

Sister Betty sat beside me and pulled me against her. I couldn't move. Rigid in her arms, the shaking intensified. "I killed her," I said into her shoulder. "She shouldn't even have been there, but I didn't make her stay away."

"No one blames you." Sister Betty refused to let go, even when I tried to pull away.

I tried pulling away again. "I killed her."

Sister Betty held me so hard, my shoulders ached. I didn't deserve compassion. Not for this. I killed someone on my team. Someone who trusted me. Who could say who would be next? No, I deserved to be treated like the monster I'd become.

The dam broke.

She held me through it all.

42

"What do we know?" I asked, pacing Father Callahan's rectory office, a paper cup of rapidly cooling coffee in my hand. More than anything, I wanted out of the Cathedral. Being here made my skin crawl. Out of anywhere on Earth, this had to be the last place I belonged. I'd showered and changed clothes, but still felt Madame Sabine's blood on my hands. I'd carry the blemish of her death on my soul for the rest of my life.

Sister Betty watched me with the wary eye she usually reserved for illness or injury. "The magical community in New Orleans has no idea who this guy is, or who his henchmen may be. We've made inquiries about the magic after the attack on you in Bourbon, but the magical signatures don't match anyone known to the local covens."

"I've checked traffic cameras, security cameras, and anything else that might have been by Charity Hospital in the past several months," Marty said, "and other than the ghost tours and their gaggle of looky-loos, there's been no one on the grounds that shouldn't be."

"Wait, what do you mean?" I sat in the chair across from my partner and locked eyes with him. "Have others been there with permission?"

"Only a few construction workers accessed LSU's medical campus next door. I counted them in, then counted them out. No changes in apparent mass, height, or shape. Whoever went in seems to have come back out. Or they faked it convincingly."

Father Callahan's chair creaked as he leaned back. "Are there tunnels under the hospital?"

Marty made a face and started typing. "I doubt it. The water table is too high in most of the city, but I'll check."

"Secret entrances are as likely here as anywhere else." I sipped the bitter, cold coffee. Whoever the hell decided to add chicory to coffee needed their head examined, maybe even more than me. I set the cup down. "If someone has a dragon to hide, I doubt a little inconvenience like environmental realities are going to stop them from making it happen."

"What about the doors Mad—" Marty looked up at me and winced. "Sorry."

"Don't be." I ignored the visceral twinge of pain at the mention of her name. Pretending would have to become a bigger part of getting the job done and keeping my team off my case. "Ask your question."

"What about the doors Madame Sabine mentioned?" He turned to Father Callahan. "She talked about doorways and places of power and the root of all things, according to your debrief."

Father Callahan's meticulous, if fussy, habit of written debriefs had annoyed me when we'd first started hunting, but now, with wisdom, I saw the value. I just hoped I'd never be forced to read any from this case.

"Yes." Father Callahan pulled his laptop from the side table to the spot in front of him. After a moment or two of typing, he read from the screen, "She called Caitlin 'Phoenix' repeatedly and said she 'must learn about the fire,' the 'doors,' and 'pathways,' and 'use the fire within.'" He shook his head. "Little of it makes sense, but she talked about doors opening, and that they'd take Caitlin where she needed to go, including 'places of power,' 'the nest,' and to 'the root of it all.' And she said, 'There are other worlds than these.'"

"That's a Stephen King quote," I said, pulling at my lip, trying to consider the words without reliving those moments.

"Dark Tower," Marty agreed.

"But how does that relate to what we're dealing with here?" Sister Betty asked. "She might have been hallucinating since she was close..." Her words trailed off. "How much of it can we trust?"

I pulled the amulet out from under my shirt and gripped it tight before pulling it off my neck to look at it. The gray stone. The chips of smoked glass. The bloody fingerprints across the center. "She pulled this free when she said all that. It opened a door before. Maybe I need to find another door and open it."

My team stared at the stone in my hand, and none of us spoke.

"The Phoenix rises from the ash to become whole again," Marty said.

But what did that tell us about what I had to do?

I did the only thing I could think of. I called Violetta.

Of course, when you're dealing with a nightmare, even one that crosses dimensions as if she had Pre-Check with the supernatural TSA, "calling" wasn't as easy as picking up the phone. I didn't know that, but Marty did. He and Father Callahan used a conference room in the hotel to set up the ritual for summoning the nightmare to the human realm during the day.

When she appeared in the circle of valerian and lavender flowers strewn on the floor, she grinned and laughed. Sheathed in a white, sleeveless dress, she stood with her hands on her hips, and I could have sworn she posed for us to get a good look at her before speaking. "Oh, my dearest, you are, by far, the most enchanting human I've ever encountered."

"Thank you for coming, Violetta," I said, trying to fake normal as hard as I could.

Her white stiletto heels dimpled the carpet as she stepped over the ring. Without acknowledging anyone else in the room, she came so close, I backed up. Of all the things I needed, the soul ablation of a nightmare's touch pretty much landed at the bottom of the list. "Oh, don't worry, cupcake, I like you too much to touch you, even by accident, though you'd be," she leaned closer, closing her eyes and taking a long sniff, "scrumptious."

"Right," I said backing up and waving her toward a seat. "Sorry to interrupt you. I'm sure you have other business to attend to."

"Nothing more urgent than finding out why you're calling." She sauntered over to the chair and took a seat, crossing her long legs and leaning back. With the exception of her bouncing mane of midnight-dark curls, she looked like she might be ready to re-enact *that* scene from *Basic Instinct*.

"Thank you," I said, gesturing toward Marty and Father Callahan. "I know you've met some of my team before."

"Yes," she gave a faint smile and nodded acknowledgment before settling her attention on me again, "but love, I'm not interested in formalities. What do you want?"

"You told me to wear this amulet that admitted me to the Compact though the next one isn't for more than a decade." My fingers grazed the stone beneath my shirt. "I've been told about doors and using something called phoenix fire to open them. I've been told there are pathways I need to learn to get to places of power, a nest, and the root of it all."

She watched me, her expression inscrutable.

"But I don't know what any of that means."

"Then perhaps you should ask the person who told you about them," she said quietly.

"I can't." I tried to swallow the lump that rose in my throat. "She's dead."

She touched her fingers to her lips and thought for a moment. Each deliberate word came out with more reserve than I'd ever seen from Violetta before. "This isn't something I can help you with. Not without... upsetting those more powerful than me."

"What do you mean?"

She laughed. "Exactly what I've said, love." She watched me long enough to make me uncomfortable. "Nightmares don't lie for personal gain or entertainment. We don't need to. We can use your emotions and fears far more easily. Besides, most humans fear the truth more than anything."

"Would you be willing to provide any information at all?" Marty asked.

"Willing?" Violetta grinned. "Of course. Especially because I so love watching this one in action. Able to, however, is another story."

My shoulders sagged, though I tried very hard to sit up straight and not show weakness. "Can you confirm anything? That these doors or pathways exist? Or anything?"

With a sigh, Violetta sat up and leaned against the table's edge. "Against my better judgement, yes, since your options are limited and you won't get help from the places you're likely to go next." Before I could ask her about any of that, she continued. "Yes, there are doors and pathways, but you already know that. You've experienced it before."

"The Compact," I said.

She nodded with a half shrug. "In a manner of speaking. That doorway's more like a dumb waiter compared to what else is out there, but it's not all that different. Every doorway has a different purpose, a different way of..." she shrugged, "opening."

"What about the places of power?" Marty asked.

"Or the nest?" I added. I needed to know about the nest. Did it mean the dragon's nest? Or did it refer to some other supernat that used nests as a home base, like vampires? If it meant a way to find the dragon and eliminate the threat from New Orleans, I had to find it. It had to be my priority.

Violetta laughed again. "Places of power are something else you already know. You live in one, my dears." She raised her hands and sang, *"Laissez les bons temps rouler!"*

I nodded. We knew about the nexus of power in the city, but how could a door take us to where we already were? And how did we find the door? I stroked the amulet, thinking as I listened to the others talk.

"Time," Father Callahan added. "She said something about time being funny."

"That it is," Violetta said, her smile dimming. "And this is my time to be going. I wish you the best, Caitlin. I'll be watching." She winked and disappeared, the chair spinning lazily in her absence.

"Well," Father Callahan said, "that was interesting."

"She told us nothing," Marty complained.

Or had she? She'd never answered my question about the nest, and she knew a non-answer would never satisfy me. Without a word, she'd given me direction. If I'd thought I could live without a soul, or survive the ablation, I'd have hunted Violetta down to give her a big hug.

"No," I said, interrupting whatever they'd been saying. "She didn't give us what we wanted, but she told us more than nothing."

Father Callahan and Marty looked at me.

For the first time in what felt like forever, I smiled a real smile. "I know what we need to do next."

From the throne of his velvet chaise, Wayne Carter regarded me with amusement and a sneer. Neither seemed out of place in his meticulously, if somewhat anachronistically, appointed apartment. "I don't know what you expect me to tell you that I haven't already," he said, his dainty hands folded on his crossed legs.

"Mr. Carter," I said, "I appreciate your generosity and apologize for inconveniencing you again." Practicing the line in my head had helped. I could barely detect the sarcasm.

He sniffed. "It is a significant inconvenience."

"We'd like to compensate you, of course," Father Callahan said.

Another genteel sneer. "Bribery?"

"Nothing of the sort," Father Callahan assured him. "Only what is due a gentleman of your standing for the assistance you provide."

"Crude." He plucked at the lace-edged ruffled cuffs peeking from beneath the sleeves of his velvet smoking jacket. "But, given that you're a product of your time, I'm sure this is all I can expect."

This time, Sister Betty shifted in her seat beside me. I could sense her urge to fire back. She didn't, of course. Her restraint didn't require regular practice like mine.

The ageless man regarded us for so long, I wondered if he'd ever speak. We endured it, though. I had to believe I'd finally figured out how to do this job. Something told me he had the answers, and Father Callahan and Sister Betty still had enough faith in me to follow that instinct. Carter had to have what we needed to get through the next phase of this mystery. He had to. If he didn't, I didn't know what I would do.

"What is it you want to know?" Wayne Carter re-folded his hands primly on his lap.

"When we spoke last, you mentioned a dragon in the city," I said.

"And you're here to recount what we already discussed?" He rolled his eyes. "Delightful. I do so enjoy wasting time."

I clenched my teeth and breathed slowly before continuing. "I believe I've found the lair, but the obstacles we've encountered have prevented us from finding a viable way in."

"If you expect me to lead you into some lizard's filthy den, you've made a grave error." His pale face flushed pink.

"Please, Mr. Carter," I said, leaning forward in my chair and taking the pressure off the Glock tucked in the holster at my back, "that's not what I'm asking."

He pursed his lips. "Then what? Be quick."

I revealed the amulet through the neck of my shirt and held it where he could see it. "I think this is a key to finding another entrance, but I don't know how to use it."

When he looked at it, I caught the briefest flash of recognition before his expression went blank. "Where did you get that?"

"It's a long story. It's already opened one door to me. The door into the Compact."

His reddish eyebrow arched, his alabaster forehead wrinkling. "How?"

I lay the amulet against my chest and caressed the smoked glass chips. "I fell into a mirror."

"Where?"

I told him the name of the hotel.

His smile grew slowly and eventually became a chuckle.

"What?" I asked. "What's so funny?"

He shook his head, regarding his fingers as they splayed against his black silk trousers. "Humans manage to get themselves into the most entertaining situations, then expect their betters to rescue them."

Irritation made me bristle, but I managed to keep my mouth shut.

"You don't need anyone to tell you how to use that stone. You already know."

"I am so tired of people telling me I already know what I clearly don't," I snapped.

Carter didn't blink, but stared in that vaguely reptilian way vampires used to study their prey. It irritated me more than his cryptic pronouncement.

"I've been told to find doors and pathways, and use phoenix fire, to find what I'm looking for, and even if this is a key, I don't know how or where to use it." This time, I launched to my feet, but before I could draw breath to continue my tirade, Wayne Carter stood before me, toe to toe, nose to nose, exuding predatory interest.

He blinked and his eyes transformed, the pupils elongating into slits, his grin baring fangs. "Oh, please, Miss Kelley, tempt me."

I stumbled back, falling into the chair like cornered prey as he hovered over me. "I…I'm sorry. I didn't mean…" Words refused to come, and I had no idea what I was sorry for, only that I regretted whatever had him salivating over me like some kind of ultra-blue Pittsburgh steak.

He glanced at the others frozen in their seats with shock. The smallest satisfied smile softened his face. "What I was saying before being interrupted," he aimed a pointed look at me as he resumed his spot in the winged chair, "was some skills are innate and we have the ability to use them without conscious effort."

Trying not to look like a terrified animal, I nodded. If I had to, and if I could draw fast enough, the Glock at my back had silver bullets alternating with white phosphorus. I tried to remember how I'd loaded the magazine and wondered if I'd survive until I fired an effective round.

"You," Carter said with a flick of his fingers, "seem to have the ability to open doors using that key. And make no mistake, Hunter, it is a key to more than you can imagine."

I stroked the amulet, the stone warmer than it probably should have been, but didn't say anything.

"You said you were told about phoenix fire?"

"Yes," I said, embarrassed by the way my voice broke. I cleared my throat and continued. "The woman who told me about it called me phoenix more than once."

He snorted. "Mythical bird you are not, but there is precedent for the title."

The room remained silent as we waited for him to finish. When he didn't, Sister Betty asked, "What precedent is that?"

"I'm not doing your work for you, human," he sneered.

"How do I find the doors?" I asked, cautious of not irritating him further.

"They are all around us." He waved a hand in a circle around his head. "We could be in Faerie, or in any other dimension you choose, if you have the right key."

"How do I use the doors? How do I find the one into the dragon's lair? And will this key open the door I need?" As the words tumbled out, I winced at the desperation and the demands they conveyed.

He held out his hand, curling his fingers in an impatient flick. When I didn't immediately rise and approach him, he said, "Come here."

After a glance at Sister Betty and Father Callahan, I obeyed, crossing the few steps in far longer than he'd taken.

"Give it to me," he said, his hand out, beckoning me with a come-on gesture. "Don't let go of the cord, though."

I held it out, the cord still looped around my neck. Leaning forward, he took the stone in his hand and closed one eye, staring hard with the other as if looking through an invisible jeweler's loupe. Of course, his vampiric sight would be better than any lens. I almost felt the urge to laugh away my embarrassed discomfort, but I didn't have time.

He looked into my eyes, and I saw fire there. Actual flames. In his eyes. Then he grinned, all vampire teeth and no charisma. He drummed his first three fingers across the glass chips and the entire world tilted and disappeared.

43

Sister Betty always promised there'd be plenty of work for a Hunter skilled in covert work. I just wished I'd stop literally falling into it. Between the unnecessary bruises and wounded pride, these sudden, unintentional entrances might send me into early retirement. At least I had the presence of mind to keep my mouth shut so I didn't yelp and draw attention to myself when I landed on my ass. It also meant I didn't bite my tongue when my jaws clacked together. So, yay, bonus.

I rolled to my belly, taking a quick physical inventory of injuries as well as surveying my surroundings as I lay in the dirt. I wiggled toes and fingers, finding nothing broken, then flexed muscles. Nothing crunched. No pain flared from sprained muscles. All appendages worked as expected. Another point in my favor. My butt would hurt for a few days, but no worse than after a few hundred split squats. Most of that could be blamed on the busted cell phone in my back pocket. Cracked beyond utility, it fought back against being the impact point, and I had no doubt I'd be wearing its image for a while.

A quick brush of my body confirmed my 1911s remained in their holsters, the amulet pressed against my breastbone, and the Glock tucked against the curve of my spine. Everyone accounted for.

Except, of course, my team. I could only imagine their reaction to my disappearance.

What the hell had Carter done to send me here? Where was "here" to begin with? The musty funk suggested underground, but for all I knew, he'd banished me to another dimension for annoying him. Hopefully nothing here would be keen on eating me.

From where I crouched, I couldn't see much, but I hoped that meant no one else could see me. The room sounded cavernous; vague buzzing and hums echoed from far away. Something like distant voices, but too indistinct to be more than weird echoes. The dim light flickered and wavered. Maybe a torch around the corner?

I'd fallen behind some low wall of rough concrete blocks on a loamy pile of dirt unlike anything I'd seen in New Orleans, but given how little I'd actually seen, I couldn't afford to rule it out. The dirt smelled strange. Vegetal. Mineral-rich. Damp. Of charcoal and...something I couldn't identify that didn't belong with the other smells, not in a space like this. It felt too much like a cave, and I couldn't imagine the water table in the city proper supporting an underground structure as large as this seemed to be. The St. Louis Cathedral had underground catacombs, but at seven feet above sea level, it marked the high ground, something most of the other large structures couldn't claim. Being underground in the city should include standing water. Or at least mud, but scraping the dirt with the toe of my Docs only revealed more damp dirt. No welling water. It didn't confirm how deep the space felt, then again, I lay on top of a dirt heap. Nothing worth wasting time on now. I had to figure out how to get out and back to the team.

I rolled to one side, both to free up access to one of my guns and to take in more of the space above and around me. This far away from the light, the overhead gloom revealed little. There didn't appear to be any spiderwebs, either fae or the terrestrial creepy-crawly kind, nor other telltale signs of the normal critter infestation triggered by human abandonment. Nothing hinted at disrepair or even neglect, at least not that I could see. I chanced a quick glance over the top of the cement blocks in front of me, only to see an open expanse of more dirt surrounded by a concrete wall. The place felt familiar. Human, at least by construction, with a hint of the alien in the air. This might not be as bad as I expected.

More sounds reached me, but slow and layered, their intensity diluted, making them unrecognizable. Something metallic clinked, and over that, other noises I couldn't identify no matter how hard I listened.

Then, a sound I'd never forget.

A dragon's roar.

Though I'd never heard it before, I had no doubt what made it. The sound rumbled in my chest, and I clapped my hands over my ears as it intensified. Grit and dirt rained on me, dislodged by the unending roar. The noise swelled, crescendoed, and pressed against my brain from inside my skull, making my head ache and eyes hurt.

When it finally stopped, my eyes watered, making it harder to see, but I still attempted to peek over the low concrete-block wall for a better look around the dragon's lair. I saw nothing I hadn't already seen. Nondescript concrete. Dirt. It didn't paint a picture of where this space existed, and then I heard something new.

A voice.

A voice like a beleaguered middle school substitute teacher trying to cajole students into their best behavior.

A familiar voice.

"You must obey, or you'll force me to give you consequences."

I didn't have to close my eyes to imagine the hooded figure we'd encountered in Charity Hospital. Or the way he'd been holding Madame Sabine when—

No.

Not now.

The next sound might have been a laugh. If it came from Godzilla. To be fair, I would have laughed if threatened with "consequences," too. A grumbled response followed, but the words dissolved in reverberating echoes.

Curiosity drove me farther up the pile to get a better perspective, not that it improved my view. Featureless dirt stretched from the edge of the pile's retaining blocks to the wall. The far walls looked like they might be covered in graffiti, but then again, it might be shadow or even moisture. Along the perimeter, uneven clumps suggested pathways. Maybe. The difference didn't look like vehicle tracks, but more like layered footprints. Which, of course, complicated things. We knew the mastermind had at least three minions, but those tracks suggested a hell of a lot more traffic and more bodies. More potential casualties. How many people were down here? How many worked for him? Did he herd prisoners through here? Or had the tracks accumulated over time? How long had they been hiding here?

Though I strained and tried to stay hidden at the same time, I caught a glimpse of indistinct shadows wobbling on the far end of the wall. A few moving vertical-ish blobs and a horizontal-ish bump. I assumed the taller, vertical splotch to be the mastermind. Even calling him that in my head made me sneer. He didn't deserve the title. Bob. Generic, lackluster, exceedingly "normal" Bob would do.

"You can't just do what you want," Bob yelled, though he sounded more petulant than like any kind of authority. The taller blob jabbed at the horizontal bump.

The dragon's response rattled through my chest like the percussion at a metal concert, more vibration than words. Whatever its actual response, Bob snapped. "Because I raised you, like my father before me. If you expose yourself—"

Another roar shook the space. Instinctively, I ducked, my arms over my head, waiting for the ceiling, or at least part of it, to crash down on top of me.

Baby or not, this dragon had a ferocious set of lungs and a clear opinion.

When the roar and the soft patter of dirt on my arms stopped, I looked up and squinted, trying to make sense of what little I could see between the terrible lighting and the cloud of unsettled dust. Nothing had changed, but I still didn't trust it not to crumble if that dragon let loose again.

"You cannot defy them again, do you understand?" The voice sounded shrill this time. Desperate. Afraid. I wondered how dragons reacted to fear from their handlers, but I didn't have to wonder long.

Howling like I've never heard shook more dust from the ceiling. Bob's shouts still broke through, though. I couldn't understand a word, but I got the gist. This dumbass was trying to shout down a toddler's temper tantrum.

Amateur. Nothing like spotting an only child in the wild.

I resisted the urge to cover my ears to protect them from the cacophony. Loud as this lizard may be, he didn't have anything on being in the pit, pressed against the metal barriers at a heavy metal concert.

"Spell him." This time, Bob sounded panicked. Smaller shadows scrambled around him, the taller, steady one. I couldn't count how many. The broad, round lumps moved too frantically to distinguish individuals.

Magic crackled through the air, and the strange purple light I'd seen from the henchmen before they'd zapped me flashed bright enough to illuminate the ceiling. Pipes. Big ones, running over my head.

Of course, I made one wrong move that unbalanced my position and I slid down the dirt pile, falling beyond the lip of the retaining wall. Dust billowed around me in a bigger plume than I would have expected in such damp conditions. I crouched into a ball, gun drawn, waiting for alarm at my appearance.

The irritated growl of a dragon might have worked in my favor as a distraction. That and I'd tumbled into an empty space with no obvious patrols or lookouts.

"Spell him again!"

Magic purple light flashed again, repeatedly, power sizzling through the air. The temporary glow gave me better visibility as I looked around. Red signs hung on the wall, identifying three-hour fire protection, another for a water main shut-off valve. Hulking transformers lurked in a far corner, and beside them, standpipes and the corner of what might be a generator. Even before I saw the sign hanging in the shadows near the ceiling that took away all doubt, I knew I could only be in one place.

Charity Hospital.

The dissipating magic left behind a strange silence and an eerily complete darkness. My eyes adjusted to the return of the dim, flickering light as I scrambled back behind the retaining wall, patted my holstered 1911 and the Glock at my back, then checked my supply of extra ammo.

We'd been right, looking over that map. Only one place existed in New Orleans big enough to conceal a dragon unnoticed, and we'd figured it out. Even if Bob and his minions didn't prove to be the entire Collectors' operation, they'd be a damned good start and a source for more information. Were the abducted supernats here? Did that explain the evidence of traffic or the random appearance of lights in the upper floors? Or were the missing beings hidden somewhere else? I tried to remember when the hospital had closed after Katrina. Surely, they couldn't have been here before then. And if they hadn't, there had to be another location. Stopping them and taking enough captives to get the information we needed would be impossible. I needed to get out and get backup.

And avoid the timoredax on the way.

Or did I?

I leaned against the cinder block wall to think.

This is what I'd wanted from the beginning. Leaving now might be throwing away a shot at ending this safely. Risking the whole team had always seemed...unnecessary, even in the best-case scenario. For all they knew, I'd been whisked away to some alternate dimension. I doubted

Carter would tell them where he'd sent me, so they'd continue working the case and end up here anyway. I had the best shot of taking down the dragon to begin with, and the advantage of surprise was on my side now.

If I prioritized the threats and planned well, I could do this on my own and still walk away with prisoners for questioning. Or at least capture them, commandeer a phone, and call for support. And if I didn't make it, my team would find back up. If I became baby Smaug's afternoon snack, Sister Evangeline's Order might be persuaded to help. And there were other monster hunters. Mason Dixon, Mark Wojcik. That mom in Ohio had been making quite a stir lately. And Bubba, if he ever resurfaced. Other supernaturals could be convinced to help, and with enough support, they'd eliminate this threat if I failed. If anything happened to me, they'd be fine. And if I succeeded? They'd never have to set foot down here.

A dragonly snarl rippled through the space, an almost musical warning, and for a minute, I wished pissed off me sounded that good.

"Fine," Bob huffed, a tremor in his words, "but leaving is still out. Of. The. Question." He punctuated the last with what must have been claps. Since I didn't hear the rush of flames followed by brief wails of death by incineration, I assumed he survived. Maybe hubris favored the douchey.

Another grumble followed, but this one sounded like the purring of a large cat. Low. Almost soothing.

"That's better," Bob said, much calmer this time. "That's more like it."

I risked a peek over the cinder blocks. The shadows on the wall melded into one big blob that vaguely resembled an extended middle finger.

As if I needed celestial commentary.

"Why is it taking so much to put him down?" Bob demanded, the shadows growing larger and fainter as they moved along the wall. "It takes too long to subdue him."

"He's getting older, stronger." The stammered response came from a human as far as I could tell. "Plus, the interaction with the magic from the—"

"I'm not interested in excuses." His voice got louder, clearer as he stalked my way.

Bob, the "mastermind" behind this dragon daycare scheme, rounded the far corner alone, following the pathway of churned dirt along the wall. His robe fluttered behind him, each step kicking up a puff of dust. He muttered to himself, his hands gesticulating at the same time.

Before I realized it, I had my weapon aimed at him.

Center mass.

My finger slid from the trigger guard to the trigger.

From this distance, I could make a head shot. Without his hood up, I doubted I'd miss. Not like last time.

And then, my hands started shaking.

His death wouldn't bring back Madame Sabine. His death wouldn't change anything. If he died right now, I'd still have to deal with a dragon, and I'd be no closer to finding the missing supernats. If he'd raised it, he might be the only thing keeping the dragon in check and preventing it from demolishing New Orleans.

I took a deep breath and tried to steady my grip against the cinder blocks.

Would taking him out be any different than killing Madame Sabine? Her death might have been an accident, but I had killed her, he hadn't. Whatever else he had done, did Bob deserve to die for my crimes?

My finger slid back to the trigger guard. The trembling muzzle of my gun tracked his progress until his dark robes blended into the shadows and he disappeared. The heavy crash of a metal door slamming shut made me jump before I holstered my weapon.

I cursed myself, heat suffusing my face. My job was to protect, to eliminate threats, and yet again, I'd failed.

What now?

Digging the heel of my hands against my eyes, I tried to slow my breathing and fight off the spiral of dark thoughts swirling in my brain.

If I couldn't end the threat he posed, what the hell was I going to do?

Plausible deniability is a beautiful thing, especially when it works in my favor.

Skulking around the underground of Charity Hospital, I planned what I'd tell Sister Betty when she inevitably reamed me out over violating the Scooby Doo rule of two. First, I'd say, I ended up here with no idea where I was. Second, the smashed phone, courtesy of yet another dramatic entrance. Third, I'd established that I'd entered enemy territory. Not exactly a place I could stop and ask for directions. Finally, alone or not, I'd been trained to do this kind of job, to make the impossible happen in the name of keeping humans, and other creatures, safe. I had an obligation to take advantage of the situation regardless of how harrowing it might be. Leaving didn't make sense. I couldn't leave if I didn't know how to get back in with reinforcements. I had to take advantage of my time whether that meant recon or eliminating threats. If, of course, I could take a damned shot without my shaking hands making it go wild. I'd deal with that when it came up again. Answering Sister Betty would prove the more difficult challenge, so that's what I prepared for.

After the door closed behind Bob the "mastermind's" departure, I crouched low and scuttled from my landing place to a broad cement support pillar in the general direction he'd left. I hid behind it and waited for an alarm, or some kind of response to my movement.

Nothing happened. Bob didn't return. No one else passed in either direction.

Vague sounds suggested activity from the dragon's general location. Metallic clinks, something that sounded like a rainfall of coins, and the whisper-hush of lowered voices. The hum and buzz I'd heard when I first landed grew louder.

I took a deep breath and crept around the round pillar, dashing to the next one, prepared for the call of alarm that never came. This time, when I peered around my cement hiding place, I caught my first glimpse of what I'd come to see.

My breath caught.

Before me stretched what could only be described as a dais. The corner of what looked like a two-foot thick marble slab emerged from a heap of shiny stuff rivaling the collection of an underwater crab with the voice of Eddie Izzard. On top of it all curled a dragon, an honest-to-god red-and-black-scaled creature of mythology at least sixty feet long and bigger than the house I grew up in. Its haunches bunched as it fluttered its wings, craned its neck, and yawned. The beast's long, split tongue extended past and curled up without touching its massive teeth. A landslide of its apparent "treasure," which included a toaster and what appeared to be car rims, cascaded to the dirt floor as it stretched its legs. The longer it stretched, the wider its toes spread and quivered, its talons extending and retracting like a cat's claws. Its eyelids closed from side to side, then another layer shuttered from top to bottom.

I shuddered and ducked behind the column, my back to it.

First the timoredax. Now, this. I slid down to the ground and rubbed my forehead.

This beast was way above my weight class. Maybe even my team's collective weight class. Unless, of course, Wayne Carter imparted some kind of dragon-killing wisdom in exchange for mojo'ing me into Trouble. Not "trouble," but *Trouble*. If anything deserved a capital letter, this situation certainly did. And, somehow, I had to figure out how to get out of it.

Sitting up on my knees, I peered around the column again and counted three cloaked minions milling about the dragon. One gave a wide berth to the creature's armored tail as it passed behind, using a rake to even out the dirt. Another stood on the far side, almost plunged in shadow, their back to me and further obscuring whatever they did. The third struggled with a bucket as it approached the raised platform of glittery junk. Engaged in such mundane tasks, I wondered if these could be the same magic users that threw purple lightning at me on Bourbon Street. I could only assume they were given the magic I'd seen, which, of course, complicated things.

I ducked back behind the column, pressing my forehead against the smooth concrete. It would really be nice to have a normal kind of fight with punching and kicking, and maybe a little gunfire. Lately, they all seemed to require some other kind of combat. Mental, emotional. Negotiation. Diplomacy. Much more of that and I'd fall out of practice with the kind of fighting I preferred. And I didn't relish Sister Betty's "conditioning" sessions when she decided I'd gotten rusty and needed to refresh my skills.

But, of course, straightforward battle wouldn't work here. Not without becoming a human bacon bit.

I considered my options. Or lack of them, without my team.

No eyes-in-the-sky scouting, my esoteric and cryptid knowledge base reduced to my respectable (but limited) capabilities, weapons limited to the twin 1911s and an emergency Glock tucked against the curve of my spine, with an extra magazine for each of the 1911s. Twenty-nine rounds of alternating silver, white phosphorus-packed silver, and cold iron already loaded, fourteen to spare. With no on-hand resources to fight magic, I'd have to neutralize the minions without getting zapped. Any of the rounds would seriously incapacitate humans, if those robed minions were human, that is. If all else failed, or if I ran out of ammo before getting barbequed, I could knock them out with a Colt-shaped club.

As for the dragon, nothing I had would kill it, though the white phosphorous rounds would fuck up just about anything's day. I could hope to get enough iron into it and slow it down, but that seemed unlikely. If I managed some super stealthy shenanigans, how many others would I have to deal with? Did they have some way of raising an alarm and alerting their boss? Or others? And all this presumed that the dragon would play nice and wait its turn in the fight rotation.

I sighed as quietly as possible.

Being totally screwed sucked. Not knowing exactly how screwed sucked more.

A colossal snap drew me out of my thoughts in time to see one of the robed figures crab-crawling away from the dragon's massive jaws, the bucket abandoned, the dirt wet under its rim. The minion's hood had fallen back to reveal a young woman, her dark hair pulled back in a low ponytail at the nape of her neck. Terrified, she shook her head as the dragon lowered its head, craning to reach her. A tendril of smoke curled out of one nostril.

Her murmured litany of "no, no, no, no no no," became faster, her panic making it an unending chant.

My chest tightened as I watched the dragon's massive jaws open, its black leathery lips curling away from teeth longer than my leg.

The woman shrank into a trembling ball on the ground.

As much as I wanted to run and intervene, I didn't. I couldn't blow my cover. I couldn't waste this opportunity. I kept watching, my stomach in knots. If I couldn't step in and save her, I'd at least do her the honor of witnessing her death.

The dragon's head hovered over the woman, but instead of devouring her, it whined.

I blinked.

Like any child throwing a tantrum, the beast kicked its back legs, and a cascade of junk clattered to the ground. It thrashed its tail, and as its head hovered over the cowering woman, its expression changed into something akin to a lizard pout and it whined again.

I could only assume words made up the whine, but I couldn't discern them. The disco ball rolling across the floor might have distracted me from attempts to listen.

"Stop it. Right now." Another of the cloaked figures stepped in front of the woman and finger-wagged the beast as she got to her feet.

This time, when the dragon moved, the third cloaked figure emerged from the shadows on the far side of the dais and raised his hands, purple sparks flashing between his fingers.

Bingo.

I might not be able to use magic, but even I could tell this was the same crap thrown at me on Bourbon Street.

I drew one of my Colt 1911s and stood, creeping up the length of the column to avoid drawing attention.

Then, the dragon drew back.

44

T he robed figure on the far side of the dais took a half step closer, and the creature cowered, crouching against its pile of shiny rubble. As the minion pulled his hands apart, the lightning grew bigger, more aggressive, and more purple light flared as Finger-Wagger sparked his own ball of lightning. Unable to retreat farther, the dragon buried its snout against the crook of its front elbows, squeezing its eyes shut.

In an instant, I understood.

These fuckers used magic for some Gringotts-level dragon abuse bullshit.

The dragon shivered, the pile of junk rattling under its quivering weight. A polished muscle car engine tumbled off the backside of the platform, and the poor creature jumped when it hit the ground.

Behind Finger-Wagger, the female had regained her feet and pulled up her hood, dusting herself off. "Okay, that's enough. He's backed off."

"He's going to learn," the magic user said, his voice a little shaky, perhaps from the effort of controlling the magic. "And if it takes hitting him with this every time he gets ugly, then that's what we'll do. It's all about consistency."

"He didn't hurt me," she said without conviction. "Let's go. He's been fed. We've got other stuff to do."

With a grunt, her companion released the magic, and the space between his hands went black again. He swiped an arm across his forehead, pushing part of his hood aside to show off an ear for a moment. "Yeah, you're right. The little prince will get pissy if we're late."

She shushed him, but with a laugh. "You shouldn't say things like that. He could be listening."

"What's he gonna do?"

"He could cast against you." The woman adjusted her hood, and I wondered if it muffled her voice, or if she'd lowered it when she spoke.

"So what? I've got a better than fifty percent chance that whatever he does won't work. I'll take those odds. He can take his lineage and stick it." He shrugged and passed her, walking away from the dragon. The other two fell in step behind him. As he passed out of my line of sight, he raised his voice in a screeching falsetto, "and his little dragon, too."

She laughed, he cackled, and they walked off, the third minion silently following.

Did three embittered minions mean an opportunity to enlist them on the side of right? Or at least the not-siccing-a-dragon-on-a-city side?

Once I heard the slam of the metal door again, I peeked out from behind the column.

The dragon curled like a cat on its pile of junk that included silver beverage cans, a hand mirror, and a bucket painted with a gaudy blue and yellow beer company logo. A sparkling string of what had to be costume jewelry wrapped around one talon, and it sucked on the pendant crystal of a massive chandelier like a pacifier. Its wings draped it like a blanket, and its massive chest expanded and shrunk as it breathed. This far away from the possibility of dying in an inferno, it kinda looked...cute. Peaceful.

But then again, who was I kidding? It could probably flame broil me from here. And if not that, I'm sure it would find another way to kill me.

Hiding behind this glorified post got me nowhere except running out of time before the minions or their brat prince "mastermind" returned to muck up my work.

"Are you going to come out, or watch me all night?"

The clarity of the words startled me. I immediately spun, gun aimed where I thought the voice had come from.

Nothing.

Empty space stretched between me and the far wall. Only the occasional footprint marked the dirt between me and the pile where I'd landed.

Slowly, I turned, step by step, inch by inch, gun in a supported grip to clear as much of the space as I could. Which, of course, only made me feel more like a stooge.

"Who said that?" The stage whisper I used felt uncomfortably loud.

"Who do you think?"

Oh, a wise guy, eh?

I shook my head. "If I knew, I wouldn't be asking."

The rasp and tinkling clink of a metallic avalanche rang through the space.

I whipped around to find the dragon standing between the dais and the pole, its massive head stopped uncomfortably close to my flesh.

"Me," it growled.

My guts dropped to my feet and, for the first time since I'd switched to carrying the 1911s on every mission, my gun felt too heavy to hold and my trembling arms dropped to my side. "Right."

The beast's nostrils flared as it studied me. Its irises...changed color, shifting from blue to purple, with flares of pink and green as its oval pupils contracted. The twin tips of its forked tongue protruded between its leathery lips. I fought the urge to step back. "What are you doing here?" it asked.

"Well," the awkward laugh that accompanied the word made me cringe, "you probably wouldn't believe me if I told you."

It didn't respond.

"But since you asked, I ended up here by accident."

"You're not one of Walter's clan."

He hadn't asked a question, but I felt compelled to answer, even if I didn't know how. "Who's Walter?"

It waited, as if it didn't understand the question.

I tried another topic. "How...how did you get here?"

It blinked, the double lids closing slowly before reopening. The slitted pupil slowly widened from the middle until blackness all but consumed the iridescent shifting colors around it. All I could think of was creepy goat eyes. A carnivorous goat that might decide to swallow me whole just to see what I tasted like.

"Or, you know, we don't have to chat," I said, cursing myself for being awkward instead of figuring out how to neutralize this threat before the others returned. At this point, if the thing ate me, it might be less painful than this interaction.

"Why have you come here?" Its head turned and its eye drew even closer. This close, I couldn't see anything but the deep, black pupil and my own reflection. At least it made it a little less unnerving.

"I didn't intend to," I said. At least I'd die with a clear conscience instead of lying. Then again, letting it get this close meant I had a chance of shooting it through the eye. Once again, I found myself trying to remember where the white phosphorous rounds were in the ammo rotation, and whether I'd be able to fire enough rounds to get to one before I died. "Do you...belong to Walter?"

"I am not a slave," it growled.

I stepped back. "No, of course not. I don't want to hurt you." I held up my hands, though one held a gun. "This is just for defense."

Why the hell couldn't I stop babbling?

It swung its head in an arc and sniffed me, dragging in air so hard my clothes ruffled in the breeze it made. "You stink."

My face flushed. "Well, it is ninety degrees and roughly seven thousand percent humidity, and there's only so much deodorant can—"

"And you reek of elf." His lip curled, drawing back like a thick curtain to bare long, sharp teeth, then it tossed its head in disgust and walked away.

"Wait," I said, chasing the dragon as it lumbered back to its dais. "What do you mean? I haven't been around any elves."

It crawled onto the pile, dislodging a crystal lamp that rolled and shattered on the ground. I jumped back to avoid the shards, and it glanced at the glittering mess and snorted. "Treasures of this world are so fragile."

"Right, but back to the elf?"

It glared at me. "No."

Oh, great. Pouting. If only I had something shiny to offer as a placating gift. Then, I realized something. "Why can I understand you now when I didn't understand how you interacted with..." I gestured in the general direction where the others had disappeared.

"Walter's clan."

"Right, yeah, that. How can I understand you now?"

"Because I want you to, Hunter."

Again. Tagged as a Hunter by some...thing I'd never met. Was I wearing a sign or something? Had someone drawn it on my forehead in Sharpie or something? "Why did you call me that?"

"It is right to call things by what they are." The dragon slumped onto the pile, resting his head on something that looked like it might have once been a Mini Cooper before it got squashed into a dragon's pillow. Metallic blue paint sparkled in the low light.

"Then you should call me Caitlin," I said, holstering my gun. "What should I call you?"

"Harold."

I don't know what I expected, but that wasn't it. "Your name is...Harold."

He snorted, and smoke puffed from his nostrils. "You're surprised."

Tact and diplomacy. Why couldn't I have been deficient in anything less essential? "No, I'm—"

"Surprised," he grunted. His massive head shifted on his pile of treasure, his eyes glinting as he sneered. "Subtlety isn't a strong trait among humans."

"Harold, I don't mean to disturb you or—"

"And yet, here you are."

I pressed my lips together, breathed, and counted to ten. "Yes, my apologies."

"For interrupting or doing so without invitation?"

"Both," I said. Lessons on manners from supernats seemed to be today's theme.

He sniffed and rubbed his snout against his clawed foot. "Humans stink." I stepped back, which only provoked another comment. "A few steps won't lessen the stench of you. State your business and be gone."

"My apologies," I said, trying to remember diplomacy and how it pertained to dragons. "I appreciate your generosity."

"I've agreed to nothing." From the deeply nasal quality his voice had taken on and the puff of smoke that accompanied his next words, the great beast must be breathing through his mouth.

"N-no," I said, stepping back again. "I only meant the generosity of your time."

It growled. "Do not insult me, human. You do not have the magic possessed by Walter's clan."

Pride. Definitely a dragon trait. I nodded, keeping my head bowed until he spoke again.

"Now, hurry up."

"I'm only here to find out why your clan is stealing—"

Harold growled, lifting his heavy head and swinging it toward me. My reflection burned in the flashing iridescence of his eye. "You dare accuse me, human? In my own lair?"

Shit. "I—"

"Silence!" The bellow rang through the building and made my ears hum. Louder than a gunshot, and longer. One of these days, I'd wake up deaf.

Harold pushed himself off his resting place to the melodic sound of his treasures sliding and lumbered toward me with two thunderous steps. "The absence of dragons in this world may embolden you little creatures, but make no mistake, your kind is still no match for mine." I could see my reflection in his wet teeth. "Perhaps it's time for a reminder?"

The reek of sulfur and smoke made me recoil more than his pithy comment about humans as little creatures.

"Dude, no one with breath like that should talk about anyone else stinking."

"Excuse me?" Harold withdrew as if slapped.

"Exactly." I waved my hand in front of my face. "You need to excuse yourself. At least until some lackey brushes those rather gigantic teeth of yours."

"Why you—" He swung a claw at me, but I jumped back and ducked as it flew by. Of course, that only pissed him off.

When he charged, I closed my eyes and stood my ground. Where the fortitude came from, I can't say.

The intensity of the hot, sour air he breathed stole my breath. It felt like I'd been standing in the sun too long, and I wondered, if I survived the next few moments, if my skin would be pink and burned. But either Harold lost interest in trying to intimidate me, or my lack of reaction confused him. Either way, I felt him retreat and waited a moment before opening my eyes.

"I could have eaten you, you know," he grumbled, laying his head on his claws. "I'm just not hungry."

And now, for my next trick, convincing a dragon not to eat me. Thankfully, I had this one in the bag.

"Harold," I said with an unintentional sigh, "humanity has a great deal of dragon lore, so I'd imagine dragons have at least some of the same legends. Are you familiar with dragon lore?"

"Of course." His brow creased, scaled wrinkles hissing as they rubbed against each other. "What of them?"

Taking it for affirmation, I pressed on. "Human legends talk about victory over the dragons. We're raised to know that dragons can be beaten, even by the weakest among us."

He laughed, his hot, stinky breath buffeting my clothes. "Perhaps, but should I desire, I could roast you where you stand or swallow you in one bite." His teeth snapped shut on the last word, as if to emphasize it.

"True," I said, trying to display a calm I didn't feel as I stepped closer and tapped his snout. "You could. But do your legends talk of a human woman named Margaret?"

The great beast recoiled, though from recognizing the name or to see me without crossing his eyes, I didn't know. "Why?"

I smiled. Bingo. "In our world, she is known as Saint Margaret, and I won't bore you with the details, but what's important is that she got swallowed whole by a dragon."

Harold snorted in amusement. "We have many such tales."

"I'm sure you do," I said, my hands on my hips, "but what might make this one memorable, or even a cautionary tale among your kind is what happened in the end."

"Swallowed whole. By a dragon. The end is she leaves through an end."

Interspecies poop jokes. Great. Because that's what I needed in my life.

"For most people," I said over the dragon's low, rumbling laugh, "but not for this one."

He stopped laughing, and leaned forward, his snout mere inches from me. When his eyes crossed to take me in, he closed one eye and tilted his head. "What happened?"

I shifted my weight from one foot to the other and subtly slid my right hand back into a good position to grab the gun holstered at my hip. "Being blessed by her God, after she was swallowed, she prayed. With the power He bestowed on her, she burst forth from the belly of the dragon."

Harold recoiled. "The only magic that works on dragons is dragon magic."

"See, the thing is," I said, tapping between his nostrils with my left index finger, "religious faith isn't magic, at least not by the strictest definition."

"The magic of the gods is still magic."

"Technically, but only if you're talking about their direct power," I said. "God blessed her, so the power belonged neither to God nor her when she used it."

Harold blinked, as if thinking his way through the argument.

"And did I mention," I asked, cocking my head, "the Christian God blessed her?"

He scowled. "I could still eat you. Or crisp you with fire and add your bones to my treasure." His claws raked through the pile beneath him, and I caught a glimpse of a bone or two under the mess.

"You could," I said. "I couldn't stop you."

"Then I shall," Harold grumbled, opening his mouth wide.

I tried not to think about how large his teeth were. That one incisor was longer than half my height. "But did I mention that I also have the backing of the same Christian God?"

Harold's mouth snapped shut and he recoiled, retreating a few steps.

"Yes, that's right. I am a human, but I am a Hunter," I continued. My gelatinous insides quivered, and if I'd had to pee, I probably would have already gone in my pants. That I still stood with some dignity intact had to count as a win. "While most humans cannot compete with the regal likes of your kind, you may want to reconsider eating one backed by the power of the Christian God and the Holy Roman Catholic Church." When he didn't answer, I said, "Or at least seriously debate it given the digestive distress it might cause."

He huffed and turned almost all the way away from me, but something told me he kept me in his peripheral vision.

"So where do we go from here, Harold?"

"You haven't told me why you're here," he grumped. "Or what you want. Or about your clan." He pretended to not watch me, then snuck glances my way, as if trying to figure out how I'd react.

And I got it. "Are you part of Walter's clan, Harold?"

He snorted, his talons curling deep into a pile of plastic coins and beads. "No."

I ventured closer, and he watched me. "Are you being kept prisoner here, Harold?"

"That's impossible." He sneered, but buried his snout in his treasures. "They can't stop me."

"But they did. They hurt you with magic."

The massive creature shrugged, and his multi-colored eye glittered more intensely. I took another cautious step closer, avoiding the shattered crystal and stepping around a textured silver side table that looked like it belonged in a hotel lobby.

Harold's front legs tensed, but he didn't move. The first layer of his eyelids closed, turning his beautiful but creepy irises from a fiery living opal to a milky rainbow moonstone.

Very slowly, I leaned over the dais and lay a hand on his warm, dry cheek.

He closed his eyes, and a single silver tear trickled over his scales.

Before I could say anything, I heard the one voice I really didn't want to hear.

4 5

"A hh, Persephone, you're here."

I didn't turn around. Showing the dragon my back might be construed as an insult. Or invitation. Maybe both, and with Bob the "mastermind" coming up from behind, I needed to keep Harold as happy as possible until I decided what to do with him. "Dude, unless you're talking to a mythological figure I can't see, you've made a mistake."

The jerk at least did me the favor of approaching Harold's lounging spot and stepping into my line of sight. Unfortunately, he had a gun aimed at me when he did and the patronizing smile that usually precedes a mansplaining. He tilted his head. "Oh, I know exactly who you are, Caitlin Kelley, Regional Monster Hunter for the Holy Roman Catholic Church. Darling protégé of the covert division's premiere operative, now settling for a safer, more mundane role covering, if I'm not mistaken, the southern United States from Tallahassee through San Antonio."

I didn't react. But seriously, how did so many strangers know so much about me?

He nodded once and continued, gesturing with his gun. "Why settle down? Cloak and dagger too much for you? Or did some other inadequacy get you demoted? Has that nasty trigger finger gotten you in trouble before?"

My teeth ground together as I went cold. "Attempting to antagonize me, however poorly, is not wise."

367

The twerp laughed, a loud braying that intensified my desire to punch him. With his free hand, he dashed a finger at the corner of his eye before regaining his composure. "Seems I've struck a nerve. Perhaps you just suck at protecting people."

The 1911 appeared in my hands, cocked and pointed at the black-robed asshole before I even thought about moving. I hated myself for reacting to his words, but I refused to back down.

"Definitely struck a nerve," the twerp said with a satisfied grin, the barrel of his gun drooping. "Good thing I'm not rattled by something as predictable as a vigilante pointing a gun at me."

Maybe I was as reckless as Sister Betty thought, and maybe I did suck at protecting people, but it was one thing for me to say it to myself and another for some worthless snot to point it out.

"How long," he said, pacing, though turning to watch me, "can you hold that heavy gun in that position? How long before your little arms tremble? Before you lose control of your muscles?"

"Want to find out?"

He laughed again. "Now, now, that's no way for a God-fearing monster hunter to behave in the face of such minor antagonism."

"Who says I fear God?"

"Oooh." The twerp lowered his gun as he touched the fingers of his free hand against his lips. "Are we ready to delve into pathology already?"

I bit the inside of my cheek, tasting blood.

"Are you going to point out all the broken bits, Caitlin? Are you really going to let me turn you into a monster so easily?"

Something inside me recoiled. "You want to turn me into a monster?"

"Haven't I already?" He gestured to the gun in my hand.

"If I can shoot you to stop you from abducting another creature, or stealing powers from them, I will. That doesn't make me a monster."

He thought for a moment, then waved his gun at me again. "I'm not sure if I'm disturbed or impressed by how bloodthirsty one murder has made you."

It hadn't been murder, but no matter how hard I tried to convince myself of that, his words rang true. Too true.

I slid my finger to the trigger guard and lowered the gun to my side.

"Aww, you're going to make me work for it?" His lower lip puffed out in an exaggerated pout. "I thought we were on to something."

"What do you want?"

He scowled. "You're not even going to let me have fun, are you?"

I didn't answer.

His scowl deepened. "You haven't even asked my name."

"And I won't, because I don't give a shit what it is. Knowing your name doesn't factor in to protecting my territory." I knew his name. Or assumed him to be Harold's 'Walter,' but he didn't need to know that.

"Doesn't it?" The stupid grin returned with his mansplaining tone. "Won't it put together the whole puzzle and prevent you from fucking up something else?"

The insinuation stung, but I didn't flinch. My finger slid onto the trigger, and I raised the gun again. "Get on with it."

He held up a hand, and when he laughed, it sounded strained and unsure. "You act like you've never played the game before, like you don't know how to flirt. Maybe that's why you can't keep a boyfriend. Or girlfriend."

Goddamn, how much had this little shit researched me?

"Talk." Though I didn't lower the gun, I put my finger back on the guard. "Before you lose the opportunity."

"Fine, you want an evil villain monologue, I'll monologue." With a heavy sigh, he shrugged. "Quick and dirty, no foreplay for you."

I waited.

He stared at me.

"Well?"

"Where do you want me to start?"

"Anywhere, before I change my bloodthirsty mind. How did you get Harold?"

He blinked. "Harold?"

I gestured at the dragon listening to our conversation.

"Why did you name him?"

"I didn't. He told me his name."

Walter shrugged, looking more like a petulant teenager than anyone capable of mastering anything, never mind a dragon. "Whatever. Not important. My family has been charged with guardianship of the Elderkind for generations. The egg from which this dragon—"

"Harold," Harold mumbled, though it sounded more like thunder.

Walter gave him the side eye, but continued, "—came was delivered to my family four generations ago. My great-great-grandfather passed guardianship to my great-grandfather—"

"Right, right," I interrupted. "We can skip all the begats and whatnot. Harold," I glanced at him and his heavy head bobbed approval, "is a sentient creature, and not your property, regardless of any guardianship legacy. What are you doing with him?"

"Ahh, but *it* is my property." He crossed his arms over his chest. "It—"

"*His* name is Harold," I said.

"*It*," insisted Walter, "is my family's legacy to this world, and I will not have the likes of you take *it* away! This great responsibility confers—"

"Dude, you've got the quote wrong," I said. "It's 'with great power comes great responsibility,' and from what I can see," I gestured at Harold's meaty head with my left hand, "the power is with this big guy right here. Not you."

I waited for him to get devoured. One bite would do it. I'd seen worse. My sister hadn't deserved her fate, but I'd be down for seeing this dude become dragon tapas. I'd even find some ketchup to help him go down. Surely, this amulet could get me to a local convenience store if I could figure out how to make it work.

Walter's face reddened. "That is *not* how this goes, you dumb redneck."

"Redneck." I looked at him, trying to figure out if I should be insulted by a shitty nickname that had zero bearing on anything about me, or because he'd done his level best to insult me and failed. "How'd you figure?"

He gestured at the guns and then made some vague circular motion at me. "You. Your guns, your muscles, your shoot-first attitude."

"If I had a shoot-first attitude, you'd already be on the ground."

"You're still a Hunter." He spat the word like it tasted foul.

"And you're an asshole."

His mouth dropped open, and he huffed and puffed without actually forming a comeback.

"Don't hurt yourself, bud. This can't be the first time someone's insulted you."

"You won't be the first to regret doing it." With a flourish, he flipped back the sleeves of his robe and started making complicated shapes in front of him while muttering.

Magic. Because of course it involved magic. His tongue flicked out, then he rolled up his sleeves.

Rolled. Up. His sleeves.

I rolled my eyes. "Dude. Seriously?"

He didn't look up as he kept...preparing. Or whatever he was doing.

"Is this the part where the montage starts and somewhere, Pat Benatar starts singing 'Hit me with Your Best Shot?' because I don't have montage kind of time."

He didn't respond. Thankfully, his preoccupation prevented him from noticing me aim the 1911 over my head and fire into the air.

The sound of the gunshot ricocheted and kept coming back in waves, making me slightly deaf, especially in the right ear. It also did what I intended.

My magical friend stumbled, tripped over his own feet, and landed on his butt. As I loomed over him, gun in my hand, he crawled backward, his mouth working. All I'd really wanted was to break his concentration. Everything else became an entertainment bonus. "You can't shoot me. If you shoot me and my family finds out—"

"What? They're going to come after me? After the Catholic Church?" I snorted a laugh, lowering the gun, but not holstering it. "Last I heard, the Church wasn't all that keen on dragons. Made a saint of the last knight to slay one, so I doubt having one hidden away for nefarious purposes is likely to garner you any favors."

"When I have dragon magic, I won't need favors from anyone."

I glanced at Harold, who sneered and rolled his eyes.

"What makes you think you're going to have dragon magic?" I asked.

Walter smiled, that smug expression that made my hand itch. "Because I have a dragon, and when it's old enough, I'll channel it."

"That sounds like it requires consent," I said, glancing at Harold again, "and I'm not thinking you're gonna get it."

"What does consent have to do with it?" He shook his head. "I have a dragon, and when it's fully grown, I'll use its power while I accelerate the growth of another one." Either he didn't notice or didn't care about the rumbling growl from the angry dragon in our midst. "Then I'll reinvent the world the way it should have been, the way my family deserves." His expression darkened and he shook his head. "The way *I* deserve."

"Really, dude? World domination?" I sighed. "Couldn't come up with anything original?"

He huffed, but before he spoke, Harold interrupted with a menacing growl, swinging his huge head and massive teeth toward Walter. "You have another?"

The not-so-masterly mind turned a little green, and between the implied threat and the stench of the sulfurous smoke Harold puffed, I couldn't blame him. "My family inherited two eggs."

Harold growled again, baring incredibly large teeth.

I took a half step back, which seemed brave as soon as Walter took off in a dead sprint.

Of course, I chased him.

He shot across the open space, running past the place where I'd landed when I arrived. Though he stumbled when he glanced over his shoulder, he didn't lose enough balance to trip.

I pushed hard, sprinting after him. For someone running in what looked like dress shoes, he had impressive traction, but it didn't compare to my Docs when he tried to cut a corner. He slid, stumbled, and just before his mad dash ended in a collision with the wall, a burst of purple light stabilized him and rocketed him forward.

Because of course he used magic. Cheater.

I ran faster, my lungs burning, a stitch in my side, but I could not lose him. He disappeared into the dark, but after a metallic crash, a squarish light burst out of the dark.

The door.

Pushing harder, I ran as fast as my legs would go, hoping the door wouldn't lock, hoping he didn't have a key, hoping I'd make it out there before he disappeared into the world.

I caught the edge of the door before it slammed shut and yanked it open, closing my eyes to avoid getting blinded by sunlight. When I opened them, he was already halfway across a courtyard and running for the chain-link fence between the hospital and the steady stream of traffic beyond. I wouldn't catch him before he got to the fence, but I hoped the razor wire across the top would slow him down until I could.

I kept running.

The screech of tires preceded him climbing the fence, but I didn't have time to look for the source.

The razor wire glowed purple and sagged as he reached the fence, but as soon as he touched the chain-link, an explosion blew him back. He landed on his back almost at my feet. I skidded to a stop, my balance precarious as I tried to avoid tripping over his unconscious body.

Nothing like divine intervention.

I bent over, panting, my lungs aching. If he was out, I was taking a minute. Especially since I didn't have anything to tie him up with.

As my breathing settled, I drew again, waiting for him to rouse.

"Caitlin!"

My head snapped up. Sister Betty ran down the sidewalk on the other side of the fence. I raised my free hand and yelled, "Don't touch the fence!" I didn't know exactly what had happened, but his minions had mentioned that his magic only worked about half the time. Or, maybe, he'd just cast the wrong damned spell. Yet another reason why magic was a pain in the ass, even if it occasionally worked in my favor. "It might be electrified." I gestured at the prone figure on the ground. "Whatever he tried to do, did...this."

She stopped and Marty, Father Callahan, and Rene almost crashed into her. "We'll find another way around."

I nodded. Cuffs or restraints could wait until they got here. The courtyard where I stood with the decidedly unconscious Walter must have once been the hospital's main entrance. The fence, however, worked hard to dispel even the implications of entrance. From where I stood, I couldn't see any kind of gate or other way in without removing whole sections. Since I couldn't risk walking away from Walter long enough to find a way to let them in, I bent over the unconscious man, patting him down to find his gun.

And that's when I got hit from behind. Just as I leaned down, a massive fist slammed square into my back and propelled me over Walter by several feet before my face crashed into the ground. The pain took a minute to catch up, but the slick heat of blood came a hell of a lot faster. I pressed the wrist of my right hand, still holding my gun, against my bloody nose. With the other, I pushed myself up to my knees, then got to my feet and turned.

Standing in the open door through which we'd run were the three robed minions, a blur of purple light fading in front of them.

Between us, Walter sat up, gun in hand.

I aimed mine at him. My hand shook.

If this made me a monster, so be it.

Before I could fire, he shot me.

I returned fire before the immediate pain in my leg drove me to the ground with an unbecoming grunt of rage and pain. His hand flew to his bicep before I hit the ground, and a small part of me enjoyed the rush of satisfaction before white hot agony blunted everything else.

"You're not going to win this, Hunter!" His face red and angry, the squealing man tried to get to his feet with his one good arm, the minions already gone.

"I don't have to win," I said, lifting the 1911 again. "I just need to not lose." As I started to squeeze the trigger, Sister Betty and Rene burst through the same door the minions had been standing in at the far side of the yard. As much as I appreciated their speed navigating straight through the oddly shaped building instead of trying to run around it with all the obstacles along the way, I cursed their timing. If my shot went wide, if I was off even a little, I could hit one of them. Kill one of them.

Murder another of my own.

The gun trembled and my arm fell, my finger already on the trigger guard. I swore and Walter grinned.

"Weak," he snarled, then laughed again.

Sister Betty got to him first, tackling him to the ground while Rene covered her, his Glock aimed at Walter's head as she disarmed him.

And I knelt there, armed but ineffectual while they handled the threat. Weak, indeed.

"Can he do magic like that?" I asked Sister Betty as Rene wrangled Walter to his feet and...encouraged him to walk back inside the hospital.

Marty didn't look up from his phone as we crossed the open space. "I'm trying to see if we can prevent him." Long ago, I'd learned the tone he used meant nothing good with an extra helping of frustration.

"Alright." I stayed close, pistol in hand. A bullet would stop a human from wielding magic, if it came to that.

Sister Betty held the metal door open as Rene stepped through with Walter. Marty followed, and I took one look back. Had the minions left the grounds? Or were we walking into a trap? "Keep your eyes open," I said to the group. "We've got three missing magic users."

Sister Betty nodded and stepped back, allowing me to pass while she stood guard.

Rene had Walter face down on the ground as Marty scrolled his phone, holding him with one hand to keep the bound man from rolling over. Only Walter looked at me, one cheek pressed against the dirty linoleum, his face further distorted with a scowl of loathing that promised retribution.

"Oh, shut up," I said to him.

Marty and Rene looked up at me, one surprised, the other annoyed, and said in unison, "I didn't say anything."

"Not you," I said waving my bloody hand at them. "Walter."

They looked at each other, then at their captive.

"Yes," I sighed, returning my hand to the agony of the wound on my thigh.

"How did you know my name?" he asked, his words slurred and muffled.

"I overheard your minions talking shit," I said. "And Harold mentioned it, too."

He snorted in disgust. "I don't know why you keep calling it that. *It* is an animal. A means to an end."

"Whether you recognize it or not, Harold is a sentient being, and *he* probably has more intelligence and emotional maturity than you."

Another huff and Walter rolled his eyes. "He's a fifty-year-old specimen that hasn't hit sexual maturity. Think of it as…I don't know, veal from Faerie."

Between bleeding, being stared at by Rene, and feeling like I'd failed yet again, rage roiled within me, unbidden and uncontrollable. I balled my fists, digging my nails into my palms. "I'm warning you to shut up, or I will shut you up."

"What are you going to do, Hunter? You had another chance to shoot me and failed. You couldn't do it. So why should I believe you'll be able to now?"

"Hey," Rene hauled Walter to his knees and smacked his head with an open hand, "shut up. She's got backup. If she can't shoot you, one of us will."

My jaw ached with tension. Though he meant to be supportive, I couldn't stand the idea that Rene thought I couldn't handle this. That I hadn't been handling it for years before him, or that I wouldn't continue handling it for as long as I could stand against whatever came for me or my territory.

"You don't need to defend me," I said, the words dripping acid.

He glanced at me. "What?"

"I've been doing this longer than you've had a badge. If I had to, I could do this alone."

Walter snickered. In two long strides, I closed the distance between us and punched him in the face.

Marty gasped, dropping his phone. Rene stared at me, gaping. Walter whimpered, bleeding from the mouth.

"Go ahead," I said to Rene, "arrest me."

He pressed his lips together until they disappeared. Without a word, he pulled a white handkerchief from the back pocket of his black jeans and blotted Walter's mouth.

"Caitlin." Sister Betty stared at me, stone-faced. "Let's wrap this up. We have other business to attend to."

"Other business" probably included a lecture and getting thrashed in the gym under the guise of a conditioning workout. I'd admit to deserving at least the latter. I shook my hand once, but didn't rub my sore knuckles.

"We need to stop him from using magic," I said. "And we can't bring him around Harold. He intends to use the dragon's magic after it reaches maturity, but I don't want to risk him being able to use it now."

Marty rubbed his phone against his shirt. "I can't find anything about inhibiting magic without some kind of elaborate ritual we don't have the components for. How does he cast?"

"You couldn't stop my magic if you tried," sneered Walter. "Like generations of my family before me, I—"

Rene shoved the handkerchief in Walter's mouth. "That's enough of that."

I nodded. "The magic I've seen him cast involved gestures and incantations." Except the fence, but had that come from him? His minions mentioned his magic failing, so did that count, or had they interfered? I shook off the questions and gestured at him with my chin. "I guess if he can't talk, he shouldn't be able to cast."

"Good," Sister Betty said. "Now, the dragon. Harold?"

"I think we've got to find a way to send him back to Faerie."

"Do you know what that would entail?" Marty asked, stepping in front of Walter's flailing and raising his voice to be heard over our captive's muffled screams. "That will take serious magic. More mojo than any of us can muster without…"

He didn't have to finish the thought.

Without Madame Sabine.

With more conviction than I felt, I said, "We'll figure out the how later. Let's check on Harold."

Sister Betty nodded, checked her weapon, and pulled out her phone, handing it to Marty. The two stepped away to chat.

I checked my thigh, poking at the raw, bloody wound through the hole in my jeans. Nothing serious, just seriously painful.

"Caitlin," Rene said, walking around Walter. "I'm sorry about running out the other day. I shouldn't have done that."

"No," I agreed, "you shouldn't have."

A muscle in his jaw flexed. "After this is over, we should...talk about things."

"What's there to talk about?" I pulled out each of my weapons in turn and checked them. I didn't relish bringing guns to a magic fight, but I didn't have much choice.

"What happened. What we said." He waited. "How you broke things off."

"You say that like I did something bad."

"Didn't you?"

"No," I said. "I did what needed to be done."

"You needed to stomp on my heart? I'll be sure to take comfort in that." He scoffed, his tongue poking into his cheek as he huffed. "All I did was try to save you from yourself."

I saw him with new eyes. He didn't see the unavoidable end of whatever we had, nor could he put it in perspective. Maybe I had more practice, but the reality stood out for me in sharp relief. I could have been anyone and he'd have "fallen" the same way. "It's a shame this is all about you."

"What the hell is that supposed to mean?"

"Only that it's good to know why I existed in your world."

"Caitlin," he made a sound something like a strangled laugh, "I loved you."

"No, Rene." I smiled, holstering my weapon. "You loved the idea of me. What you dreamed I'd be in your life. You don't love the real me, only what I represent in your world. The dream girl you've imagined and projected onto the closest female that looks like her."

"That's crazy."

"Is it? You said you wanted to save me. From myself."

"You were drowning."

"No." As much as it felt like a lie, it wasn't wrong. The me he saw didn't exist, and what existed, he couldn't see. I pressed on. "You needed to *see* me drowning. You needed to rescue me. Don't you get that I'm not the damsel in distress you're looking for?"

He scanned me up and down as if I'd morphed into something incomprehensible. His eyes shone with terror when they finally met mine.

"Exactly," I said, my voice barely a whisper.

46

Hey, Harold, I'm coming back and I'm bringing friends, so be cool, okay?" My voice echoed through what must have once been a garage level, but got no response. "Harold?"

"Should we be worried he's not responding?" Marty asked.

Sister Betty shushed him, listening, then whispered. "We've always got to be worried. It's how we stay alive."

But worry didn't provide much armor, something I sorely missed though it wouldn't protect against magical assaults. "I don't know if it's an issue," I admitted. "But I don't like it. Not with the magical minions possibly wandering around here."

"Right."

"Harold!" I called again, taking point as I led my friends to meet a dragon. Sister Betty swiveled, clearing the sides of the room as she kept pace with me and Marty. We followed the trail around the perimeter. As counterproductive as it felt to walk through such undefended space, at least we could see everything coming or going. At least, I hoped it made some tactical sense. I didn't need another regret before I died. Or before someone else did.

"I don't see anything," Sister Betty said.

I nodded, gesturing ahead where something shiny from Harold's dais glinted.

"What…is that?" asked Marty.

"You'll have to see it to believe it." I kept walking, sweeping with my gun.

Approaching the massive dragon lounge might have been more impressive from this angle rather than the way I first saw it. Perhaps that's why the pathway took the circuitous route before being presented to Toothy McDragonface. Nothing like a hulking mythical beast to scare the shit out of your captives.

Harold didn't lift his head or open his eyes as we approached.

"Harold. Wake up." This far away, he had to hear me. The echoes made my voice annoyingly loud. Of course, that also meant the minions would hear us, but I'd rather that than sneak up on a creature that might flambé me if startled.

"It's not a good idea to antagonize creatures big enough to eat you," Marty said, his voice thick with awe as he stared at Harold.

"That's my entire job description, bruh." I held the Colt in a two-handed grip, aiming low as I approached the great beast very slowly, trying to see if minions lurked in the shadows behind him. Sister Betty turned her back to me, clearing the rest of the room.

"Baby or not, dragons will still eat you, weapons and all," Marty warned.

"Unlikely," I said. "Humans aren't part of their diet."

"Okay, fine, roast you where you stand. Does it really matter how it kills you?"

"He," I reminded him. "Besides, everything I encounter wants to kill me at some point. Why should he be different?" When Marty didn't answer, I nodded. "I stick with what I said before. I don't want to use more force than necessary unless it's the only option to save our own lives."

He sighed. "I swear you have a death wish."

"Ethics, death wish." I tried to conceal the shiver that raced through me. "Potato, po-tah-to."

As we got closer, I felt the rhythmic warmth from Harold's breathing. Gesturing to Marty and Sister Betty to hold back a few steps, I approached Harold, but not close enough that he might nip at me if he woke up grumpy. "Hey, Harold."

This time, the beast moved, swinging his head in my direction.

I stepped back on instinct, but not before I saw the book perched open on his pile of treasure. The tip of one talon held it open. "Sorry to wake you."

"I wasn't sleeping. I was reading," he said, a touch petulant, a touch indignant. "What do you want now, Hunter?"

Nodding, I holstered my weapon and held out my hands, palm up. "I've come to make you a proposition."

His eyes narrowed, his multiple eyelids squeezing from all directions until I stared into a pupil that reflected my face. "Why?" The next burst of his breath smelled faintly of char and sulfur.

"Because you're stuck here, separated from your kind, separated from a world you can actually move around and be free in, and that sucks. You deserve better."

He moved back, but his scowl deepened. "Go on."

I gestured back at Sister Betty and Marty. "My friends and I want to offer you the chance to go back to Faerie where dragons belong."

"I know where dragons belong," he growled.

"Right, okay." I held up my hands. "I'm sorry. I don't know how much you know about this world or that."

His lips puckered, almost pursed as he turned back to his book. "I know more than you think." With unimaginable delicacy, he closed the book with his talon and pushed it across a pile of spoons into a stack of more books. "I've been alive longer than you, and I've used that time learning. Other members of Walter's clan were kind enough to teach me to read and shared their knowledge." He scowled. "What does Walter say about this...proposition?"

"I don't give a damn," I said. "We're going to deal with him. He'll never get anywhere near a dragon again." I hoped my words wouldn't prove me a liar.

"And what do I have to do?" Harold asked.

"Nothing," I said. "You just have to agree. It might take time to make it happen, but the only thing you have to do is say yes."

Doubts assaulted me. Would sending him back on his own be ethical? As a juvenile of his species, he'd need protection, guidance. Some kind of integration into whatever society the dragons had established. And what about to the residents of Faerie? Would they reject a dragon introduced into their world? What if my offer sent him into a worse situation than Walter had already devised? Would I be sending him to the slaughter?

Sweat trickled down my back. Sweat from the intense heat and humidity, of course.

I tried to shake off the distraction and focused on Harold.

"And if I say no?" His words came out in something like a purr.

Fear of promising more than I could deliver grabbed me by the throat, stifling potential words. It might have been more concerning had words come to mind.

"We'll work through another solution," Sister Betty said.

Harold stretched his neck up, his scales hissing as they slid over each other. He angled his massive head with imperial yet reptilian creepiness, shifting to look down on all three of us with one of his multi-colored, iridescent eyes. His nostrils flared, each breath pouring hot, sulfur-tinged puffs of air down on us.

I wondered if I should draw, or prepare to die.

"You travel with powerful companions, Hunter." Harold primly folded his front claws and nestled deeper into his pile, jostling a goblet-shaped trophy loose and sending it tumbling to the dirt. "You have built your clan wisely."

"Thank you." I glanced back at them. "I'm proud of them."

"It is clever to include a technomancer. But the elf may prove a poor choice."

"Techno—"

"Elf?" Sister Betty interrupted.

"What do you mean?" I asked when she finished.

"Your mage." His claws flicked up, releasing an avalanche of coins and books from where his claws rested. "Mages glow. Easy to recognize, even in humans."

"Who are you seeing glow?" I glanced at my own hand. Nothing but the sheen of blood from my gunshot wound and bloody nose. Not even a healthy glow under that. I might be pale enough to glow in the dark.

"Him."

I turned to Marty, who looked horrified.

He stared at his hands, flipping them to check the backs. "I'm not glowing."

"You can't see what a dragon sees, and it is unwise to try."

I sighed at the timbre of the familiar voice. Again? Really?

The weight of everything on me increased until the only thing I felt was exhausted.

Turning around, Walter stood behind us, holding a gun. He held it all wrong, of course, more like Rick Grimes, the barrel dipping but still pointed it in the general direction of our feet. I had more fear for my Docs than my life since he had no way of accurately sighting his shot, but I didn't want to get shot again, either. I hoped to remain the only one who got shot today and pushed thoughts of Rene out of my mind as I locked eyes with this tall drink of crazy. "Walter."

"Don't patronize me," he snarled. "You won't stand in my way. You won't find the cryptids I've taken, and you won't take my dragon!" His scream echoed, the shrill sound piercing my eardrums.

I stuck a finger in one ear and wiggled it. More for dramatic effect and to piss him off than anything. Plus, if he thought I didn't take him seriously, he'd be easier to take down. I quashed another rush of concern for Rene, and focused on the twerp that had, somehow, gotten free. "That was…impressively high, but the last time I checked, Harold isn't 'yours' and neither is the magic you're stealing from your captives. And make no mistake, however this ends, we will find them and free them."

Walter's manic stare flicked from me to Sister Betty to Marty, then to Harold as he lowered his head. The way Walter's eyes widened, I'm sure Harold had bared his teeth, but I didn't turn around to check.

"I don't think you comprehend how deep the shit you're in really is," I said, bringing his attention back and keeping it on me as my team shuffled. "The smartest thing you can do is give me that gun and surrender."

"I took down your boyfriend; I can take you out, too." When I drew the 1911 and aimed at his chest, he jumped, then stepped back with a laugh. "Again with the big guns?" But his bravado didn't cover the waver of fear in his words.

"You wanna see what I can do with a big gun? Fine, let's dance." I stepped forward.

He puffed up his chest. "You can't do it."

"I can," Marty said from Walter's right.

"And so can I," Sister Betty said from his left.

His head swiveled between them and I could almost see him trying to figure out how they had flanked him, how he hadn't noticed them moving. How I'd gotten this whole thing over on him. Then, he raised the gun, and it might have been a trick of the light, but it seemed to glow purple. "I'll shoot you first."

"So do it," I said, "but I'll take you down with me. And if not me, one of them will."

I could almost feel Sister Betty stiffen, but I ignored it.

Walter swung his aim to her with a sick grin. "I'll take her out. You won't survive losing her and killing me. But if I'm not here, others will take on reshaping the world with dragon magic."

The sliver of truth in his words wormed its way through my heart.

Sister Betty had been shot on my watch before, and I'd vowed not to let it happen again, not to let harm come to any of my team again.

"You won't shoot me, Walter," Sister Betty said with unnerving calm.

"Not when you want to shoot me," I baited him. "Come on, point that thing where you really want to shoot."

He stepped forward and cackled, his eyes gleaming, and I wondered if I imagined the purple light gleaming in them. "Oh, I want to shoot her more than I want to shoot you. I want to kill you without killing you, because that will be my legacy. I'll be the one who ended not one, but two monster hunters. I'll be the one who cleared the path for the new world order!"

I sighted down the barrel of the Colt, aiming for center mass. Taking a slow breath, I readied the shot.

Rene ran up behind Walter, Father Callahan fast at his heels. They couldn't see my gun, and if my bullet went stray, or if it went straight through Walter, they'd be at risk. What bullet had been in the chamber when I checked? Could I fire, knowing the risk?

"Marty," I sounded calmer than I felt, but the wobble in the tip of the gun betrayed what I felt inside, "take the shot."

He had to see Rene and Father Callahan behind Walter, that my aim wouldn't hold true, or, even if it did, I still might murder someone else. I already had blood on my hands, and I couldn't do it again. Marty had to take the shot. He had clear line of sight. But I couldn't say that, couldn't telegraph anything to Walter because I couldn't let him shoot the woman I loved.

"Marty, take the fucking shot!"

With the gunshot, the tension left the room.

And I fell to the ground.

I n my line of work, getting shot is sometimes part of a day's work. Getting shot twice, though, is insulting.

Blood ran between my fingers as I held it over the wound in my right shoulder. The wound in my thigh burned, but my shoulder hurt like a bitch, maybe because I'd been holding my gun when he winged me. That pissed me off more. As I waited for him to fall, to be taken down by... someone, I noticed the silence. More than there should have been, even with the percussion deafness of close-range gunfire.

I looked around.

Everyone, except me and Walter, stood frozen in mid-stride. A faint purple mist hovered around each of them.

"What have you done?" I asked, the whisper of sound thin in the silence.

"Magic." He giggled, the gun still pointed at me.

"You won't win this," I warned, though I didn't know if I believed it. If he had the juice to stop all of them, if he killed me, what else would he do? And how could I stop him?

"Like you said, Hunter, I don't have to win, I just have to not lose." He raised his gun and took another menacing step.

My wounded arm refused to lift the heavy pistol in my hand. I couldn't make it move. It hung at my side, inert. Useless.

The man stood over me.

He'd kill me before I could draw with my left. I couldn't draw the Glock at my back.

It had come to this.

I closed my eyes and prayed.

I welcomed the void to swallow me whole.

Hell came for me in a roar of sound and rush of heat.

The Black Dog approached with a whimper. I couldn't tell the difference between my tears and the rain. Maybe that's why I didn't smell brimstone this time, but I could see it. Him. Glowing red eyes and all.

He should have seemed threatening, especially since I knew what he was.

Instead, he approached slowly, head down and whining.

And I let him.

In the rain, soaked to the skin, the Black Dog lay beside me. Wiry fur brushed my skin as he snuggled as close as possible. Reassuring weight anchored me, and the heat radiating off him warded me against the chilly rain. I stroked his head as he laid it on my folded knees.

He looked up at me without moving, giving only a soft whine in response.

My hand stroked the dog's thick fur, stopping only to dig my fingers into his coat. "You're not so bad, are you?"

He lifted his big square head, looked me in the eyes, and licked my face.

I laughed and scratched between his ears as he put his head back on my knees. "I don't see how people are so scared of you, you big baby."

He yawned, then whimpered, his burning red eyes on mine.

"It might be the eyes," I said, shifting to lean against his thick, warm body. "But you're no menace, are you? You just want to keep me company and warm me up." Despite the rain and the nasty muck pooling in the cracks of the street, I wanted to lie down and snuggle against him. I wanted the Black Dog's heat to warm me until the cold inside just stopped. Even if it took forever. Even if it meant never moving again. Everything weighed on me; even my thoughts felt heavy. Rene. Walter. Harold. The missing supernats. Responsibility for the huge territory I'd been given. Sister Betty. I couldn't carry it any longer. I wiped the mingled rain and tears from my face and pressed it against him. "You know, don't you?" My throat closed hard on the question, cutting off the words I couldn't say, making me cough. Tears burned, distinguishing themselves from the rain for the first time.

The Black Dog whined.

I looked into those red eyes but saw nothing to fear. "I can't let you down because you don't expect anything from me."

Of course, he didn't answer.

"All I've done," I dug my fingers deep into his fur, scratching until his eyes closed, "everything I do creates more work for my team. Or hurts them. Or leaves someone in pain."

The Black Dog's eyes opened.

"Or dead," I said, the words nothing but a whisper.

Maybe it was time.

He scrambled to his feet and nudged his head under my hand again. I obliged by scratching an ear. His eyes locked on mine, giving a tentative "boof" of a bark.

"What, boy?"

He leaned forward and licked my face. I couldn't resist hugging him, burying my face in his neck, and releasing the sobs I couldn't control any longer. My strength drained away. The exhaustion from holding it all together and being strong took over.

Maybe leaving would relieve the burdens on my friends. Sister Betty wouldn't be tempted to violate her vows. Father Callahan could find a worthy Hunter to stop Walter and his magic minions. Rene could daydream me into whatever he needed without ever being hurt by reality. And Marty...Marty would be safe doing something other than hunting monsters. Not to mention my parents. No one would be more relieved than my parents.

After an encouraging lick on the cheek, the Black Dog backed up, his warmth retreating.

I shivered but made no move to follow.

The dog stepped back again, lowered his head, and gave another tentative bark.

"What?"

He retreated with a whine.

"You want me to go with you?"

His tail wagged, water flying from his saturated fur, mouth open in a doggy grin.

The bone-deep cold of the rain penetrated to the center of me, and I couldn't stop shivering. Not even the numbness could stop it, and I didn't have the strength to make it stop. Having the dog close would keep the chill at bay. In his presence, I could sense the relief I needed.

The Black Dog looked behind him and took a half step back. It lowered its head, as if beckoning me.

When I stood, he wagged his tail, hurrying to my side, stepping under my hand and looking up at me, his pink tongue lolling. After a moment, he stepped forward and all I wanted to do was follow.

But I stopped. Something stopped me.

Nothing I could explain, just a sensation that tugged at my core. As much as I wanted to go with the Black Dog, my feet wouldn't move. Frustrated tears streamed down my face, and I dropped to my knees, heedless of the rain, of the chill in the air, and the effluvium my jeans absorbed from the street.

The warmth of the Black Dog anchored me as it leaned against me.

I buried my face in its hot, thick fur and wept, angry and helpless.

All I had to do was go. All I had to do was let go. I desperately wanted to.

But I couldn't.

Nothing hurt more than that.

The Black Dog didn't smell like brimstone. I caught the tang of wood smoke before I heard the peaceful chorus of crickets or peepers. Looking up, everything had changed. A smooth, easy-to-travel road stretched out endlessly under a canopy of stars. Live oaks lined each side, fireflies glittering around the twisted trunks. The peace of the void called from somewhere down that dark road. I could feel it. Sweet relief waited for me.

"Get up! You have to fight!"

Sister Betty's voice sounded so far away, an echo from the other side of reality. Had she died too?

If I followed her voice, would we go into whatever came next together?

I had to find out.

S he's not responsive."

"Caitlin!" I felt the shake, felt my body jerk and shudder. The rain on my face. "Wake up! You have to fight this, Cee!"

But it had always been a fight. Every step. Every move. Every single thing I'd managed to accomplish had been a knock-down, drag-out fight, and to my bones, I was tired. They had to be, too. They had to be weary of carrying everything I put on them, and of all of the bullshit that made their lives chaos. If I just let go, I could save them all. I could give them peace if I let go and went...wherever I went next.

"Goddamn it, Caitlin, you fight back right now!"

Sister Betty.

It had been a long time since I'd heard her blaspheme.

She sounded as tired and as scared as I felt.

If I left, what would happen to her? Or the rest of them? Would they walk away from the hunting, or would they stay to help the next Hunter? Would the next Hunter love them like I did? Would the next Hunter protect them? Anyone could protect a city, but how do you trust your loved ones to someone else?

"Caitlin, come on," Marty said, and I heard his fear, too.

Would walking away be the right answer? Could I really walk away and find the peace I needed so badly if I knew I'd abandoned them to the things that go bump in the night? Could I give up and walk away from a chance to show Shannon I'm stronger now? That I'm sorry I couldn't fight for her?

"Caitlin Fiona Kelley, you open your goddamned eyes right now, and come back to me," Sister Betty demanded. "You are not leaving like this."

I opened my eyes.

47

The rain wasn't rain.

I awoke in the garage level turned dragon's lair. Greasy smoke, sulfur, and the heavy smell of water on stale earth hung in the air. Sprinklers poured water from the overhead gloom as I tried to look up into Marty and Sister Betty's worried faces. "I'm okay," I said, sitting up, surprised when neither of them fought me.

"You need to stay here," Sister Betty said. "Harold can keep you safe. We'll call for back up to deal with the magic users, and check for the captives."

"What about Walter?"

The two of them glanced at a charred husk on the ground.

"I killed him," Harold said. "I am leader of the clan."

I turned to look up at the dragon, his neck extended high over us. "You saved me."

His head dipped, and he closed his eyes for a moment. "You proved worth saving, Hunter."

"Thanks." What else do you say when a dragon compliments you?

"You are part of my clan," he continued, "and I will protect my own."

I bowed my head, mimicking the movement he made. "Thank you. I am honored."

"And these members of your clan will become part of mine as well."

"Thank you," I repeated, not sure what else to say.

Harold inclined his head, then lowered to look into my eyes. "You are formidable, Hunter. But fragile."

"Goes with the human gig," I said, pushing myself up to my feet.

"No, Cee, stay here."

"No," I said. "The job's not done. We're not done."

Sister Betty looked at me, her expression grim. I understood. She wanted to demand that I stay behind, but she needed me. She looked up at Harold. "Will you agree to our proposition?"

"I will...consider it," he said, then lay down and watched us through droopy eyelids. "After this is done. There is much to think about."

My eyes met Sister Betty's, and without a word, we agreed. Later. We would deal with this later.

"And the captives," Harold said, gesturing with a talon to the shadowed behind his dais. "He kept the captives there."

"Caitlin!"

I only had enough time to brace myself before Rene crashed into me, sweeping me into a bear hug that lifted me off my feet.

"Thank God you're okay."

Pain flared in my wounded shoulder, but I didn't stop him. I let my uninjured arm wrap around him. "I'm glad you are, too," I said.

"Walter, he used magic." He put me down, then noticed the blood. "You're hurt. That gunshot...the flames?"

"Yeah, he shot me. Again." I gave a one-sided shrug that didn't use my wounded shoulder. "Then Harold roasted him."

Rene turned, noticing the charred remains. "Sick burn," he said.

I wanted to laugh, needed to, but it got stuck inside. Instead, I nodded while Marty chuckled. "Let's go," I said, gesturing to the dark side of the dais. "Harold said Walter held the abducted supernaturals in there."

"He kept them close to make transferring their magic easier," Harold said, his head resting on his talons. "The spell is still draining them, so you'll need to stop it."

"How?" I asked.

He shrugged. "I don't know."

Sister Betty studied me but didn't say anything. I nodded in response to her unasked question. Yes, I could make it. Yes, I would be okay, for now, at least. We needed to move.

"Come on," I said to my team, retrieving the 1911 from the ground. "I'm down to one hand, and it's the weaker one, so keep that in mind."

With that, we passed Harold and walked into the gloom until we found the door.

I almost wished we hadn't.

The room beyond the dais had once been some kind of storage or maintenance room. The stench of bodies, of waste and death, permeated the air. Cement walls stretched up to narrow horizontal windows letting in slashes of light. Hospital gurneys crammed the room, each one holding at least one supernatural creature, some holding two or three. Too many children filled those beds. I steeled my stomach and passed between two half-shifted were adults that reached for me. Pain radiated off them in waves. Though I wanted to, I couldn't stop to comfort them. I kept walking, as if drawn to the center.

My chest ached.

They'd been here all along. They'd been in agony, and I'd been not even a hundred feet away on the other side of a wall and hadn't known. Hadn't heard, hadn't sensed anything amiss. They'd suffered while I wasted what little time they had left.

"Oh my God." Rene breathed the words, but he was the only one who spoke.

I walked deeper into the room, Sister Betty's presence behind me.

Another gurney's occupant stirred as I approached, an ancient creature that looked human, but couldn't be. He opened one rheumy eye, his cracked lips uttering a soundless plea. I took his outstretched hand, trying not to flinch as his bony fingers did their best to squeeze mine.

His immediate neighbor lay shackled to her gurney. Blackened skin ringed her wrists, ankles, and neck under her bonds. They had to be silver. Silver injured the fae like that. "Can you get these off her, Rene?"

He fumbled with his keys and tried to release her.

I kept walking.

Agony pulsed from every direction. Plaintive cries of pain and despair. I struggled to breathe.

If this used magic, there had to be a focal point. There had to be something we could destroy and break the spell.

"Walter, you sick fuck, what have you done?" I murmured, walking past hands that tried to clutch at me, to grasp my clothes. I ignored the burning pain when someone jostled my arm or grazed the wound in my thigh. For them, I could endure. I had failed them in so many ways, it was all I had left to offer.

The vague suggestion of a path wound between the gurneys, wide enough to pass through without moving any, but a gauntlet of suffering people begging for help.

Sweat streamed down my body, but I kept going, walking to the inevitable center, determined to face whatever waited for me.

Everything hurt. Every step took monumental effort.

The noise in my head became nothing but an unintelligible howl.

I reached for the comfort of the void's numbness.

Nothing responded.

Heat poured off me and I shivered.

One gurney stood alone, a ring of empty space separating it from the others. The bristle of hot, wiry fur against the back of my left hand gave me strength as I drew nearer the center. To a small form shrouded in a weak purple glow.

I stopped, gasping for breath, unable to continue. I leaned over, unable to brace myself without hurting some injury. Sister Betty caught me and offered support. I looked into her blurry face and blinked away tears I hadn't been aware of shedding. "I can't."

Her tears flowed freely. "You can. We're here."

I struggled to believe her. To have the same faith in myself she had in me. It wouldn't come, but I couldn't tell her no. So, I stood up, nodded, and kept going.

When I stood over that central gurney, whatever determination kept me going died.

A little girl in a pink dress lay motionless on the dirty padding. Her dull, honey-brown hair spilled over her shoulders in greasy clumps. Her skin looked gray beneath the grime, but her rapid, shallow breathing proved she lived.

Had Walter known? How had he known?

I couldn't breathe. My chest burned.

The little girl looked almost exactly like Shannon.

Her once-plump limbs looked withered, and she jerked in her sleep with a cry that broke my heart. Night terrors? Like the ones that made Shannon crawl into my bed late at night?

"Caitlin?" Sister Betty put her hand on my uninjured shoulder.

I knew little about magic, but I knew I had to destroy the focal point to end the spell. If it hadn't died with Walter, destruction was the only option.

"We don't know it's her," I said, staring down at the child that could have been my little sister's haggard twin.

Sister Betty reached out, and as her finger entered the nimbus of light around the child, sparks jumped and the glow intensified, all the creatures around us howled in pain.

And with that, we knew.

Why couldn't it have been an object? Why did it have to be Shannon?

No, *not* Shannon. A girl that looked like her.

"I can't do this," I whimpered. I turned to look my mentor in the face, to beg her for help. "I can't hurt her."

She stared at me, tears in her eyes, her pain evident. She knew. She understood.

Before she could answer, Rene interrupted. "You don't have to," he said. "You didn't do this. You don't have to do anything. This isn't your responsibility."

I looked past Sister Betty to confront the anger and frustration in his voice. He looked at me like he stared down a monster.

"This isn't something to debate." Marty scowled at Rene, then stepped around a gurney to get in front of him. He held out a hand, his knife in the other. "The spell didn't end with Walter. This girl's the focal point of the magic, and that focal point has to be destroyed to end it. If she dies, everyone else here has a chance."

I stared at the blade.

"This has to be done," he said softly, "but you don't have to do it alone."

His words hurt.

I hated magic. I hated blood magic.

I stared at the knife, knowing it would be the compassionate end, the one that caused the least trauma to any who'd survive. The quiet, quick end would be merciful to Shannon.

No.

Not. Shannon.

To the girl who looked like Shannon.

"You have to make the decision you're comfortable living with." Sister Betty struggled with her emotions, the battle evident in her expression. Whatever mercy she wanted to offer, razor-sharp responsibility still bit deep. "There may be other options, but they may suffer while we try to find them. You can release them all now with the loss of one." She stared down at the little girl and paled. "No one can tell you what the right choice is," she said. "But we're here with you, whatever you choose."

I nodded, then turned back to not-Shannon and stared at the wriggling child.

Ending her suffering meant ending all their suffering.

I held out my left hand behind me, palm up and open.

Marty placed the hilt of his knife in it.

The heat in my chest increased, burning my skin.

I looked down, noticing the glow of the amulet.

Without thought, I pulled it out of my shirt with my right hand, wincing as my shoulder complained with each movement. The stone burned my fingers. Fire blazed behind the glass chips. I held it tight, fire ripping through me, the knife igniting in my other hand. Power like I've never felt before coursed through me. Lava filled my veins. I feared burning to ash as I stood there, but I knew, even if I did, it would begin again.

The Phoenix would rise.

The Black Dog leaned against my leg, my companion through the Void.

And I knew.

I was the conduit, and I had a job to do.

Holding the knife over the little girl's heart, I closed my eyes and cried.

Everything became flame as it plunged home.

Power drained out of me as fast as it had filled me. I collapsed, the wound in my thigh tearing, the jarring impact shooting flares of white-hot pain from my fingertips to the top of my head. The cold concrete floor felt good against my feverish flesh, despite the pebbles digging into my skin.

I felt the Black Dog close, but kept it at bay as I struggled to sit up.

Sister Betty reached out to help on one side, Marty on the other. He nodded, then stood, looking at the gurney. "It's over," he said softly. "You did it."

Tears poured down my face, and my breath shredded my lungs with each sob, but I still managed to say it. Though the words hurt, I still said it. "I need help."

Sister Betty pulled me to her fiercely and squeezed me tight. "I know."

Everything fell away.

The anger.

The shame.

The misery.

The numbness.
None of it mattered.
She had me. She forgave me. She still loved me.
With her strength pouring through her embrace, the void retreated.
I could start over here.
With her refusal to give up, I had a place to start.
"Come on," Sister Betty said, helping me to my feet. "Let's go home."

THE END

for now

AUTHOR'S NOTE

Woo. That got...heavy. But, as "they" say, art imitates life and the reality is that far too many people suffer with untreated, and sometimes undiagnosed, mental illness. While the stigma around mental illnesses like depression, anxiety, and a multitude of others is lessening, it certainly still exists and prevents people from getting the help they need to feel better. Sometimes, like Caitlin, they are tempted to take matters into their own hands and put a permanent end to their temporary crisis. If you are one of those people, you are not alone.

What you feel is valid.

What you feel is *real*, and you *deserve* to feel better.

If you are in crisis, call the National Suicide Prevention Lifeline at 1-800-273-8255. Not everyone can talk on the phone, especially when hurting, but you can chat them at https://suicidepreventionlifeline.org/chat/.

If you are suffering, there are resources out there for you and a community of people who have been where you are right now. Your illness may lie to you and tell you all kinds of negative things, but here is the truth: the world is better with you in it, and you *can* and *will* get through this. Even if you don't know what to do, you can make the first step.

- Figure out what to do with help from the National Alliance on Mental Illness https://nami.org/help
- Find more resources at the Substance Abuse and Mental Health Services Administration, including finding treatment for mental illness and substance abuse https://www.samhsa.gov/find-treatment
- Contact a therapist near you, or one that provides telehealth (virtual) appointments. Popular websites like betterhelp.com are easily accessible, or search national organizations like the Anxiety and Depression Association of America at https://members.adaa.org/page/FATMain for local providers.
- If you need hope, please visit www.HoldontotheLight.com or follow #HoldOnToTheLight, a blog campaign encompassing blog posts by more than 100 fantasy and science fiction authors around the world in an effort to raise awareness around treatment for depression, suicide prevention, domestic violence intervention, PTSD initiatives, bullying prevention and other mental health-related issues.

This is not a complete list of resources, but a place to start. Sometimes, you may have to try out a couple of therapists, or doctors to get what you need. It can be frustrating. It can be infuriating. Stick with it. You've come too far to only get this far.

No matter what lies your illness is telling you, you are worth help and what you're feeling now will not last forever. Please get help as soon as possible. Don't wait. You are worth it, I promise, even if you can't see it right now.

Don't worry, Caitlin will be back. It will take a lot more than this to keep her down.

And it will take more than what you're going through to keep you down, too.

Hold on to the Light. The world needs *you.*

It gets better.

ABOUT THE AUTHOR

Theresa Glover spends her days plumbing the dark depths of the human psyche in search of new, frightening character inspirations from the relative comfort of her marketing job in North Carolina. When not writing or crafting her ass off, she can be found buried in a book, playing Magic, or watching horror movies alone in the dark.

FRIENDS OF FALSTAFF

www.ingramcontent.com/pod-product-compliance
Lightning Source LLC
Chambersburg PA
CBHW051521100726
47898CB00005B/1541